EVERSON SOLSTICE

MATT BANNISTER WESTERN 17

KEN PRATT

Published in the United States by Wolfpack Publishing, Las Vegas

CKN Christian Publishing
An Imprint of Wolfpack Publishing
9850 S. Maryland Parkway, Suite A-5 #323
Las Vegas, Nevada 89183

cknchristianpublishing.com

Paperback ISBN: 978-1-63977-467-8
eBook ISBN: 978-1-63977-466-1
LCCN: 2023944303

Author's Note

The history of Portland, Oregon, is very interesting. Portland is a hundred and thirteen miles away from the Pacific Ocean, but Portland was the busiest sea harbor on the West Coast, aside from San Francisco. Portland was known as the shanghai capital of the United States and is well known for the Shanghai Tunnels, but in recent years, those have been debated. In Fact, the whole reputation of being a shanghai city has come under debate in recent years.

Most of the time, I use fictional towns, but this story takes place in Portland, Oregon, in 1884. This story is a work of fiction, and I took some fictional liberties of the city itself to add buildings, change street names and create the waterfront.

There were crimps, sailor houses, and an abundance of crime and corruption in early Portland. I did my best to show how that sailor's system worked back then with the crimps and sailor houses. I find it fascinating; I hope you will too.

This story is by no means a reflection upon the city of Portland itself or the Portland Police Department. I have the utmost respect and admiration for Police Officers and the work they do.

—Ken Pratt

Chapter 1

Floyd Bannister gazed out his apartment window from the fourth floor of the Silver Casterlin Tenements building at the beautiful blue water of the Willamette River, reflecting the sunshine like glittering diamonds that enhanced the excitement that bubbled within him. It was a beautiful summer's day, and for the first time, he had a family member coming to Portland to visit him. His Grandson, Gabriel Smith, was coming to spend a week with him. Gabriel's adopted brother Evan Gray was also coming, which was fine. Floyd planned to treat Evan like family and make the two boys feel at home while taking a few days off work to show the boys around town.

Floyd planned to take the boys to various restaurants and stores to show them there was more to the world than Willow Falls. He planned to take the boys to Oregon City to see the roaring Willamette River Falls. He also planned to take a sternwheeler up the Columbia River to the beautiful Multnomah Falls in the Columbia Gorge so the boys could gaze at the majestic one-hundred-and-forty-seven-foot waterfall to appreciate its full beauty and splendor. Both waterfalls would be there long after Floyd passed away, and someday, when Gabriel brought his grandchildren to the natural wonders, Gabriel would remember being there with his grandfather. Floyd didn't have much to give as a lasting legacy except his time and the memory of the time spent with his grandson, as short as it may be.

The two boys had just finished school, and this trip to visit him was their reward. Life was just beginning for them, and Floyd knew by experience that when the schooling ended, the work started, and there would be less time for having fun. He doubted Gabriel would ever have a week to spend with his grandfather again. This opportunity with his grandson was a once-in-a-lifetime treat, and Floyd had every intention of making it so unique that the memories would last Gabriel's lifetime.

The front door opened, and his wife, Rhoda, walked into the two-bedroom apartment in the heat of arguing with her twenty-six-year-old son, Bob Mears. Floyd turned from the window to listen while he sipped his coffee quietly.

Bob followed Rhoda inside, complaining, "It's not my fault they're coming. Why do I have to pay for your guests? They're not related to me."

"You're not paying for them," Rhoda replied impatiently.

"If I have to rent a room somewhere so your

guests can stay in my room, then I *am* paying for them!" Bob argued.

Rhoda turned to face him. "If you had stayed true to Ingrid, you'd have a nice home. I told you the storage room isn't your home; it is just a place you can stay for now. I need that space for Floyd and my grandson and his friend. It's only for a week, Bob. Certainly, you can find a place to stay."

"He isn't your grandson, Mom. He's Floyd's. By the way, I would be with Ingrid, but the crazy woman came at me with a knife. She's crazy."

Floyd snickered. "Her catching you smooching on that harlot didn't have anything to do with that?"

Bob cast a bitter glance at Floyd. "That's my business, not yours."

Floyd offered a slight grin. "That's true. Except now you're camped out in the space reserved for my grandson. You've already heard your mother say you must vacate for a week. There's no reason to argue about it because that's how it is."

Bob Mears was five foot ten inches tall with a slim build. He had short dark brown hair, a thin mustache on his upper lip, and large blue eyes like his mother's that the ladies apparently found handsome as he never lacked for a lady's attention. Bob dressed nicely for a man of his blue-collar means as a part-time bartender at the Silver Casterlin Saloon for Floyd and a full-time bartender at the Maroon Squid Tavern on Water Street along the Willamette River. Two business partners owned the Maroon Squid Tavern; one was looking to move out of Portland and wanted to sell his half of the business to

Bob. It was a golden opportunity for Bob to become a half-owner instead of an employee. He had been saving his money but was still significantly short of the needed funds, and the idea of being forced to waste a single cent on a room for a week aggravated him.

"Fine!" Bob exclaimed irritably. "I'll waste my money on a room, but if I lose out on buying the Maroon Squid because of this, I'll never forgive you two."

Rhoda's patience had run its course. "That's your problem, not ours. Apologize to Ingrid and get that straightened out. Maybe she'll loan you money and let you move back in."

***

Ingrid Moller was a fifty-five-year-old widow to a former sea captain whose ship was lost at sea four years before. She owned her home and had raised two sons; the oldest was lost at sea with his father when he attempted to enter the safety of the Columbia River during a fierce winter storm. All hands were lost less than a mile from shore; losing her husband and oldest son nearly broke Ingrid's will to live.

Ingrid's second-born son, Sven, had a young lady he was betrothed to in town and wasn't willing to leave her to go to sea with his father. Sven worked at a warehouse on the wharf loading ships and got to know Bob while having drinks at the Maroon Squid Tavern after work. Sven introduced Bob to his mother, and over the next year, a romance began to build between the much older widow and her son's young friend. Ingrid made a secure living as the owner of three rental houses and a fleet of seven barges leased to be towed up and down the Willamette and Columbia Rivers. Her husband had bought them as investments to supplement his retirement in the growing and prospering city where the rivers were the highway to the world beyond the American shore.

***

"Ingrid would rather stab me than look at me," Bob said. "She was going to loan me the money to buy the Maroon Squid, but that loan is gone now too. I should have known better than having Rose stay in the house with me while Ingrid was gone. I never considered Ingrid might come home a day early. It was bad judgment. Mother, can you put Floyd's grandson in here with you or have Maggie get a room? She has more money saved than I do."

"No!" Rhoda snapped. "You can leave your things in the storage room, but I need the bed and will take a mattress out of Bill's apartment for the other boy. Be sure to save room for that. They are arriving today, so pick up your things and leave."

"Are you going to pay me back for room expenses?" Bob questioned.

"No! Now get out of here," Rhoda finished. "We have to go get those boys pretty soon."

The glower on Bob's face revealed his hostility

as he spoke to Floyd, "You were never excited to do anything with me."

Rhoda complained, "For crying out loud. You never wanted anything to do with Floyd when he tried because you didn't want a *stepdaddy,* as you'd say. Well, Bob, your stepfather did everything he could for you, and yes, he did try to spend time with you. Stop acting like a baby and get a room for a week or stay with one of your friends."

Floyd shook his head slowly as Bob left. It was Floyd's experienced opinion that Bob was as much of a fool as Floyd had been at his age. "That young man had a good thing going with Ingrid. It's too bad he couldn't keep it."

"Well, we all live and learn. I just hope he learns quicker than either of us did. Well, shall we go wait for the train? It should be arriving within the next hour or so."

Chapter 2

The train station was on the east side of the Willamette River, so Floyd and Rhoda had to take the Stark Street Ferry, a steam-powered flat-keeled craft with a tall wheelhouse and smokestacks expelling coal smoke and steam across the river. Once on the east side of Portland, they had to walk a fair distance to the rail station and wait. The Oregon Short Line steam locomotive arrived a little later than expected but eventually pulled into the station expelling thick plumes of steam as the three passenger cars lined along the decking.

Floyd could hardly contain his excitement when Gabriel stepped off the train carrying a traveling case. He was a handsome young man with dark hair, a youthful square-shaped face, and brown eyes that immediately reminded Floyd of his deceased wife, Ruth Fasana. Gabriel had the height and broad shoulders that came from his grandmother's Fasana bloodline.

"Gabriel! Hey, Gabriel." Floyd raised his hand to be noticed among the others waiting for the train's arrival.

"Grandpa." Gabriel grinned. The train had been a new experience that started exciting but soon grew tiresome, despite the amazing ride through the Columbia River Gorge. He gave his grandfather a quick hug, followed by one for Rhoda. "This is my brother, Evan. He's never been here before either."

"Hello, Evan. I'm Floyd. You might as well call me Grandpa, too."

"Hello," Evan shook Floyd's hand uneasily.

Rhoda gave the slim, blond-haired sixteen-year-old boy with blue eyes a hesitant hug. "Well, Evan, if you're going to call him Grandpa, you might as well call me Grandma. How was the train ride, Gabriel?"

"It was weird. I've never been on a train before. I've never gone so fast."

Evan added, "It's much faster than traveling by horse."

"Oh?" Rhoda questioned, doubting the boy had ever been outside of Willow Falls, "Have you traveled by horse very far?"

Evan lifted his brow with a sad nod. "Yes, Ma'am. My parents brought us here from New York by wagon." He didn't feel the need to tell her about losing his family on the way, meeting Donovan Moskin and John Birch in The Dalles, their crime spree ending in Willow Falls, or losing his older brother Rodney.

"I suppose you would know about horse travel

then. That's a long way. Well, boys, we should get you home and some food in those bellies. I can make a thick ham and bean soup and plenty of it."

"Thank you," Gabriel said. His eyes were drawn to the tall masts of the ships anchored on the Willamette River waiting to dock and those along the piers stretching along the river's far side. He had never seen a sea-faring ship before, and the port of Portland was busy with a wide variety of boats, tugboats, and skiffs. "Do you think any of those are pirate ships?" he asked. Gabriel had read *A General History of the Pyrates* several times; it was one of his favorite books from his Grandpa Ash's library. The book was now a treasured belonging of his.

Floyd chuckled. "No. The only treasures those boats carry are wheat or other goods like that. The harbor is our main business, and the warehouses along the waterfront are full of just about everything except a pirate's treasure."

"This is the Columbia River, isn't it? It goes to the ocean?" Evan asked.

"Portland is built on both sides of the Willamette River, but the Willamette enters the Columbia not far outside of town. The Columbia River reaches the ocean about a hundred miles west of here. Maybe later today, we'll walk down to the pier and look at the ships, but let's get you boys home, unpacked and situated." Floyd smiled warmly. "Welcome to Portland, fellas. Have either of you ever been on a boat?"

"No."

"Today is the first of many things, then. Your first

9

train ride, your first ferry ride, and once we reach the west side of the river, your first street trolley ride. You two may not want to return to Willow Falls once you discover how exciting Portland can be."

***

The Silver Casterlin Saloon & Tenements was the only signage the four-story brick building advertised on a large sign hanging over the concrete sidewalk. The Silver Casterlin building was already one of the tallest buildings in the city at four stories high, but to make it more noticeable, a large flag pole was on the roof, proudly flying the American flag. The saloon was on the first floor and was one of the larger saloons in the city that offered a wide variety of drinks, food, and game tables.

Like any port city's saloon, it could become a rowdy place, and to keep the rowdiness from getting out of hand, the bar had security guards working every night. During the day, meals were the primary source of income, but as night fell, the alcohol flowed faster than the setting sun and continued until the early morning hours. Running such a business took committed employees, and Floyd was pleased with the employees he had working for him to make the business flow as efficiently as it did.

The three floors above the saloon were filled with sparsely furnished apartments referred to as tenements for whoever wished to rent one on a monthly basis. There were thirty-six apartments in all. Some, much smaller than the others, provided nothing more than a bed, small table, and chair. Thirteen square blocks of Portland had access to clean water through the Portland Water Works, including the Silver Casterlin building though it was only plumbed to the first floor.

A centralized sewer line was built two blocks away to carry the city's sewer to the river and had been connected to the Silver Casterlin Saloon a year before. Two water rooms were built near the stairs to accommodate the residents and the saloon patrons with commodes and wash basins. A single bathtub was in a locked room for the residents and saloon employees, with hot water from the boiler in the basement that heated the water and the first floor.

Cold or hot water was made available for the residents at a large sink near the water rooms to fill buckets of water to carry upstairs. Eventually, the tenement rooms would be plumbed for water and radiator heat, but for now, the apartments were kept warm by their cookstoves which burned coal and vented out of the two large chimneys on the roof of the building.

The expense of upgrading the building's water and sewer had been considerable but served the saloon patrons as an easy place to relieve themselves without leaving the premises and cut down on the waste thrown out from upstairs windows to the streets below. Now that indoor plumbing was readily available on the first floor, anyone caught tossing their waste out a window was immediately evicted. It was a rule that Rhoda, being the tenement manager, strictly enforced.

Floyd was humored by how impressed the two boys were by the ferry ride and learning how to use the water closets and the quick access to hot water. Such modern conveniences were far from coming to Willow Falls, as was the gas lighting that the building provided. Of course, not all of Portland had access to the water or sewer lines yet, but it was in the works to reach every home and building eventually. Plumbers were in demand, as were laborers for the trenches and ditches that needed to be dug. Portland was a thriving city with work readily available for anyone looking for a job. It was in Floyd's mind to let the two boys know jobs were easy to find if they wanted to stay in Portland when their weeklong vacation was over.

"And this is where you two will be staying," Rhoda said as she unlocked a door without a number on it. It was a storage room at the end of the hallway on the fourth floor. It had no window or light and was merely an eight-by-twelve-foot room. Inside was a pile of clothes on a locked trunk, a lantern for light, a bed with a wood frame, and another mattress on the floor; each had a blanket and a thin pillow.

"Thank you," Gabriel said.

Rhoda continued, "My son, Bob, has been staying in here for the past two weeks. But for now, he's staying elsewhere while you two are here. Here is the key; don't lose it. You're free to come and go as you please."

Floyd added, "Rhoda makes dinner about six o'clock every night, and we go to bed around nine. If you get hungry after that, you can go to the saloon and order a bowl of chili, but I do not want you two boys wandering around Portland after dark. When the sun goes down, this town can become dangerous. So, to be safe, promise me that you'll both stay in the building, okay?"

"Yes, sir," Evan and Gabriel both agreed.

**

After having a good meal in his grandparent's apartment, Gabriel stared out the window with a birds-eye view of the river. The beautiful, radiant blue water of the Willamette River was stunning all by itself, but Gabriel's attention was on the tall ship's masts rising noticeably above the piers and anchored in the middle of the river. The variety of ships with two, three, and four tall masts with their sails hoisted and tied to the yardarms was a world away from Jessup County.

The only boats Gabriel had ever seen were canoes and a rare rowboat on the Modoc River. He was fascinated by the intrigue and mystery of the tall ships. A steam-powered sternwheeler passed by the anchored vessels with its black smoke and steam plumes rising above the water while a smaller steam-powered tugboat with paddlewheels on both sides pulled an empty barge up the river. Occasionally they could hear the Stark Street Ferry blow its steam-whistle for the start of another river crossing.

"Grandpa, can we go to the river and look at the boats?" he asked.

"I suppose we can, yes."

***

Walking on a concrete sidewalk beside a brick-laid street was a new experience for the boys. The curiosities of Portland and all the many things that were new and fascinating to Gabriel were quickly diminished by the need to step over a splattered puddle of dried vomit from the night before. The closer they strolled towards the beautiful blue river, the more pungent the foul stench of sewer and piles of rubbish filled Gabriel's nose. Willow Falls may not have had gas lighting, plumbed water, or an indoor commode, but the air was fresh and the streets were free of human waste. Gabriel couldn't believe his grandfather was so used to the stench that he didn't notice it.

Water Street ran the length of the waterfront, lined with piers built out over the river. Being a port town, warehouses extended out onto the piers in either direction as far as his eyes could see. Each warehouse had private docks, and the company name was painted boldly on both sides of the buildings so the ship captains or masters, as they were sometimes called, knew where to moor their ship. Each warehouse brought goods in by rail, freight-wagon, or the river and shipped goods out the same way.

Portland was a busy port that imported and exported goods of all kinds locally up and down the Willamette and Columbia Rivers, up and down both coasts of the United States and around the world. The port of Portland was busy with crafts of all kinds, from locals fishing in small canoes to skiffs transporting sailors to and from anchored ships, river-dwelling single-mast boats to the much larger two, three, and four-mast ships that traveled the seven seas. Smaller sternwheelers hauled passengers all over Oregon on the rivers, and the larger steam-powered paddlewheel ships regularly traversed up and down the West Coast.

Tugboats were the busy bees of the harbor as they assisted the vessel in docking and leaving port, along with pulling barges. Tugboats were the little working boats that helped make the port of Portland function as well as it did. The Stark Street Ferry crossed the river back and forth repeatedly until midnight, and then a rowboat was used if someone needed to cross the river. The black coal smoke of the double stacks on the ferry, tugboats, and other steam-powered vessels left a discolored trail hanging over the river that slowly filtered and settled over the city when there was no breeze.

Floyd turned on Water Street and walked two blocks until he turned onto a pier separating two warehouses. He walked across the heavy beams of the dock towards a magnificent ninety-foot, three-mast merchant ship loaded with hundred-pound bags of Oregon wheat. The laborers pushed wooden carts stacked with bags to the edge of the dock, then carried them up a ramp to the ship and then down into the ship's hull to stack them in an organized manner, careful to distribute the weight as evenly and securely as they could to keep the weight of the cargo from shifting.

Floyd waved towards the ship. "Here it is, boys, the heartbeat of Portland, the harbor. Ships come from all over the world to pick up loads of wheat, corn, lumber, and everything else to be shipped just about everywhere. If you want to see the world, joining a ship's crew might be a good job for you. The men that work on that ship get to see things none of us ever will."

"That ship is so big," Gabriel said in awe of the three-mast ship. He couldn't take his eyes off the impressive, green-painted ship with a gold railing. The ship's name was painted gold on the bow, *Rosenberg's Accolade #3.*

Floyd explained, "This pier belongs to the Haslett-Jones Shipping Company and I'm friends with the general manager. He won't mind us watching his people work for a bit. You don't want to just come to the docks and start loitering like we're doing because most places are not too friendly if you're not working."

A short, stocky, grizzled older man exited an opened warehouse door holding a writing pad. He wore work boots and faded bib coveralls over a lightweight faded red shirt. "Floyd, what the heck are you doing down here? You know Amos has a beef with you. Right?"

"Speak of the devil. Harry, I was just telling my

16

grandson that you'd be fine with us watching your people work for a bit." He shook hands with the older man named Harry.

"Yeah. I'm fine with that," Harry said good-naturedly. "Amos has the beef, not me. You took most of the man's paycheck in our last poker game."

Floyd grinned as he chuckled lightly. "Well, a man shouldn't bet his paycheck if he can't afford to lose it. I learned that many years ago. This is my grandson, Gabriel. And that's a—" His mind went blank as he tried to remember the blonde-haired boy's name.

"Evan," Gabriel replied.

"Evan, yes." Floyd explained to Harry, "Evan is Gabriel's friend. Gabriel is my boy Matt's son."

"The marshal?" Harry questioned as he shook both boys' hands.

"Yep. These two are visiting from over near Branson. It's their first time in the city. And by the way, you can tell Amos, if he has a beef with me, he has a beef with Matt. And my son is not a man he wants to meet on bad terms. Is he, Gabriel?"

Gabriel shook his head. "No, sir."

Harry smiled. "I suppose not. Well, look around, but there isn't much to see."

Gabriel asked, "Can we go look on the boat?"

Harry shook his head. "They're called ships, son. Some of these sailors will slap you silly for calling her a boat. To answer your question, it's not my permission to give, and I can't let you on her. Captain Pete is a good man, but you never, and I mean never, go aboard a ship unless the captain invites you aboard."

"Oh," Gabriel said, disheartened.

Harry frowned. "Captain Pete is not around right now, or I'd ask him for you. Listen to me, boys; I live here, you don't. I'm sure your grandfather has told you not to wander around after dark down here. These streets get mighty dangerous at night, especially near the river. So, stay with your grandparents and do as they tell you. You'll see women around here trying to wave you down or taking a sudden romantic interest in you; stay away from them too. Things are going around that you don't want to happen to you. And don't make any fast friends around here. That's the best advice I can give you."

Floyd said, "I haven't gone into great detail yet, but I did tell them to stay inside the building after dark."

"Well, listen to your grandfather and enjoy your visit. I have some real work to do, Floyd. Not all of us get to sit in a comfortable chair, look pretty and talk to young, pretty waitresses for a living."

Floyd smiled as he nodded, "Ahh, but a wise man does. I'll see you later."

Chapter 3

Maggie Farrell's mouth opened with excitement when she entered her home and saw Gabriel sitting on the davenport. "It is so great to see you again!" She hugged Gabriel. She had met Gabriel when she went to Branson with Floyd and her mother for Thanksgiving nearly a year before. "Welcome to Portland. Are you considering moving here now that you are out of school?"

"No..." he said unconvincingly. The tall ships had him intrigued.

"You don't sound so convinced about that," she chuckled. "I've not met your brother. I'm Maggie. I'm Rhoda's daughter, Floyd is my stepfather, but he is more of a father than not."

"I'm Evan Grey..." he hesitated before continuing, "I live with Gabriel and his family."

Gabriel corrected him, "You do more than that; you're my brother."

Evan gave a half smile and nodded. He had always felt welcomed in the Smith family, but there was an unspoken division where his personality, humor, and peculiar traits revealed a separation of family ties. He was made welcome, loved, and taken care of, but they were the Smith family, and Evan was still a Grey. It had never felt more evident that he wasn't family than now that he was visiting Gabriel's grandparents. He felt out of place and wished he had not come with Gabriel.

"Are you thinking about moving over here, Evan?" Maggie asked.

"No," he answered plainly.

Rhoda stood near the cookstove and sighed loudly. "It's too darn hot to cook. I'm ordering dinner from the saloon's kitchen. Today's a special day because our grandson is here. I'll order some beef stew with some biscuits. You boys will love it."

Floyd offered, "Tomorrow, we'll be taking a sternwheeler up the Willamette to Oregon City to see the Willamette Falls."

Maggie frowned. "If you wait until Saturday, I can go with you. I want to go."

Rhoda added, "It would be fun to take Maggie with us, Floyd. There is enough to see right here in town until Saturday. We can ride up the Columbia on Sunday to see Multnomah Falls. I have plenty of work that I plan on doing tomorrow."

Floyd wrinkled his nose. "Well, we don't have to do it all immediately. Alright, Saturday it is. Tomorrow we'll wander around the city."

***

An hour later, a cast iron kettle of beef stew was carried upstairs and delivered to Floyd's apartment by one of the cooks. Once set on the table, Rhoda ladled out bowlfuls of the thick stew as they sat at the table to have dinner. The table was too small for all of them, so Floyd sat in his chair and ate.

A quick knock on the door sounded, then it opened as Bob Mears entered the room. His eyebrows lifted with a friendly expression as he noticed Gabriel and Evan. "Oh! Hi, I'm Bob. I'm Rhoda's son." He shook their hands as introductions were made.

"How do you like the city?" he asked.

"It doesn't smell good," Evan replied dryly.

Bob chuckled. "I notice that too sometimes, especially down by the river. But that's where the sewer goes, so I suppose it's to be expected. Living downtown here, you get used to it, but you don't smell it where I lived near the hill on the edge of town. But I'm back living here now. Well, I was until you two took my room."

"It's not your room," Rhoda expressed impatiently.

"Ma, you know what he meant," Maggie said, sticking up for her younger brother. "It's just temporary."

"That's right," Bob agreed. He grabbed a biscuit and bowl to fill with stew to eat. "I did find a place to stay for the price of splitting a cord of wood. So, I'm good."

"Does the elderly old woman know you're only staying for a week, or did you buy her a ring?" Maggie teased.

Bob laughed. "Oh, that's low, Sis. You assume it's a woman, but it's not. I'll be staying with my pal

Edgar and his wife."

"I'm glad you found a place to stay," Rhoda said sincerely.

"Me too, Ma. I can't afford to spend any money. I'll be splitting that wood this weekend. Like Floyd always told me, a little sweat equity never hurt anyone."

Rhoda said, "We're taking the two boys on trips this weekend, Oregon City on Saturday and the big falls on Sunday. I hope you might want to go with us as a family. We haven't done anything like that together in a long time."

"Wish I could, Ma, but I have other plans. I'll be working my butt off and trying to earn enough money to invest in my future. If there is one thing I learned from Floyd, it is how to run a saloon and do it right. I want to buy half of the Maroon Squid Tavern and turn it into something you two can be proud of."

Floyd's lips curled upwards slightly with the compliment. "I wish you luck."

Bob spoke awkwardly, "I don't need luck. What I need is about two thousand and seven hundred dollars. Hugh wants out and is giving me six days to come up with the money, or he's selling his half of the tavern to whoever comes up with the money first. This is my chance to make a name for myself, and I only have six days, five days tomorrow, to come up with the money. Is there any way you two can help me, just this once? Or you, Maggie?"

Floyd sighed. "Bob, I just can't do it. We don't have that kind of money."

"Could you get a bank loan? I promise I'll pay it back. I can't miss this opportunity. You know I'd make you proud of me."

Floyd shook his head. "I'm sorry."

"Sorry?" Bob questioned, becoming obstinate. "Are you afraid I'd run the Silver Casterlin into the ground if I owned the Maroon Squid? You could get the money to help me if you wanted to," he accused irritably.

"I suppose I could, but I won't put myself in debt and depend on you to pay it. That comes directly from the Proverbs, the book of wisdom. The answer's no, Bob."

"I'd pay you back!" Bob shouted irately.

Maggie spoke softly to ease her brother's temper, "In Floyd's defense, you haven't ever proven yourself to be a man of your word, Bob. How much do you owe our parents right now? How much do you owe me? We've helped you many times before and never received a penny in return."

"This is different; it's an investment! Don't you understand? You're supposed to be my family."

Maggie continued, "The ferry you were going to build with Hank across the Sandy River was an investment too. So was—"

"Hank stole that money and disappeared! That wasn't my fault," Bob argued.

"That is my point," Maggie said calmly. "It is never your fault, but it always costs someone else a lot of money for you to fail."

Bob pointed an angry finger at his sister and bitterly cursed at her with a raised shout.

"Hey!" Floyd yelled as he stood from his chair. "That's enough. Your sister isn't doing anything to deserve language like that except speaking the truth. Maybe you better cool down or leave, Bob."

Bob tightened his lips and held up a hand in surrender. He picked up his bowl of stew and leaned angrily against the small, cluttered counter to eat. He brought his spoon halfway to his mouth and paused to speak gently, "I don't need luck. I need help. I have youth, passion, and imagination. I'd bring excitement and fun into the Maroon Squid and make it one of the most prosperous saloons in town. I know I could do it if I had the chance. I'll make you equal partners until I can pay you back. I know you three could come up with the money if you wanted to. I have a lot of great ideas that will make a fortune."

"We gave our answer," Floyd stated firmly to bring the conversation to a close. He added to Gabriel, "Well, shall we sit down and talk? I'm sure you have questions about your grandmother or great-grandparents."

Rhoda's upper lip twitched with the mention of Floyd's departed wife.

Bob asked through a mouth full of food, "You are my parents, and you won't help me?"

"No, Bob, we won't. If you'll excuse me, I'd like to talk to my grandson."

"You never wanted to sit down and talk to me," Bob complained under his breath.

Rhoda answered bluntly, "That's not true at all. Floyd's always been there to talk to you. You didn't listen and cared more about having fun with your friends."

Bob had no response to his mother's slight rebuke. He looked at Gabriel, sitting at Bob's usual place at the table. "How long are you in town for?"

"Just for five days."

"I don't know that there is much to see in town, but the falls are both nice. You'll have fun. You're Marshal Matt Bannister's son?"

Gabriel nodded.

"I met Maggie's beau, William Fasana. Do you know him?"

Rhoda answered sarcastically, "They're family. Of course, he knows that cockroach."

Gabriel's eyes widened with surprise to hear her call William such a repulsive insect.

Maggie covered her mouth to not drop food from it as she laughed at Gabriel's expression. She swallowed, careful not to choke on a chunk of beef. "She means nothing by it. It's just the relationship they have," she explained to Gabriel.

"Oh."

Bob continued seriously, "William spent a week here sometime back to visit with Maggie. I didn't get to know him because I had my own woman at the time and lived on the hill. He seemed like a pompous man to me though. Is he?" he asked Evan.

Evan shrugged. "I only met him once or twice. I'm not related." He wasn't particularly fond of William himself ever since William teased him about the town hanging him before they entered Willow Falls after being rescued from Donovan Moskin and John Birch two years before.

"So, you're a friend of his?" Bob questioned while pointing at Gabriel.

Evan nodded.

"No. He's my brother," Gabriel clarified. "He moved in with my family." Gabriel didn't want to go into the details of Evan's life and left it at that.

"Why? Where is your family?" Bob asked.

Maggie spoke softly, "Perhaps he doesn't want to talk about it, Bob. Besides, that is none of our business. I think we should just make sure Evan is welcomed and treated as a member of our family."

Evan's cheeks reddened slightly. His eyes misted just a bit as he explained quickly, "My family is dead. My parents decided to come to Oregon, so we left New York and came west. My mother and younger siblings died on the trail, and my father died in The Dalles. My older brother and I were left alone and got mixed up with two bad men who turned out to be outlaws, and we were all arrested in Willow Falls. They killed the deputy, kidnapped Gabriel's mother, and made her show them where a cabin was on a lake. That's where I got to know her. Matt Bannister came and killed the two outlaws, and that's why I live with them."

"Does your brother live there too?" Maggie asked.

Evan blinked a few times to fight the moisture that clouded his eyes. He missed his brother, Rodney, a great deal. "He was killed too."

"By Matt?" Rhoda asked.

He shook his head slowly. "No." He didn't want

to explain that his boss, Charlie Ziegler shot and killed his brother.

Maggie reached over and placed her hand on Evan's. "You've been through so much tragedy. I'm sorry. But you have a new family now, and I'll make sure you enjoy this week." She leaned over as far as she could to embrace him affectionately. "You're family here."

"That was at my cabin?" Floyd asked.

Gabriel turned his head and answered, "Yes."

Rhoda's brow lifted as she put her attention on Floyd. "We own a cabin?"

"Lee does now."

"That's right, you have a rich son," Bob said from the counter. "That makes him my stepbrother. I wonder if he'd give me a loan. Do you think he would?"

Floyd answered dryly, "You have no collateral, nor would he know you from anyone on the street."

"What's that mean?" Bob challenged his stepfather with a sneer.

"It means he won't loan you a dime."

Rhoda was displeased. "He might. I've met Lee, and we got along well. I'm the only mother he has now, and if I wrote to him, he might give Bob a loan to buy into that saloon."

Bob's eyes brightened. "Would you, Mother? I'd be forever grateful. I don't know where I can come up with that kind of money on my own."

Rhoda nodded thoughtfully. "I never thought about it until now, but yes, I will wire Lee tomorrow."

"No, you won't!" Floyd strongly exclaimed. "I won't have anyone in this house bugging my son for money. He worked his butt off for what he has, and if you want something, go work for it like he did."

Bob narrowed his eyes disparagingly. "You told me when I was younger that you considered me your son too. If that's true, then I'm the same as him. If we're brothers, then why not ask him for a favor? I'd pay him back over time. I only need less than the asking price because I worked my butt off, too, and I've saved three hundred dollars so far. That may not sound like much to him, but I've worked hard for it. Can't you trust me just once? I'll pay him back."

Floyd had some compassion for the young man, but Bob was as unreliable as a rotting board, and it was a lot of money he wanted to borrow from someone else. Floyd knew Bob may have meant every word about paying the money back, but those sincere words are quickly forgotten when there is money in his pocket and a loan to pay back. History repeated itself time and time again. Floyd's voice was firm, "The answer's no. And I'll wire Lee first thing in the morning to tell him so, just in case your mother decides to sneak a wire to him begging."

Rhoda threw a spoon at him that hit the wall and bounced off with a loud clang. "How dare you?" she shouted. "I wouldn't wire Lee without talking to you first! You are such a…" She glanced angrily at Gabriel and struggled to hold her tongue. She slammed her fist on the table and then pointed at Floyd. "We'll talk about this later when your grandson is not here! You need to decide if I'm considered your children's mother or not!"

Floyd's brow wrinkled. "Honey, you'd have to ask them, not me."

"No, I'm asking if *you* consider me their mother. Is this my grandson or not?" she pointed at Gabriel.

"Of course he is. We're married."

"Is Bob your son or not?" Her glaring eyes dared him to give the wrong answer.

Floyd grinned uneasily. "Can we talk about this later?"

"No! It's a simple question. You asked Gabriel if he had questions about his *grandmother*," she emphasized with a bit of jealousy, "I'm the only grandmother he'll ever know. Your old wife is dead and gone. You need to quit talking about her because I'm here!" She pointed at Gabriel. "I'm his grandmother, and I'm Lee's mother now. I'll wire him any time I feel like it, and I don't need you trying to interfere with that! Do you understand me, Floyd?" Her eyes burned into him like a growling dog threatening to attack.

"You can write to him anytime you want, just don't ask for money. If Bob wants money, he needs to work for it or figure it out on his own."

"I am!" Bob shouted. "I work all the time, but you can't make three thousand dollars earning four dollars a night! I need help, and you're refusing to help me. You act like you want me to fail with everything I do. And I don't know why. I'm not a thief, beggar, or scoundrel, I'm just a man trying to do what's right, and no one will help me. I'm not robbing anyone; I'm just looking for some help to get a loan to buy a legitimate business."

Frustrated and embarrassed to argue in front of his grandson, Floyd rubbed his eyes quietly. "Bob, the answer's no."

Bob turned around and hit the wall with a loud bang. "Fine! But you know, I'm going to get the money, and I'll run the Silver Casterlin out of business. You'll be begging me to give you a job!"

Floyd's lips rose slightly. "Probably so. Goodnight, Bob," he said, nodding towards the door.

Bob stormed out of the apartment, slamming the door behind him.

Rhoda sat back down at the table with her chest rising and falling slowly with a sneer on her lips as she fought to keep her temper under control. "I think we are being unfair to Bobby and need to reconsider helping him this time."

Floyd carried his empty bowl to the small kitchen counter. He looked forward to the day when the apartments had plumbed water, so he didn't have to carry buckets of water upstairs to clean the dishes and carry the water back down to dump into a sewer drain. "We don't have that kind of money, Rhoda."

"No, but we could ask the bank."

"I'm not going into debt for him."

"I wouldn't either," Maggie said softly. "He won't pay anything back."

"Then what about asking Lee?" Rhoda questioned, ignoring Maggie's comment.

"No."

"Then what are we going to do, Floyd? Bobby's my baby boy."

"We're going to worry about ourselves because your baby boy is a grown man now. He can manage on his own. Disappointment is a part of life. He'll get over it."

Chapter 4

The next day, Floyd had spent hours walking the two teenagers around Portland, showing the two country boys various things around the city, including the downtown corner where Floyd's father, Fredrick Bannister, had slipped on the ice and broke his back. Fredrick was campaigning in the Oregon gubernatorial race at the time and passed away shortly after that. Floyd took them on the horse-drawn trolly and showed them the sights that came to mind, along with various stores and other things that might interest the two boys. No matter how interesting the sights were, the waterfront's boats and river traffic fascinated Gabriel the most.

The boys had never seen sea-faring ships or busy docks where men labored to load and unload a ship's cargo. There were some areas along the waterfront that Floyd preferred to avoid, but he did take them back to the same warehouse and dock belonging to the Haslett-Jones Shipping Company they had visited the day before.

The tall ship they watched being loaded the day before had already left port and was on its way to the Pacific Ocean for a sea-faring journey. In its place, tied to the dock, was a flat barge loaded with crates of canned salmon from Astoria that the men were unloading. Other men were stacking various supplies and goods on the dock to be pulled back to Astoria by a steam-powered tugboat before returning with the next load of canned salmon to be disbursed accordingly.

"Floyd, you old coot, how dare you show your face around here after taking my money?" Amos Garvin said with a friendly grin. "I suspect you'll be at the poker table on Saturday night so I can win it back?"

"Not this week. I have my grandson visiting, and I want to spend time with him. This is my grandson, Gabriel. He's my boy Matt's son. Oh, and this is Evan; he's my adopted grandson."

Amos shook their hands. "I can only imagine how much fun you're having with this old coot. Don't play poker with him, boys. He'll rob you blind."

"Oh, I wouldn't take money from the boys, but you, I will anytime," Floyd said.

"I'll win it back. What are you doing down here anyway?" Amos asked. He worked for the Haslett-Jones Shipping Company as a warehouse supervisor and played in a weekly poker game with Floyd in a backroom at the Silver Casterlin saloon.

"The boys wanted to see the ships. It's their first time seeing them. They're from over east."

Amos shifted his eyes over the river. "It's pretty quiet today. We have the barge to finish loading, and that's it. I know Pacific Crest Distributing has a couple of ships docked and another waiting, and so does Keefer Winds Trading Company down the road. They'll be lined up here and there, but we haven't got much going on today. We'll be going home early. Say, is that boy of your wife's going to buy the Maroon Squid? He's been going around asking for twenty dollars here and thirty dollars there with the promise to pay back double within three months of his ownership, plus free drinks for a month."

Floyd exhaled with a touch of frustration. "He's trying to buy it. Is he getting any money?"

Amos Garvin spoke through a sarcastic chuckle, "Double your money and get free booze; he's getting some takers. But I gotta tell you, Floyd, from what I heard, he's borrowing big sums from people who are probably not the types of people he wants to cross or cut short."

"I didn't know he was doing that," Floyd answered.

"Well, he better keep his promises to Big Richard and Potsy Jones, or he'll end up floating downriver or wish he was. Your wife's son bragged to Harry earlier that Felix Rathkey gave him hundreds of dollars this morning. If you ask me, he's digging himself into a hole he can't get out of."

Floyd nodded irritably. "Thanks for letting me know. I don't need any of them coming into the Silver Casterlin looking to collect his debt. I better see if I can find Bob and talk some sense into him."

***

The Maroon Squid Tavern was a red single-level building on Water Street in a rougher section of town than Floyd generally liked to go. Inside was like many low-end taverns with cheap liquor behind the bar, scuffed-up tables, and a billiards table on a filthy wooden floor. A hallway at the back of the tavern led to several rooms where a man could find a prostitute.

The Maroon Squid Tavern lacked the class, cleanliness, and good food that the Silver Casterlin prided themselves on. To turn the Maroon Squid into a successful business that would rival, let alone run the Silver Casterlin Saloon out of business, was an immature pipedream—to say the least. The most the Maroon Squid Tavern offered someone was a drink of watered-down cheap liquor, a chunk of dry bread, and possibly a venereal disease.

The tavern was owned by a partnership between Hugh Ogle and a silent partner who lived in San Francisco and had never been to Portland. Hugh wanted to sell his half of the tavern and retire to Salem to live with his recently widowed sister and manage a store his deceased brother-in-law owned. Hugh liked Bob and wanted to give the young man a chance to buy his half of the tavern, but the price was non-negotiable. It was Hugh's retirement money, and if Bob couldn't come up with it, someone else would.

Hugh and Floyd knew each other well enough to know they would never be good friends, but when it came to Bob, they both had his best interest in mind. Floyd explained to Hugh what he had heard about Bob borrowing money from people, including some of the city's more well-known criminal elements.

Hugh rolled his head, exasperated. "I don't think Bob understands that borrowing money from that many people is a darn foolish idea. I told him I needed the money by next week or I'd be making the sale public. I don't have a choice, Floyd. I wish I could do payments for him, but I can't afford to. I gave him a chance, but I don't want him getting into trouble over this. He'd never be able to pay them all back, giving free drinks away. How stupid can he be? Dang, Floyd, I wish I could do more to work with him, but I can't afford to. I'll let Bob know I can't sell it to him and he needs to return that money right away."

"I'd appreciate it. He'll be mad for a while, but better mad than enslaved to everyone he borrowed money from. He'll get over it. Thank you, Hugh. And good luck to you."

Hugh waved a finger as a sudden thought came to him. "You know, Felix is a pretty good lawyer and probably doesn't know that Bob is your son. As a respected businessman in town, it might be a good idea if you pay Felix a visit, explain that Bob has made a foolish decision, and ask Felix to take the money back and use whatever legal means he can to void the other agreements. Being as well respected as you are, Floyd, he might agree to that and help get Bob out of this mess. Big Richard and those folks make me a bit concerned."

***

Felix Rathkey was a lawyer who had come to Portland ten years before to set up a law practice. The Rathkey Attorneys at Law office was a two-story brick building on Sixth Street with a brown canvas awning over the entry. Two other attorneys worked as part of the Rathkey team and were free to have their own clientele but were also assigned clients needing representation by the court of law that Felix was not interested in representing.

In the courtroom, Felix was a competent debater and had a successful reputation as one of the best defense lawyers in the city, if not the state. However, a good portion of his clients were common thieves, ruffians, and as some of the higher society would say, the city's filth. In the courtroom, Felix was a smooth-talking, highly intelligent man who strived to be the District Attorney's worst nightmare for arguing the smallest holes in a case into a sinkhole that most often allowed his clients to walk free.

Felix was married with a seven-year-old daughter and went to church every Sunday as a faithful Christian man for the upper west side to see. He gave free legal advice to his fellow church members and kept his upper and lower society relationships as separated as the East is from the West.

Behind the nice suits and clean-cut man was a cunning individual who had used his talents as a defense attorney and inflated legal fees to become a partner or acquire an interest in several shadier establishments in Portland's lower west and east sides. If his upper society friends knew he owned or was in partnership with some of the unrespectable businesses that he was, it would ruin his reputation. To combat such a threat, Felix set up contracts and a local bank account with a false name and address in a different state. A power of attorney signed by both parties gave Felix complete control of the man's endeavors.

Felix Rathkey claimed he liked to help people and was known for making financial loans. Floyd Bannister had taken a hundred-dollar loan out from Felix once. Getting that loan paid off had cost him nearly three hundred dollars. It only took one time for Felix's collector to arrive at Floyd's door and demand money or pay the consequences of missing a payment to understand the error of borrowing money from Felix. It had taken a long time, but Floyd had paid the loan off with the added high-interest rate. Since then, he had never asked for anything from Felix again.

Floyd left the boys in the waiting area with the office secretary while he entered Felix's private office.

Felix Rathkey was in his mid-forties, an average-height man at five foot nine inches tall and a bit chubbier than he wanted to be at two hundred and thirty pounds. Felix had a round, friendly face that was cleanly shaven—a pair of silver-plated spectacles set on his nose over his intelligent brown eyes. A slightly chipped tooth was the only flaw of his smile. Felix's light brown hair was kept short and respectably combed over to one side with a touch of hair pomade to keep it in place. He had broad shoulders and a short neck that made him look like a concrete block in a light gray pinstriped suit with a white bowtie over a soft blue button-up shirt. A gold chain pocket watch was stuffed in his matching suit vest pocket.

"Floyd Bannister, my goodness, how are you?" He shook Floyd's hand vigorously. "Come in and sit down. Cigar?" he waved to a cigar box on his oversized desk.

"No, thank you." Floyd had learned not to accept anything from the attorney, who was as tricky as a trap-door spider and pliable as a snake. He sat down in a leather back chair.

"So, how can I help you, Floyd? Are you here for a loan? Legal representation by chance?"

"No." Floyd shifted uncomfortably in the chair. He knew the warm and friendly face across the desk could turn cold and unfriendly with the slightest breeze. "I'm here to ask a favor of you."

"Oh? What kind of favor?" Felix asked curiously.

"My stepson, Bob Mears..."

"Oh, yes, Bobby Mears. What about him?"

"I heard he borrowed money from you and many

others to invest in a partnership in the Maroon Squid Tavern. He can't buy it. I talked to Hugh and the deal is off. So, I came to ask you to let Bob give you the money he borrowed back."

Felix frowned as he rested his chin on his folded hands. "Of course, he can bring the money back. That's how deals are done; he pays me back. How many other people did he borrow from?"

"Apparently, quite a few. He's trying to borrow upwards of three thousand."

"Huh. Bob asked me for five hundred."

"He apparently asked Big Richard, Potsy Jones, several men on the docks, and even Laura Eggers for money too, or so I was told."

"Really? Huh," Felix said with a noticeable frown. "Well, tell him he can pay me back today without much interest; five dollars or so. You know, I don't give out loans for free."

Floyd stood. "Thank you."

"Yeah, it's fine. Make sure he pays Big Richard, Potsy, and Laura back today and anyone else of their character. I'll walk you out. Did you hear they spotted a whale in the Columbia River about twenty miles from here yesterday?"

"No. A whale?"

"Yeah. That's what I heard. I was told it was an orca whale. It was swimming along one of the boats heading upriver. It must be lost, but wouldn't it be exciting if it came to town here? I've never seen a whale, but I'd sure like to," he said as he led Floyd out of his office and down a hall to the waiting room.

"That would be exciting, especially for my grandson. He's visiting from the Branson area. He's already fascinated by the ships."

"They must be fascinating if you've never seen one before. But for us? They're as common as a crow. I think we overlook how amazing the engineering of those ships really is. These must be your grandsons?" Felix asked, pointing at Gabriel and Evan.

"Yes. This is my grandson Gabriel and his friend, Evan."

Felix shook their hands. "Felix Rathkey. If you boys get in trouble with the police, look me up, I'm the best lawyer in town."

Floyd offered, "He better not get in any trouble. His father is my son, Matt, the U.S. Marshal. Matt would bust his butt; I'm pretty sure."

Felix's mouth dropped open. "Matt Bannister, the U.S. Marshal, is your son?" he asked, astounded.

Floyd nodded proudly. "Yeah. You didn't know that?"

"No, I didn't know that. And this young man is *his* son?"

"Yeah."

"Huh. I didn't know the marshal was married and had a family. How old are you, Gabriel?" Felix asked.

"I am seventeen. Evan's sixteen."

"Wow." Felix put his attention back on Floyd. "Well, do me a favor; if Matt ever comes to town, I'd like to meet him. Maybe we could have a social dinner and invite some of the more influential people in town and let them know that you're Matt Bannister's father. That might give you a few contacts to help build your career and reputation."

Floyd shook his head doubtfully. "I don't think Matt will ever come here, but if he does, I'll bring him by."

"Excellent." He gazed at Matt's son quizzically. "It was nice to meet you. Gabriel, is it?"

"Yes."

"And you're Evan. Is your father famous too?"

Evan shook his head.

"Well, enjoy your visit." He turned to Floyd. "Have Bobby come see me." He waited in the lobby for his guests to leave and then turned to his secretary. "Send a runner to fetch Big Richard and Laura Eggers. I want them here in an hour. If Bobby Mears comes in, tell him to come back at four. Tell Bobby I'm out of the office or something. Do not accept anything from him. The loan he took he needs to hand to me personally."

Chapter 5

Bob burst into his mother's apartment furiously. He pointed his finger at Floyd and shouted with tears of rage clouding his eyes, "You had no right to tell Hugh not to sell to me! Why can't you stay out of my life? You ruined my chance to make something of myself. Don't you understand? I could own that place!"

"I did what I needed to do to—"

"I can't believe you!" Bob cut Floyd off, outraged. "You'll do anything to make sure I don't do better than you. What is it about me that makes you dislike me? I've never done anything to hurt you, Floyd. Sure, I was a pain in your neck when I was younger, but you have no right to interfere with my life!"

Rhoda walked into the apartment behind Bob, wondering why he was angry. She was in her manager's office on the second floor when Bob barged in looking for Floyd. She had followed him upstairs. "What are you shouting about? They can hear you downstairs. Now lower your voice and tell me what you're mad about instead of just barging into my office and making a scene."

"That man you married ruined my life! He told Hugh not to sell the tavern to me!"

"Floyd, what's this all about?"

Floyd ran a hand through his silver, well-groomed hair. "If I could *speak*, I could explain, but he keeps screaming."

"I have a reason to!" Bob screamed as loud as he could.

Floyd tried to explain in a gentle tone, "Bob, I did you a favor..."

"Some favor!" Bob shouted. "What's the favor, working for you for pennies when I could have made a fortune? You went behind my back and intentionally betrayed me. I'll never ask anything from you again. I'll never speak to you again, and I'll never forgive you." Bob's chest rose and fell quickly as he fought to control his emotions.

Floyd's patience had run out. He stood from his chair and moved across the room to shout in Bob's face, "Damn it, Bob, listen to me! Do you know Felix charges two times the amount you borrow? You'd owe him one-thousand dollars immediately and then interest on top of that! You won't be paying back five hundred dollars. By the time you pay him back, you're at least looking at three thousand or more if you're not fed to the fish by the criminals you borrowed money from because you won't be paying them on time either. By borrowing from Big Richard, Potsy Jones, and Laura Eggers at the same time, you're writing your own death sentence. Or, at best, your selling yourself to be their slave and working yourself to death to pay your debt!"

"I can make that tavern into a gold mine! I have

ideas, and I know I can pay them all back!" Bob argued.

Floyd exhaled and took a breath before continuing in a softer voice, "By giving them all free drinks for a month while the interest climbs higher on several large loans that have already doubled? No, Bob, you can't. I told Hugh what I heard, and we both agreed for your own good not to sell you that tavern. And then I went to see Felix, and you can return the money. You can return it to all three of them, but it needs to be done today. Bob, I know you're upset, but son, I only did it because I don't want to see you get hurt. There will be other opportunities. That rat trap is not the only one you'll come across. You're running head-first into quicksand, and I'm trying to help you. So please, trust me this once and return that money."

Bob sat down heavily in a dining table chair. "I really wanted to be the owner."

"This isn't the best way to get anything. I wish we could help, but I don't have the money. Now, I know you're disappointed, but go return that money to Felix, Potsy, Big Richard and Laura, or anyone else you borrowed from. They're a dangerous bunch, Bob. Go clear this mess up."

Rhoda was stunned to hear what her son had done. She spoke softly, "Go do as he says right now, Bobby."

***

Broken dreams lead to the sorrow of disappointment, which leads to discouragement, which can drag a man's spirit down to the lowest levels of de-

spair when all hope fades away like the wilted ped-
dles of what once was a beautiful flower. Bob was
not heartbroken when his relationship with Ingrid
Moller ended. He was far more heartbroken to lose
her financial support. The loss of her promise to
spoil him with her wealth did not compare to the
brokenness Bob felt to see the opportunity of his
life slip through his fingers, and there was nothing
he could do about it.

Bob had collected over a thousand dollars to return to the lenders. The largest investor was Felix
Rathkey, and being so, Bob walked towards Sixth
Street to return what he had borrowed that morning. He was confident that his ideas and vision for
the future would make the Maroon Squid the most
popular tavern in town. As his anger subsided, he
began to reason with a calmer mindset and knew
Floyd was right about one thing; the last thing he
needed was debts he couldn't pay.

Bob turned onto Sixth Street and walked two
blocks to enter the brick two-story law office
that Felix shared with his assistant attorneys. He
approached the secretary and was informed Felix
had left the office and would return at four that
afternoon.

Bob stepped out of the office and remained under the canvas awning for the shade it supplied to
decide where to go next. It was around two o'clock,
and he had other people he could return money to.
He walked six blocks to a large two-story white
Victorian house with black trim and black curtains
that covered the windows. The Silk Shades Plea-

sure Parlor was owned by Portland's controversial Madam, Laura Eggers.

He entered the front door into the home's foyer, a small room with a middle-aged man sitting on a high stool behind a desk with a single piece of paper on it for him to keep track of who entered the home and what room they visited. He lowered a book he was reading and eyed Bob curiously. "Can I help you?"

Bob knew everyone entering the parlor would be searched for weapons and be forced to empty their pockets for the security of the waiting ladies. He could never afford to visit the high-class ladies for an hour's cost at a minimum, but he had entered the day before to speak privately with Laura Eggers for a loan. "I'm here to speak with Laura," Bob said.

The man, dressed in an expensive tan suit, answered, "She's not here. She is gone until tomorrow."

"Oh…well, I borrowed some money from her this morning and want to return it."

"Come back tomorrow."

"Can I leave it with you?"

"No. I don't want to be responsible for it. She'll be back tomorrow."

Bob walked eight blocks to the Mariner's Union House Tenement building. It was a white three-story wood structure with flaking paint where Big Richard Burkhalter kept his office. Initially, the first floor was a tavern, and the two top floors were rented to sailors coming off ships who wanted to drink and indulge themselves in every way while in port.

Big Richard had discovered it was hard to conduct business in the building while the rowdy and drunken sailors were carousing in the tavern and the floors above him. He closed the bar and turned it into a store specializing in sailor's clothing and goods, along with alcohol and other vices. The two upper floors were now tenements rented to local working men who worked or slept during the day. Big Richard owned other houses to board the drunken sailors and opened the Wavering Wharf Tavern on Water Street.

Bob discovered his long walk across town to be for nothing, as Big Richard was also out of the office for the day. Looking at his watch, Bob wandered along the docks and paid back a few men he had collected small loans from. He eventually walked back to Sixth Street, entered the Felix Rathkey Attorneys at Law office door, and was told to sit down and wait by the secretary.

After a short wait, Felix exited his office and shook Bob's hand. "Hello Bob, I apologize for making you wait. I understand the business opportunity you wanted to invest in when we signed that loan contract closed?"

"It did," Bob said, unable to hide his disappointment.

"That's too bad. Come into the office, and let's take care of this business."

Bob followed and was surprised to see Big Richard and Laura Eggers sitting comfortably in chairs beside Felix's desk facing a lone empty chair that

Bob was invited to sit in.

"I just went to both of your places to pay you back," he said to Big Richard and Laura Eggers. He was relieved to be able to pay them all at the same time instead of walking back across town.

"Sit," Big Richard said with his deep voice. He was a large, robust man with greased black hair combed straight back and a thick black mustache. His round face and cold, steady eyes watched Bob with as much concern as looking at a harmless bug.

Felix sat behind his large desk. "I'm glad to hear that, Bob, because you owe us some money."

"I have it. I have all of it," Bob said, reaching into his pocket.

"Good. I invited Richard and Laura to have lunch with me, and over a lengthy discussion about contracts, we came to an agreement, and I bought your debts from them. We're all businessmen and must profit from all our loans." He paused to exhale noticeably. He waved at Big Richard and then at Laura Eggers with his hand. "They're tough, and you're lucky you're dealing with me, not them. I hate to tell you this, but they raked me over the coals when I bought your contracts from them, but here is the good news. I probably saved your life." He pushed some papers across the desk for Bob to grab. "Here are the agreed-upon contracts and receipts for your debt that I covered for you, signed by Miss Laura Eggers and Big Richard, freeing you from any debt owed to them."

Bob grabbed the papers and gasped. "I only borrowed a hundred dollars from Laura. This says five hundred dollars!" He flipped the page to stare at the one for Big Richard. "Uh...a thousand dollars!" he shouted. "For a two-hundred-dollar loan? Are you crazy?"

Big Richard took a deep breath and exhaled irritably but spoke calmly, "You read and signed my loan agreement. It states the first payment was due in thirty days and no earlier or a penalty would be added to the interest. The penalty, it is clearly written on the contract, is up to my discretion."

Laura added firmly, "You should always read a contract fully before signing. Your eagerness is your stupidity. Well, my business is done here. Richard, shall we leave?"

Big Richard stood. "Yes, my dear friend, I'll take you home." He turned to Felix. "Nice doing business with you. Until next time."

Felix told Bob to wait as he walked his two friends out of his office.

Bob shook his head in horror as he stared at the two amounts. His stomach was tying itself in double knots until he felt sick enough to puke.

Felix entered the office, followed by two men dressed in suits. They stood by the door to block Bob from leaving. Felix sat behind his desk and peered at Bob with a friendly smile while he tapped his desk thoughtfully.

Stunned, scared, and suddenly feeling helpless, Bob shrugged his shoulders. His eyes watered as he spoke with a troubled voice, "I can't afford to pay them that. I make three dollars a night, sometimes four."

"Bob," Felix said slowly, "were you not listening? You don't owe them anything. I paid your debts. You owe me." He shuffled some papers on his desk and lifted one to look at it. "You owe me a total of five thousand dollars."

"What?" Bob gasped, nearly choking over his saliva. "I make three dollars a night. I just borrowed the money this morning. I borrowed less than eight hundred dollars from all of you. How..." He was speechless.

Felix answered, "Compound interest, penalties and fees, taxes too, if that makes you feel better."

"No, it doesn't make me feel better!" Bob stood, beginning to feel a sense of panic gripping his soul. "I can't pay that, and you know I can't pay that. How can I pay you five thousand when you wouldn't loan me one thousand because I don't make enough money to do so! Floyd said you would take the money back. He said you told him so."

Felix nodded. "Floyd's right. Give me what you have."

Bob pulled a large wad of crumpled bills out of his pocket and tossed them onto the desktop. "There, we're even!" Bob exclaimed. He tried to leave the office quickly, but one of the men guarding the door shoved him fiercely to the floor. He landed on his buttocks and stared at Felix with frightened tears clouding his eyes.

Felix shook his head with a slight smile. "Settle down, Bob. You're acting like a mad woman. Have a seat and relax. I'm not going to hurt you," Felix said calmly.

Warily, Bob watched the man that shoved him and caught a glimpse of the grip of a revolver in a shoulder holster under his suit jacket. He sat and wiped a bit of nervous moisture from his upper lip.

"Bob, relax," Felix said calmly. "That being said, I hate to tell you that this money you gave me is nothing but a drop in the bucket because the interest will build up quickly. You're in a great deal of debt. You're right; three dollars a day won't cover the interest," he chuckled. "You're in deep water, Bob."

One of the men at the door asked, "Deep enough to throw him overboard with an anchor tied to his ankle?"

The words sent a cold chill down Bob's spine as it straightened involuntarily. His heart began to pound, his palm sweat, and his breathing became labored. His heartbeat pounded in his ears while his face flushed, and his upper lip began to sweat while waiting for Felix to answer.

"No, Tony," Felix laughed good-naturedly. "I think I have another way to collect my debt this time. Bob, do you think you could work with me, or would you rather the fellas take you for a boat ride?"

Bob couldn't tell if they were being serious or not. He answered quickly, "Um...I...can work with you. I can do anything you want." His willingness to work was never more sincere.

"Good." Felix paused as he watched Bob's hands shake like a wet scrawny dog left in the cold rain to freeze to death. His expression changed from sympathetic to as rigid and emotionless as a tombstone. "Bob, I wrote up a contract for you to sign, and if you don't fulfill it, these two men and others under my employment will hunt you down for long as it takes to find you and bring you to me. And I will personally see to it that you disappear for good. Are we understood on that part?"

"Y...Yes," he stuttered.

"Good. You see, this isn't so bad, right? Bob, I'm easy to work for. You just have to do your part, and this debt I bought is paid for. It's just that easy. Whoosh, vanished, and you don't owe me that any-more. You'd like that, wouldn't you?"

"Y...yes, sir. I would indeed."

Felix nodded slowly, studying Bob carefully. "Good. To make this all disappear instead of you, all you have to do is give me the two boys that were with your stepdad today. Matt Bannister's son and his friend."

"What?" Bob gasped, dumbfounded.

Felix held up the palm of his hand to stop any more questions. "I will only tell you a time and place to have them; how you get them there is up to you. That's your end of the contract to fulfill, not mine. Once that is done, we'll meet back here and wipe the slate clean. You'll be free to go and live on your three dollars a day with no threat from me. I might even give you back the money you gave me as a bonus. But, if you *ever*, meaning in your life-time, tell anyone about this agreement with me or if I hear a single rumor from just one person you told, the first clause of our contract will be applied.

Understand?"

He shook his head. "What clause?"

"I'll make this so clear that even a stupid man can understand," Felix said shortly. "If you fail to bring the two boys when you're told to or speak a word of this to anyone, *ever*...you'll disappear. That means *dead*! Do you understand now?"

Bob nearly choked as he swallowed nervously. He nodded quickly.

"Good. That big man there is named Tony. He will take you into another room with a chalkboard and give you the details of when and where to meet. And maybe, if you succeed and prove yourself trustworthy, we can work together again on a more permanent basis where your three dollars a night becomes a fire starter. Don't fail me, Bob. Tony, he is all yours."

The stern-looking man named Tony pointed at Bob and motioned for him to follow. Bob obediently obeyed.

Chapter 6

"Did you get everything taken care of, Bob?" Floyd asked when Bob came into the apartment.

"Yeah," he answered uneasily, "I did; it's all been taken of. Thanks for your help," he added with a lack of sincerity.

"You're welcome. At least I feel better about that now." Floyd was at the dining table playing a game of chess with Gabriel.

Bob asked Gabriel, "Are you pretty good at Chess?"

"Not really. Grandpa's beating me."

Floyd motioned to an empty chair invitingly. "We're having a chess tournament. Evan beat your mother, and I'm trying to beat Gabriel. It appears Evan and I will be facing off for the title tonight."

Bob sat and scanned the game pieces on the board. "Where is Maggie?"

Floyd said while studying the game board, "Hitchens didn't show up to work tonight. She's downstairs waitressing, so I don't have to be. You could take her place if you wanted to make a little extra money. She's working until eleven."

"Hitchens," Bob said with a hint of frustration. "Are you going to fire him?"

"Depending on why he's not here. He might have a good excuse; I don't know. Check," he said to Gabriel as he moved a bishop in line with a poorly protected king. "I would be down there working myself, but with my grandson here, Maggie was nice enough to volunteer."

Bob exhaled to help him relax. "If you need help tomorrow night, I'll do it. I have to work at the Maroon Squid a bit later. I told Hugh I'd be late to take care of the loan business. I just wanted to come by and let you know it is taken care of."

Floyd offered a kind smile and tapped Bob's shoulder affectionately. "I'm glad to hear that."

Bob faked a quick smile in return. "I was thinking about it, and if the invitation is still open, I'd like to go to Oregon City with you on Saturday."

Rhoda answered from her padded chair in the small family room, "We'd love to have you, Bob. It will be wonderful to have the whole family take a trip together."

"Absolutely," Floyd agreed.

"Good. I figure if I'm Gabriel's step-uncle, then we should be getting to know each other while we can."

Gabriel agreed. "It would be fun. The biggest waterfall I've ever seen is in Branson."

Floyd chuckled. "Well, where we're going puts

the Premro Island Falls to shame."

Rhoda asked, "You didn't see Multnomah Falls when the train passed by it?"

Gabriel shook his head. "No. I was facing the river."

"You didn't see the Columbia River Falls?" Rhoda asked, bewildered.

"No."

Evan volunteered, "He was sleeping. I caught a glimpse as we passed, but not much of one. I was reading or *trying* to."

Floyd offered a slight smile of anticipation. "I can't wait to see your faces when you see them."

Bob frowned heavily, knowing it was never going to happen. "You sound excited."

"I am. I can't wait to show these two boys what a real waterfall looks like."

***

It was Wednesday night, and Bob was not given much time to devise a plan. Maggie working until eleven in the Silver Casterlin Saloon was a concern that Bob had to keep in mind because there was only one staircase down to the first floor. Once there, they could go out the back door, but he feared running into Maggie on the way downstairs, or if bad luck persisted, she stepped out of one of the water closets as they passed by. He did not want to be seen leading the two boys out of the building.

He waited until eleven thirty, not knowing if

Maggie had decided to take a bath after work or not. There was someone in the bathtub. He had knocked, but the person had not answered. He would bet his last dollar that it was Maggie.

He went up to the fourth floor, stepped past his parents' apartment to the end of the hallway where the storeroom was, and knocked on the door. Every breath was a silent prayer, if one could call it prayer, that Maggie would not come up the stairs. He didn't know if she was in the bath or inside the apartment. What he did know was he had very little time to have the two boys at a specific place, or his life was in danger.

The door opened slowly as the sleepy face of Gabriel met him. "What?" he asked.

Bob whispered, "I'm sorry to wake you, fellas, up. I need to get into my trunk real quick to grab something. Do you mind if I come in?"

"No, come in." Gabriel opened the door and stepped back to sit on the bed.

Evan slept on a thin mattress on the floor and moved over as far as he could to let Bob get by him in the dark room. The room had no gas light mounted on the wall like the hallways. Gabriel turned up a small lantern to allow Bob to see.

"Thank you. Again, I'm sorry to bother you two. A Seventeenth Century galley docked here today, and I want to tour it. I have a knife I'm going to trade to go aboard. Do you two want to go? It's an old pirate ship that once belonged to Blackbeard. It has the cannons and everything still."

"We can see it tomorrow," Gabriel said with interest.

"No, you can't," Bob stated. "It's leaving at first light. This is my only chance to see a pirate ship from the seventeenth century that belonged to Captain Blackbeard. I'll probably never see another real pirate ship in my lifetime, and I get to go inside and have a tour of it. If you want to come with me, we can stand where Blackbeard stood. I met the captain tonight at work, and he'll show us around the whole ship and tell us the story behind everything. But if you want to go, you better get dressed."

Evan spoke in a low voice, "Gabriel's grandfather told us not to leave the building at night."

Bob scoffed with a wave of his hand. "Are you a baby? I've lived in Portland my whole life and work at night. It is safe as long as you know where to stay away from. Trust me; this will be one of the most amazing experiences you'll ever have—a real seventeenth-century pirate ship. If you are too afraid of the dark to miss this opportunity, you'll always regret it. I'm going." He grabbed an eight-inch hunting knife from his trunk. "Are you two coming or not?" he whispered.

"I don't know, you're Grandpa might get mad," Evan said to Gabriel.

Gabriel was interested. "Can we wake up Grandpa? He'd like to see it."

Bob put his palms out with a shake of his head. "No. That would be a bad idea because once my mother wakes up, she doesn't go back to sleep, and you both saw how tired she was tonight. Trust me; I'll be with you, so it's perfectly safe. We'll wake Floyd up as the sun rises and take him down there, but he won't get to board it. A pirate's ship, fellas! Come on, don't be babies. Get dressed, and let's go. You'll love it."

"I'm going," Gabriel said, grabbing his pants.

Evan was hesitant. "Your grandfather said not to leave the building after dark. We promised him. Remember?"

"I know, but if it's the only time we can see it, he'll understand," Gabriel reasoned. "Besides, we'll be with Bob. I mean, what's the worst Grandpa could do, be disappointed in us? Mad? He'll understand. Come on, Evan, it's a real pirate ship where Captain Blackbeard lived. We might even find a lost gold piece in a crack, a quill pen he used, or something on board. Can you imagine how neat it would be to own something Blackbeard owned?"

"I don't think we should," Evan said.

"I'm going but don't want to go without you. In fact, I won't go if you don't. But I really want to go aboard that ship and see what it looks like inside. Please, come with me, Evan."

Evan sighed. "Okay."

"Great! Get dressed. Do we need to pay too?" Gabriel asked Bob.

"No. I'm trading my knife for it. It was my grandfather's knife; he was killed in the Alamo. I told the captain about having the knife that killed a few Mexicans at the Alamo, and he offered a trade.

This knife is historically significant."

"Really?" Evan asked doubtfully. "What was his name?"

"Why? Do you know the name of every man killed at the Alamo?" Bob asked with a scowl.

"No," Evan admitted. "I was just wondering."

"Honestly, I found the knife on the street a few years ago. It doesn't mean anything to me. I overheard the galley's captain talking to a man about collecting war relics, and I made up the story and offered to trade it for a tour of his ship. We made a trade, and I don't want to be late to meet him. So, let's go."

"You lied to him?" Gabriel asked while pulling on a boot.

"Yes. It's the chance of a lifetime. You two can thank me later but hurry up. Remember, we must be very quiet, though. I don't want to wake up my mother." Bob had to come up with something to convince the two boys to leave the safety of the Silver Casterlin building with him. Having heard of Gabriel's interest in the tall ships, the idea had forged in his mind throughout the evening. When it came to boats, there was nothing more interesting than pirates.

They walked down the stairs and exited the building without being seen. They walked quickly for some distance before turning towards the river when Bob led them into an alley behind a three-story square-shaped building with no identifying marks or lights on upstairs. A single lantern dimly lit hung near the back door. Bob told them he was meeting the captain there and knocked on the back door. A man with short curly black hair and a thick mustache wearing a suit opened the door and invited Bob and the two boys inside. He closed the door behind them.

They walked into a faintly lit room that appeared to be a laundry or a storage room, with bedding and liquor bottles filling the shelves. Another man, bigger than the first, wearing a derby hat over his short brown hair and a tan suit, stood behind a table with an opened brown bottle of whiskey and five shot glasses filled with a golden liquid. Gabriel and Evan both began to feel uneasy as neither expected a ship's captain to be wearing a clean suit, let alone two of them.

Bob handed the knife to Tony, who stood behind the table. "Captain Jones, here is that knife I promised you that belonged to my grandfather before he was killed in the Alamo. Are you ready to take us aboard one of Captain Blackbeard's ships?" He hoped Tony would catch on to the lie.

The man named Tony nodded as he caught on. "Yeah. But before we go, let's have a drink." He handed the two boys a shot glass of golden liquid.

"No, thank you," Gabriel replied graciously. He was beginning to pay attention to the bad feeling that swirled around in his gut.

Tony reached inside his jacket, pulled his revolver from his shoulder holster, and aimed it toward the boys. "Drink it, now!" Tony demanded with a fierce snarl.

Gabriel's eyes widened as a cold chill of terror worked its way down his spine.

"I'm joking," Tony said with a chuckle and replaced the gun inside his jacket. "But it is customary to have a drink before boarding a ship. It's bad luck if not. So please drink it if you want to come aboard the ship."

Bob laughed uneasily. "Fellas, just drink it."

"If you say so," Gabriel said uneasily, swallowing the shot. "It's apple juice," he said with relief.

Evan exhaled and began to smile as he drank it.

Tony laughed. "Scared you, didn't I?"

"Yes," Gabriel replied with a relieved grin.

Tony turned to his friend, "Open the hatch and let's give these boys a tour."

His friend, Howard, slid a table across the room; the sound of the table legs scraping across the wood floor was unsettling, and caution churned in Gabriel's stomach as a hidden hatch door appeared from under the table's long tablecloth. Howard pulled it open, revealing a dark stairway that led down to what seemed to be the cellar. "We have something to show you, boys."

"I thought we were going to look at a pirate ship?" Gabriel asked uneasily.

Tony walked around the table and grabbed a lantern on the shelf. "We are. You wanted to know about pirates; this is where it begins. This way to where the pirates hid their treasure chests when they'd come to Portland. Follow me." Tony descended the stairs, leading them down into the cool temperatures of the cellar. He walked to a door and pulled it open, exposing what turned out to be a tunnel lined with boards. It was lit by lanterns that hung from the ceiling.

"Pirates never came to Portland," Gabriel stated as he followed the men down the stairs.

"You're wrong. In fact..." Tony made up a fictional pirate story with a rumor of a lost treasure buried somewhere under the tunnel's floor as they slowly moved along it. Before too long, Evan stumbled and spoke with a slur, "My head's feeling a little funny."

"It's the lower atmosphere," Howard explained, "keep walking."

Tony stopped at a heavy wood door along the side of the tunnel about a hundred feet from the cellar and pulled out a key. "This is where the pirates hid their treasure years ago. Some people still do."

"Like what?" Gabriel questioned quietly. His head was feeling lighter and wobbly as well. "I don't..." He was quickly feeling faint as an overwhelming tiredness came over him.

Tony guided him through the door and down a faintly lit tunnel to a brick cell built into the side of the tunnel. Inside, there were about four inches of loose straw on the floor. Tony let Gabriel fall to his knees, and he slowly turned to sit. Evan fell flat on his stomach, unconscious.

"Bob?" Gabriel questioned with a slurring of the

name. His head wobbled to one side before he fell over in a deep sleep.

Tony closed the cell's heavy wood door blocking out most of the available light from a lantern across the tunnel. With the twist of the key and a good jerk, he made sure the heavy door was locked. He glanced at the two unconscious boys and spoke through a narrow-barred window in the door, "You two are the pirate's treasure."

Bob, relieved to have accomplished his task but guilt-ridden, closed his eyes and sighed. A big hand fell on his shoulder. "Good job, Bob. Your debts are paid. I need you to sign those debt release forms, and then you are free to go."

Howard was unrolling a scroll on top of an old wine barrel revealing three pieces of paper. "Here is a pen. Please sign them, and that is it. You're a free man."

Bob glanced back at the door where the sleeping teenagers were as a wave of guilt settled in and took root in his inner being. He wasn't sure how he would ever be able to look Floyd in the eyes once Floyd realized his beloved grandson was missing and might never be seen or heard from again. "What's going to happen to them?"

"Bob, sign," Howard repeated.

"I will. I just want to know what's going to happen to them."

"They're going to become sailors. Bob, sign these so we can go home," Howard said.

Bob stepped over to the wine barrel and signed

his name three times. He handed the fountain pen back to Howard. "I'm done?"

Howard nodded. "You're done."

Suddenly, an arm wrapped around Bob's chest from behind, trapping his left arm in a tight clench like a boa constrictor while another hand slapped a handkerchief soaked in ether over his nose and mouth. Bob struggled to break free, but breathing the ether into his lungs quickly took his will to fight away as the tunnel faded to black.

***

Bob awoke with a gag inside his mouth held in place by a sash of cloth tied around his head. His hands were tied behind his back, and his ankles were chained together and padlocked. He could hear the steam engine's power thudding away and the paddlewheels churning water on each side of the tugboat, moving it along the water's surface without a single lit light aboard the boat as it glided up the Willamette River in the darkness.

Bob was lying on the floor inside the wheelhouse and could see the captain holding the protruding wheel handles while keeping his eyes forward on the dark river. Bob grunted, trying to get the captain's attention, but the man refused to look his way and ignored him. After a short time, the captain slowed the tugboat to a stop. Bob's desperate cries through the gag alerted Tony, standing just outside the pilot house door.

Tony entered the pilot house, heartlessly grabbed

Bob under the arms, and dragged him out of the pilot house onto the short deck as the forward momentum of the tugboat began to slow with the slowing paddlewheels.

For the first time, Bob could see the tugboat had left the city, and they were up the Willamette River surrounded by dark forests with thick walls of black reaching into the night with the treetops illuminated by the starry sky and moonlight. With his fate quickly becoming realized, Bob tried to scream for someone to take the gag out of his mouth so he could plead for his life, but the gag remained to keep his cries muffled while the two men padlocked a short chain connected to a fifty-pound anchor to one of the chain links around his ankles.

Terrified, Bob screamed through the gag until he choked and tried to regain his breath. Sweat dripped down his face as he tried to break the binds around his wrists and kick his legs free from the two men that held him. He squirmed and turned every which way to break free, but the best he could do was flare his nostrils with rage and panic. His eyes were wide, muscles tense, and veins standing out in his neck while his fists were clenched in a continuous effort to break free. The knowledge that his death by drowning was imminent terrified him. He had kept his part of the deal and would pay for it with his life.

Tony waited for the tug to stop drifting and lit a match for his cigar, letting the match burn so that Bob could see his face. He sucked in the cigar smoke and slowly released it from his mouth. His eyes watched Bob squirming on the deck like a worm trying to escape its fate of a fishing hook. "Sorry, Bob. You did well, but the risks of you talking are too high. Let's throw him in."

Bob hollered through the gag in an attempt to beg for his life. He shook his head and began to sob. He screamed with all his might as the two men raised him from the deck.

Tony and Howard lifted Bob, despite his efforts to fight them, and dropped him in the river with a sudden splash that was louder than the two men expected. Bob frantically tried to keep his head above water by kicking his feet, but the chain around his ankles was connected to the anchor still on the tugboat, limiting his motion significantly. Each desperate kick brought his mouth out of the water just long enough to scream and beg for his life through his pleading eyes, and then he'd go underwater again only to kick his legs and try to plead again.

Howard chuckled. "Look, Tony, Bob's bobbing."

Tony picked up the anchor and dangled it over the side. "Not for long." He dropped the anchor overboard. The last thing Bob heard was Tony say, "Bye, Bob."

Chapter 7

"Rhoda, have you seen the boys?" Floyd asked, coming into the apartment.

"No. Why?"

"I went to wake them up, and they're not there."

"They're probably in the water closet or taking a bath. I'm sure they'll be up here soon enough. They better be, or their breakfast is going to get cold. What do you have planned today?" Rhoda asked.

"I don't know. I should have been more prepared to find fun things to do to keep them entertained. We walked all over this city for the past two days; I don't know what else I can show them in town. I don't have any fishing poles and don't know if either boy can swim, so I'm hesitant to rent a rowboat just in case. I'll ask them what they want to do. Maybe they have an idea or two."

Rhoda suggested, "You could walk to the butcher shop, say hi to Maggie, and bring some bacon home."

"We could certainly do that. I think I'll wander downstairs and see if they are there. It seems a little later than usual for them not to be wanting breakfast."

"Stop worrying about them. They can have a cold breakfast if they want a cold breakfast. They are two teenage boys, probably curious about how a water faucet works and what the city offers without their Grandpa holding their hand. They're fine."

"I suppose you're right. I'll go down and check on the saloon and see what the boys are doing while I'm at it."

***

Evan opened his eyes to the strange sight of yellow straw on his face and the scent of mildew in his nose. His head ached as he sat up and rubbed the side of his temples. Grimacing, he took a moment to gaze at the strange surrounding of brick walls and a heavily beamed ceiling. A heavy and thick wooden door with a three-by-six-inch opening with three iron bars inlaid into the wood let the available light from a lantern in the tunnel inside the dark cell. He twisted his head with alarm and was relieved to see Gabriel sleeping beside him. He leaned over to prod him. "Gabriel. Where are we?"

Gabriel grunted and squeezed his eyes tighter with a throbbing in his head. He flung his arm outward to hit Evan as he turned over to his back. "What?" he griped.

"Where are we? Wake up." Evan was increasingly

becoming more anxious the more the night before came back to him.

Gabriel opened his eyes and focused on the heavy dark beams over their head and the brick walls. He gradually sat up, becoming more aware of his surroundings. "A cell? Are we in a cell? Where's Bob?"

"I don't know. The last I remember was drinking that juice and going down into a tunnel."

Gabriel's expression grew concerned. "You weren't feeling good. I wasn't either."

"We didn't get drunk, did we?" Evan asked.

"No. I think..." Gabriel tried to swallow with a dry throat. He was thirsty. "I think we were drugged. Where's Bob?"

Evan stood up slowly and tried to open the cell door. "It's locked."

Gabriel got to his feet and tried to look down the horizontal boards of the corridor from the small window. "Help!" he yelled. Gabriel grimaced with a sharp pain that throbbed in his head. He kicked the door, trying to break it open, but it held secure. He kicked it repeatedly until he felt weak and out of breath. He sat down against the cold wall.

"Help!" Evan yelled out the small opening as he took over, trying to kick the door open to no avail. He sat down, winded and weak.

"I'm thirsty," Gabriel admitted.

"Same here. Hungry too."

"I don't know what's going on, but I think we're in trouble," Gabriel said with a higher-pitched tone than usual. Realizing they were being held prisoner brought overwhelming fear and uncertainty.

"Trouble with the law?" Evan asked anxiously. "This can't be a jail, can it?"

"I wouldn't think so; we were drugged. We had to have been…" His breathing began to increase. "We've been kidnapped."

Evan's bottom lip began to quiver. "For what?"

"I don't know."

***

An hour later, the sound of a door opening echoed down the tunnel, and then the sound of a key turning the lock of their door sounded before the heavy door was pulled open. The curly dark-haired man with a mustache who had opened the door in the alley the night before held a silver-plated revolver in his hand and aimed it at the boys. A small Chinese man in his forties set a tray carrying bowls of food and a silver pitcher of water with a tin cup in the cell near the door.

"Why are we being kept here?" Gabriel asked as he rose to his feet slowly.

The Chinese man backed out of the door while the man holding the gun answered with an iron-plated expression, "You'll be fine. Don't worry." He closed the door.

Gabriel shouted out a desperate threat, "My father is Matt Bannister, and he'll come looking for me!"

The man who locked the door peeked through the window like he would say something but left wordlessly.

"Why are we here?" Gabriel shouted. "Come back!" They heard a heavy door close at the end of the tunnel, and then it was silent. "Evan, we're not here by accident."

Evan reached for the pitcher and filled the cup to quench his thirst. He handed the cup to Gabriel to get a drink. They each ate the small bowls of rice and drank some more water. Before long, their heads began to feel light, and they again laid down to sleep.

***

Floyd was growing frantic. It was past noon and there was no trace, sign, or sight of the two boys. Concerned, he set out to find Bob to see if he had seen the boys, but to Floyd's dismay, he could not locate Bob either. He had learned Bob had worked the night before for a few hours and then went home sick around eleven, but Bob had not gone back to his friend's house where he was staying. He had not been seen since the day before. Various scenarios filled Floyd's mind, from maybe they went fishing to perhaps they got drunk somewhere and were sleeping it off, despite how unlikely it seemed.

There were bad elements in town, and the more severe scenarios also crossed his mind. Floyd walked all over town checking restaurants, saloons, taverns, and even bordellos to see if anyone had seen Bob and two teenage boys matching their description. He had no luck finding them or anyone who had seen them.

Growing more frantic, he went to the police department to ask about any bodies found the night before or any arrests matching the three missing young men. However, the police had not found any bodies nor arrested anyone fitting the names or descriptions given. The hospital had no patients by those names or fit the descriptions. Floyd was out of ideas. He had spent hours searching before going home, only to learn the boys had not returned. Becoming increasingly concerned, Rhoda as well began to search for them.

As the day came to a close, Floyd was desperate to find his grandson, who was entrusted into his care. It was becoming more likely that if he could locate Bob, he'd find the boys. Several times Floyd had stopped and thought of where Bob might be, but one thought that kept nagging at him was that Bob had borrowed money from some of the more infamous people in the city with less than honorable reputations. Floyd had walked miles back and forth across the city asking anyone he could think of about the boys and had learned nothing. Every hope he had was running dry, and eventually, he found himself standing in front of the Rathkey Attorneys at Law Office.

"Miss," Floyd said to the office secretary politely, "Have you seen Bob Mears today?"

"Who, sir?"

"Bob Mears, my stepson. He came in yesterday to pay Felix back some money. He and my grandson have disappeared. I can't find them anywhere."

"Well, sir, he's not been here today. But I hope you find them."

"I would like to talk to Mister Rathkey, if possible."

"Mister Rathkey is with a client right now. You could have a seat and wait if you'd like."

Floyd was running out of time and didn't want to wait for an unspecified amount of time to ask a simple question. "Miss, I don't have time to wait. I'm looking for my grandson, so please get Mister Rathkey for me now."

"I'm sorry, sir, but he is in a meeting."

Frustrated, scared, and desperate for any helpful information, Floyd shouted, "Felix!"

The secretary stood from behind her desk and pointed at the door. "Sir, please leave!" the secretary ordered sternly.

Floyd stepped past the lady, down a hallway, and abruptly opened Felix's office door. It was empty. "Where is he? Felix!" Floyd shouted.

A side door opened in the hallway, and Felix Rathkey stepped out, closing the door behind him. "Floyd, I am having a consultation with a client. But since you rudely interrupted me, what can I do for you?" He was irritated about the abrupt interruption.

Floyd didn't care about being polite, the only thing he cared about was finding his grandson, and he was determined to turn over every rock and buried stone to do so. "Bob and my grandson are missing."

Felix grimaced. "I'm sorry to hear that, but what

does that have to do with me? I don't know why you'd be looking for them here."

Floyd lowered his voice while his eyes hardened into a glare. "The last I knew, Bob owed you money."

Felix's head lifted with understanding. "Oh...I see. Come with me." He invited Floyd into his office and closed the door behind them. He immediately went to a wooden file cabinet, opened a drawer, fingered through the files until he found what he was looking for, and pulled it out. He handed a piece of paper to Floyd. "Read this."

Floyd read a receipt stating that Bob's five-hundred-dollar loan was paid in full. It was signed by both Felix and Bob the day before.

Felix wasted no time to explain, "Bob paid me back the five hundred dollars he owed me, and we are clear. Like, I told you I would do, no interest was added. If you thought I would have anything to do with his disappearance, you should be ashamed of yourself. Now, can I get back to my meeting?"

Floyd handed the paper back to Felix. "My apologies. I'm just worried."

Felix put a hand on Floyd's shoulder affectionately. "Floyd, I'm sure they'll show up. Teenagers aren't always reliable. I'm sure they're fine, though. Now, I must get back to my client."

Floyd walked across town to question Laura Eggers and Big Richard and was shown the same type of written receipt signed by them and Bob. There had been several people Floyd had questioned that mentioned that Bob had paid their money back.

If there was one individual who Floyd didn't want to talk to, it was Potsy Jones, the owner of Potsy's Sailor's Lair. Potsy was a known crimp and had approached Rhoda in the past about working with him to shanghai men from the tenements when he needed them. Having been told that Bob borrowed some money from Potsy, Floyd questioned Potsy and was shown a register book indicating that Bob had returned the money with an added one-dollar interest.

Floyd walked home, growing more defeated and afraid yet desperate to find his grandson. He prayed as he walked that he would find them at home when he arrived. But to his dismay, all he found was a concerned wife and stepdaughter wondering where the three boys could be. They were worried, and they asked if they should send a wire to Gabriel's parents. Floyd hesitated to cause an unwarranted panic because there could still be a reasonable explanation. There was a chance that the boys had joined Bob on some excursion early that morning and hadn't made it home yet. That was their hope.

"If they are not back by morning, I'm wiring Matt," Floyd said.

***

Gabriel barely opened his eyes when he heard someone speaking. In the haze of being half asleep and barely conscious, he could see the blurry image of two men standing in the doorway watching them. The two men were talking together, but the words faded in and out with his consciousness.

"Kid!" the man shouted. He chuckled and then told his friend, "He's out."

"Give them a few pitchers of pure water to wash some of that crap out of their system. Give them more than just rice. Throw some meat and fruit into their meals to keep them strong. When they start getting too loud or out of control, put the Morphine back in the water. Unlike the other bums we've sold, I want them taken care of, Tony. These boys are gems. Do you hear me?"

"Yes, sir."

"Floyd Bannister has been asking about them. He's been running all over town asking questions. Don't be surprised if the Marshal, Matt Bannister, comes to town." He nodded at Gabriel. "That's his son."

Tony Hurner took a deep breath. "Don't you think the marshal might cause some trouble if he comes here?"

Felix shook his head. "No. We covered our bases, and these boys will be gone in three or four days for a one-way trip around the world to Africa aboard the *Everson Solstice*. The ship's having some repairs done." He smiled contently. "Don't fret, Tony, we're not involved."

"And if they come back?" Tony questioned.

Felix padded his friend on the back of his shoulder. "So what? They have no idea who we are. Let's get out of this dingy place and get something to eat. Do you want to have some fun? Let's go to the Silver

Casterlin for dinner and see how Floyd is doing."

Tony Hurner wasn't amused. "Did you know that boy was the marshal's son when we took him?"

Felix nodded proudly. "I did. That's why I did it."

"Why? I don't understand the reasoning. We're supposed to take vagrants without families," Tony said.

Felix offered a casual smile. "I know that's generally the rule, but Matt Bannister is famous. He is perhaps the most famous lawman in America, and no one has ever gotten the better of him. A hundred years from now, long after we're gone, he will still be known as one of the greatest of all time, right? But his son will disappear, and that is one mystery he will never be able to solve. It will be a mystery that will haunt him and the nation forever, but I'll always know I got the better of him. On my deathbed, I will let it be known that I did it. I'll put an affidavit in my will explaining exactly how and why I did it. I may never become famous for being a lawyer, but I'll be the man behind the greatest unsolved mystery that haunted Matt Bannister to his grave."

Tony replied, "You know Matt Bannister is not a city policeman, right? I doubt our police will try to stop him from tearing this town apart to find his son. I've read about him, Felix. He's brutal."

Felix grinned with a silent chuckle. "So are you, Tony; that's what I pay you for. You two country bumpkins will get along fine. Maybe you can even help Matt look for the boy."

Tony wasn't convinced it was a good idea. "I

think we should take these two across town and let them wake up in the woods and avoid any risks that we don't need."

"It's not like you to worry about the law. You know I'll keep you safe. Besides, they were with you and Howard last night. We can't afford to let witnesses go free."

"It's not the local law I'm concerned about, Felix. That boy's father will come here and raise hell. Why are you intent on doing this? We should just let these kids go and avoid any trouble. His father is a bloodhound that doesn't stop, and he won't stop looking until he finds the truth. That's what I've read about him anyway."

Felix was unconcerned. "Tony, I'm doing it simply because I can. Relax. I have it all under control. If the marshal shows up and starts snooping around, those boys will be gone, and there's nothing to find. But if by chance he starts digging too deep, we got rid of Bob, and we can get rid of the marshal the same way. In fact, maybe we will anyway. That would be a much greater mystery than his missing son." Felix watched Gabriel sleeping soundly on the straw bedding. "Make sure Pan empties the waste bucket before he goes home. Let's go see how Floyd is doing."

Chapter 8

Matt Bannister stepped off the train and into the humid Portland air of a hot afternoon with his Parker shotgun in his left hand and his saddlebags thrown over his shoulder. He wore a comfortable blue pinstriped suit and put his gun belt on before departing the train. His long dark hair was in a ponytail, and his beard and mustache were neatly trimmed. The trip to Portland wasn't a pleasure trip, and the seriousness was reflected in his expression. He pulled the brim of his hat down to shield his eyes from the glare of the sun's reflection off the blue water of the Willamette River bordering the rail station. Matt looked across the river towards West Portland. It was a solid line of piers cluttered with warehouses with company names painted across them all along the riverbank as far as his eyes could see.

Despite the congestion along the river, the blue water had a certain beauty, with several tall ships moored along the piers and several more spread out and anchored in the middle of the river. The ships varied in size and number of masts, but all had their sails furled, revealing the bare masts standing tall and proud in the air. A long rowboat transferred the sailors from one anchored vessel to shore. Black smoke rose like a wildfire from the smokestacks of the coal-burning steam-powered tugboat, slowly pulling a barge with a dozen swine past an anchored three-mast ship in the center of the river.

Beyond the busy river, the downtown buildings varied from two to three stories tall. They were mostly built of wood and close together, but the city spread out in a vast area at the foot of a beautiful tall hill thick with evergreen trees. Matt had been to big cities in his travels but doubted he had ever been to one with a more intriguing first impression. The train had come through the east side of the city, which was big enough to make the starting point of looking for the two boys a rather daunting venture. Getting his first look at the city from across the river, he could see how vast Portland was compared to Branson and the other small towns he had grown used to.

Morton Sperry stepped off the train in awe at the city's vastness and humid air of a hot sweltering day without a breeze. He was dressed in the closest to a suit that he could come up with—black pants, a black vest, and a tan shirt with sweat staining his underarms and back from a hot train ride. His worn and dingy hat covered his head to shade his eyes as well. His neck-length brown hair was unbrushed and dangled freely, while his hardened features and thick goatee made him look far more like a dangerous criminal than a lawman. The forested high rolling hills above West Portland were more of a welcoming sight to him than the city or waterfront lined with piers, buildings, and ships. Morton carried his rifle over his shoulder with one hand while his saddle bags were flung over his shoulder as well.

He stared at the barge passing by with an odd expression. "Sailing pigs. You won't see that in Natoma."

William Fasana stepped off the train with a giant grin on his face. He had been to Portland not long before to visit his Uncle Floyd and newly discovered favorite Aunt Rhoda when he came to see the woman he was courting, Maggie Farrell. William was excited to be back in the city and took a deep breath into his lungs as he stepped onto the train stop platform. "Don't you love it? The smell of city sewer, steam, and coal smoke just makes my day spectacular! Mmm, I love it! Don't you, Mort?"

"Not really, no," Morton replied. He was stifled by the humidity and heat bouncing off the concrete under his feet. It was Morton's first time west of the Cascade Mountains, and the summer heat of Western Oregon wasn't the same as the dryer heat of Eastern Oregon.

"Where do we go from here?" Matt asked William.

"Follow me." William wore a tan suit, with his

double reversed gun belt on his hip, and held a carrying case for his clothing and personal effects. His clean black Stetson hat was placed over his free-flowing blond wavy hair that fell over his shoulders. A neatly manicured goatee covered his weathered face. William quickly walked from the train station to the Stark Street Ferry, which they rode across the Willamette River. A trolley ride and a few blocks of walking on concrete sidewalks eventually led them into the Silver Casterlin Saloon.

William passed the saloon's bar with a wave to the bartender as he continued towards the office, where he found Floyd working. "Uncle Floyd!" he thundered as he opened the door. "I need a free drink after roasting on that train, but we're here."

Floyd stood with a pleased smile. "William, my favorite nephew, or the only one that claims me, anyway. I'm glad to see you." He embraced him in a hug. "Did Matt come?"

"I'm right here, Dad," Matt said as he stepped into view.

"Son." Floyd stepped forward, hesitant to hug his son. He reached an awkward hand out to shake. Matt shook his hand firmly. "I'm glad you're both here. Matt, I'm sorry about Gabriel. I don't know where he is."

After hearing the words, Matt's breath escaped his lungs in an exasperated gasp. "I was praying he'd be here when we arrived. He hasn't shown up?"

Floyd shook his head.

"This is my new deputy, Morton Sperry. Morton, this is my father, Floyd," Matt introduced them as he turned his head to hide a slight moistening of his eyes.

Floyd stared at Morton as a small smile lifted his lips. He had been good friends with Morton's father when the two men standing before him were little boys. "Morton," he shook his hand firmly. "Welcome to Portland, fellas. Let's go upstairs, and I'll tell you what I know. Lord willing, you three men can find Gabriel and Bob."

"His name's Evan," Matt corrected sourly.

"Evan's missing too, but so is Bob."

"Bob's missing too?" William asked.

"Yes. He went missing at the same time. I'm figuring they were together, but I don't know how because I told those boys not to leave this building after dark. They promised me they wouldn't. They went to bed and were gone in the morning."

Matt raised a finger curiously as he asked pointedly, "Who is Bob?"

"Rhoda's son. He's twenty-six. Let's go upstairs, where we can sit down and talk. Rhoda's near frantic trying to locate Bob. He's her baby boy, you know. William, grab a drink if you'd like; either of you as well. It's on the house. If you're hungry, we can put in an order, and they'll bring the food and drinks up."

"If they could bring up a pitcher of water, that would be great for me and a meal," Matt said. They all ordered food and followed Floyd to the fourth floor to his apartment.

William entered first with a loud, "Hello, Aunt

Rhoda, or should I start calling you *Mom*, just in case I marry your daughter?"

Rhoda was sitting in her chair weeping as she looked at Bob's picture in a family photograph taken three years before. She set the photo down, rose quickly, tightly wrapped her arms around William, and sobbed bitterly. "Thank you for coming," she blubbered through her sobs, "Find my son, Willie. Help me find my son." Her tears fell heavily enough to wet his shirt.

William was surprised to have the strong and independent woman who had shown so much strength, fire, and vitality in the past, sobbing on his shoulder. He put his hands on her back and spoke softly. "That's what we came here to do, Aunt Rhoda. We'll find him."

***

An hour later, they were seated in the small family room in a circle with dining chairs surrounding the davenport and padded chairs. Floyd told Matt and the others all he knew about Bob and his life, including borrowing the money to buy the Maroon Squid Tavern and the proof that he paid it all back. He told them everything he and the boys did, and when questioned, there was nothing that stood out as suspicious or that he could suggest as a starting point.

Floyd finished, "I looked everywhere I could and questioned everyone Bob knows. There's no trace of him or the boys. My first suspicion was Big

Richard or Potsy, Jim Weathers, Felix, and Laura Eggers, but I asked them all, and Bob signed the receipts freeing him from any debts owed to them."

Matt stood and turned towards an opened window to stare out over the city. His eyes went to the beautiful blue water of the Willamette River. He spoke coldly, "I knew I didn't want Gabriel coming here. Portland is known for people disappearing. '*Shanghaied*' is a better word for it. This is exactly what I was afraid of!" He turned around to ask his father sharply, "Do you know anyone involved in that?"

Floyd was surprised by the fury in Matt's eyes and tone. "Not personally. There are rumors about some people, but I can't say for sure."

"What name comes to mind?" Matt asked pointedly.

Rhoda answered sharply, "Potsy Jones. He's a crimp. He owns a sailor house on Water Street, and he's involved in that. I know because he asked me to send single men his way."

Matt shot a hardened glance at his father. "I thought you just said you didn't know anyone involved in it?"

"I don't!"

Rhoda answered plainly, "Potsy didn't talk to your father. Everyone knows Floyd is too honest and weak to do that, even for money..."

"Weak?" Floyd questioned abruptly.

"Yes, weak. You haven't got the jewels," Rhoda said with an upwards thrust of her palm and a firm grip with her fingers. She put her attention back on

Matt. "Potsy spoke to me in my office; I manage the tenements here. He wanted me to point out single men renting rooms that wouldn't be missed. And any available woman too. I told him to get lost." She nodded with tightened lips.

Floyd frowned questionably. "Is that what happened to that young man named Jack that disappeared from here? That young French fellow, too?"

"I don't know!" she exclaimed with a hardened glare.

"Not Big Richard or the lawyer, Felix, though? No one else?" Matt questioned. The news of borrowed money was a red flag and perhaps a motive. It was stated that Bob had borrowed the most significant sum of money from Felix Rathkey.

"No, just Potsy," Rhoda answered.

Floyd added, "There are rumors that Big Richard may also have a hand in shanghaiing. I've heard Felix isn't so innocent himself when it comes to the law. The story is he owns a brothel on Third Street that has a trap door leading into a tunnel system, but again, that's just hearsay. I don't know whether Felix owns it or if the trap door story is true. I've never been there."

William couldn't resist, "Liar! That's the one you took me to the last time I was here. Did you ever get rid of that more southern-ish lice issue?" He laughed at Rhoda's scowling expression toward Floyd.

"William," Matt said, not appreciating the joke. "Dad, please, continue."

Floyd smiled at William's humor. "I did, by the

way, William. You should have seen the barber's face when I told him I needed a shave." He laughed for the first time in days.

William's laughter roared.

"Excuse me," Matt said irritably. "My son is missing, and I'm not finding the jesting funny. I want answers. I'm not here to visit! Dad, finish what you were saying."

Floyd shrugged as his smile faded. "I don't remember what I was getting at. I had a point, but I don't know what it is now."

Matt glared harshly at William for interrupting the conversation with a stupid joke. "That's too bad because it may have been important." He rubbed his beard thoughtfully as silence fell over the room.

Morton suggested, "Maybe we should start with the most obvious. The people that we know are involved in taking people. That Potsy fellow."

"Oh!" Floyd exclaimed. "I remember now. Tunnels. The trap door I mentioned supposedly drops down into a tunnel. There are tunnels underground for delivering supplies that I know. But I heard the Chinese have a maze of tunnels that they use for all kinds of things, including shanghaiing. That's what I've heard."

Matt sat down and buried his head in his hands. "I have spent some time in Chinese tunnels, which are not much fun." He removed his hands and twirled his thumbs which could still ache occasionally. "Where is your Chinatown from here?"

"They have a twelve-block section of town not far from the river, about seven blocks north of here."

"Twelve blocks?" William gasped. "No one's run them out of town yet?"

"No. Everyone leaves them alone. The Chinese make up much of our workforce, digging trenches for the waterworks. They're good people. I have two working in my kitchen."

Matt looked at his two deputies. "I'll tell you all right now. At the moment, I'm as lost as Gabriel is. I'm looking out over this city, it's massive, and there are tunnels underneath too. If we stick together, we won't find anything. I'll be perfectly honest with you all; this is out of my expertise because it's hard to follow tracks on concrete. And that's the world we're in."

"Are you saying you can't do anything?" Rhoda asked bitterly.

"No," Matt answered sharply. "I am putting my faith in the Lord and relying on God's grace and mercy to lead us to the boys somehow and someway." He told his deputies, "We need to split up to cover more ground and try to find an avenue that might lead one of us to the boys. We need to attack this from three different angles; I just don't know what those angles are.

"I think our best bet is to leave those angles in the Lord's hands and see where they take us. But while we are here, we can not be seen together or know each other. Just like that reporter who wore the leatherman costume and played a role, so are you two. So, take your badges off and hide them. You're no longer deputies. I want you both to find a fake last name and history in case your reputation has reached this far. I'll confront all those people Dad mentioned and raise some hell to get the attention of whoever took my son. That's what I'll do.

"William, your role is to say you don't know me, and we're not related. You're just courting Maggie and don't like me. I don't know what to tell you beyond that. Do what you must to get to know Potsy Jones or Big Richard. Use your best judgment to try to learn anything you can."

William shrugged. "I don't like you, so that will be easy."

"What about me? Boss?" Morton asked.

"Morton, you look mean enough to flow in and out of the saloons and places on the riverfront that those types of people frequent without raising any suspicion. Make friends and try to learn what you can. See if you can't make some friends with the worst of them. If anyone can get away with that, it's you."

William explained to Morton, "What Matt's saying is you are one of them, a criminal."

Morton smirked. "So, it should be like going home for me, then?"

"You'll be calling some old barmaid *Ma* before sunset," William agreed.

Matt ignored his two deputies' lighthearted teasing. "Dad, Rhoda, I don't want anyone knowing William and Morton are with me. It's better if the people involved don't know who they are. So don't tell anyone, or we will never find out what happened to Bob, Gabriel, and Evan. Secrecy needs to be kept as our top priority. Understood?"

"Yes," they agreed.

"Good. Morton, why don't you wander the docks and snoop around to see if you can make friends or get a job with Potsy Jones or Big Richard. I already know where William is going. Maggie has a hold of him like a bull's nose ring. I'll go to the Maroon Squid Tavern, announce my arrival, and see where that takes me. Keep your wits and stay alert and sober. We'll meet back in here after dark." He asked Rhoda, "Do you have any rooms we can stay in?"

"Two of you can sleep where the two boys were, and one can sleep on our davenport."

William volunteered, "I'll sleep on the davenport since I'll be talking to Maggie until late anyway. And speaking of my dear lady, I'm going to see her. Don't worry, boss, I'll be working too. Gamblers familiar with this area often have a lot to say with enough drinks and good luck. I may sacrifice some money, but I'll get you what you need to know."

"You do that," Matt said. He questioned his father, "Where would I find the Maroon Squid Tavern? I'll start there."

Chapter 9

Matt entered the Maroon Squid Tavern and was quickly aware that he was the only man wearing a suit and Stetson. The other patrons were dressed in clothing for manual labor; loose-fitting flared trousers held up by a belt pulled tight at the waist or suspenders over sweat-stained, long-sleeved cotton shirts. He knew he wasn't in Branson anymore when he noted that all the men wore heavy work boots on their feet and flat or knit caps and an occasional sweat-ringed bowler on their heads. He stood out like a sheep amongst hogs and got their attention immediately by entering and standing at the bar.

"What can I get you?" a middle-aged man asked as Matt approached the bar.

Matt's eyes scanned the patrons around the filthy tavern filled with smoke and a musty stench that tickled Matt's nose. A homely prostitute in her mid-forties was sitting in the corner, trying to use her loose clothing to entice an old gray-haired man. The old timer appeared about as interested in her as he was in the dog crap clinging to his boots. His interest was in the glass of alcohol he gazed at with the sagging expression of a lifetime of regrets.

"Are you the owner?" Matt asked the bartender.

"No, I'm not," the bartender answered roughly. "Do you want something?"

"Where would I find the owner?"

"Not here, but he'll be back. Do you want something or not?"

"No," he stated. Matt noticed in the mirror behind the bar that a skinny, poorly dressed man in baggy clothes was approaching him from behind. Matt could see the curious expression in the man's eyes as he approached.

The stranger leaned on the bar beside Matt and rubbed the material of Matt's suit coat between his fingers. The man was about Matt's age, in his early to mid-thirties, and hadn't bathed in a while. His balding, short brown hair was unkempt and greasy. His face was thin with sunken cheeks and unshaven. He smelled of stale beer, filth, and body odor. "That's a nice suit. It tells me, Mister, that you could afford to buy me and my friend a drink."

"Does it?" Matt asked.

"Yep. Doesn't it, Frank?" he asked the bartender.

"That's up to him, JoJo. You know you're not supposed to pester other customers," the bartender, named Frank, said.

Matt scanned the mirror to see where the fellow's friend was, but he could not identify an obvious friend of the man beside him. The foul-smelling man named JoJo leaned closer to him. "You might want to buy me a drink, you know?" It came across as more of a threat than a request.

Matt's suit coat covered most of his holster, but the man should have noticed the gun belt as it wasn't hidden. Matt spoke as his right hand moved slowly toward the holster. "I have an idea. How about we make a trade? I'll buy you a drink when you tell me where Bob Mears is."

"Huh?" JoJo grunted.

Matt slowly drew his revolver, stuck the barrel in the man's belly, and pulled the hammer back until it clicked. "You heard me. Now where is your friend?" His eyes hardened like a cold stone. Unable to identify the man's friend, Matt was concerned about being blindsided when he least expected it.

Immobilized by the shock of a gun pressed against his belly, JoJo froze as panic seized him. His blue eyes began to water while his hands and bottom lip trembled noticeably. His voice had become strained as he choked out with a stutter, "D...don't k...k...kill me." His quivering lip strengthened against his top lip, forcing a frown while his brow lowered, wrinkling his face emotionally just before he blurted out frantically, "Don't kill me!" He collapsed to the tavern's floor, curled into a ball, and wailed like a whipped child with loud uncontrolled sobs. Reaching into his baggy jacket, he pulled a black rat from an inside pocket and held it close to his face as he bawled.

Matt stared at him, stunned by the man's emotional breakdown. Matt lowered the hammer and replaced the gun in his holster. He quickly realized JoJo's emotional fortitude was troubled.

"Hey!" the bartender shouted with a pointed finger at Matt. "What the hell do you think you're doing? What did you do to him? JoJo," Frank, the bartender, called as he walked around the bar and knelt to help JoJo to stand. "Are you hurt?"

"No..." JoJo cried. He sat up against the bar, blubbering while cuddling his rat.

"What happened? Did this man hurt you?" Frank's eyes shot an angry glance at Matt.

"No..." JoJo continued with a high-pitched whine, "He was going to sh...shoot me." His face crumbled as he began weeping. JoJo reached his arms around Frank for a comforting hug.

Frank glared up at Matt with a fierce expression. "Get out of this tavern, and don't ever come back! He's like a child, you bast—"

Matt held up his hands in surrender as he interrupted Frank, "I'm sorry. I really am. I had no idea. I was trying to identify his friend before I was blindsided."

"What friend?" Frank shouted abrasively. "JoJo doesn't have any friends except his rat. Now get out of here!"

Matt knelt to speak to JoJo, "Please forgive me. I shouldn't have scared you like that."

Frank was angry as he helped JoJo to his feet. "What right do you have to point a gun at him anyway? He has enough people picking on him around here without a stranger scaring him to death. Get out before I grab my club and bust your head!" He patted JoJo on the back. "I'll get you a drink, JoJo."

"You will?" JoJo whined.

Matt said, "How about I pay for it." He reached into his pocket and set a silver dollar before JoJo. "I'm sorry to scare you."

JoJo wiped his eyes and touched the coin. He sniffled and caught his breath. "Thank you. This is Florence. She's my friend," JoJo said and kissed the rat's head. "Bob is nice to me."

Matt could feel his chest falling downward like an avalanche with the weight of guilt for scaring the man. "I'm glad to hear that. Do you know where Bob is?"

JoJo shook his head like a child. "Frank, I got a dollar." He grinned.

Frank walked back with a tall glass of foamy warm beer and set it in front of JoJo. "I'll take that dollar once you get your fourth beer."

"Right," JoJo said with a smile.

Frank spoke to Matt harshly, "I told you to get out!"

Matt raised one finger and then pulled his coat back to show his silver badge pinned to his shirt. Frank's eyes narrowed to peer at the badge and widened just a bit when he acknowledged that Matt was a U.S. Marshal.

Matt asked JoJo softly, "What do you do for work?"

JoJo took a long drink and wiped the foam off his upper lip. "I trap rats. I raise them too. I have a full barn of rats. Do you want a pet rat?"

Matt shook his head, repulsed. "No, I don't want a pet rat. Your name is JoJo?"

"Yes. JoJo Perkins. What's your name?"

"Matt." He put his hand out to shake. JoJo stared at his hand awkwardly and then slowly shook his hand. "Again, I apologize for scaring you. I should not have done that."

JoJo grinned, showing a mouthful of badly yellowed teeth. "I've been scared worse. The other night four men attacked me, and I thought they would kill me, but they didn't. They just wanted money, but I didn't have any. That made them mad, and they took all my clothes off and pushed me into a restaurant while everyone inside ate dinner. I tried to leave, but they held the door closed, laughing at me." His eyes watered as he added with emotion, "They took my papa's knife. It belonged to my papa. Mama gave it to me after Papa died." His eyes filled with thick tears and one dropped down his cheek as his bottom lip quivered with emotion. "Now Mama's gone to heaven too."

"Is that the only thing you had of your father's?" Matt asked gently.

He nodded. His bottom lip puckered. "My sister doesn't like me. It's all I got was my papa's knife."

"Do you know who took your knife?"

He nodded.

"Who?"

"Dillon. He likes to push me around and give me a bad time. Him and his friends. I would fight them, but I don't have muscles like you." He felt Matt's bicep with both hands. "You're strong!"

"Thanks. What does Dillon do for work?"

"Do you want me to buy you a beer?" JoJo asked Matt.

Matt smiled. "No, thanks. I don't drink, JoJo."

"You must drink some, or you'd die."

"Water or tea mostly. Do you know where Dillon works?"

"For Potsy," he said with a snarl to his lips.

"And who is Potsy?"

"A creep."

Matt waited for an explanation, but none came. "You don't like him? Is he mean to you?"

JoJo nodded slowly. "They make fun of me and do things." His eyes watered again.

"Like what?" Matt asked, leaning against the bar and watching JoJo's expressions closely.

JoJo took a long drink of the beer to finish it, slapped the bar, and called for another. "Nothing," he said with a hostile upper lip twitch.

Frank brought him another tall glass of beer. Frank explained, "Potsy and his boys like to humiliate JoJo. He's not the brightest candle in the room and can't defend himself, so he's an easy target. Hugh, the owner, felt sorry for him and built JoJo a room in the old barn out back. That's where he farms his rats. Someone has to take care of him, so we give him two free daily beers and food. JoJo is a good-hearted man and as harmless as a child, but he is harassed a lot."

"You live in a barn?" Matt asked JoJo.

Frank answered, "He can't keep a job, and his sister has nothing to do with him. She's too high and mighty now that she married Potsy. JoJo embarrasses her, so Potsy and his thugs target him."

Matt looked at JoJo, who was staring at his beer sadly. Matt turned his attention back to Frank. "My name is Matt Bannister, United States Marshal. I'm looking for Bob Mears. Do you know where he is?"

Frank stuttered with surprise, "No...no one knows where Bob is. You're Matt Bannister?"

"I am." He reached into his pocket and pulled out another dollar coin. "It was nice to meet you, JoJo. This is for you." He looked at Frank with a touch of anger burning in his eyes. "Where would I find Potsy?"

***

Matt followed the directions he had been given and walked along First Street to a single-level building with a false front with a large painted red sign stating simply, Potsy's Sailor's Lair.

Matt went inside and found a saloon like most others, but it was decorated with heavy rope, netting, a four-foot-tall anchor inside the door, and other things to represent the sailing industry. Plenty of men were inside drinking, but a table of four men wearing suits and playing cards watched Matt curiously.

Matt leaned his side against the bar and rested his chin on his left hand as the bartender approached him.

"You look like a bourbon kind of man, am I right?" he asked Matt.

Matt shook his head slightly. "Is Potsy here?"

"Yeah. Who can I say wants to see him?"

"An old friend." He made eye contact and nod-ded to the four men playing cards. The bartender walked towards a door that led behind the wall.

A moment later, he returned, followed by a me-dium-height man in his mid-forties with balding, short brown hair and a full beard graying on the chin. Potsy Jones had come out of his office hop-ing to see an old sailing friend, but his cheerful expression faded upon seeing Matt. "I don't know you. Why would you tell him we were old friends?" Potsy's eyes shifted toward the four men's table to ensure they were aware of a stranger with un-known intentions.

Matt pulled his suit coat back to reveal his badge. "I'm U.S. Marshal Matt Bannister. Do you have a moment?"

Potsy was alarmed to see the famous marshal in his place of business. "Sure," he said uneasily. "What can I do for you?"

"For starters, is Dillon around here?"

"Dillon," Potsy shouted, waving one of the men at the table to come forward.

Matt watched a medium-built young man ap-proach the bar in his early to mid-twenties. He was a handsome man that wore tan plaid suit pants and a matching vest over a white shirt. He had neatly combed brown hair and a clean-shaven oblong face. His general appearance was of a respectable young gentleman that might be found at church. Dillon wasn't what Matt expected a bully who humiliated a helpless man to be.

"Yes, sir?" he questioned Potsy.

"This is U.S. Marshal Matt Bannister. He asked for you by name."

Dillon gazed at Matt curiously. "It's an honor to meet you." He put his hand out to shake.

Matt looked at his extended hand and said, "You might not want to shake my hand in a minute. You appear like a young gentleman, and I hope you have that in you. I met a man named JoJo Perkins, who I took an immediate liking to…"

Dillon grinned with a slight laugh.

"Is something funny?" Matt asked.

"JoJo is the town idiot," Dillon explained.

"Maybe, but I consider him a personal friend of mine now. You and I know he can't fight his way through a rice paper wall, so I'm making it my business to fight his fights for him. Leave him alone from now on, or you'll be fighting me. And I promise you will lose that fight. Are we clear?"

"Yes, sir," Dillon said, stunned to have been threatened by the marshal.

"Now, I'll shake your hand as long as we're clear."

"Yes, sir," Dillon said. He shook Matt's hand with a new understanding to leave JoJo alone.

"Now, if you would be so kind as to give me back his father's knife," Matt said, extending his palm expectantly.

Dillon nodded towards the door. "I tossed it in the river."

Matt's eyes narrowed irritably as he questioned slowly, "You took the only thing he has that meant anything to him and threw it in the river?"

"Yes, sir," Dillon swallowed noticeably under Matt's glare.

Matt breathed in deeply before exhaling. "Then I suspect you better take your pals, strip down, and jump in and find it. Because I'm coming back tomorrow and bringing him with me. If you don't have that knife, I'll beat the snot out of you and scar up that handsome face."

Dillon glanced at Potsy questionably. "We'll never find it out there."

Matt raised his voice, "You better go swimming and *try* while there is light. Wouldn't you think so, Potsy?"

Potsy was the boss of his crew and had never had someone else order his men around. He could pay off several Portland police officers, but Matt Bannister wasn't one of them, and his reputation was well known. Potsy wasn't about to challenge the hardened eyes of the famous marshal. "Go find it," Potsy agreed. "And make sure you find it. You boys, go help him."

Matt watched them grudgingly walk out of the saloon.

"Are we done?" Potsy asked irritably.

"No. I'm looking for Bob Mears. Do you know where he is?"

Potsy lowered his brow. "No."

Matt tapped the bar slowly with a slight snarl forming on his lips. "I heard you are involved in the shanghaiing business. My son disappeared a few days ago." He watched Potsy's eyes and facial features carefully.

Potsy shifted on his feet uncomfortably. "I have a few sailor's houses, sure enough, but I run a legal business. I may skirt the law here and there, but I'll put my hand on a Bible and swear to you that I know nothing about your son. And that's the truth."

Matt spoke slowly, "Bob Mears, a teenager named Evan Gray, and *my son*, Gabriel, went missing four days ago. Someone knows something, and here is the message I want you to spread to everyone so that the person responsible hears my words: *Let my son go while they can.*" Matt's eyes hardened as he spoke, "Because I'm not leaving here without my son, and I will kill the men responsible if they do not let him go, whether that person is you or someone else."

Potsy had met all kinds of dangerous men and women over the years, but there was something about Matt's eyes that sent a chill down his spine. He sputtered, "Marshal, I swear to you, I know nothing about that. I swear I don't."

Matt leaned over the bar to speak privately, "If I find you are involved and are lying to me, you will be a dead man. You tell everyone you know I'm here to find my son, and someone better release him or tell me where he is. And if, God forbid, he is gone, someone will die. His name is Gabriel, and I want him back. I'm not leaving without him and will make your lives hell until I know who is responsible. Get to spreading the news. I'll be back tomorrow to get that knife. And Dillon better have it."

Chapter 10

Mark's Meat Market was on Ninth Street next to the popular Gypsy Wagon Restaurant, which had a brick patio in front with tables under sun umbrellas where the customers could enjoy eating outside. On the other side of the meat market was Polly's Bakery, which made the best pies in Oregon, or so their sign claimed.

William Fasana stood across the street watching Maggie Farrell work behind the counter. She was busy as there was a short line of waiting customers to purchase meat for supper. When William wasn't watching Maggie, his attention shifted to the bakery sign, and he wondered if the pies were really that good. He had been standing on the sidewalk waiting for Maggie to notice him, but in her busyness, she had not. He strolled across the street to the bakery and was impressed by the different kinds of pie he could purchase. William was skeptical of something called ricotta pie, so he bought an old, reliable apple pie. He carried his pie to the line of waiting customers at the meat market and casually watched Maggie focus on what she was doing with each customer ahead of him.

"What can I get for you?" she asked while wiping the perspiration from her forehead with her sleeve before writing down the last purchase in a notebook to track the sales.

William sighed heavily. "How about two forks and a pretty lady's company?"

At the sound of his voice, Maggie looked up quickly. Her lips tightened as her eyes filled with moisture. She quickly stepped around the counter, wrapped her arms around him tightly, and wept as her body trembled with emotion. Her brother's disappearance was a heavy burden on her usual lighthearted soul. "I'm so glad you're here."

"Me too, beautiful. But I'm holding a pie here that's getting heavy," he said, holding it outward with one hand while holding her with the other. "Can you join me? We'll go next door and eat it."

She sniffled and wiped her eyes as she released him. "I get off at six tonight."

"You can't take a break to eat some pie?" William questioned.

"No. There's already a person behind you waiting. I must get back to work. Save some of that pie for me. Polly's really are the best." She smiled sadly and went back behind the counter.

Her boss, Mark Henning, met her at the other side of the counter and said to William, "Please, take her home, William. All she's wanted to do since Bob went missing is work. Maggie, I can handle this. Go home and spend some time with William. He's come a long way to see you."

She washed her hands in a faucet and met William out front, where they sat at a table in front of the Gypsy Wagon restaurant. They ordered two iced teas and promised a nice tip if the waitress brought them the necessary utensils to eat the pie with.

William listened as Maggie talked about her brother and what she knew about his disappearance, which wasn't anything helpful. She didn't want to think that anyone would want to hurt her brother, but the longer he was missing, the closer the thought came to taking over any hopes she had of seeing him again.

"I love my little brother, William. Floyd thinks they were shanghaied, which scares me to death."

William put his hand gently on hers from across the round table. "We have the same fears for Gabriel. But I guarantee you if they were, we'll find who is responsible. Matt and I are determined to stay here until we do."

Maggie sighed. William was missing the point of her misery. "It wouldn't make a difference. My brother would still be missing. I don't know if we'll ever see him or either of the boys again." She sniffled.

William spoke sincerely, "I have to believe we will. I already lost my niece this month. I don't know that I can handle another loss. As you know, I'm not the praying one in the family, but I *am* praying about this. Despite my gambling, drinking..." He paused. "I wish I was more like Matt sometimes so I could be as sure that God is listening to my prayers the way God listens to Matt's. I guess that's my way of saying I really want to find Gabriel alive, and I'm praying to Jesus about it. I just can't promise he's listening. I sure hope he is."

Maggie's eyes moistened as she watched him affectionately. "He is. But if you're in doubt, then point your eyes at the Kingdom of God, pick up your mat, and start walking. We can never go back, William, but we can always go forward with the Lord."

He nodded, "I'll work on that."

"Don't try to be perfect before you can believe God hears your prayers or knows the anguish of your heart. That will only discourage you. Jesus cares about you from the inside out, so your vices may be the last things to go, but inside, you'll be a new or revived creation. I know your heart's still broken from Hannie's death, and now Gabriel's missing. William, now is when you should know God wants to listen to you from in here." She patted her heart. "When it comes from the heart, he hears you the loudest. No matter how sinful we are, God wants us to pray to Him. That's how he makes us right, from the inside out, not the outside in."

She closed her eyes and prayed, "Lord, William and I are both hurting, and we come before you to ask, please help us find Bob, Gabriel, and Evan alive and well if they are still in town. If not, then we pray that you will watch over them and bring them back home to us. And in the meantime, help us trust you during this time of not knowing what the future will bring. But we *do* know, even if it hurts, that you will never leave us. And Lord, let William know you love him just the way he is."

"Amen," William said.

A gentleman pulled a chair out for his wife to sit at the table beside theirs. "Look at that, Nora, we're just in time for a prayer meeting," the man said. He sat across the table from his wife.

"Don't interrupt their prayer, Felix. That is rude." Nora Rathkey looked at Maggie and apologized. "I am so sorry. Oh, Maggie, I didn't recognize you with your head lowered. Have you met my husband, Felix? Felix, this is Maggie, the best woman butcher in town. I get our meat from her," Nora explained to her husband.

"No, I haven't," Maggie said. Her eyes fell upon the man that loaned her brother money and happened to be one of the last people to see Bob.

Felix's eyes scanned her from head to toe. It wasn't too often that he saw an attractive lady wearing pants. Maggie wore gray cotton pants with a button-up plaid blue shirt over a white undershirt. They appeared like men's clothing which was most unladylike, yet she was too cute not to find attractive. "Hello. I'm Felix Rathkey, Attorney at Law. It's nice to meet you. Do you work next door?"

She nodded. "Yes, I do."

William recognized his name and reached a hand over to shake Felix's hand. "My name is William Craig. I'm an old friend of Maggie's down here visiting from Seattle. Did I hear you're a lawyer? Business law, by chance?"

Felix shook his hand without much interest. "I'm certainly knowledgeable on business law, but my office specializes in criminal defense." He scanned William over and wasn't quite sure what to make of him.

Maggie didn't know why William lied to Felix, but she said, "Misses Rathkey, this is my old friend, William."

Nora smiled at him. "Pleased to meet you."

"Likewise. I bought this pie, but it might be too big for Maggie and me. Would you two like to have some? It's a free meal."

"Well…" Felix said hesitantly while questioning his bride with a gaze. She shrugged. "If you don't mind, we'll accept your offer." He waved at the waitress to get her attention and said, "We'll have two saucers with forks and two iced teas."

"Right away, Mister Rathkey," the waitress said.

William scoffed. "We had to bribe her with a big tip to get saucers," he complained.

"I come here for lunch enough that they know me. So, what do you do, William? I can't help but ask, what's the deal with the gun setup? You might notice you don't see many people wandering around with guns. Do they commonly wear them in Seattle?" Felix questioned. He silently guessed that William was a gambler, but the double silver-plated reversed gun set on his waist made him question whether he was a gunman. Either way, he knew William was not local.

"Generally speaking, no. But I have to tell you, I own a large and prospering gambling hall and saloon on the lower west side along the harbor called the Tall Sea Palace. I'm a gambler by trade, and I made my share of enemies over the years. I don't usually wear my guns, but new cities make me nervous. I figured while I was in town visiting my friend, I'd look around and see if there was room and opportunity enough for me to move on over here."

The waitress delivered the two saucers and a pie spatula to lift the pieces out easier than using a butter knife. "Thank you," Felix said.

William snorted. "You get special treatment, and I'm the one leaving a tip."

Felix chuckled lightly as he got a piece of pie for his bride and himself.

Nora Rathkey asked William, "So, you're old friends with Maggie?"

"I sure am." He tried to block Maggie from seeing him as he leaned across the table to speak privately with Nora. He said in a slightly lower voice, "Don't tell her, but I'm working on courting her, if you know what I mean. She could use a friend and a piece of pie with her brother missing and all."

Nora's growing smile at William's blatant attempt to make his attention known faded with the last sentence. "You have a missing brother?"

Maggie nodded sadly. "He went missing four days ago."

"Oh heavens. I will be praying he comes home," Nora said empathetically. "Is that what you two were praying about when we interrupted?"

Maggie nodded. "Thank you. We'd appreciate your prayers."

Felix asked, "His name isn't Bob, is it?"

"Yes. Do you know him?" She had never met Felix, but she knew the name of the man that loaned Bob the money.

"Yes. I gave him a loan. He paid it back, and Floyd told me he was missing the next day. Bob is still missing?" he questioned innocently.

"Yes," she answered awkwardly. "Bob and two others that came here for a week's visit. We're praying they come home."

"Oh, Lord, we will be praying, too," Nora said sincerely.

Felix exhaled through fluttering lips. "Now, that's a bit of really sad news, and I brought my wife out to have lunch because today is her birthday. It's supposed to be a special day."

"Well, happy Birthday, Misses Rathkey. You can't be more than what, twenty-two?" William asked with a flirtatious wink.

She snickered. "Charming man. I like him already," she said to Maggie. "I'm a bit older," she said with a smile.

William raised his eyebrows at Maggie. "Well, my dear friend, shall we leave these two love birds alone? Maybe we'll go make our own nest."

"Oh, hush," Maggie said with a sad grin as she stood.

William set the pie on Rathkey's table. "Happy Birthday. It was nice to meet you both. Do you have any suggestions about who I should talk to about investing in a business here?"

"How long will you be in town for?" Felix asked. "I have friends in the mortgage business that might know of one or two places willing to sell if the price is right. My office is just down the block on Sixth Street. Come by sometime."

"Sounds good." He shook Felix's hand before leaving a tip on the table and walking away with Maggie. When they had walked a safe distance, Maggie asked, "Why did you lie to them?"

"Who said I was lying? I *am* here to court you."

She gave him a playful shove across the sidewalk. "You know what I mean."

He stopped and faced her. "We just met one of our suspects. Floyd said Felix might have dirty hands. If so, I want to toss out some bait like a fisherman and reel him in slow. So, sweetheart, I'll be right back."

William hurried down the block and approached Felix and Nora. "Excuse me, I don't mean to interrupt, but could I meet you in your office tomorrow to maybe meet your pals, look at properties, and discuss business? I didn't want to say so in front of Maggie, but I love the girl and know she'll never leave her mother. Now that might be a curse all on its own, but if our love is...well, love, then it will have to bloom like a weed here. I'll have plenty of money to spend, but I'll still need to sell my business and rebuild it here. I'm always looking for an investor or two if you're interested. Is it possible to meet tomorrow?"

Felix nodded thoughtfully for a moment. "Yes. I can meet you in my office around noon?"

"That works. I'll see you tomorrow."

"Oh, and William, could you leave the guns at home? They draw a lot of attention."

William smiled. "You bet."

Chapter 11

Morton Sperry carried his saddlebags into the Mariner's Union House Tenement building, which was owned by Big Richard Burkhalter, to ask about a room but was sent away for lack of vacancies. He was referred to Lottie's Shore Leave Boarding House down the road a few blocks. Morton discovered Lottie's was nothing more than a two-story house, with the downstairs transformed into a small tavern with a bar and billiards table. It had a kitchen that made three meals a day and tables to sit and eat. Upstairs was opened into a vast space with a few support beams and twenty bunk beds with wooden storage boxes to rent stacked at the foot of each bunk bed.

The bed, sheets, blankets, pillow, storage box, and padlock to lock the box were all individually priced rentals and seemed a bit steep to Morton as he checked in. He was told he could pay by the day or start a line of credit that would be paid later by a ship's captain when hired onto a ship.

"Why would a captain pay my debt?" Morton asked the old man that stood behind a small counter. He had a registry book to keep track of every guest that signed in and every penny a man owed for rentals, food, or drinks.

"The captain deducts the cost from your wages when you get paid. You don't look like a sailor to me anyway," the old timer said, looking Morton over.

"I'm not," Morton replied. "But I'm up to learning a new trade within reason. I'll pay since I don't plan on going to sea."

"That's fine. Would you like to leave your gun belt with me for safekeeping? We don't like to have armed men staying here. Drunk men and weapons are a dangerous combination, you'll understand."

Morton's eyes gazed at the man evenly. He seemed uneasy under Morton's cold stare. "I'm not a drunk. I'm keeping my gun."

The old man shrugged his shoulders. "If there is any trouble, the police will be notified immediately, and you'll be removed to the city jail. Any debts incurred will be paid before you leave, or the police will be notified, and you'll be charged with robbery. Understand?"

"There won't be any trouble or debt." Morton took a padlock and key from the old timer and walked upstairs, where he found three rows of bunk beds.

An old man with a long gray beard reclining on a bottom bunk removed his pipe from his mouth and said, "You don't look like no seadog to me." A pair of crutches leaned against the bunkbed as his injured left knee was tightly wrapped in gauze.

"I'm not," Morton said coarsely.

The old man chuckled. "This home is for sailors, not plow boys like poor Henry over there crying in the corner or drifters like you. But you'll do, I'm sure."

Morton ignored the old man and looked at the other men in the room; most looked as rugged, mean, and weathered as himself, except for a teenager who looked out of place and anxious. Morton spoke loudly, "My name is Morton Myers, former leader of the Myers-Finn Gang. If any of you get into my stuff, I will not hesitate to kill you. That's your only warning."

"Shipmates don't steal from each other," a man answered simply from the bottom bunk three over from the old man with a hurt knee. "That bed is empty, the last bottom bunk." He pointed at a bed near his.

Morton approached the bed and sat down on the mattress. It was two inches of a mattress on board slats. It wasn't the worst bed he had ever sat on, but it wasn't comfortable for the price he paid. He nodded to the man. "Morton Myers."

"So you said. They call me Swansy, but my name is Peter Swan. I am originally from Maine. I've been at sea for my whole life and have seen ports all over the world. What's your story?" he asked as he approached and extended his hand. Peter was about the same height as Morton, broad-shouldered but lean. He had black hair that covered his ears and a matching thick beard and mustache about three inches long. Peter had blue eyes that were solid, confident, and sincere.

Morton shook the man's strong hand with a firm grip. "I've been an outlaw all my life and finally hit my end. I figured I needed a new start where no one knew me. The sea is the only place I've never been."

Peter raised his brow. "You aren't the first man running from the law that's gone to sea. I just signed on with the *Everson Solstice*. It is undergoing some repairs before departing for Africa. The Atlantic starts getting rough about the time we'll reach it, so the captain wants it in tip-top shape. I can't say I disagree with him on that. I've been through some Atlantic storms, and they'll make you a man real quick. I could introduce you to Captain Smithrud if you want."

Morton yawned. "No. If you want to know the truth, I'm looking for a job on land, but doing what I'm good at. I hear there may be something I could do that's more hands-on and rough. I don't know who to contact, but I think I might be good at taking people and putting them on ships."

Peter narrowed his eyes, repulsed. "I don't know what you're looking for. If you're talking about working for a crimp, talk to the man downstairs. He may be able to help you. I'm a sailor and don't believe in half of the crap that goes on in ports like this one. I have no business talking to a man like you."

"We all have to make a living," Morton said to finish the conversation. Knowing the conversation was over, Morton opened a box, set his saddlebags in it, and locked it with a padlock. "Thank you for the advice; I'll go downstairs and talk to the old man."

Peter reclined on his mattress. He spoke with a touch of venom, "Well, cockroaches, rats, and snakes can all be found around the trash together. Men like you make me sick."

Morton stopped and peered at Peter for a long moment. The man's eyes remained on Morton without shifting down or away as the two men's will for dominance clashed. Morton's lips turned upwards with a smirk before he went downstairs to question the old man behind the counter.

The old man had moved behind the bar to make drinks for two men who had no money but added the cost to their debt. In the following twenty minutes of trying to learn anything helpful from the old timer, Morton learned his name was Tom. When Morton expressed an interest in finding employment in shanghaiing people, Tom explained shanghaiing was impossible because, by law, every man hired onto a ship had to sign the ship's Articles of Agreement of their own free will. The Articles of Agreement was the contract between the Shipmaster and the newly hired man. Extracting any other information from Tom beyond that was like squeezing juice from a carrot by hand.

Morton watched Peter come downstairs and walk out the back door toward the privy. The city water and sewer systems had not yet reached the city block they were on. Morton waited five minutes and then walked out into the fading light of the day to wait.

Peter stepped out of the privy and held up a defensive hand, uninterested in talking when Morton tried to speak. "We have nothing to say to each other," Peter said sharply. "Men like you are why that young man up there is trapped here. Oh, yeah, you'll fit right in with these other vultures scavenging off the ignorance of fools."

"Are you talking about that kid upstairs? Maybe you could explain what you're talking about?" Morton asked, not understanding what Peter was saying.

"That kid, Henry, is a stupid teenage farm boy from the valley who came here with three friends a week ago to frolic with the women and city frills. His two friends returned home, but Henry met a pretty young lady who fawned over him and asked him to stay a few days longer. You might have noticed he's not the most handsome kid, and she's quite a beauty, that she is. She brought him here, and now he's trapped. She comes by every few days to keep him quiet and content, but it's a scam," Peter said irritably.

"I don't understand," Morton said. "Are they courting or something?"

Peter rolled his eyes impatiently. "She works for a crimp. She brought Henry here to accrue so much debt he can't pay it. That kid is naive as a spoiled pet pig being led to the slaughterhouse. Henry is just dumb enough to believe she cares about him enough to pay his debt." Peter shook his head. "The reality is he's waiting for a ship. That boy is trapped here. He can't leave without paying that debt, or he's facing robbery charges which will put him in jail. Henry thinks he is waiting for the lady of his dreams, but at any time, some thugs like you will come get him and escort him to a waiting ship. I'll tell you right now, that kid hasn't got what it takes to be a mariner, and he'll be thrown overboard intentionally or fall overboard from his own stupidity, guaranteed. Boats come in day and night, so they could get him anytime."

Morton questioned, "Did you tell him that?"

Peter scoffed. "You better learn quick how things work around here. If I uttered a word to Henry about that girl being hired to lure fools like him here or what his future looks like, I'd end up like the old man with a broken knee, if not worse. It's a cold world, and there is nowhere colder than the harbors and ports around the world." He spat a glob of mucus on the ground. "If that's what you want to be, you're in the right spot. But I think hell is a good place for all of you."

Morton looked around him carefully. "I lied," he said softly. "I'm a U.S. Deputy Marshal here with Matt Bannister looking for three young men that disappeared. His son is one of them. But if you tell anyone that, I promise you will be sorry. Matt is on a blood hunt, and you don't want to be the man that tells people who I am. I could use your knowledge and help, though."

"You're lying."

"No. I'm not." He reached into his front pants

pocket and pulled out his badge. "I'm being honest. I can help that boy, but I need your help. Where should I go to get in with the criminals and the people doing the dirty work? How do I get their attention? How do I get invited into that business?"

Peter eyed him, weighing what he was shown carefully. "Hide that badge, first of all. You'll be killed if they see it. I don't know anyone in this port, but I know how to help you. Give me half an hour, and then come into the Wavering Wharf Tavern as you came into the bunkhouse, loud and obnoxious. Let them all know you're an outlaw, bank robber, or whatever you were, and I'll take it from there.

"Morton, if that's your real name, I will start a fight with you and put up a fight, but you better win. I can take the bumps and bruises, but I'm do-ing it for that kid up there. You better help that kid get out of here safely, or I'll let everyone know who you really are, and they'll take care of you. Make no mistake; these are dangerous people you will be messing with. So, you better have eyes on the back of your head and be tougher than sturgeon's skin because they'll kill you at the drop of a hat."

Morton offered a half smile. "Those are exactly my kind of people."

***

Peter Swan hadn't been in Portland long, but the reputation of the Wavering Warf Tavern made it the most likely place to find someone in the crimping and press-gang business. It was the largest tavern on the waterfront—rowdy, dark, and full of men that worked on the docks or sailed the rivers and seas. It was the perfect environment for crimps to approach sailors coming ashore and invite them to stay in their sailor houses, bunkhouses, or brothels.

Immediately when a ship drops anchor in the middle of the Willamette River, it was common to see boats rowing out to it, inviting the sailors to come ashore. It was a thriving business, and every crimp and boarding house owner knew that after months at sea, the sailors were anxious to go ashore to drink, gamble and visit the brothel. Like loggers on weekends were known to come to Portland and spend their pay on wild times, so were the sailors coming ashore. Some were faithful to their ship and remained aboard to wait for the ship to properly dock before taking shore leave, guaranteeing they would receive their full pay.

Others gladly grabbed their belongings and climbed into the skiffs, abandoning the ship and leaving their pay for the past month's labors behind. They knew the pleasures of Portland were at their fingertips, and there were several sailor houses they could choose from to stay and get whatever they wanted on credit. An experienced sailor—whether a cook, surgeon, carpenter, boatswain, or basic crewman—was a skilled commodity always in need when the next ship arrived. The ship masters, also called captains, saved money when their crew members jumped ship after anchoring, and paying the credits owed to a sailor's house for a new crew was cheaper than paying the wages owed. It was a financial gain for all parties involved, except for the sailor, who gained nothing except a week or two of pleasure and maybe new clothing for the next voyage.

Every port worked the same way. The skiffs were manned by men working for one sailor's house or another and competed with their rivals to tempt the men to stay at their facility. The first skiff to arrive was usually the fullest, but they came back luring more of the crew with cigars, alcohol, and at times, a scantily dressed woman aboard the skiff. It was all free for the taking, and all a sailor had to do was climb overboard into the skiff.

When the ship was moored to the dock, and the sailors came ashore with their full pay in hand, they were met by vultures inviting them to one sailor's house or another, promising a hot bathhouse, good food, all the liquor they could drink and even a free ticket to use at one bordello or another. Every sailor's house was ready to welcome the sailors to live, thrive and enjoy their stay until the next captain came looking for men. Such marketing and means of temptation kept the businesses flowing. They kept a constant revolving door of sailors coming and going while all along profiting the men and women who found a place to secure their means on Water Street and the surrounding area.

Every ship that came into port after a long sea journey lost men to the temptations of the city and the ease of staying at a sailor's house. Sailors like Peter Swan knew how it worked and watched the wharves looking for the type of ship he wanted to work on, and when he saw one, he approached the captain of the *Everson Solstice* and made himself available to join the ship if the captain paid his debt at Lottie's. Captain Smithrud agreed to hire the experienced sailor on the spot.

It was far better to pick your own vessel to live on than to risk letting someone else sell your fate. Because once a captain paid a man's debt, the sailor, whether experienced or not, was boughten and, if necessary, was taken under guard to the captain's ship for a long journey at sea. In some ways, it was a form of volunteer slavery to be bought and forced to labor for months at a time in harsh and dangerous conditions.

A sailor's life was a career where the living was free, and the crewman didn't have to concern himself with anything except doing his job until the next port, where it started over again. Not all sailors lived free like that. Peter finished each journey and collected his pay before resigning his position to enjoy shore leave and signing on with another ship. He saved his money and let the captains pay his debts. He knew too well that someday his body would become too old and injury ridden to continue and would need the money he had made over his career to live on. But too many sailors never saw a dime they worked for, and the ship captains and crimps earned their wealth from those sailors eager to get to shore.

Peter Swan was no fool. He knew very well that the crimps and those associated with them would be where the action was. Every crimp had men that worked for him as bodyguards, strong men, and thugs that roamed the streets seeking sailors and drunks needing a place to sleep. A drunk sailor who had gotten paid stumbling back towards his moored ship was a potential gold mine. Not only could they befriend him, knock him unconscious, rob him of his money, and leave him in a sailor's house overnight, accruing a small debt he couldn't pay the next day when he woke up, especially after having a hot breakfast at an inflated price. Such means of collecting sailors took hired men of low moral caliber, precisely the kind of men Peter had every hope of helping Morton gain their attention.

Peter entered the Wavering Wharf Tavern and complained loudly about a former gang leader threatening to kill anyone who touched his things in Lottie's Shore Leave Boarding House. He said the man was lawless and expressed an interest in joining a press gang. Peter stood at the bar having a drink while sharing his disgust with whoever would listen for about twenty minutes before Morton walked into the tavern wearing his gun belt. "Oh, crap, here he is," Peter said with annoyance.

Morton Sperry walked into the tavern and let his eyes scan the bar like an angry bear looking for a fight. He shouted to get everyone's attention, "My name is Morton Myers—the former leader of the Myers-Finn Gang. Anyone can wear a gun belt, but only two types of people use them: lawmen and outlaws. I am no lawman. I'm not bragging when I say I'm mean and dangerous, but I'm also loyal and looking for a new job. Who has one?"

Peter stepped away from the bar. "I told you; we don't want your kind around here. Go back to wherever you came from. You're not welcome in here."

"Really? And who's going to stop me?" Morton asked as he approached Peter.

Peter spat on Morton's chest to draw his attention from a quickly thrown, unexpected hard right swing toward Morton's head. Morton ducked just as the arm breezed over him.

Morton came up with a hard right fist into the solar plexus of Peter's abdomen just below the sternum. Peter grimaced as the wind was sucked out of him. He froze momentarily as his body reacted to the well-connected hit. Morton spared no mercy as he followed with another punch to the stomach and then a swung elbow to the temple that sent Peter to the floor, where Peter pulled himself into a fetal position and gasped for breath.

Morton quickly drew his revolver and pointed it at the barkeeper, who was handing a wooden club to a patron across the bar to end the fight. "Put it away, or I'll put a bullet through your hand, just for starters! Do it!" Morton yelled with fierce glaring eyes.

The bartender, a round, heavy man with an elongated face, fearfully did as he was told.

Morton spoke loudly, "I'm not here to cause trouble. I know what I am capable of and what I'm good at. Pass the word around, Morton Myers is new in town, and I'll work for the highest bidder. I'll do whatever you want. That's all I have to say."

He glanced down at Peter. "I thought you'd be tougher." He pointed the revolver at Peter's head. "Does anyone want him dead? Just say the word." He paused as Peter stared at him with alarm. Morton holstered his weapon and approached the bar. "I'll buy that man on the floor a drink. He at least dared to challenge me."

Overhearing Morton, a large man, well over six feet tall and well over two hundred pounds, who looked like a burly lumberjack with the power to snap Morton in two, said, "Without the gun, you don't look all that tough to me. Do you think you could beat me without the gun?"

Morton knew Peter staying down gasping for air was partly acting, but he didn't want the big lumberman to ruin his moment by beating him senseless. Morton's back was against a proverbial wall, and he couldn't back away from the challenge without appearing cowardly. His lips rose slightly into a dangerous smirk. "Let's see what you got, big man."

Morton raised his hands to fight as the big man stepped forward. His heart beat quicker, knowing he would be in trouble if the man got a hold of him. The man's hands were clenched tightly into large balls of pain if they connected with his face. When the man drew his arm back to swing, Morton drew his revolver and leaped forward to slam the butt of the grip into the bridge of the big man's nose. Morton's body bounced off the man's chest as the strike had its intended effect of breaking the large man's nose while splitting the skin open. The man turned away from Morton to hold his bleeding nose, wincing in pain.

Ruthlessly, Morton slammed the revolver across the man's head repeatedly until the big man dropped to his knees while bleeding profusely. One more hard swing of the gun over the man's head, and he fell face forward to the floor, unconscious. It would have been more impressive if it had taken one swing to put the man down, but despite the means, Morton was still standing and holstered his revolver victoriously.

Knowing all eyes were on him, he spoke loudly. "I don't always need my gun, but I'm no fool. You all heard what I said a moment ago. I'm staying at Lottie's." He walked out of the tavern onto Water Street and exhaled with relief.

Chapter 12

Matt Bannister stood on the roof of the Silver Casterlin building, looking over the city lights of Portland. He let his eyes fall on the Willamette River's dark water, reflecting the city lights glow. Watching the river traffic throughout the day was interesting, but now nearing midnight, the Stark Street Ferry's steam whistle signaled its final journey across the river for the night.

Matt's heart was heavy as he leaned one leg on the two-foot raised edge of the roof. Millions of people were in the world, but he only had one son. There was a good possibility that Gabriel was the only child he would ever have since it was unlikely that Christine would ever bear a child. To admit Gabriel was his son, brought a good deal of guilt because Matt knew he was not the father he wished he had been. He had no knowledge of Gabriel two years before, and if he had never returned to Willow Falls, he would have no knowledge of Gabriel or feel the fear and anxiety that filled him now.

Seeing Gabriel for the first time was like looking in the mirror, and it was the most brutal punch to the gut he had ever faced. It was heartbreaking to realize he had run away just when his dreams may have been realized, and he could have raised Gabriel with Elizabeth as his wife if he had the perseverance to stay in Willow Falls all those years ago.

Life doesn't promise a person's dreams will come true or that true love always ends happily. A person's choices on the road of life can thwart every good opportunity that comes their way and leads them to the grave or down roads they never intended to be on. One wrong choice can change the entire trajectory of a person's life and have lasting consequences that may be painful, crippling, and life-altering.

Matt had certainly made his fair share of mistakes, and they left scars that still hurt. He was thankful to know Gabriel and to have a relationship with Elizabeth and Tom that allowed him to get to know Gabriel as his biological father. Tom Smith had raised Gabriel, and the young man's parents guided his values and influenced him to be the wonderful young man he was. Matt was still an outsider and knew he might never be close to his son.

Matt was hard to get to know, and Gabriel was now a young adult starting a life of his own. The window of time to build a lasting relationship was closing fast, and the weight of it, knowing his only son may never be a part of Matt's life, left an emptiness that no one except his son could fill.

Life gets busy and good intentions get put aside when something more urgent arises. Matt had tried to spend time with Gabriel, but too often, those rare occasions were interrupted by one thing or another. There was a general knowledge that although he was Gabriel's biological father, he would never be considered Gabriel's *real* father. That honor was reserved for the man that invested his life in raising him, Tom Smith. Gabriel's surname was Smith, not Bannister, and it would always be. The Bannister name would end with Matt.

Sadness carries a weight that could sink the strongest of ships, as the anchor of sorrow can weigh far more than the body supporting it. For some people who let the keel of their lives become uneven and inconsistent, allowing each wave of life to sway their world without a balance to bring them back, the weight of sadness could tip the scale and become a tragedy before the storm is over. Storms end, and calm seas return, but a damaged ship needs to return to port and find that solid ground of their lives again.

Lee Bannister had loaned his carriage and hired a driver to take Matt, William, and Morton to Natoma, where Lee arranged by wire to have new horses ready for the carriage and a new driver to take them to the next stop and so on to get the three men to Walla Walla, Washington as quickly as possible, to catch the train to Portland. On the way, Matt insisted they stop in Willow Falls, and although it was getting late, Matt told Elizabeth and

Tom about Floyd's wire and informed them that he was on his way to find the son they all shared. Tom Smith wanted to help, but Matt refused to let him come along. Matt explained that if bad news were found, Elizabeth would need Tom then and there, not three or four days away.

Elizabeth's terrified tears had broken Matt's heart just like her tears always had. He promised Elizabeth he would bring their son home and intended to keep that promise. Now his eyes scanned the large city below him, and of the hundreds of lights that shone around him, he had no idea where to begin. It was overwhelming. He had never felt more lost and overwhelmed than he did now in a strange city seven times the size of any he'd been in before. He made a promise to Elizabeth that he didn't know he could keep because he didn't have a clue where to find their son.

William was spending time with Maggie like a henpecked baboon, which Matt never imagined he'd ever say about William. Morton had told Matt that he was playing a role on the waterfront, but Matt wasn't exactly sure what that role was or what Morton meant by it, as their evening meeting had been short and Matt's mind was spread out over many things, but nothing more important than finding his son.

Matt gazed over the city and wondered what light his son was under or what boat leaving the harbor he might be on. Was Gabriel already out at sea? Portland streets were known for shanghaiing young men and making them virtual slaves on ships. However, finding the men involved in such a wicked activity was harder than he first thought it might be. Nobody claimed to know anything, and even the city police claimed to be ignorant of such men and means. Every door he tried to open had closed abruptly in his face, and time...well, he didn't know if he was too late or not.

The anxiety of his son disappearing in Portland brought a level of desperation that Matt wasn't experienced with trying to control. To help keep his emotions on an even keel and not be swayed by the giant waves of the unknown, Matt looked up at the clear night sky at the bright moon and prayed, "Jesus, my Lord, I am looking over this city and wondering what light is closest to Gabriel and Evan. What light shines on them, if any? This city is bigger than I can search, and this is so much larger than I can bear.

"Jesus, I'm scared I won't be able to find Gabriel. I love him, Lord, and I don't want to lose him. Please, guide me to him somehow. I can't get any answers and don't know who to go to for help or where to search. I feel like I'm walking in circles. I know Gabriel and Evan both believe in you and are praying too. I know they have to be, and if you would be willing, help me to find them. I'm lost without you, Lord. And Jesus, I fear they were shanghaied, and if so, then I pray that you will be with them and keep them safe until they can come home. If they are still here, then help me find them. Give me the strength to get through this because I don't know if I can."

Matt wiped his eyes dry from a slight moisture

that had filled them when he heard footsteps approaching on the roof behind him. He glanced back to see his father, Floyd.

"It's not a bad view, is it?" Floyd asked. "I didn't mean to interrupt you. I just wanted to see how you were doing."

"It's a nice view," Matt said.

Floyd put a hand on Matt's shoulder. "How are you holding up?" He could see the watery eyes in his son's expression.

Matt nodded slowly. "I'm alright. I just don't know where to look. You live here; you must know more than you're telling me. Gabriel's life is in danger, Dad, so if you know anything you're not telling me, please do."

Floyd grimaced irritably. "Son, I can't tell you something I don't know about. Do you think I'm hiding something from you like I'm involved in that crap? I'm not, Matt!" he glared at his son, more hurt by the unspoken accusation than upset.

Matt sighed. "I'm not accusing you. I'm just grasping at straws or anything that will help."

Floyd waved an arm towards the river. "Everyone knows that the waterfront down there is the epicenter of most of our crime in one way or another, but the people who control it won't be found there. Like anywhere, there is a certain amount of corruption in our city, and it all has to do with money. I still can't understand why the boys left the building. I told them to stay inside after dark because the streets get dangerous, and they each promised me they would."

"Dad, I didn't want to ask in front of Rhoda or Maggie, but if Bob owed money or was looking for money to buy that tavern, would he have the connections to, in essence, *sell* Gabriel and Evan?"

Floyd shook his head. "No. Bob would never do such a thing. Bob is a lot like I was at his age—irresponsible and immature, but he's no criminal. I initially thought that maybe he took the boys to one of his friend's places to get them drunk or fix them up with some of his female friends, but now I don't think so. He knows I'd wring his neck. No, something isn't right. Bob knows too many people around here to be messing around."

Matt clenched his jaw with remorse as a wave of emotion hit him like an unexpected rogue wave. "I ah…I've only known Gabriel for a year and a half. He found out I was his father last November. We don't have much of a relationship, although I would like to have one with him. Christine probably can't have children, so Gabriel is the only son or child I'll ever have. It might be too late to get to know him, as he's basically grown up now. I'm afraid if I never see him again, I'll have missed my only opportunity to know my son."

Floyd glanced at his boy as the words hit his heart with a hardened punch. His eyes watered slightly. "Gabriel's the only grandson I have that has given me the time of day, and I'm not giving up on the boy," Floyd said. He hesitated before adding, "But you know, Matt, how you're feeling is exactly how I feel about you and your siblings. Of course, I did that to myself and never forgave myself for it. I understand what you're feeling, Matt. I really do."

Matt turned his head to look at his father. "You have to forgive yourself, Dad. What's done is done, and it was a long time ago. It's easy to blame someone when you're not walking in their shoes. You've been forgiven by all of us. You need to forgive yourself."

"Easier said than done, Son. It isn't just about forgiving myself; it's not having that bond with my sons like you're finding out. My life's been a mess, but despite my failures, just know I love you all. I love Gabriel too. We'll find him, Matt," Floyd said with a nod as he stared out over the city. He blinked repeatedly to wash the tears away.

Deep within, Matt wanted to tell his father he loved him and rose into his throat but was choked back down. "I pray so," was all Matt said.

Chapter 13

Tony Hurner entered Felix Rathkey's office first thing in the morning. He sat down across from Felix and sipped his coffee before saying, "Have you ever heard of a criminal named Morton Myers? He ran a gang called the Myers-Finn Gang?"

Felix furrowed his brow thoughtfully. He sat behind his large ornate desk, reading through some court papers. One of his clients was Oscar Petrovic, accused of manslaughter for causing the death of his best friend after playfully pushing his friend on the pier, causing the drunk man to stumble and fall into the river. His friend's head hit the edge of a floating dock during the fall, killing him almost instantly. Felix was reading through the file to ready himself for the trial. "It sounds familiar, but I can't place it. Why? Was he arrested?"

"No. That Morton fellow came into the Wavering Wharf last night and caused some trouble. I've never seen anything like it. He said he was looking for a new beginning working around the docks doing what he knows best: crime. He's tough. He beat one man, some sailor who shares his boarding house. And you remember big Lyle Bert? You defended him last year for a drunk and disorderly case? That Morton fella knocked Lyle out by pistol-whipping him nearly to death. We don't get his kind around here too often; he's a real fast draw, gunfighting outlaw."

"Huh. Was he arrested?" Felix asked again, thinking he might have a new client to represent.

"No. Morton's looking for a job, and I thought it might be better if he worked for us instead of working for Potsy or Big Richard. If we wanted to run them out of town, which I know you have mentioned in the past, then that man might be a better friend than a foe. He's a shootist and killed his share of people; you can see it in his eyes. He might be just the kind of man we need if we run into trouble with our competition or the Chinese. Whoever hires him first will have a dangerous man."

Felix gave his full attention to Tony. "Do you know where he is staying?"

"I do."

"Then go talk with him and if you still think he has what it takes, bring him here about one o'clock or so. Tony, you need to test him for all he's worth. I'll contact a few prosecutors and see if they've heard of him. Where is he from?"

"That I don't know. But I'll find out all I can."

***

Morton knew that a man seeking an honest job arose early to pursue one, but a man seeking employment in more of a criminal aspect searched at night. He had been out late and slept later than some other men. He was eating breakfast at one of the tables near the billiards table when a man called his name.

Morton turned his head and gazed at a big man nearly six feet tall with broad, muscular shoulders. He wore a clean tan suit with a matching vest and a derby hat over his short light brown hair. His clean-shaven face was oval-shaped, with cold, narrow sky-blue eyes that were alert and fearless. He was a handsome and clean-cut man of some means and had a confident formidability about him that warned he was not a man to be messed with. If he was not dressed like a city businessman, Morton might suspect him of being a man of Cass Traver's murderous caliber without the scars and rough exterior. "I'm Morton. What do you want?"

Tony Hurner nodded his head towards the door. "Can we take a walk?"

"Are you a lawman?"

"No. Let's go talk for a bit."

"Alright."

Once outside, Tony extended his hand. "My name is Tony. I was in the Wavering Warf last night and heard what you said. Are you as tough as you say?"

"Did you ask me out here to find out?" His cold green eyes searched Tony for a weapon. He guessed there was a .38 caliber revolver in a shoulder holster under Tony's jacket. Morton was confident he could draw his revolver much quicker than Tony could reach for his.

Tony's lips rose slightly. "That wasn't my intention. I might have a job you'd be interested in. But I need to know more about you. Where are you from?"

"A small dot of a town called Cold Water."

"Never heard of it."

"I'd be surprised if you did. There's nothing there, and that's what put my cousins and me into a life of crime. I ran the Myers-Finn Gang for years, but times change. Am I as tough as I say? I don't know, but I'm not afraid of anyone. Now who are you?"

"I'm the man that might be your boss if I decide I could use a man like you. The first thing I need to know is if we can get along. Can you follow directions when given?"

Morton grinned with a short chuckle. "I can follow directions just fine as long as they are not foolish. I won't put my neck in a noose for anyone. I work smart or not at all. What's the job?"

Tony was looking for a yes or no answer. "The job is you doing what I say. Can you do that?"

"Depends on what it is. If you say go into the police station and start shooting, then no. I won't do anything stupid."

"Are you willing to follow orders or not?" Tony asked sharply. "If not, we have nothing more to talk about," Tony said with finality. "If you worked for us, there wouldn't be stupid requests because our business is all about secrecy, trust, and longevity. You being killed or arrested wouldn't do us any good at all. Now, can you follow orders or not?"

Morton exhaled to think it over. "Do you pay well?"

"You'll be able to afford an expensive suit before you know it."

"I'll play along. Yes, I'll do as you say. I need the money."

"Good. Let's find out." He pointed down the sidewalk. "Do you see that bum walking towards us? Take these and go break his ribs." He held out a pair of brass knuckles.

Morton peered at the skinny man talking affectionately to a black rat he held in his left hand and carried a small wicker cage in his right hand. "I wouldn't need those to break his ribs. He looks half-broken already. Can't you find someone that will put up a fight?"

"If you want a job doing what you do best, as you said last night, then do as I say and don't ask questions. He's a worthless bum. Take these, put them on, and break his ribs for no reason other than I say so."

Morton was torn. He did not want to hurt the fragile man who was entirely innocent of deserving the pain of broken ribs. He could not justify doing it, but for the chance of finding Gabriel or what happened to him, Morton took the brass knuckles and slipped his four fingers through the finger holes, leaving a solid brass plate across his fist.

He kept his right hand slightly behind his hip as he approached the shabbily dressed man and pointed towards the sun as he exclaimed, "Look at that!"

The man turned slightly to expose his ribs and raised his left arm, holding the rat to block the morning sun from his eyes. "What?" he asked.

Morton threw a hard right fist to the center of the man's ribcage. The man gasped as he collapsed, releasing the rat that scurried a short distance away before stopping. The bum withered on the ground gasping for breath while holding his ribs. A breath of air was sucked in and expelled with a loud cry of agony through a pain-filled grimace and gasping breaths. Every breath inhaled, expanded his lungs and pressed against his ribcage bringing forth a great deal of anguishing pain. His body convulsed with his heavy sobbing, but each convulsion of his body and deep breath brought more excruciating pain. The pain caused him to weep harder, which brought more body convulsions with his sobbing. "It hurts! It hurts!" the man kept saying through a steady flow of tears and loud wails.

Morton's brow narrowed with the guilt that filled his chest as he watched the man writhing in pain, just like a child that had fallen off a horse into a briar patch. The man's reaction was unexpected and haunting.

The bum looked into Morton's eyes for an unspoken explanation of why Morton hurt him with tears so thick that Morton could not look away. "It hurts," the man whimpered through his sobbing gasps as he held his ribs. "It hurts."

Tony stepped beside Morton and said, "Kick him in the face."

Inwardly, Morton felt sick but followed orders

and brutally kicked the hurt man in the face with his boot. The man cried out as it jarred his body. He sobbed with gasping breaths that brought more anguish. A new split lip dripped blood steadily down his chin.

Tony knelt beside the bum. "JoJo, I heard you were talking to the U.S. Marshal Matt Bannister. I suggest you avoid him like the plague your rats bring if you know what's good for you. I won't be so nice next time. I caught your friend for you before she ran too far away." He set the black rat on JoJo's chest; she was dead from being crushed under Tony's foot. He tapped JoJo's cheek with a few light taps while JoJo picked up his beloved rat with horrified eyes and deep, grieving groans.

Tony chuckled and turned to Morton. "You passed the test."

***

Tony knocked on Felix's office door and opened it. "Oh! My apologies. I didn't realize you had company."

"William, this is my assistant, Tony Hurner. Tony, this is William Craig. He's looking to buy a tavern or other properties here. We were discussing business."

William Fasana stood from his chair to shake Tony's hand. He was surprised to see Morton with him. "It's nice to meet you, Tony." He shook his hand firmly. He looked at Morton and reached his hand out. "I'm William Craig. Are you an assistant too?"

Tony answered, "This is Morton. He's interviewing for the job of putting a new roof on the building here."

William grinned and looked at Felix before asking Tony, "Do roofers always wear a sidearm around here? We have plenty of bandits in Seattle, but it isn't so bad that the roofers need to carry weapons." He laughed. "It's nice to meet you, Morton."

Tony's cheeks reddened, realizing how ridiculous his words sounded.

"Nice to meet you," Morton said with an uncomfortable smile. "I'm not working today. I took my wife to collect her children from her ex-husband a bit earlier, and he's a violent man. I just put this on to show him I wouldn't tolerate any nonsense."

William was genuinely impressed by Morton's quick thinking. "That sounds like it worked."

Morton nodded. "It did."

Felix spoke, "William, I'm afraid I need to discuss roof prices. Could you talk Maggie into joining my wife and me for dinner at the Pengelly Restaurant around six? I think we could do some business together."

"Yeah. I think we could do that."

Felix shook his hand. "Excellent. I'll see you tonight."

Once William left the office, Tony closed the door and motioned for Morton to sit. Tony sat in one of the other chairs. "Felix, this is Morton Myers from the town of Cold Water. He just moved over here looking for a change, and I think he has the skills we are looking for. He taught JoJo a lesson. I don't think we need to worry about JoJo talking anymore."

"Good," Felix said softly as his eyes gazed at Morton. "You are one rugged-looking man. Life hasn't been easy on you, has it?"

"It's been rougher on others," Morton said.

"You recovered well when William questioned about your sidearm. I know you're not a roofer. I asked around about you. Your gang's reputation is known to our District Attorney's Office. I can't say I know of it, but I'm a defense lawyer, so I wouldn't be so inclined to know unless you needed my services. You've never been arrested for your crimes?"

Morton was almost humored to hear the Portland District Attorney's Office had heard of a gang he made up off the top of his head. He answered Felix's question with a shake of his head. "Most witnesses can be persuaded not to testify. I was arrested once but found innocent of the crime I committed." He smiled. "I have a large family, and all my cousins are outlaws too, so not many of us served time."

"Who are your cousins?"

"The Burke brothers from my town and the Jester brothers from central Oregon."

"I think I have heard of the Jester brothers. They are your cousins?"

"Yes, sir. And we've always protected each other."

"How's that?"

"Well, sir, we've convinced witnesses, jury members, district attorneys, and judges that it might be best for them and their families to ensure our relatives walk free. I guess you could say we act as our own defense attorneys. We've never needed to hire one."

Felix laughed. "You just don't get paid as much, huh?"

"Not usually." Morton smiled slightly.

Felix looked at Tony. "I like him."

"I thought you might."

Felix turned his attention back to Morton. "I don't hire anyone without signing a contract, and there is an affidavit for secrecy in it. Of course, if you break that, it isn't a lawsuit or jail you'd face, but certain death. Understand? That means if you decide to partner with us, it is a brotherhood, probably like your gang, like your family for sure, with expectations of total loyalty, devotion, and commitment to our business. You're an outlaw, a criminal, and we do a little of that too. We'll bring you in slowly, but if you decide to join us, you'll be cared for in every way. Are you married?"

"No."

"I usually expect my people to be clean-cut, like Tony, but I think I want you looking as rugged and intimidating as you do. Tony, have the barber maybe comb his hair back and shave around the goatee, but don't cut his hair or touch the goatee. I like how rough and dangerous he looks, and I don't want that changed."

"Okay."

"Morton, Tony's going to buy you some suits, and I do want you wearing those. And you'll have to exchange your gun belt for a shoulder holster and smaller caliber of weapon, by the looks of that one." He nodded at Morton's .44. "Here in the city, a snub nose .32 that can be easily concealed seems to work best. That is what I have."

"Where I'm from, that's a woman's gun," Morton said plainly.

Felix chuckled. "It may be, but it still kills." He paused, pulled out a two-page contract, and set it on the far side of the desk for Morton to read and sign. "This contract has your name on it. All you have to do is read it, sign your name, and this five hundred dollars will be yours to purchase new suits and boots and get yourself cleaned up. Buy a new weapon and shoulder holster too. Tony will set you up in a place to live; if you want a woman, he can arrange that too. But as I said, there will be no turning back once you sign your name."

Morton furrowed his brow as he took hold of the contract and read it. He stood and took hold of the fountain pen and signed his name.

Felix stood behind his desk and reached out his hand to shake. "Welcome aboard, Morton. Your life is about to change for the best it's ever been. Those hard times are behind you now. We'll take good care of you. This money is yours. Tony, get him set up and take him under your wing."

Chapter 14

Matt went to the Portland Police Department and waited to speak with the Portland Police Chief, Bruce Schlemer. He had been waiting for over an hour in a waiting room and was growing impatient. Finally, an average-sized man in his late fifties with well-groomed short gray hair and a manicured short gray mustache stepped out of a hallway and pointed at Matt. "Marshal Bannister? It is an honor to meet you. I understand you wanted to speak with me?"

Matt stood to shake the man's hand. "Are you the chief, Bruce Schlemer?"

"Yes. Forgive me. I apologize for making you wait so long. As you can imagine, I get busy. I was in a meeting. Well, let's go to my office and talk for a bit. Maybe you can tell me what this is all about?"

They entered a small office with files, a standard desk, and chairs. Nothing stood out as unique about the office; it was small, simple, and efficient.

"What brings a man like you here to see me?" Bruce asked as he closed the door behind them and took a seat behind his simple desk.

"My son is missing. I suspect he may have been shanghaied along with his adopted brother and a local man named Bob Mears. They all went missing at the same time about five days ago now."

Bruce frowned. "I'm sorry to hear that. What makes you think something bad happened?"

"Because it's been five days!" Matt said sharply.

"And surely that is very alarming, I understand. I know you mentioned shanghaiing, but that really doesn't happen here. Perhaps your son and his pals are out drinking on a four-day drunk binge or passed out in a Chinese opium den. That happens all the time."

Matt's eyes hardened. "They are not on a four-day drunk or smoking opium. I'm a little taken back, Chief Schlemer. Are you the only person in Portland unaware of the shanghaiing in your city?"

Bruce laughed lightly. "Trust me; it's all gossip and rumors. It's like the story of the Legend of Sleepy Hollow. It's not a true story, but yet, it has become a legend, and I'm sure over in New York, there are teenagers terrified to go out at night in fear of seeing the headless horseman. I'm the police chief, right? If that crime happened on our streets, I'd know it. I'm telling you, Marshal Bannister, you're barking up the wrong tree. There must be a more reasonable explanation of why those three are missing. I will do everything I can to help find your son because I have my own children and certainly empathize with you. Still, the fact remains that the headless horseman isn't patrolling the roads of Tarrytown, New York, any more than the Chinese stealing white men to become sailors." He chuckled.

Matt spoke pointedly, "I didn't say anything about the Chinese or white men. I just know my son is missing, and I know the reputation of your city. It's funny how you can sit here and say that, but my father's wife was approached by a white man who offered her money to send drunk men his way to do exactly what you said doesn't exist here—"

"No," Bruce interrupted with a shake of his head. "I'm sure your father's wife is mistaken. And if that did happen, why didn't she come to us and let us know so we could investigate it? Marshal Bannister, men come to Portland every day to celebrate their payday. Most go home after a weekend drunk, but some fall off the ferry and drown. Some think they can swim across the river and drown.

"The Willamette River isn't like some of these smaller rivers and streams that most men from out of town are used to, so they decide to go swimming in what looks like calm water, unaware that there is an undertow that will pull them down and drown them. Some are found, but some get tangled in the debris below and are never found. They go missing, but it doesn't mean they were shanghaied. We have that reputation because we are one of the largest shipping ports on the west coast." He chuckled.

"Every port town has that reputation. It just goes with the nature of the business, like the Legend of the Headless Horseman goes with Halloween. But again, you could go to Terrytown, New York, and walk around all night in the cemetery; the headless horseman isn't there." He finished with a careless shrug.

Matt slowly stood. "I'm going to find my son with or without your help. When I do find the people responsible, I'll end it myself. I'm not leaving town until I do."

"Marshal, I remind you that you have no real jurisdiction here," Bruce said pointedly. "If I were you, I'd be very careful where you tread. I'm not saying we don't have dangerous people here; we do. But you might find yourself in over your head. Literally. Go back home, and let us try to find your boy."

Matt took a deep breath. "You haven't even asked what his name is. That tells me that you have as much interest in finding him as you might a dog crapping in the grass. I'm done talking. Have a good day."

***

Matt stopped by the Rathkey Attorney at Law Office and was told that Felix was at the courthouse for a trial. Matt found the courthouse and entered the courtroom quietly to watch the trial of Oscar Petrovic, a man accused of manslaughter for causing his friend's death.

Matt watched the last twenty minutes of the trial and followed Felix outside of the courthouse while the jury of twelve men considered the evidence.

"Felix Rathkey," Matt called to get the lawyer's attention. A man with black curly hair that walked beside Felix spun around sharply when Matt hollered. Matt took notice of the slight bulge under the man's suit coat, revealing a shoulder holster.

Felix turned around and noticed Matt's badge immediately. "Yes?" he answered. He knew who Matt was but didn't want to display that in his expression.

"I'm U.S. Marshal Matt Bannister. Do you have a moment?" He looked at the black-haired man with Felix, who suddenly appeared nervous.

"Absolutely. What an honor to meet you." He shook Matt's hand firmly. "My wife won't believe me when I tell her I met you. You're quite a famous man." He gazed at Matt with a friendly grin.

"I shouldn't be," Matt replied. "I understand you are one of the last people to see Bob Mears before he went missing..."

"Bob is still missing?" he interjected with a touch of surprise in his voice.

Matt nodded slightly as his eyes studied Felix carefully. "So is my son. They went missing simultaneously, and I am intent on finding them."

"Of course," he answered understandably. "So, how can I help you?" Felix's concern appeared genuine.

153

"You could help me by telling me who else Bob owed money to or who might have a reason to make him disappear along with two teenagers. I know shanghaiing happens here, and I need to know who is involved in it. You're a defense attorney who certainly knows the criminals around here. I need names and addresses that you might have."

Felix raised his brow and exhaled. "Well, as a representative of law enforcement, you know about attorney and client privilege. Gosh, even if I knew anything, I'd be liable to lose my license if I shared it." He grimaced as he debated on a decision. "Give me a…no. Well…" He shook his finger at Matt indecisively. "Oh, gosh, you know your son is missing…let me ask around. I have never represented anyone arrested for that crime. I don't know if it even happens here, but I know Bob owed money to a low-life hood named Potsy Jones.

"I loaned Bob money to invest in a business, but he paid it back the same day. I have his signed receipt to prove that. Bob borrowed from Potsy Jones too. In fact, I recall Bob mentioning he had to pay everyone back. I loaned him the most, so Bob paid me first. I met your son, actually. Your father brought him to my office when he asked me to return the loan from Bob without interest. Your son was a handsome young man. Yes, I'll do whatever I can to help you find him. Let me scan through some of my old files and see if I can locate any names you may want to talk to."

"I met Potsy yesterday. I gave him a fair warning.

He approached my father's wife about shanghaiing men some time back. So, I know it exists here, and I'm going to end it, at least the lives of those who took my son. Even if it is five years down the road and Gabriel comes back from overseas and tells me who did it, I will come back here and kill those responsible. That's a promise that you can spread around town for me."

Felix gazed at him awkwardly. He spoke slowly, "I'm not in that kind of a social circle to mix with anyone who knows anything about that kind of stuff. As I said, I don't know of or have ever represented a client knowingly involved in such a crime."

"I didn't say you were, but maybe your clients do. I'm offering a five-thousand-dollar reward for information about my son's whereabouts or who took him. The money will be wired as soon as the information turns out to be true. Some of these folks will start talking soon."

"I imagine so," Felix said quietly. "I hope you find him very soon. And as I said, I'll help however I can."

"Much appreciated."

"Matt, I hope you don't mind me calling you that. Have you met William Craig?" Felix asked curiously.

Matt's brow narrowed. "Who?"

"William Craig. He's Maggie's friend from Seattle. Have you met him yet?"

Matt nodded. "Yes, for a moment. I can't say I enjoyed his company much. Why?" William had told

Matt that he had met Felix and was going to his office for a meeting, but William never told him the last name he used. They knew it would be hard to act like strangers since Maggie was Matt's stepsister, but that didn't mean they had to like each other.

"He and I are talking about doing some business together. It sounds like he has plans to marry Maggie. I met her yesterday as well. She's a very cute and hard-working lady."

Matt shook his head with disgust. "She could do much better than him. I think he's a jackass. I don't trust him with Maggie or around my family. In fact, he's not out of my suspicions for my son's disappearance."

Felix's brow raised with interest. "Really? As far as I know, he wasn't around when Bob and your son went missing, was he? He told me he just got to town."

Matt's eyes shifted to the man with curly black hair and mustache, whose lips curved slightly upwards. "I'm not sure. As I said, I just don't like him. I'll probably throw him out of my father's apartment window before too long or force him to use those pretty guns of his for more than impressing the ladies. I'm a gunman; I doubt he is." Matt motioned to the black-haired man, "Who is your friend?"

Felix pointed at the courthouse. "In my profession, I make enemies of the victims of the crimes my clients are accused of. Some folks are furious when my clients walk away free men. Therefore, not being a violent man, I hired protection. This is my bodyguard, Howard."

"Howard, nice to meet you." Matt shook his hand. "I'd appreciate it if you'd let your clients know about my reward. It's a lot of money for just telling the truth."

***

Felix closed his office door and sat heavily in his chair behind his desk. He gazed at Howard Nicol and thoughtfully pressed his bottom lip against his upper teeth. "A five-thousand-dollar reward can buy a lot of talk. Loose lips sink ships, and sunken ships hold a lot of skeletons." He shouted, "I wish they'd get those damn repairs done and get that ship out to sea!" He lowered his voice not to be overheard, "We have to move the boys in case someone talks, but I don't know where. I'm worried the marshal will get a search warrant, bring a force of men into the tunnels, and break every door open. The marshal's right; that's a lot of money for just talking. We must get them two boys out of there or eliminate them like Bob and give the captain his money back. Any ideas, Howard?"

Howard nodded slowly. "Pan Ching and I could watch over them at that abandoned cabin along the river I use. No one ever goes there, and I could paint the windows black and put a lock on the door. I could prepare it today and take them there tonight. That way, they'd be out of town, and the marshal could search to his heart's delight but never find them."

Felix nodded in agreement. "Make darn sure you shackle and bind them securely. We can't afford for them to escape, Howard."

"They'll be too drugged to escape. Don't worry, boss, I know what I'm doing. I'll prepare it today, and we'll move them tonight. Do you want the new guy to help?" Howard was in his early forties with black curly hair that was kept short. He had a long, narrow face, large brown eyes, and dark brows. He was a big man at nearly six feet but not as broad as Felix or Tony. Howard seldom wore a hat and kept a thick well-groomed mustache.

Felix didn't think beards or facial hair were respectable for professional men and didn't allow anyone in his office to have any except for a well-maintained mustache. He had made an exception for Morton because he believed Morton appeared far more menacing with his goatee than he would without. He had plans for Morton to keep him outside the office, where a man of his wild nature would be better served.

"No. We can't trust Morton yet. His job, for now, is to collect money and intimidate people. He inspired me to tamper with witnesses and jury members in a whole new way. A way that he's very experienced with. I think Morton Myers will be a great asset for us, but we'll bring him in slowly."

"Felix, what the marshal said about his son returning in five years is a scary thought. There is no promise those boys won't come back," Howard said anxiously.

Felix's forehead wrinkled. "I'll meet with Captain Smithrud and offer some of his money back if he can promise me those two meet their end off the African coast. It will be in his best interest too."

Chapter 15

Matt entered the Maroon Squid Tavern to find JoJo Perkins and take him to Potsy's Sailor's Lair to retrieve his pocketknife and have Dillon apologize to him. Matt was angered to learn that JoJo was in the hospital with several broken ribs. It seemed someone had given JoJo a pretty good beating while on his way to check his live traps under the piers and granary. A fellow who knew JoJo brought him to the tavern, and the owner, Hugh Ogle, had taken JoJo to the hospital. Hugh had questioned JoJo about who attacked him, but JoJo was too afraid to say.

Matt walked to Potsy's Sailor's Lair and entered with the leather thong removed from the revolver's hammer in preparation to draw if needed. "Where's Dillon?" he asked as he stepped through the door. His words caught everyone's attention as he scanned the tavern and found Dillon leaning against the bar, talking to a pretty waitress. "Have you got JoJo's knife?"

The furious glare in Matt's eyes scared any will to fight out of Dillon. He swallowed nervously and spoke in a cracking voice, "The water was too deep; by the time we got to the bottom, we had to come back up. Gilbert nearly drowned searching. Marshal Bannister, we spent three hours trying but couldn't find it. There is no way to find it. In replacement, I bought JoJo a brand new knife, their best knife." He held out a fine-looking wood-handled knife with a folding blade.

"He's telling the truth. We all tried," one of his pals offered sincerely.

Matt didn't seem to hear them as he shouted, "I told you to leave JoJo alone, didn't I?"

Dillon's brow lowered, not entirely understanding the purpose of the question. "Yes. I bought him a new knife. A better one," he answered.

Matt's eyes roamed the room taking notice of any potential threats willing to protect Dillon. Matt pulled his revolver from the holster and pulled the hammer back as he aimed at Dillon. His hardened eyes glared harshly at the young man, who stiffened, immobilized in fear.

"Uh... Sir..." one of Dillon's friends grasped at something to say. "He got JoJo a new knife. A nicer one!"

"Shut up!" Matt snapped with a quick, fierce glance at the man. "The only person that needs to talk is Dillon. I told you just yesterday that I'm doing JoJo's fighting for him, and you still attacked him and even killed his rat!" Matt yelled furiously. "I'm stopping any more attacks on him today. I won't kill you, but I will cripple you. What knee do you want to be blown away? You won't be such a nuisance to him with one leg, will you?"

Dillon's face contorted in terror as his breathing turned into short, troubled breaths. His voice trembled in a higher pitch, "I didn't do anything to him. Please, I bought him a new knife. I'm sorry for taking his. I tried to find his."

Matt lowered his aim and pulled the trigger. The gun's percussion was amplified inside the tavern, but it was overridden by the screaming of Dillon as he jumped into the air and then fell to the floor, sobbing in terror. The bullet penetrated the bar's solid wood base, missing Dillon's foot by four inches.

Matt walked intently forward and knelt to grab Dillon's hair with his left and yanked his head back to shove the revolver in his face. "Shut up!" Matt yelled ferociously as his burning eyes watched the cowardly bully weep. "Stop your crying; I didn't shoot you! Listen to me... Shut your mouth and listen!" Matt shouted over Dillon's crying.

"Why didn't you listen to me? Huh? I warned you, and you beat JoJo so bad that he's in the hospital! And then you had the nerve to kill his rat even after I warned you? Now you expect me to have mercy on you? Oh, no; it doesn't work that way with me. Before I disfigure your pretty face, tell me why you and your pals attacked him?" He glanced behind him towards Dillon's friends to let them know he was aware of them.

Dillon stared at the gun's barrel and the fierce eyes of a man who had killed more men than Dillon had ever beaten up. He was perplexed by the question. "I didn't do anything! I haven't seen JoJo. I tried to find that knife. I swear it! I got him a new one," he wept as he held up the knife.

"Which one of you beat JoJo up this morning?" Matt demanded to know.

"It wasn't us," Dillon shouted. "I swear it wasn't us!"

"Last chance," Matt said coldly.

"I don't know!" Dillon screamed before covering his face protectively with his hands. "I don't know what you're talking about!"

Matt's expression remained a cold snarl with the .45 caliber barrel inches from Dillon's face. He could see that Dillon was on the verge of a panic-stricken emotional breakdown and knew lies could be discerned by an unexpected question at that level of emotional distress. Ferociously Matt shouted, "Do you know where my son is?"

Dillon's emotional restraint broke. "I don't know! Oh, lord, I don't know anything about your son. I swear, I don't." He began sobbing uncontrollably. Dillon tried to speak but was too emotionally strained to say anything. He slid horizontally to the floor, withering and jerking with silent sobs when Matt released his hair.

"Marshal," one of Dillon's friends said nervously, "We don't know anything about your son or JoJo being hurt. Honestly, we don't. Bob Mears is a friend of mine, and no one knows where he is."

Matt stood. He took a deep breath to calm the fury that had gotten the better of him and holstered his revolver. "Any ideas on who might know?" he asked with an emotionally exhausted voice.

The man shrugged. "No. And I'm not just saying that; I mean it."

"None of you beat up JoJo this morning?"

"It wasn't us. Marshal Bannister, we liked to humiliate and scare him sometimes, but we have never hurt JoJo. He's Potsy's brother-in-law. His wife is ashamed of him, but that doesn't mean she wants him hurt. We didn't touch him."

Matt looked down at Dillon and exhaled. He knelt and grabbed the knife Dillon had bought. He spoke to Dillon softly, "I'll take this to him for you. Someone hurt JoJo pretty bad, and I assumed it was you. I apologize for being wrong. That knife you threw into the river was the only thing he had of his father's. To you, that may mean nothing, it's just a knife, but to him, it was priceless. And if you can't understand that, then you're a worse person than I already think you are."

Matt stood and announced, "I am offering five thousand dollars to anyone who can tell me where my son is or who took him. I'm staying at the Silver Casterlin. If your information's true, you're five thousand dollars richer. You don't have to be afraid of who took my boy coming after you because the people who took my son will be dead or wish they were. Spread the word for me."

***

Morton Sperry was eating lunch with Tony Hurner in the Wavering Wharf Tavern when Matt Bannister abruptly entered the tavern and announced who he was, followed by a large monetary reward for any information leading to the return of his missing son or who may have taken him. After saying what he had to say, Matt walked out as abruptly as he entered.

Tony Hurner finished chewing his bit of salmon and pulled a thin bone from his mouth that he didn't see on his fork. "Have you ever heard of him?"

Morton nodded while watching the door. "Certainly. You?"

Tony nodded. "Never thought I'd see him here, though. He certainly made you uncomfortable, didn't he?"

Morton nodded. "He's the reason I left home. He built an office in Branson. I have never seen him in person, though. He's not as mean-looking as I expected him to be."

"He does have a wild reputation. If you'll excuse me for a second. Wait here." Tony left the table and hurried outside. He called for Matt to wait as he approached him. "You are *thee* Matt Bannister from Wyoming?"

"I worked in Wyoming."

"Tony Hurner is my name." He shook Matt's hand with enthusiasm. "Five thousand dollars you're offering, and I'd gladly take it. But I must be honest; if I could help you get your son back, it would be an honor to me. Do you know what happened to him?"

Matt answered sharply, "If I knew what happened to him, I wouldn't have to ask for help, would I?"

Tony chuckled at the stupidity of his question. "I meant do you have any suspicions? If not, you might want to poke around Potsy's Sailor's Lair. I have heard that he and his thugs, press gangs are what they are, take people off the street and lock them up in a warehouse until they're out to sea. Potsy is notorious for crimping; shanghaiing is what I mean."

"Who are you?" Matt asked.

"Tony Hurner is my name, but don't tell Potsy and his boys I told you anything, please. I don't want to go missing."

"What do you do?"

"I'm an assistant attorney at a local law firm."

"You're a lawyer?"

"No. Let me rephrase that. I'm an attorney's assistant. I run errands for the most part. I was having lunch with a friend of mine. The Wavering Wharf makes the best salmon in town," he explained. "Listen, I'd like to help you if I could. Let me poke around a bit. I know Bob Mears; he was in our office the other day to pay a bill. Let me ask around, and maybe I can come up with something."

"Do you work for Felix Rathkey?"

"I do." He seemed surprised.

"I spoke to him earlier. He didn't think he could help me much."

Tony raised a finger. "Felix stays in the office. I get out here on the streets and ask around quite a bit. I know more people than he does. Let me see what I can do for you."

"I'd appreciate it."

"Say," Tony said thoughtfully, "have you ever heard of the Myers-Finn Gang?"

Matt nodded. "Scum, one and all. Why do you

ask?"

"I met a man a couple of nights ago who claimed to be part of the gang. He was catching a train to Seattle the next morning. I've heard of many outlaw gangs but never heard of them. I didn't know if he was lying or not."

"I can promise you that there are many more outlaw gangs that you've never heard of, which are more deadly than the ones you have heard of. Did the man have a name?"

"He introduced himself as Morton Myers."

Matt's brow raised with interest. "He was going to Seattle? Once I find my son, I'll be going to Seattle then."

"He was telling the truth?" Tony asked to verify that Morton Myers was who he claimed to be.

Matt's lips smiled faintly. "Not many men would claim to be him if they were smart. He'll either die by my gun or hang when I catch him. Thanks for telling me where he went. I'll find him."

Tony felt better about trusting his new friend. "I'll keep in touch. I suggest you investigate Potsy Jones and his press gang. They are the most notorious shanghaiers in town. I bet they grabbed your boy. I hope not, but that's what they do."

"I'll do that, thank you. Please let me know if you hear anything about who beat up a man named JoJo Perkins this morning. I'd like to know who put him in the hospital."

Tony questioned, "The rat man? Who in the world would want to hurt him? I'll do my best to find out."

Chapter 16

"Well, let's just say I don't like pompous lawmen with bitterness against someone with a nicer gun set than his. I just met the man, but I don't think we'll be friends, if you know what I mean." William chuckled. He sat next to Maggie in the Pengelly Restaurant across the table from Felix Rathkey and his wife, Nora. Felix had asked him how he liked Matt Bannister.

Nora Rathkey was an uncommonly tall lady at five feet and ten inches tall with broad shoulders and a thick body. She didn't appear obese or over-weight; she was just a bigger woman than most others, and some men too, including her shorter husband. Nora had pretty long brown hair with a natural wave that she often wore down on her shoulders. Her face was oblong with intelligent, large almond-shaped brown eyes. She had a prom-inent Roman nose that her husband criticized occasionally, but she was a very attractive lady in her mid-thirties with a bubbly personality that matched Maggie's own like a pair of gloves being reunited.

Nora had always appreciated Maggie while purchasing meat at the butcher shop but had never spoken to her at length. The more the two ladies talked over dinner, they discovered they had much more in common than they knew, and a mutual friendship quickly grew. However, Felix had an agenda he was interested in, and the two ladies talking non-stop hindered any business discussion between the men. After a delicious meal and dessert, Felix and Nora invited William and Maggie to their home for drinks.

The Rathkeys lived in an elegant white two-story colonial home with a large four-columned front porch set in the beautiful Northwest corner of Portland at the base of the west hills, otherwise known as snob hill. Their home stood alone on a city block surrounded by trees, groomed hedges, and rose bushes that Nora took great pride in. She loved flowers and had a variety of flowering bushes surrounding their home.

The newest neighbor was over a block away, but to the annoyance of Felix and Nora, a newly constructed framework of a large Victorian house was being built directly across the street. The hammering of the carpenters was enough to drive Nora mad daily. Neither she nor Felix looked forward to having such close neighbors.

The Rathkey's home was large but comfortable, warm, and inviting. Nora's mother lived with them and had been watching their only child—seven-year-old Gretchen. Felix and Nora excused themselves momentarily as the doting parents left their guests to tuck their daughter into bed for the night. Upon returning, the four of them shared drinks and a time of socializing with Nora's mother before Felix excused himself, escorted William into his home office, and closed the door.

Felix offered William a fresh drink and a cigar as they sat in two padded chairs facing a large desk that they angled towards each other to talk comfortably. Bookshelves filled with law books and other interests lined an entire wall, there were prints of tall ships and other things on the walls, but William's attention was drawn to a large pencil sketch of Nora's side profile that was a fair likeness of her beautiful hair, but her nose had been insultingly exaggerated to an embarrassing degree. The drawing was mounted in an oversized wooden frame.

"That's...Nora?" William asked, pointing at the drawing, unimpressed.

Felix chuckled as he lit his cigar and leaned over to light William's. "Yeah, that's a caricature of her; I paid an artist to do it. Nora hates it. I think it's funny, although not far from the truth. She also has big ears, so she wears her hair down. I swear she can hear the geese leaving Alaska every Fall and smell the geese leaving Mexico every Spring. I'm pretty sure her father was an elephant." He chuckled as he sat back and crossed his leg to get comfortable. "I wanted a wife with childbearing hips, and I got an elephant. The funny thing is, she isn't fat; I am."

William said, "I think Nora is very nice."

"Oh, she is. So tell me, William, do you have

much trouble with the police in Seattle? I know here, the police pretty much leave the drinking establishments alone for the most part, but just talking with you tonight, I get the feeling that you don't always do things legally."

William let the cigar smoke slowly drift from his mouth. "I run a perfectly legal establishment from closing time to sunup," he said with a wink and a smile. "I heard all your dogs barking when we got here, so I'll put my philosophy to you like this; I think the police are a lot like dogs. You have to kick them occasionally and sometimes rub their nose in their own crap to teach them their limits. Honestly, the police don't bother me. They're bought and paid for like trained monkeys."

"Do you have an interest in dogs? Do you want to see my kennel?" Felix asked. Behind the Rathkey home was a white building with black wrought iron fencing five feet tall with pointed spires rising another six inches, creating four cages on both sides. Each pen had six by ten feet of outside space and six by five feet of space inside the building where the dog's bedding was. Each pen had a wrought iron gate to access it from the outside and a door inside along the center aisle to make caring for the animals easy. Felix was very proud of his kennel, but Nora didn't share his enthusiasm about dogs and disliked having them on their property.

William waved off any interest. "I have no time or interest in pets. I think they're a nuisance."

"That's too bad. Dogs are a hobby of mine. You said you were a gambler. Do you like horse racing?"

"I do if I know the horses I'm betting on. The

poker table is where I'm at my best; high-stakes poker games are where my interests lie mostly."

"If you're not busy tomorrow night, why not come with me to the races? You're the kind of man who might enjoy our group. It's a high-stakes, invitation-only thing, though. You'll understand."

William was intrigued. "You have my attention."

"Good. Bring some money to gamble with; I'll help you pick winners. We have a good night planned. You'll double your money, I promise."

"Sounds good."

Felix offered a pleased smile. "After tomorrow night, you'll want to move your operation down here for more reasons than just Maggie. I think you're going to love it."

William nodded sincerely. "I am a gambler, so maybe so." He hesitated. "I can't say I'll ever be the world's most faithful man or the most honest when it comes to women, but I've always been hooked on Maggie. I suppose if anyone can make me an honest man by outside appearances anyway, then it might be her. I wouldn't mind having a son or two to carry on the Craig name. I'm moving over here with that in mind."

"Having a family is the greatest thing in the world," Felix said, sipping his drink. "You're moving here at the right time, too. Portland is an expanding city with plenty of opportunities to build your fortune. I trust we can work together and make a lasting friendship and a successful partnership." He raised his glass in the air to toast.

"Partners," William said as he lifted his glass to toast. "As long as I'm on top of the totem pole, Felix.

You're the man for all things law and order as my lawyer, but unless you have some experience in the gambling halls and saloons, I'll follow my own advice on how to run my business."

"Of course." Felix agreed. "What did you think about the Maroon Squid Tavern? Have you considered anymore about buying that?"

William shook his head and waved a finger. "It's not what I'm looking for." William paused. "But if we're going to be partners, then you probably ought to know that I can be a little rowdy and step outside the law here and there when need be."

Felix gazed at William with a bewildered grin. "William, I'm your attorney; everything you say to me is confidential. Well, once we sign a contract. But a drink and a handshake will do for now. So, have any places caught your attention?"

William exhaled with an animated show of smoke rings. "The Wavering Wharf looked promising. There were a few others, but most were too small for my needs. I see missed opportunities all along the river and want to take over the entire waterfront." William held up a finger to add pointedly, "There is legal and illegal money to be made by the thousands."

Felix stated, "I'm not sure I understand what you mean. Opening a saloon with gambling tables is perfectly legal with the right licensing and city permits."

William raised his brow questionably. "Are you sure you're a criminal lawyer? You should already have a pretty good grasp on what happens on the waterfront."

"Theft? Burglary?" Felix probed.

"On the waterfront?" William asked sarcastically. "What are you going to steal, written I owe U's from sailor's pockets? You know as well as I do that the price of labor is a golden profit. The ships come here every day from months at sea and lose sailors to the pleasures of shore leave. They all know they can be hired on the next boat or any boat that comes in. It's the nature of the business. Am I right?"

Felix shrugged. "I work in the courthouse, not the docks. I don't know."

"You can't be that blind and dumb. Someone in town probably scooped up Matt Bannister's son, stuck him on a schooner, and put the cash in their pocket. I'm not telling Matt that because what he doesn't know won't hurt him. But I think there is a pretty good chance that his boy is seasick right about now. You're my lawyer, so I trust this will go no further because Maggie would drop me like a maggot-infested puppy if she heard me say this, but I intend to take over this town and make all that shanghaiing business mine."

"You think Matt's son was shanghaied?"

"Do you have another explanation?"

"No, I suppose not."

William finished his drink and strolled over to the small cabinet bar to refill his glass. "I have been studying you, Felix. You are undoubtedly a good lawyer, but I know you're not as clean-cut and dumb as you are pretending to be. Floyd Bannister mentioned you loan money, so do you blackmail people? How do you make your living? I mean, you have a beautiful and expensive place here. You can't be that innocent; otherwise, you wouldn't want anything to do with me."

Felix smiled. "I own an attorney's office with lawyers working under me. I don't have to blackmail people. I loan money at a fair interest rate to help other people reach their dreams as I have reached mine. I help people."

"Right," William said doubtfully. He carried his drink back to his chair and sat, crossing his leg comfortably. "And what if those clients don't pay? That's where your assistants Tony and Howard come in, right? Don't worry, Felix, I have men like them too."

Felix's frown was noticeable. "They collect the debt, yes."

"And the roofer with the sidearm from this morning?"

"A new assistant. What is with all the questions?" Felix asked, growing weary of being questioned.

William rubbed his eyebrow with a slight smile on his lips. "You may be my lawyer, but I don't trust men too spit-shined, polished, and on the straight and narrow to be my partners. I cross the borders of the law, and if you were so inclined, you could betray me and have me sent to prison while you take over my business. That doesn't work for me. You're too honest of a man to be tied with the likes of me."

Felix smiled to himself and slowly said, "I may not be as blameless as you might think. As your attorney, I can assure you of my confidentiality, but I can't assure myself of yours. I think we have the same lack of trust in each other, William."

"Sounds like, but you know my intentions; I intend to open a saloon and gambling hall, where I intend to shanghai men until I can run the others out of town. I don't know one dishonorable thing about you. And that concerns me."

Felix chuckled as he watched William. "Okay. You see my life and think all is blissful. And it is, but I have a wandering eye."

"I saw you watching Maggie. Don't think I overlooked that."

Felix nodded. "She's a pretty lady. Nora thinks I'm as faithful as a coon dog, but I keep a lady or two on the side."

"Painted ladies?" William questioned.

Felix took a deep breath before saying, "I keep a little hideaway in town here where I meet my ladies. I'm not as straight and narrow and clean-cut as you may think. Everything must remain confidential, Partner," Felix said. "Everything."

"I figured you did. A man that keeps a picture like that of his wife, doesn't honor her much," he said while pointing at the humiliating drawing of Nora.

Felix grunted a short chuckle. "I honor her enough. I believe we'll make great business partners, after all, William."

Chapter 17

"Marshal Bannister? Can I speak with you in private?" a man asked. He had followed Matt to the stairway of the Silver Casterlin building. He had been waiting for Matt to return.

"Who are you?" Matt asked, looking the man over carefully.

"My name is Eric Stiles. I am a Portland Police Officer sworn to protect the citizens of this city, and I think there are some things you should know." He was a tall, lean, muscular man in his late thirties with short dark brown hair and a thick mustache. He had a stern countenance about him that warned that he wasn't a man to be messed with. He had a broad square-shaped face, flattened nose, and brooding dark eyes dulled and hardened by life's misfortunes but still genuinely sincere. He was dressed in a gray and white striped shirt and black pants, with scuffed-up boots from use on the concrete sidewalks.

"Like what?" Matt asked warily. He had spoken to the police chief earlier that day and was not impressed by his lack of interest. He had never met Officer Eric Stiles and didn't know the man from anyone else on the street. Matt, uneasy and vigilant, kept his eyes on the stranger.

"Can we talk in private?" Eric asked.

Matt invited him to the roof where they would not be seen or heard, but he refused to turn his back to the man and asked him to walk up the stairs first. Once on the roof where they were alone, Matt asked, "Who are you again?"

"My name is Eric Stiles. I was a sergeant with the Portland Police until I stood up to Chief Schlemer. I'm now demoted back to nothing and one complaint or irritation away from being fired. I'm on Bruce Schlemer's blacklist."

"Do you have information about my son?" Matt asked.

"No. I saw you at the police station and heard what the chief said after you left. Chief Schlemer isn't interested in finding your boy because he is bought by every crimp, scoundrel, and criminal element in this city. The reward you offered has him and others worried because there are no true secrets in town. Somebody always knows something, and they'll talk if the price is right. In the next day or two, I expect to find a few dead bodies or more missing people associated with the harbor. Those who took your son will be securing their loose ends. I'll bet you on that."

"Any idea who it is?" Matt asked.

"You need to understand that there are four of five press gangs that work for certain individuals that make up a good portion of the shanghaiing around here. It does happen here, and it happens often. The Potsy Jones crew, Big Richard Burkhalter, Theodore Marks, Laura Eggers, China Joe, The Fifth Street Tong, and Sebastian the Greek are all involved in shanghaiing poor souls to ship captains. They all have sections of town and sailor's houses that pay Chief Schlemer and others to be left alone.

"We have all kinds of illegal activity happening here, including the Chinese bringing in illegal immigrants from China, young girls in particular, for prostitution and then shipping them to Chinatowns all over the west from here. That's a big business for them. The Chinese have their own pier, and no one cares what they do there.

"Last spring, the body of a police officer I knew well, Marvin Harrison, was found in the river. He had been shot in the back of the head. His murder has never been solved. The public doesn't know it, but Marvin had evidence proving that Chief Schlemer had several scams and dirty dealings worked out and was being paid quite well by several criminals.

"The day Marvin died, he was sent to Laura Egger's bordello by Chief Schlemer to investigate an assault on one of the ladies. Officer Marvin Harrison was found floating in the river later that night. Oddly enough, his house was ransacked, and the evidence disappeared. I should add no girl was ever assaulted, either.

"Chief Schlemer denies he ever sent him there, but Marvin was my friend, and I heard the chief tell him to go there myself. I was demoted for saying so. That's our police force; the chief and lawyers get rich while we honorable patrolmen repeatedly arrest the same people for the same things. Not all patrolmen are honorable either; some profit from being on the take."

"You think the chief had your friend killed?" Matt asked.

"I know he did. He has too many scams going on to risk losing them. Now who pulled the trigger? I don't know. It could have been one of our own or Laura Egger's security man. Who knows? But that's not what I came here to talk to you about."

Matt remained quiet to let the off-duty patrolman say whatever was on his mind.

"Three men going missing at once is not unheard of, but Bob Mears is a local and well-known. To my knowledge, Bob wasn't involved in any of that underhanded business, but being a bartender, he met people who were. Marshal Bannister, I believe your son was shanghaied. It is possible that those three young men found themselves in the wrong place at the wrong time. But Bob has lived here most of his life and knows just about everyone in the crimping business. I just don't believe he'd become a victim.

"Now two healthy teenage boys who are strangers to Portland, absolutely. They're perfect victims, but not Bob. This leaves me with three possibilities: someone thought they could get a good price for the teenagers and killed Bob to get away with it.

180

Second, Bob was shanghaied with them, which could have happened. Or third, Bob was desperate for money to buy half interest in the Maroon Squid Tavern, so he made a deal to deliver the two boys to someone for a set price.

"I know Bob personally and don't think he'd have the heart to do something like that. So I wondered if there was any evidence that he had left town. I checked the stage, train stations, and stern-wheeler passenger lists, and his name was nowhere to be found. He didn't buy a horse that I could find. There is no trace of him at all. It makes me think whoever has your boy may have killed Bob to keep him from talking because Bob is, in my opinion, a tender-hearted man. But who *they* are, I don't know."

"Where would they hide the boys? I hear there are tunnels?" Matt asked with a twitching upper lip.

Eric wrinkled his nose. "I've wandered around down there, and I've never found a thing."

"Then why are the tunnels there?"

Eric waved towards Chinatown. "The Chinese were the first to dig tunnels, but the idea expanded to the Americans. Just look at our harbor; we have miles of warehouses, and all have deliveries to make. The Chinese inspired the idea of creating a tunnel system to make deliveries underground to the basements of the businesses, which would be easier and faster than interfering with the trolleys and street traffic. We can give the Chinese the credit they deserve; they are very efficient. But there is not much down there to see."

Disheartened by another dead end, Matt asked, "What about Felix Rathkey? What do you know about him?"

Eric snorted with frustration. "Felix Rathkey is the reason all these criminals are still flourishing. He gets rich while everyone else suffers because of his wretched clients."

"Is he involved in shanghaiing? He's one of the last people to see Bob."

Eric shook his head. "Felix is a scoundrel, no doubt, but there is no evidence that he's involved in shanghaiing."

"Alright," Matt said with a discouraged tone. He was suspicious of Felix and encouraged Morton and William to get to know him now that fate or providence had lined them all together. All the lies, deception, and effort to root out the man were for nothing. Matt's original inclination to trust his gut that there was more to Felix than meet the eye was proving to be a waste of time, and there was no time left that he could afford to waste.

Eric continued softly, "I'll keep trying to find out who took your boy, but chances are he's already at sea. I'm sorry to say."

Matt was tempted to tell Eric about his two deputies playing different roles and how successful they had become, but now Matt doubted his two deputy's efforts were worth the effort.

Matt ran his hand over his hair, frustrated. "In your opinion, where should I start spending my time looking?"

Eric thought momentarily. "There is a crimp named Oliver Sweat. He had a grudge against Bob because of Bob's ex-fiancée, Ingrid Moller. From what I understand, Oliver had a great interest in courting the widow and invested months trying to win her heart, and just when he thought he had, Bob stepped in and stole her away. Now she's single, and Oliver is back trying to court her. He's the only one I can think of with a motive to get rid of Bob."

Matt turned around with interest. "Where would I find him?"

"Oliver's Place on Second Street."

***

Oliver Sweat had two men row a long boat out to the newly arrived *Perch Michelle*, a three-mast English Schooner that belonged to The Westland Shores Shipping Company, which anchored off Pier #14.

Oliver boarded the ship with the captain's permission and invited the crew to stay at his boarding house while they were in port. The invitation was quickly followed by handing out slips of paper with a map indicating the location of Oliver's Place and a list of benefits of staying there. The sailors, desperate to leave the confines of the ship for a time of shore leave, were eager to accept the invitation. Several sailors grabbed their few belongings, quit the ship's employment, and boarded the boat to be rowed back to shore. Others who wanted to be paid their wages and return to England with the ship stayed on board, patiently waiting for the vessel to be moored before going ashore.

Those who got into the boat and left with Oliver, willingly forfeited their earnings because they knew there was no need for money with men like Oliver Sweat to supply their every need. At the same time, Oliver gave the captain a map with a note stating he had experienced seaman for hire.

***

Matt was told by a man at Oliver's Place where to find Oliver and waited for the longboat to be rowed back to the pier.

A man in his late forties was first to climb the ladder onto the dock. He stood off to the side as the others made the climb. "Gentleman, you have made the right decision to come with me. I am going to treat you right." One at a time, he shook the hands of the foul-smelling sailors who took their first steps on solid ground after months of rolling with the ocean swells.

"Oliver Sweat?" Matt asked as the man began to lead a group of ten sailors toward his place. The two men that rowed the boat had already started their return to the anchored ship that set against the moon's light on the river to load more men.

"Yes. Do you need a place to stay?" Oliver reached into his jacket pocket to hand Matt an invitation.

Matt grabbed him by the breast of his jacket, swung Oliver around, and threw him down to the heavy planks of the dock. Matt stomped on his chest, slid his boot to the underside of Oliver's chin over his throat, and pressed down. He drew his revolver and pointed it at Oliver's face. Matt's snarl was visible in the light from the gas streetlights on Water Street. "Where is my son?" he snarled.

Oliver was terrified to have been attacked by a stranger and now moments from death. He was shocked and clueless about what the madman was demanding. All he could see was the fury of a man's eyes, which terrified him. "What...who?" He struggled to speak with a boot pressing down against his throat.

"My son!" Matt snarled furiously. "Where is my son? You better start talking!"

With the surprise of the attack quickly passing, Oliver was filled with rage. "I don't know your son," he stammered. "Get your foot off me or pull the trigger. But there are witnessed right there, you stupid son of a—"

Matt pressed down to increase the pressure on his throat. "I'm Matt Bannister, and I want my son Gabriel back now! Where is he?"

Oliver grabbed Matt's ankle to release the pressure on his throat. Matt lifted some of the weight, and Oliver began to cough. "You got the wrong man."

Matt reapplied the weight. "Where is Bob Mears?"

Oliver again tried to free the weight from his throat. "I don't know!" he said through a cough. "You jackass, I have nothing to do with his disappearance or your son."

The righteous anger revealed on Oliver's face was one of an innocent man being punished for a crime he didn't commit. Convinced that Oliver was telling the truth, Matt removed his foot and let the man sit upright on the dock while Matt holstered his weapon. "I was told you might be involved," Matt explained plainly.

"No, I'm not involved! I don't take people like that! Who told you I might be involved?"

"That doesn't matter."

Oliver's eyes glared at him. "The hell it doesn't! Well, you can tell them they're dead wrong. True, I hate Bob, but I'm not a killer. I'm just a broker of experienced seamen and those wanting to go to sea. Now if you'll excuse me, I have men to attend to." He stood, humiliated and angry.

"Is Eric Stiles a corrupted policeman?" Matt asked.

Oliver grimaced irritably, "Go to hell." He turned away from Matt.

"Is he corrupt?" Matt asked.

Oliver turned around bitterly. "Why should I tell you anything after what you did to me? You didn't ask me anything. You just threw me down, stepped on my throat, and pulled a gun like I was the worst of criminals in front of my clientele. Why should I tell you anything at all?"

Matt exhaled and rubbed his beard, feeling helpless, defeated, and suddenly lost as another dead end only led to him mistreating an innocent man. "You're right. I apologize to you. I am sorry." He sighed and shrugged helplessly like a lost kid in a rainstorm. "I just want my son back."

Oliver glared at him for a moment. "Good luck with that."

"He's the one that gave me your name," Matt said as he watched Oliver walking away."

Oliver turned around angrily. "Eric told you that? Why would he tell you that?"

"Because you don't like Bob."

Oliver chuckled bitterly. "Yes, as a matter of fact, I hate Bob. I hope he is gone forever. But I don't take people, nor do I hurt people. Eric should know that already; I'm shocked he'd name me. No, by the way, Eric is one of the few policemen that are not on someone's payroll. He'd be better off financially if he were, but that's not his way."

Oliver led his new guests toward his boarding house. Matt sat on a heavy beam on the edge of the dock to watch the boat approach the *Perch Michelle* and more men climb down a rope netting to get into the longboat.

He looked up at the sky and closed his moist eyes as he prayed, "Lord, I am getting scared. If Gabriel is still here, help me to find him. And if not, help me to find out what happened to him." He took a deep breath to calm his nerves. "Jesus, you've always been faithful. Please help me to trust you now too. I'm looking in the wrong places and can't find my way. I have no clear direction and keep hurting the wrong people. Please shine a light on Gabriel and Evan and lead us to them. I don't know if I can keep doing this without knowing. I need your help, Jesus. In your name, I pray, Lord. Amen."

Chapter 18

Morton was a bit uneasy by the courtesies and expenses that Tony Hurner arranged for him. Tony had bought him three suits, new boots, a shoulder holster, a new .38 caliber silver-plated revolver, and a derby hat. He arranged for Morton to move into the Cinder-Hess Hotel until they found him a nicer place to live permanently. Morton had bathed at the hotel and put on a gray pinstriped suit with his shoulder holster under the jacket. It felt uncomfortable at best, as he felt naked without his gun belt and the weight of his sidearm on his hip.

Tony invited Morton to his home for dinner but insisted that Morton couldn't meet his wife looking like an old buffalo hunter from the Kansas plains. They went to a barber shop and had a barber comb Morton's neck-length brown hair straight back and used some pomade to hold it in place. His face was shaved except for his thick goatee, which the barber trimmed just enough to look respectable.

With the new black derby set on his head, Morton felt a bit silly, as it was a dandy man's hat, and he was no city businessman like Lee Bannister. Morton looked in a mirror and knew William Fasana would have a good time teasing him for playing dress up like a little girl. It was the best he was ever dressed, and he looked good, but the strangeness of a new look made him a bit self-conscious.

When Adam and Eve ate the forbidden fruit in the Garden of Eden, the first consequence of their sin was becoming self-conscious. They were ashamed of being naked and hid their bodies with leaves and tried to hide from God. Self-Consciousness and fear have walked hand in hand in people's lives every day since then.

Morton knew he was dressed well and looked much better than before, but he still felt self-conscious about his appearance and feared being laughed at by strangers on the street.

**

Tony Hurner entered his house and was greeted by his wife, Beth, with a quick kiss.

"You're going to be so happy. I made meatloaf, green beans, and cornbread with a honey glaze, one of your favorite dinners. Oh, I see you brought a friend," she said with her eyes falling on Morton.

Tony padded her rump and turned to face Morton as his arm encircled her waist. "This is Morton Myers. He is working with Howard and me at the office. I thought I'd bring him home for dinner.

There is enough food, isn't there?"

"There is always enough," she said with a polite smile. She put her hand out, palm down, to be grasped by Morton's. "Pleased to meet you, Mister Myers."

Morton looked at her hand awkwardly and grabbed her fingers to shake. "Nice to meet you, Miss."

Tony chuckled. "Beth, Morton is from the backwoods and a little rough around the edges. I'll spend the next few days teaching him to greet a lady properly."

She gazed at Morton with a bit of curiosity. "A real mountain man, huh? Well, we don't get those around here too often. No matter. Please, come in and get comfortable. Dinner will be served in a few moments. Would you two gentlemen like a drink before dinner?"

Tony answered, "I'll make the drinks, sweetheart. Those mountain folks like Morton like their drinks a bit stronger than you usually make."

"Not too strong of a drink for me, please," Morton said with a wave of his hand. His attention was drawn to the multiple potted plants around the family and dining rooms. There was a variety of green plants, such as a large fern in a corner, which seemed odd to Morton. Ferns were all over the woods, but he had no idea why someone would want one in their house. Yet, the fern was quite stunning in a blue and white clay pot set against the white paint of the wall. There was a small cactus on the window seal, and other green plants that Morton could not identify. They were not garden plants that would feed the family through winter, and garden plants were the only plants Morton knew too much about. There were some pretty orange succulents on a side table and other small flowers scattered about, but a vibrant white jasmine plant in a large blue and white clay pot filled the home with a welcoming sweet fragrance that only a jasmine can provide. "You have a beautiful home," Morton said sincerely, as he admired the paintings on the wall.

The Hurner home was on 12th Street, several blocks into the residential area of the lower to middle working class. It was a narrow two-story home next to many others of the same design with one or two bedrooms upstairs and a kitchen, dining, and family room downstairs. The house was clean, bright, and cheerfully decorated by a lady's artistic hand. Tony explained that his wife loved to paint, which explained the many canvas portraits of flowers decorating the walls. Sunflowers seemed to be her favorite, as many of the paintings were of sunflowers.

"These paintings are great. My..." Morton paused. He almost let the word *fiancée* slip out, "sister would love them. I love them."

"Thank you," Beth said with a beaming smile to have someone appreciating her artwork. "I think sunflowers are joyful flowers. They just make people feel good. How could a giant bright flower not make you feel good?"

Beth Hurner was a stunning twenty-four-year-old young lady with straight, shoulder-length blonde hair tied in a ponytail with a red ribbon. Her face was triangular and flawless, except for a slight scar on her dark eyebrows that revealed the depth of her brown eyes. She was of medium height and shapely. Throughout the day, Tony talked about Beth, and Morton wished he had a dollar for each time Tony commented on how beautiful his wife was. To Morton's surprise, Tony's wife was as beautiful as he claimed, even prettier than his own fiancé, Audrey Butler.

"Yes," Morton agreed. "Your paintings are beautiful." Somehow the brightness of the yellow in the portraits reminded him of the artist. There was joy in Beth's presence, yet a sadness hidden in her brown eyes. Despite the beauty and brightness of the paintings, an unknown sadness crept into Morton's heart. An unexplained feeling that she was going to break his heart.

Tony asked, "What's for dessert?"

"I didn't make anything for dessert. But I can go to the bakery while you two eat."

"Hmm, no, the bakery's closed," Tony said as he glanced at the clock on the mantel.

"Barely. If I hurry, I might catch Sally cleaning up or on her way home. Certainly, she would sell me another cake or pie that didn't sell today. It will only take twenty minutes or so."

"Well, if you wouldn't mind. I can set the food on the table and make our drinks," Tony said.

Morton didn't want to be a burden. "Miss, I don't need any dessert if it will cause you any extra trouble."

Beth smiled appreciatively. "It is no trouble. Tony always likes having dessert after his supper." She wrinkled her nose and admitted, "I ate the last piece of cake today. Wouldn't it be nice to sit down with a piece of pie and talk after dinner? I think so. I'll be right back."

Once Beth left the house, Tony sat in the family room and said, "It's not a mansion, but Beth makes it beautiful. I'm the luckiest man alive, Morton. I really am. Not every man can marry a woman that they love more than life itself, but I can. One day you will too. Now that you're working for Felix, you'll earn enough money to live comfortably. You have to provide for a wife, so that's a good start. Have you ever been in love, Morton?"

"Yes." His mind went to his fiancée Audrey back in Branson. He missed her.

"Did she break your heart?" Tony asked.

Morton nodded slowly. "Yeah, she did."

"I never loved anyone until I met Beth." Tony continued, "Her parents were missionaries to some Indian tribe along the Columbia, and about fourteen years ago, a smallpox epidemic hit. All four of Beth's siblings and her mother died. Beth was nine years old, I think. She was raised by her father, and being a religious man, her father wasn't so willing to let her marry me, but I persuaded him over time. He was old and dying, and I went to church a few times." He laughed lightly. "Her father's gone now, but he used to say the Lord was the light of his life. Have you ever heard one of those Christians say the Lord is their light in the world? Well, Beth is the light of my life."

Morton couldn't say he was a Christian under the circumstances, but he understood exactly how dark the world could be and how hopeless and dreary life becomes when there is no light to offer some hope. Jesus brought that light that changed Morton's life in ways he never knew were possible. The bitterness he once felt daily had become a lighthearted joy, and hope replaced a hopeless future. "Is she still a Christian? You know, from growing up like that?"

Tony's expression turned slightly bitter as he shook his head. "She used to attend church with Felix and Nora, but now she goes to one with a friend of hers down the road. I told her I didn't want to hear about it or want to see a crucifix or cross in our house. She keeps her Bible in her bedstand drawer and reads it after I'm gone."

"You don't believe in God?" Morton questioned.

"I believe there's a god, but how can there be only one true one when there are so many, right? I spent my youth in a Catholic orphanage. I don't know who my father was; my mother was a shady lady in New Orleans when I was born. I grew up in the slums with her until she answered an ad for a wife and married a man who gave her a choice— lose him or me. She chose to keep him, so off to the orphanage I went. I had just turned six. I never saw my mother again. One of the priests there beat any goodness right out of me," he said with a hardened edge. "If I went back and found him still alive, I'd like to kill him slowly." He lifted his glass and took a drink with a far-off, angry glare. "What about you, Morton? You can't believe in God with all your crimes."

Morton shrugged uneasily. "I guess you could say I'm on the jury stand about that."

Tony chuckled. "Well, I'd be the prosecutor of that trial. I've never seen anything good come from religious people. I have seen plenty of hypocrites that preach one thing and then do what they say you shouldn't do. Felix is a Christian, you know. He speaks at his church occasionally and plays the whole *I'm Holy* role for the church. But I know all of Felix's secrets, and he's as far apart from Beth's father as a man could be. I respected Beth's father. He lived what he believed in and was always fair with me."

"We went to church for funerals," Morton offered. "My two brothers married in a church, too, I guess."

"You didn't go, and I was forced not just to go, but live it daily, along with the beatings and everything else. I will never say the word *father* again unless I have Father Wilkinson tied to a table and a knife in my hand."

Before any more could be said, the door opened, and Beth carried a rhubarb pie into the house. "I apologize for taking so long. Sally told me the gossip about her friend being arrested for stealing money from the store she works at. Sally asked if her friend should use Felix as her lawyer."

Tony's brow lowered slightly. "Of course, she

should."

"Is there a circus in town?" Beth questioned. "I ran into Felix and Nora on the way to the bakery. They were with another couple. The woman that works at the butcher shop, I always forget her name, and some weird-looking man with long pretty hair wearing a gun belt with two fancy guns. I thought maybe he worked for a circus or something, I don't know, but he looked like a trick shooter or something. Felix didn't introduce us."

"Huh," is all Tony said with a grunt. He didn't like William and found it interesting how quickly Felix and William were becoming fast friends.

"Morton, I hope you like meatloaf, cornbread, and rhubarb pie because we have plenty of it," Beth said.

Morton was chuckling. "It sounds delicious."

***

Two hours after Morton left, there was a knock on Tony's door. He answered it to see a delivery boy that Felix often used who lived near his home. The boy handed a sealed envelope to Tony and ran home. Felix had already paid the boy for the delivery.

Tony opened the envelope and read the note:

Everson Solstice was delayed by unforeseen repairs but is projected to sail in two days with the outgoing tide at 4:00 am. Until then, we must move the two parcels to a new loca-

tion. Meet Howard at midnight at our wharf for details. This is urgent. No Morton.

"Who was at the door?" Beth asked. She was in her night clothes and preparing for bed.

"A note from Felix. Sorry, hon, but I have to work late tonight. I don't know how late I'll be." He sighed heavily. He was tired and wanted to sleep.

"What time are you leaving?" she asked.

He looked at the clock. It was nearly eleven. "Half an hour from now. I'll try not to wake you when I come home."

***

Tony and Howard Nicol found the two boys sleeping heavily in their cell. Choral Hydrate and Morphine were used interchangeably in their water occasionally to keep the boys calm and quiet, and for tonight, sleeping peacefully. Tony and Howard placed the two boys on top of one another in a wooden crate painted with the word *Deceased* and nailed the lid on. They put the crate on a pushcart and pushed it along the maze of tunnels until they came to a locked door; unlocking it and pulling it open revealed a rope and pulley counterweight elevator that lifted them inside a warehouse filled with various goods.

A tugboat waited for them at the far side of the warehouse, where it was most concealed from the view of the city. They opened the crate and carried the boys out a backdoor and down some stairs to a floating dock, where they placed the boys in the pilot house floor of the tugboat. The tug's steam-powered engine turned the paddlewheels and left for a journey up the Willamette River without a light of any kind burning aboard.

Four miles upriver, the tug slowed to a gliding stop in the shallow water near a dark forest where a man waved a golden lamp on the shore. There was a small abandoned log cabin set back from the river that was hidden from view by the trees and overgrown brush from the river that had been vacant for many years. Howard Nicol had used it for a fishing cabin and kept it in decent shape, claiming it as his own.

They carried the boys to the cabin, put wrist and ankle shackles on them, and then used padlocks and chains to connect both ankle shackles to an iron bar bolted securely into the log wall.

They got a pitcher of water from the river and put Choral Hydrate in it to help keep the boys quiet. A small Chinese man named Pan Ching had a tent outside the cabin and unloaded the tugboat with the food supplies for their stay.

Tony ensured the two boys were bound securely and boarded the tugboat to go home. He waved goodnight to Pan and Howard, who would watch over the two boys while Marshal Matt Bannister did his best to find them in town.

Chapter 19

Morton had the hotel wake him up at six in the morning so he could meet with Matt and William on the roof of the Silver Casterlin building. He dressed in the same gray pinstriped suit he had worn the day before, applied a scoop of pomade to his hair, and combed it straight back as the barber had shown him. Tony Hurner assured him that the barber's homemade pomade in an unlabeled silver can was the best hair grease in the city.

Morton considered wearing the new derby over his slicked-back hair, but he felt like it was too pompous for him to wear. He was a country boy and preferred his old worn flat-brimmed hat that was misshaped to his liking, but it wasn't up to the standards of his new employers, so he wouldn't wear a hat today. Looking in the hotel's mirror, he adjusted his shoulder holster, preferring the weight of his sidearm to the awkward shoulder holster.

Morton went to the fourth floor of the Silver

Casterlin, knocked on Floyd and Rhoda's door, and got a cup of coffee.

"When William comes back, tell him to join us on the roof," Matt told Floyd. William had gone down to the water closet.

"Morton, do you want to explain the suit?" Matt asked as they reached the roof. Morton was supposed to play the part of a dockworker, but seeing him in a gray pin-striped suit and shiny black boots with new slicked-back hair made Matt curious. He had not spoken to Morton for nearly two days.

"I'm working for Felix, as William probably told you. He had his man, Tony, buy these for me and this stinking shoulder holster. I feel naked without my sidearm."

"What kind of work?" Matt asked.

Morton shrugged his shoulders. "I'm not sure yet. Collecting overdue money from his clients, watching people, and so on. I don't really know."

Matt sighed, disheartened. "Nothing was mentioned about the boys?"

Morton shook his head. "No."

"I met a police officer last night named Eric Stiles. He thinks the boys were shanghaied, and Bob may have had something to do with it; if so, he is probably dead. Eric thinks the crimps wouldn't risk Bob talking. He could have been shanghaied too, but Eric doubts it because Bob is too well known around here. Do you think Felix is involved in that kind of activity?"

Morton shrugged. "Nothing I've heard from Tony has indicated so. I made myself known as I said I would, and sure enough, the next morning, Tony Hurner came to seek me out. I know we're not supposed to hurt innocent people, but I had to prove I could follow directions, so I beat a homeless man yesterday morning with a pair of brass knuckles, but then I was—"

"Wait!" Matt nearly spat out his coffee. "You beat up a homeless man? Was he wearing green wool pants and an ugly yellow shirt?"

Morton could see the anger building in Matt's eyes. He nodded, growing slightly anxious. "He was. Why?"

Matt took a deep breath before speaking, "His name is JoJo. He has the mind of a child in some ways. I was wondering who hurt him. Certainly, you could tell he was helpless, right?" Matt asked irritably. "His ribs are broken, Morton."

"I didn't want to do it, Matt," Morton answered sincerely. "Tony came looking for me, which is what we hoped would happen. I didn't know who Tony was, but I knew whoever he was, he came to me for a reason. Tony handed me some brass knuckles, and I had to break that man's ribs or lose the chance of finding the boys. And we might be on the right trail because Tony wanted that man hurt because he heard that fellow JoJo was talking to you. So that tells us something. And that makes me wonder if we're on the right track. I met Felix and was hired. That's when William was there. How they met, I have no idea. Anyway, I had to sign a contract swearing never to say anything about what we do. If I do, it means my life. So, whatever they do, it can't be legal."

Matt rubbed his beard irritably. "Now I know who hurt JoJo and why. Tony had you break JoJo's ribs because he was talking to me? They have to be hiding something. Stay with it."

The stairway to the roof led up to a small shed-like building on the flat top of the building called a bulkhead with a full-sized door that squeaked when it opened. William Fasana stepped onto the roof carrying a cup of coffee and nearly spilled it when he bent over, bursting into laughter while pointing at Morton. "Look at that suit on you and a new hairdo too!" He laughed. "You got enough grease there that we could rub your head on the tracks and stop a train."

Morton's cheeks reddened as he nodded passively while William laughed at him. "I knew you'd have something to say. Go ahead." He motioned for William to continue.

William's grin widened. "Matt, you don't want to slip and fall and break your back like your grandfather did years ago, so be careful today. It's going to be hot, and that grease will be dripping right off Morton's head onto the sidewalk." He laughed.

Morton asked, "Did I put too much pomade in my hair?"

William answered with a chuckle, "I don't know, is your hair usually black? Maybe you could get some used axel grease for your goatee. Better yet, Maggie would appreciate you going to the butcher shop and standing around there catching flies with that grease trap. Maybe you could strike up a deal of a penny per fly, comb those puppies out at the end of the day, and score a fair day's wage. But no, seriously, Morton, you look great. Keep it the way it is." He turned to Matt and asked, "So, what's up today?"

Morton was confused. "So, do I look okay or not?"

Matt chuckled. "You look fine. William had dinner with Felix and his wife last night and has reason to believe Felix has some illegal dealings too. It is just hard to say in what."

Morton nodded, "Tony's wife said she ran into them. I had dinner at their house." He looked at William before continuing, "She thought William was funny looking. Like a clown, or how did she say it, a trick shooter at a freak show?"

"Huh?" William grunted. "What do you mean? What does she look like? Is she the ugly redhead that was built like a two-hundred-year-old oak stump? I don't care what she thinks."

"No. Tony's wife is named Beth. She's a very pretty blonde-haired lady."

"That was Tony's wife?" William asked. "She was very pretty. She thought I looked funny? Funny, like how? Like unusually handsome or like fun and exciting?" He explained to Matt, "Humor can go a long way to winning a lady's heart. You wouldn't know that, though."

Morton answered slowly, "No. More like a clown."

William stared at him for a moment in silence. "Well, that just proves that a pretty face doesn't mean she's intelligent. After dinner, we went to Felix's house for drinks, and I questioned him because he couldn't keep his eyes off Maggie. I'm not stupid; he's a snake trying to slither her way. How do I know? Because I'm one too!" William laughed. "Anyway, I got him to admit he's got a woman on the side. I caught him looking at Tony's wife the same way he was looking at Maggie; lustful. That blonde beauty of Tony's didn't seem to like him very much, though. That snake probably tried for her and got his head stomped in." He looked at Matt and said, "Rory Jackson always stomped on my head when I'd try to court her."

Matt answered, "Maybe that's because your idea of courting was meeting in the hay loft."

William nodded agreeably. "Probably."

Morton scratched behind his ear where a dab of the pomade was clinging to his skin. "Tony's wife is a great artist too. She's a lot like Christine, if you don't mind me saying."

William spat through his teeth. "Pretty women always have great secrets. Isn't that right, Matt?"

"I wouldn't know. You're the ladies' man, not me."

"That's right," William said as if he forgot some information, "you're not married yet. I'm sure Christine has some secrets that will ruin your life soon enough."

"Shut up," Matt grinned. "You're offended that Tony's wife called you a clown, aren't you?"

Morton added, just to watch William squirm, "A freak show trick shooter is what she said."

William glared at Morton, perplexed. "How in the world...why would she say that? I don't look like my buddy, David, now do I? You better tell her to get some spectacles."

Matt chuckled slightly. "You are offended. Well, get over it, William, because we're still no closer to finding the boys than before. Gabriel and Evan are out there somewhere, and my first initial suspicion was Felix, but after meeting Eric last night, I'm not sure we're on the right track. He knows this city and says he's never heard of, or suspected, Felix of shanghaiing anyone. He agreed Felix is as dirty as a rat, but not with that type of business. He suggested I speak with Oliver Sweat, which I did. I roughed him up a bit, and it still brought nothing."

Morton raised a questionable finger. "Boss, you got mad at me for hitting a man, but you're the one raising hell?"

"It's *my* son that's missing, and I promised Elizabeth I'd bring him home. I'll do what I must to keep my promise to her. She's his mother, and I can't stand to see her cry."

William asked, "So...what are you saying? Do you want me to drop the charade with Felix and find a new fool to court?"

Matt was torn. His gut and instinct couldn't let Felix go, but the police officer Eric Stiles knew the city better than Matt did and indicated Matt was looking in the wrong place. Matt had questioned Oliver Sweat and Potsy Jones and walked away, convinced that both were innocent of knowing anything about the boys. However, he had not been able to speak with Big Richard Burkhalter. Each time he tried, Big Richard was not available.

Matt answered slowly, "Not yet. I haven't met Big Richard, but I will today, even if I must wait all day to see him. I'll let you know if I get a suspicious feeling about him. If Felix is innocent, then we need to focus elsewhere and in a hurry. Eric said Big Richard is in the shanghaiing business."

William lowered his brow with contemplation. "I'm not offended!"

Matt looked at William questionably. "Good for you. In the meantime, while you're dealing with that, I'll find Big Richard and a few others that Eric named and apply some pressure. I feel like I'm still on the outside, barely causing a ripple within the inner circle of that wretched business, and what I want to do is burst down the door and shoot every one of them."

"It's just a matter of time," Morton said to encourage Matt.

William walked to the edge of the building to look at the five stories below. He sucked up some phlegm from the allergies that had risen since coming to Portland and spat over the edge. He watched his wad of phlegm fall before stepping back with a short laugh, not to be seen by whoever he tried to spit on. "We'll find them, Matt. And if Morton happens to go missing today, it will be easy to follow the grease wherever he goes. Basically, like a trailing a slug."

Chapter 20

Big Richard Burkhalter was a large man. He was robust; some would even say obese at nearly three hundred pounds. He had black hair, slicked straight back with a dab of the barber's pomade. His face was round with a thick black beard. His beady dark eyes revealed the menacing evil within him. He had walked the two blocks from his home on Fourth Street to his office at the Mariner's Union House Tenement building, where he kept his office on the main floor.

Richard didn't have a secretary, but he did have a guard sitting outside his office named Elijah, who decided who got to see Big Richard and who didn't. Elijah knocked on Big Richard's office door before entering the office and closing the door behind him. "The Marshal is here again. He watched you come in, so I can't send him away this time."

Big Richard followed Elijah to meet Matt Banister in the small waiting room. Matt was a tall, lean, muscular man dressed in dark blue suit pants with a tan button-up shirt with black stripes; the sleeves were rolled past his wrists, and his star-shaped badge was pinned to his left lapel. He was a handsome man in his mid-thirties, with a dark beard on a square-shaped face and a long ponytail. He held a Stetson with a flattened brim in his left hand while his right was near the wooden grip of his Colt .45.

Richard was slightly perturbed to learn Matt had been waiting for him to guarantee a meeting. He reached out a hand with a forced smile. "Marshal Matt Bannister, I am sorry to have missed you the past few days. It is an honor to meet you. So, what can I do for you?" He asked as he shook Matt's hand.

"I'm looking for my son and hear you may know something about that," Matt said bluntly with a coldness to his eyes.

Big Richard was quickly on the defensive. "How so? Who would even suggest that I knew something about that? I did hear through the grapevine that you were looking for your son, but I assure you, I know nothing about it."

Matt focused on the man's eyes. "Eventually, I will find out what happened to my son, and if you had anything to do with it, I will come back here and put you in the grave. You have my word on that."

Big Richard gasped. "I was hoping for a more friendly meeting."

"I don't have time to be friendly. Every day that I don't find my son, I get a bit angrier. I'm not here to make friends, and I'm not leaving until I find my son, even if it takes years. I'll find the tunnels and hound you and everyone else to the grave to find my boy. Count on it."

Big Richard was incensed. "Marshal Bannister, what do you want from me? Do you want to see the tunnels? Is that what you want? I can show you them and let you search to your heart's content. If you do find your boy, it won't be me he points a finger at. Come, I'll show you to the tunnels."

Big Richard took Matt to the back of the building to a hatch door that opened to reveal a stairway descending into what appeared to be a dark basement. Richard grabbed a lantern and turned the gas up as he took three steps down before pausing to say, "Well, come on," before continuing down the stairs. "Please look around. Go explore, do whatever you want, but I reject the idea that I may have anything to do with your boy or any others."

The basement walls were stone cemented together with a wood beam ceiling. The basement was cluttered with empty bottles, trash, and broken furniture. The far end open doorway led into a faintly lit tunnel with walls lined with horizontal twelve-inch-wide boards.

Matt took the lantern that Richard invited him to take. His attention went to the sound of two men's voices as they laughed with each other while leading a donkey with a heavy cart behind it, filled with various goods to be delivered at various stops. They passed by the basement door without interest.

Big Richard spoke, "You see, Marshal Bannister,

the tunnels have a purpose, making deliveries from the docks, not stealing people off the street. This is our basement and storage area. But you are welcome to wander around and look to your heart's content. I have work to do, so I'll be upstairs when you finish. Don't wander too far, or you might get lost and wind up in Chinatown."

Matt walked freely in the tunnel. It was broader than the ones in Branson's Chinatown and higher. Depending on what was available for each new tunnel section, the walls were lined with wood, bricks, or stone the further Matt walked. The floor was hardened except for areas covered by planks that were consistently muddy from the groundwater. There was nothing amiss that he could find.

There were not many, but he found a few locked doors that raised his curiosity, and he shouted for Gabriel and listened carefully for a reply that never came. After walking through the tunnel, which connected with others, and spending more than an hour underground, he eventually returned to the Sailor's Union House and Tenement building's basement. His heart was heavy as he ascended the stairs.

"Did you find anything, Marshal?" Big Richard asked sarcastically as Matt entered his office.

Matt shook his head quietly.

"I didn't think you would. Listen, I don't know what happened to your boy, but I hope you find him; I truly do. But I will ask you to leave my people and properties alone."

Matt wandered outside in the noonday sun to

Water Street, then walked block after block until the piers and warehouses no longer lined the water's edge and took a seat on the ground beside the river. He tossed a pebble he had pulled from the dirt into the water.

Moisture burned his eyes; frustration, discouragement, and a heavy dose of helplessness overwhelmed him. He shook his head while biting his bottom lip emotionally.

He looked up into the blue sky. "I don't know where else to look, Jesus. I have tried and found nothing, not even the slightest clue of what happened to them. I have repeatedly asked for your help, and you're silent. I know you're faithful, and I know your ways are not our ways, but Jesus, if I can ask you once again, please, let me find Gabriel. I don't know your plans for him or where he is, but I just started to get to know my son and would like to get to know him better. His mother will be devastated if I can't bring him home. I gave my word to her; I promised. Jesus, if it is in your will, let me take my son home, Evan, too. And if Bob shanghaied them, expose him so I can find him. Jesus, my Lord, this is bigger than me, way bigger. I need you, Lord, and I need you now."

***

Putting his discouragement aside, Matt stood from the riverbank. Morton had told him about a promise he had made to a man named Peter Swan that helped Morton make an impression to get him noticed. The promise was to help a young man named Henry. All Matt knew of the young man was that Henry was caught in a dangerous situation that he may not have been aware of. If Matt could not save his son, he could at least save another father's son from a similar fate. He brushed the dust off his pants and left the river's bank to walk to Lottie's Shore Leave Boarding House.

Matt wrinkled his nose as he entered the boarding house. He had thought he had become used to the foul smell that lingered in the air near the wharves of Portland, but he was wrong. Lottie's Shore Leave Boarding House was filthy and smelled of stale alcohol and the body odor of several men that sat downstairs drinking in the makeshift tavern. The men didn't seem to notice a trash can in the kitchen that attracted flies by the dozens with the remains of rotting fish and other trash that gave off a foul odor.

A grizzled old man with an unshaven face and uncombed short gray hair came out from behind the small bar and squinted his eyes as he leaned closer and stared at Matt's badge. "Is that real?" he asked.

Matt's eyes scanned the other men sitting at the tables. Morton had described Peter, and Matt recognized him immediately by the black eye Morton had given him. Peter stared at Matt curiously.

"Of course, it's real. My name is Matt Bannister, U.S. Marshal. I'm looking for three young men, my son, Gabriel, Evan Gray, and their friend, a teenager named Henry, who has been missing for about a week. Do any of them sound familiar?" Matt asked, including Henry's name with the two boys.

"Nah," the old man groaned. "I heard your boy's missing, though. Sorry, I can't help you."

Peter approached Matt and volunteered, "There's a teenager named Henry upstairs."

The old man responded pointedly, "He's not your boy's friend, though."

"How do you know?" Matt asked sharply. "I'll ask him myself."

"No," the old man objected. "He's having some alone time with his lady friend. I told him I'd keep everyone out of there while she visits. Young men like their privacy. If you know what I mean?"

"He'll get over it," Matt said.

Peter stepped forward, "I'll introduce you." Peter led the way upstairs into a stuffy and humid large room where an old man lay in bed and smoked his pipe while resting a bad knee. Across the room, Henry sat on the bottom bunk holding the hand of an attractive young lady wearing a fine dress.

Peter spoke cheerfully, "Say goodbye to her, Henry. You're leaving this dump."

"Huh?" Henry questioned.

"What do you mean?" the young lady questioned.

"This is Matt Bannister, and he's taking Henry home."

Henry gazed at Matt. "The marshal?"

Matt nodded. "Get your stuff, and let's go."

"Where? I don't want to go anywhere. Am I in trouble?" Henry asked.

Peter pointed at the young lady. "Henry, she won't

pay your debt for staying here. She's a hired whore to keep you content while your debt grows—"

"Shut up, Peter! Don't talk about Rose like that!" Henry exclaimed. "We're in love, and I'm taking her back home with me," Henry argued.

Peter chuckled. "She's not here because she likes you, dumbass. She's here because she gets a cut of your blood money when they ship you out to sea."

"Shut up, Peter! Just leave us alone. I'm not going anywhere," Henry griped with a scowl.

Matt sat on the bottom bunk across from the young lovers. The young lady avoided his eyes. He spoke gently, "Rose, is that your name?"

"Yes," she replied uneasily. She was a young lady in her early twenties with shoulder-length brown hair tied in a braided ponytail. Her triangular-shaped face was soft and fragile, with an innocent appearance, bright brown eyes, and a delicate nose and mouth that gave her the impression of a Sunday school teacher. She was dressed in a dark purple, almost the shade of black, dress with a white breast and collar.

"I'm here to do you a favor, Rose. I'm going to take Henry back home, but first, we can go by your place and get your things so you can go with him. Are you ready to go?"

She released his hand and crossed her arms over her chest nervously. "Um, I'm not ready."

"You're not ready to leave with Henry?" Matt questioned. "If you're worried about paying his debt, I'll cover it. Let's go to your place, pack your things, and we'll take a coach to introduce you to his parents. You two can start living your romantic dream right now." He hesitated while she gazed at the floor silently. "No?" Matt questioned. "Tell Henry the truth."

Her leg began to bounce anxiously, but she didn't answer.

Henry stood up. "Let's go, Rose. This is great."

"Sit down, Henry," Matt said with a harsh tone.

"What is this all about? What's wrong?" he asked as he sat.

"Ask her," Matt replied. Peter chuckled lightly.

Henry asked her quietly, "Rose, why are they asking you about this?

"I...I...don't know," she answered uneasily.

Matt's voice grew stronger, "Look at me, Rose!" She turned her head to meet his hardened eyes. "You better tell Henry the truth right now."

"Rose?" Henry asked in anguish.

Suddenly the innocent young lady's expression transformed into a bitter scowl as her hardened heart revealed itself in her brown eyes as they glared at Matt. "Fine." She turned her head to speak, "I don't feel anything for you, Henry. Like all the others, you are just a stupid boy desperate for love. You're all so stupid! No, I'm not paying anything for you; I *get* paid for you." Sometimes the prettiest snakes have the most venomous bite, and her voice revealed the venom of the bitterness within her.

Henry gasped as his eyes filled with the moisture of his first heartbreak. "But...I stayed here for you. I love you."

Rose chuckled with a coy smile. "You love the

215

idea of being in love. I just let you believe I felt the same, but you're just a customer to me."

"But...Rose..."

"Henry," Matt said plainly, "she's a prostitute hired to swoon you. Leave it at that. Get your things and get out of here. If you need money to get home, come by the Silver Casterlin Tenement building later today, and I'll help you. Grab your stuff and go. Rose and I are going to have a conversation. Peter, take him down and make sure the old man knows Rose is paying his bill after all."

Once Peter walked a heartbroken Henry out of the room, Matt asked softly, "Is Rose your real name?"

"Does it matter?" she asked spitefully.

"It matters a lot. You have a name; is it really Rose or not?"

"My name was Edna Ford, if you must know, but I go by Rose now."

"Edna, you are a very pretty young lady and could easily find a wonderful husband if you—"

"Who do you think you are to lecture me?" she snapped. "You don't know me or know anything about me other than I'm a whore. So please, don't try to pretend like you care about me. All you care about is finding out who hired me or maybe how much I charge because I am pretty. All you men are exactly the same! So, Marshal Bannister, shall I undress?"

Matt shook his head. "No. I just thought I'd try to help you get out of this kind of life and maybe into something more honorable. But if this is the life you want, then I won't bother. I'm a nice man, but I can make life very hard for you if you don't tell me who pays you to do this to young men like Henry."

"Oh?" she questioned with a coy smile, "How hard? Are you going to throw me around the room a little bit, slap me around or give me a real beating like a man? I've had it all! Are you going to point your gun at me and threaten to shoot me?" she asked with a skeptical grin. "Do you want an answer? Here it is, I had a romantic interest in Henry, and you ruined it. No one hired me, and that's the only answer you'll get from me. I loved him, and now I may never see him again," she said with such sincerity that it would almost be believable if she had not admitted the truth a moment earlier. There was even a trace of tears clouding her eyes.

"You're not going to tell me anything, are you?" Matt asked.

"I just did. And far as I know, falling in love with a nice young man isn't a crime yet. So, either arrest me for something, or can I go now?"

"Little Miss Edna—"

"Don't call me that! My name is Rose," she snapped.

Matt said gently. "I'll call you whatever you want. My son is missing, Rose. Maybe you have become so hardened that you don't care about people anymore, and if so, I feel bad for you because that's no way to live. Life is supposed to be worth something tangible you can hold and love, like family and friends. Gabriel is the only child I have and probably will ever have. I'm looking for the people who took him and Bob Mears, who you may know. If you know anything about their disappearance or know of any crimps who may have taken them, I'd appreciate you telling me."

"I never met anyone named Gabriel. I know Bob, but I haven't seen him lately. I wish I could help you, but I can't. That is the truth. Can I go now?"

Matt sighed as another dead end raised its head. "You're free to go, but before you do. If you want out of this life, let me know. You're wrong; there are men who want to help you simply because they care about human beings without asking for anything more. If you want to start a new life and get away from all this," he waved around the room, "I can help you do that."

Her eyes narrowed questionably. "Why? Why would I want to leave *this,* and why would you help me? I told you I would strip down here if that's what you want."

"No, that's not what I want," Matt said firmly. "I'm not telling you this to benefit me. I see a young lady with a whole life ahead of her that she can live to its fullest if she chooses to. Jesus loves you just the way you are, but you live a very sinful life, and I think you know that. You can't feel good about what you do when you look in the mirror. You might see a pretty face, but inside, it must be hollow and empty. Perhaps dark, like there is nothing to live for except money and whatever vices numb the pain.

"Rose, I don't know you or your past wounds,

but Jesus is the brightest and warmest light that could change your world around and turn those hurt-filled brown eyes that are filled with anger and bitterness into eyes that shine with brand new life. The Gospel Mission down the road that tells you about going to heaven when you die might overlook the importance of knowing Jesus right now while you're alive.

"Jesus gives meaning, purpose, comfort, peace, and hope to anyone who comes to him. It is his nature, and that nature becomes a part of who we are because he lives in our hearts. I can introduce you to Jesus just like the Gospel Mission can, but if you want to change your life, get out of this city, and start over somewhere else with new friends that care about you and a place to stay, I can help you do that. But that is a choice you have to make."

Rose had listened and wiped her nose quietly. Her eyes had softened as he looked at Matt sincerely. "I don't know anything about your son. Honestly, I don't."

"Doesn't it feel good to be honest?" Matt asked with a sad smile. "You could always live like that and have a long life that means so much more than what…money? I don't know what your biggest passion in life is, but if you're willing, you could come back to Branson with me and have the opportunity to achieve it."

She wiped a silent tear away before it could fall. "I'm a harlot."

"No," Matt said softly. "You're so much more than that. If you take a chance and trust me, I'll prove it. You're a beautiful young lady that, somewhere along the way, got that heart of yours all tangled up with thorns, and we need to dull their edges and untangle them. You'll become a whole new person once you realize not everyone is out to hurt or use you. There are a whole lot of us that might just come to think you're a wonderful person just because you are. I'm staying at the Silver Casterlin. Come by and ask for me if you are willing to take a chance to make a better life for yourself."

She looked at Matt awkwardly. "Are you asking me to marry you?"

Matt laughed. "No. I'm already engaged. Let me explain: my fiancée works at a dance hall, and she'll be moving out. I thought you could live, work, and dance for a living. It is a respectable place where the ladies are treated properly, as a lady should be. It would be a good place to make new friends and rebuild your life."

"I'll think about it," she said softly, thoughtfully. "How did you know I don't feel good about what I do?"

"How could you? You have to be heartless to do stuff like this, and I believe within that tangle of thorns, we'll find a good heart." He smiled kindly. "Will you tell me who hired you?"

She shook her head quickly. "I can't." She looked into his eyes. "But I will tell them I am leaving. I want to leave." Her lip began to quiver as her eyes filled with thick tears. Her voice shook, "Did you really want to help me, or was all this talk just to ask who hired me?" Tears slipped out of her eyes and rolled down her cheeks.

Matt was stunned. He could see how fractured and scared she was of being left alone now that a ray of hope had shone a way out of the life she knew. Matt leaned forward, extending his arms towards a frightened child. Rose fell forward into his arms and burst into sobs as he held her. "Rose, you never have to tell me who hired you. I meant every word I said, and I keep my word. You better believe I want you to return to Branson with me; yes, I do. You're going to be okay. All I want in return is to see you change your life, and that's all the reward I need."

Chapter 21

Gabriel Smith had woken up in a strange new environment of log walls instead of the expected brick cell he'd come to know. He had been moved to a small cabin, and to his horror, he and Evan were chained like prisoners with ankle shackles chained to an iron bar secured to the wall and wrist shackles with a twelve-inch length of chain. The same Chinese man bringing them food and watching over them over the past few days brought them some food and set a pitcher of water on the cold steel of the unused cookstove beside a tin cup. He had also brought in the same metal bucket used to relieve themselves they used in their brick cell.

Gabriel wasn't sure how many days had passed due to being kept underground and not knowing how long they slept after drinking the tainted water. There was no way to tell day from night underground, but now he could see the sunlight shining under the door. The single window was painted black, but the sunlight still shined through the paint. It was the first glimpse of the sun since being taken.

The Chinese man had never spoken to them nor looked at their faces, despite their questions, pleads, and shouts. Once, Gabriel had tried to attack the man in the cell, but he was quickly hit in the throat, stopping any further attempts to attack the little Chinese man.

Evan and Gabriel had often spoken at length about their circumstances, plans to escape, and their family and often prayed together. Gabriel always felt that the Chinese man understood and listened to every word they said.

The door was pushed open by a white man with black curly hair and wearing a light gray suit that had gotten dirty on the river's edge. The man held a fishing pole in one hand and a stringer of seven fish—a combination of trout, bass, and perch—in the other. He smiled. "I hope you boys are hungry because I caught some fish. Pan will mix all that up in rice for you, I bet. It's about all he knows how to make, I think. I'll fry the trout up for my supper with little flour and pepper; you can't beat it." He was one of the same white men that Bob let take them into the tunnel.

"Where are we? What are you going to do with us?" Gabriel asked anxiously. He was grateful to have someone who could answer his questions, which had never been answered.

Howard Nicol answered, "You're out of the dungeon. That ought to be good enough, huh?"

"No. Why are you keeping us prisoner?" Gabriel pressed. "How long have we been here? My mom is going to be worried," Gabriel's strength was fading as his voice cracked with the mention of his mother.

Howard ignored him and handed the fish to Pan, who immediately took the fish outside to clean them.

"Where are we?" Gabriel demanded as the desperation and fear moistened his eyes.

Howard leaned against a small counter and folded his arms. He yawned. "Somewhere you can scream as loud as you want, and no one will hear. But before you do, just know I'm not opposed to shoving a towel down your throat instead of hearing it."

Evan warned, "His father is Matt Bannister. You should let us go while you can."

Howard smirked with a slight chuckle. "So you've said. Listen to me, both of you." He pushed himself off the counter and stepped closer to the boys. "Matt Bannister is already here looking for you. But this is Portland, our city, not the prairie where he can follow horse tracks. He's as lost as you two are; he just doesn't know it. You only have one more day here, and then both of you are leaving on a ship bound for Africa. Your mother will be missing you for quite some time."

"W...what?" Gabriel gasped as a wave of sheer terror ran up his spine and took root in his chest. His mouth went dry as he tried to swallow nervously. He choked out, "Africa?"

Howard grinned, enjoying the two terrified faces that stared at him. "That's right. And do you know what's funny about that? Your daddy will probably watch the ship be towed down the river while he's wondering where you are."

Gabriel spoke desperately, "We have a family waiting for us to come home. My mother and father, brother and sisters. How could you do this?" The moisture building in his eyes puddled and slipped down his cheeks.

Howard pulled a billfold out of his front pocket, opened it, and pulled out a few dollar bills to show them. "You're worth more money to us than you are to them."

"Matt will kill you," Evan said plainly. He was too frightened to weep.

Howard laughed. "He hasn't yet. He's still trying to find someone to tell him anything, even with his five-thousand-dollar reward. Do you two know why you were taken? This should tell you how intimidated we are by your father." He paused with a pleasure-filled smirk on his lips as he watched Gabriel. "You were taken because you are Matt Bannister's son. That's why. We are pretty good at what we do, so I wouldn't put your hopes in him finding you. You're better off thinking of the brighter side of things. You'll enjoy seeing the world."

"God will hold you accountable for this," Gabriel said.

Howard was unconcerned. "Pray if you want,

but I'd save those prayers for one of those high sea storms if I were you. Maybe if you're washed overboard, a whale will swallow you up and bring you back home before spitting you out like a...what's his name in the book of...a...numbers? What was his name, Jima? Jerimiah? He was in the whale for three days or so, right?"

Gabriel answered, "Jonah. And it wasn't in the Book of Numbers. Jonah is important enough to have his own book in the Bible."

"That's right! Jonah," Howard grinned. "Yeah, I remember that story from being a kid. He fell overboard and was saved by a whale. It's a happy little story."

Gabriel's eyes glared at Howard as he spoke pointedly, "It isn't that happy of a story. The message that Jonah was sent to Nineveh to tell the people is the same message I should tell you. Repent and turn your life around to serve God before it's too late. You need to repent from your wickedness, accept Jesus as your savior and let us go."

Howard laughed with a shake of his head. "Well, you just keep reading your Bible stories, and I'll keep filling my wallet with money. You two religious boys are already boughten like two wiener pigs at auction."

Gabriel's eyes hardened with a sudden burst of rage, and he kicked the bucket they had urinated in over, splashing it onto Howard's pants.

Howard cursed as he looked at his pants. They were the only clothes he had to wear until the boys were delivered onto the ship. Angry, Howard rushed forward, forcing Gabriel backward onto the mattress by the throat. Raising his right arm, he swung downward, hitting Gabriel's face with a hard right fist. He raised his arm to beat Gabriel again, but Evan stood, slipped his shackled arms over Howard's head from behind, and yanked the twelve-inch chain across Howard's throat to strangle him. Evan leaned back with all his weight and turned towards the bed, forcing Howard to release Gabriel as Evan pulled Howard on top of him. Howard grasped at the chain around his throat, fighting to get a breath while Evan strained with all his might to strangle him.

Gabriel wasted no time fretting about his swelling eye. He stood upright, locked his hands together, and slammed them down on Howard's face like swinging a maul.

Howard could not budge the chain from choking him, which was a greater concern than trying to stop the thundering pair of hands that pounded down upon his face. He was in dire straits and reached for his .38 caliber revolver in his shoulder holster.

"Get his gun!" Evan grunted as he used all his strength to keep the chain tight. The bed limited the space his elbows had to pull any tighter.

Gabriel had been so blinded by anger that he forgot about Howard's gun until now that Howard got a firm grip on it and was pulling it out of his shoulder holster. Gabriel grabbed Howard's wrist with both hands and fought to keep the gun from being pointed at himself or Evan.

Howard's face was reddening, and his eyes bulged as he struggled to breathe. Howard brought a desperate knee up and connected with Gabriel just below the lower ribs. He gasped as the blow paralyzed him for a moment. The wave of pain moved through his body like an ocean swell rolling up through his abdomen. Despite the pain, Gabriel refused to release his grip on Howard's wrist and fought to control the weapon. Howard was a strong man, but he was losing his strength the longer he couldn't get a full breath.

Howard, in an act of desperation, pulled the trigger and shot into the wall. The loud percussion startled Gabriel, but he could feel Howard getting weaker, so he fought harder for control of the gun. Howard squeezed the trigger again, firing another shot into the wall. He was losing strength quicker now that he was exerting himself and unable to get a full breath. His arm holding the gun weakened, and his hand loosened on the revolver's grip. His head began to tilt backward, and his eyes began to close as he was losing consciousness.

The door was kicked open, and Pan ran inside; jumping into the air, he drove a forceful knee into Gabriel's kidney. Gabriel gasped at the debilitating blow and fell onto the bed before rolling to the ground in anguish. Pan landed on the bed and drove an unmerciful elbow into the side of Evan's head, ending the death grip on Howard.

Pan removed the chain from Howard's throat, and immediately, Howard sucked in a deep breath and rolled off Evan sliding to his hands and knees on the floor. He vomited and then coughed repeatedly as he caught his breath.

Pan, enraged, fired a hard fist into Evan's sternum, driving the boy's breath away. Evan turned to his side and began to weep as he recovered his breath; the pain was severe.

Howard stood slowly and stumbled away from the bed to the small counter. After clearing his throat, he turned towards the two boys with rage burning in his eyes. "I wish I could kill you both right now and be done with you. I want nothing more than to shoot you both!" He nodded thanks to Pan, who handed Howard his revolver as he looked at Howard's throat.

"You'll be okay," Pan said with a thick Chinese accent.

Howard, his neat hair messed up, red-faced, and starting to breathe normally, wiped the sweat from the exertion from his forehead. "Pan, I'll talk to you outside."

Gabriel got to his hands and knees and glanced at Evan when the two men closed the door behind them. "We almost had him."

"You should have grabbed his keys," Evan complained.

Gabriel sat on the floor against the side of the bed, catching his breath from fighting. "The gun was more important. But I think I'd rather die than go to Africa. I won't get on a ship, Evan. I won't do it."

Howard burst through the door and knelt before Gabriel to glare into the boy's eyes. "So, you'd rather die than get on a ship? Fine! Tomorrow when we take the tug back to town, I'll chain an anchor to your ankles and throw you overboard. And I'd be glad to do it! Shut your mouth, or I'll sew it closed. I swear I will!"

***

Tony Hurner wouldn't tell Morton where they were going as they rode a street trolley into Portland's Chinatown. Unlike Branson and other places, Portland welcomed the Chinese and had one of the largest Chinatowns on the West Coast.

Morton had never met many Chinese people, but the little old Chinese lady in Natoma named Tillie was a beloved woman in his hometown. He nodded respectfully to a pair of smiling Chinese men they passed on the sidewalk of Chinatown.

Branson's Chinatown, which the Chinese built, had a strange architecture from their homeland with arches, low hanging roofs, and ornamental details to make the buildings more homelike. But in Portland, the buildings were two or three-story buildings like the rest of the city.

Tony explained that most of the buildings were owned by Americans and rented to the Chinese for businesses and tenement buildings. However, the Chinese brought their heritage to Chinatown by transforming the buildings and streets with their artistic and efficient touch to make the city their home. They built covered balconies and elevated walkways between buildings, built hip roofs to some buildings, and hung colorful drapes and signage in Chinese spread across the twelve square blocks that housed thousands of Chinese men, women, and children who made Portland their home.

"Where are we going, Tony?" Morton asked.

Tony Hurner pointed at a two-story wood-built tenement building that was painted brown. Other than the address above the door, it had no other markings. Depending on the tenement renter, the window coverings varied from silk curtains to blankets. From the front, the building appeared like a standard building with a flat roof, but the side view revealed that horizontally, it was an entire city block long and had what seemed to be a long single-level house in the center of the roof. The long bunkhouse on the top was added more recently to house another thirty men in living quarters of bunk beds, a kitchen, tables, and chairs. The building's profile looked a lot like a train's caboose or, as Tony's wife, Beth, had once commented, Noah's Ark.

"That's the brown caboose. It belongs to Felix, it's nothing more than a tenement building he rents out to Chinese tenants, but we're going downstairs into the basement." Tony smiled before adding, "You're going to love this."

"It's not an opium den, I hope. I have no interest in that or a harlot, to be honest," Morton said, growing concerned that he was being taken to a brothel and expected to participate. He was willing to do a lot of things to find Gabriel Smith, but being unfaithful to his fiancée wasn't one.

"No, I promise you, it's not either one. But I could point you to either if you were interested."

They entered the front door, walked to the middle of the main hallway with tenements on either side, and then entered an alcove to a door guarded by a large and powerful Chinese man wearing a suit with a double shoulder holster blocking a doorway.

The man's stern expression melted into a broad smile. "Tony! I took your advice and bet on Lola last night. I don't know how you knew she'd win, but she did. I won a lot." He grinned. "Lola never wins."

"Perfect. The next time we meet for lunch, you're paying," Tony teased.

"Deal. Thank you for the tip," he said with a heavy Chinese accent.

"I don't know who Lola fights next, but you don't want to bet on her twice in a row. Never do that," Tony offered.

"Ahh. Good tip." The man's eyes went to Morton as his smiling face faded. "Is he with you, Tony?"

"Yes. Bolin, this is Morton Myers; he works with us now. Put him on your welcome list. Morton, this is Bolin Zhao. He also works for Felix, just in a different part of town."

Morton shook the big man's hand, surprised to see such a large Chinese man and feeling the strength of Bolin's handshake. It had become clear that Bolin guarded the door to the basement for a reason and only let certain people in.

The basement was large and separated by load-bearing walls supporting the building above that broke the large basement into sections. The sound of a crowd could be heard as they made their way to the center section that opened into a large area of bleachers surrounding a twelve-foot square pit three feet deep. The pit was surrounded by an added two feet of boards around the edge of the pit, making it five feet deep.

A large crowd of white and Chinese men and a few women sat in the bleachers or stood in groups, talking. Morton found it interesting that it was a mix of well-dressed upper-class citizens joining with the poor and Chinese laborers in conversation. A bar sold liquor, beer, and wine, while next to it, a busy kitchen made various Chinese foods for the spectators. The smell of the food made Morton's stomach growl.

Felix Rathkey walked through the crowd to greet Tony and Morton. He was holding a small but muscular white short-haired dog with black spots and a partially black face. The dog was missing an eye and had bits of its ears missing and a small red sore scabbed over on its upper cheek. "Morton, welcome to our Wednesday night fights. This is my little man, Brick." He pointed to a table where a small crowd was making their bets. "Be sure to bet on Brick, and I suggest you bet on Turk. There are other fights, but those are my two dogs. Hurry up and make your bets and take your seats. I'll meet you there."

"Dog fights?" Morton asked Tony.

"Tonight, yes. Last night they had the women's fisticuffs. Lola, who Bolin bet on last night, won, but we can fix the fights as needed. We have men's fights with or without gloves and rules occasionally. This is the kind of place where anything goes, but it's always different, and the gambling is huge. See that man over there with the gray hair holding the white flag? That's the Chief of Police, Bruce Shlemer; he's a great man. We have a lot of good policemen that come here. Even the Mayor sometimes."

Morton was stunned. "You let women fight in that pit?" Morton asked, pointing to the pit's concrete floor and three-foot walls.

"No. They cover it with boards and a white canvas covering. See those holes in the corners? Posts slide right down into them, and they build a ring. The nature of people never really changes, Morton. The Romans had a coliseum where they watched various kinds of fights. We have the brown caboose." Tony chuckled. "Come on, let's make our bets. You'll see. I think you're going to love it."

Around the pit, two men held watches, and two others held a small tablet and a pencil; each man wore a blue or red silk sash draped over one shoulder and under the other to separate teams. The police chief, Bruce Schlemer, held a small white flag, and four Chinese men wearing red or blue sashes held long poles with a wicker net. Four fifty-gallon barrels were brought out, two painted red and two blue and placed at both sides of the pit so that a barrel of each color waited on both sides of the pit.

Felix Rathkey held his small dog with a blue-collar while his opponent held his small dog with a red collar and waited at one end of the pit. Morton had no idea what they were waiting for as he watched with interest. He could see his friend and fellow deputy marshal, William Fasana, ordering a drink and some Chinese food.

A door opened, and a roar of applause erupted from the audience as four Chinese men carried a wooden six-foot-long crate with tiny air holes to the pit and set one end over the pit. One of the men pulled the rope opening the slat door at the end of the box while the others lifted the crate and emptied one hundred wild rats into the pit. Excited to be free, the rats scurried quickly around the pit, searching for a way out. Several tried climbing or jumping over the walls but fell back into the mess of rats. Verifying all the rats were in the pit, they pulled the crate away.

Bruce Schlemer held up a white flag and spoke loudly, "Welcome. The contest and the timekeepers will begin when the flag is dropped. The contest is not over until every rat is dead. Any rats collected by the teams that are not dead will be placed back into the pit with the dog, with time being added until the rats are dead. The dog that kills the most rats in the shortest time wins the contest. Ready competitors? Begin!" He dropped the flag, and the crowd stood up with anticipation with a loud cheer and shouts of encouragement for the dog they bet on.

Felix and his competitor released their dogs into the pit of scurrying rats. Both men screamed at their dogs like frantic children encouraging their friend to win a foot race.

Brick, a spotted Staffordshire Bull Terrier, quickly sunk its teeth into a rat's head, shook its head violently, and tossed the rat away. It was quickly noted by the man with a pencil and tablet wearing a blue sash, who kept track of how many rats Brick killed. One of the young Chinese men with a pole expertly scooped the rat Brick had killed from the pit and tossed it into the closest blue barrel to be counted and verified dead at the contest's end.

Brick pounced on another rat, trying to scurry past him, but it was seized, shaken, and tossed to the ground. The dog moved expertly from one rat to another as its training taught him to do. One large brown rat was grabbed on the back, shaken and tossed, injured; it began to crawl while its back bled. Seeing it was alive, the man with the net withheld from pulling it out of the pit.

Felix Rathkey ran around the pit, pushing one of the polemen out of his way. He leaned over the wooden barrier and pointed at the injured rat while screaming for Brick to follow his commands and return to kill the wounded rat. Brick obediently returned and broke the rat's neck with a vicious snap of his jaws on the rat's head and harsh shaking of the rat.

Brick's opponent, a Rat Terrier named Peaches

wearing a red collar, chased a sizeable brown rat into the corner and nipped the rat's hindquarters. The rat spun around and fiercely attacked Peaches snout with a deep bite of its own. Peaches repeatedly yelped in pain as he ran away from the rat, only to find the pit was full of rats that turned and bit at the rat terrier's legs, tail, ears, and sides. Peaches no longer tried to kill a rat but ran in circles, yipping with his tail tucked between his legs, bleeding from the bites it had received. Each rat it ran into in a blind panic, turned around, and attacked the terrified dog. It was Peaches' first time being put in the pit, and he wasn't trained to be a ratter like Brick was.

The basement was loud, with the crowd shouting for the dog they bet on and the loud yipping of the little dog being terrorized by rats. The basement was suddenly enveloped by the loud and deep laughter of William Fasana, who had wandered over to the pit's edge with his drink and eggroll. He pointed into the pit and shouted across it to Sam Waller, the owner of Peaches, "Sam, I don't think Rat Terrier means what you thought it did." He laughed and then took a bite of his eggroll.

Felix laughed at his new friend as he proudly watched his champion ratter kill one rat after another. Peaches spotted Sam and tried to leap out of the pit to the safety that Sam's arms promised, but fell back into the pit on top of a rat that spun around and bit him. Peaches finally froze in place with his tail tucked underneath him hyperventilating and yipping in pain.

It took nearly fifteen minutes for all the rats to be killed by one dog. It was an easy win for Brick, but he had some wounds to add to his collection of scars. Rats, when cornered, become fierce creatures as the tell-tale sign of Brick's missing eye, missing chunks of his ears and snout, and hairless spots of past bites revealed. Brick's front leg, neck, cheek, and ear bled from being bitten by a rat fighting for its life when the competition was finished.

Morton had won his minimal bet but was disgusted by what he had witnessed. He had never heard of *ratting* or watched such a crazy event. The rats were large, ferocious, and it was a strange and bloody sport to see.

Felix didn't want to get blood on his suit, so a Chinese man wiped Brick down with a wet towel and put an ointment on the bites before taking Brick out of the arena to a back room. The other dog, Peaches, was mangled with several bites and scratches while he whimpered in pain. Morton overheard Sam tell the Chinese man not to bother cleaning his dog up or giving the ointment of herbs to heal the wounds because he would immediately put the worthless animal down now that he had lost so much money.

Felix heard Sam say those words, too, and turned around to make an offer. "Hey, Sam, if you're just going to kill your dog, how about we make a wager? I'm bringing my pit bull out next to fight Hu Lee's chow. How about we wager on how long it takes my pit bull to kill your terrier?"

Sam tossed the rat terrier towards Felix's feet

carelessly. "Do it. I don't care."

Morton, already repulsed, watched the rat terrier hit the concrete floor with a yipe and quickly left his seat to pick up the bloody dog. "Can I have him? I wouldn't mind having a dog like this." He couldn't stand the idea of letting the frightened dog become a victim of a much larger dog. He didn't know what kind of a dog a pit bull was, but the wager Felix made Sam made it clear that Peaches didn't have a fighting chance of survival.

William Fasana watched Morton oddly and then laughed. "The roofer's got a soft spot. You might want to toughen up before you start leaking tears over a mutt."

Morton cast a harsh glare at William. "Shut up."

Felix spoke, "Morton, William's a friend of mine. Normally, I'd say yes, keep the dog, but we already have wagers being placed on how long it'll take my dog, Turk, to kill it. Keep a hold of it until the referee drops the flag, and then toss that loser in with Turk."

Morton's heart fell. The little dog that was whining and bleeding on his shirt was shaking like a leaf in a strong breeze. Typically speaking, Morton wasn't too attached to dogs, but watching the tormented little fella run from the rats in terror touched his heart. He'd hate to throw the dog to its inevitable death, but he couldn't show weakness. William's words sounded like a mockery, but he knew William had a much deeper meaning to his words. Both of them were there to find Gabriel and Evan, and it took cruelness to fit in with the cruelest of people. If Morton showed his detest for watching an animal being hurt for entertainment, it would show a heart of weakness to those watching him.

A Chinese man led out a large black Chow wearing a muzzle and a red collar. Behind him, Morton watched Felix's employee, Bolin, lead out a large and powerful tan pit bull wearing a muzzle and blue collar. Morton's eyes widened at how powerful the animal appeared to be. He had never seen a dog with such muscle definition or looked fierce and intimidating. Turk was scarred from previous dog fights and looked as mean as his deep growl sounded. A chill ran down Morton's spine. He liked the scared little dog in his arms. He nodded at Felix with finality. "I thought I'd try. Mark me for five dollars at fifteen seconds."

A policeman wearing a uniform approached Chief Schlemer and spoke for a moment. It was a serious conversation, and Chief Schlemer spoke to Felix and handed him the white flag before hurrying out of the basement.

"William," Felix said, "You're now the referee. Morton, drop the dog in when he lowers the flag." He told the timekeepers, "Don't start the clock until Turk is released."

William finished his drink and chuckled at Morton. "Ready, set, go!"

The anguish and pressure in Morton's chest to release the hurt little dog into the pit were overwhelming. The flag went down, Morton dropped the small dog into the pit, and it immediately began yipping and jumping up the wall for Morton to reach down and save him. A moment later, Bolin released the pit bull, and within a few seconds, it was over to the sound of a cheering crowd. Morton grinned with the others but wanted nothing more than to go home. He didn't want to watch anymore. But for the sake of Matt's son, he sat in the front row and watched for the remainder of the night.

Chapter 22

Matt sat alone at a corner table in the Silver Casterlin Saloon with an untouched drink. He felt good to have freed the young man named Henry from the grip of some unknown crimp and the prospect of changing a young lady's life for the better. He could celebrate his victories, but the lack of information about Gabriel tainted any celebration. It was looking increasingly like Gabriel, Evan, and Bob had disappeared out of thin air. Knowing the five-thousand-dollar reward had not brought a single person forward was disheartening. The only explanation was either those involved in their disappearance were dangerous enough to hold a death grip on the city or no one knew anything about it. Either way, it was another discouraging dead end. Clearly, someone didn't want that reward out there, as many of the flyers he had put up across town were taken down.

He felt like there was more he could be doing,

but he had already walked all over the city several times and visited the more well-known crimps, and there was nothing he could grasp onto as a ledge of hope. He tried to hold onto the faith that he could find his son, but he was losing that hope. It had been too long, and now there was nothing more he could do. The reality of going back to Willow Falls, looking into Elizabeth's eyes, and telling her he failed to find their son was beginning to sink in. Even worse, under the circumstances, he'd have to tell her he could not find the people responsible. There would be no justice, and his journey to Portland would become completely worthless.

The Portland Police Chief, Bruce Schlemer, came into the Silver Casterlin with two other officers wearing their uniforms. The Portland police uniforms were dark blue single-breasted coats with brass buttons and a large star-shaped badge stating *police officer* with a single to two-digit number to identify the officer. The two officers escorting the chief were numbers eleven and seventeen. They wore matching dark blue vests with another badge and matching pantaloons. The officers wore matching wide-brim black hats, except for the chief, who wore a white sailor's captain hat with a pin that said *Chief* on the front.

They approached Matt's table, and Chief Schlemer said, "Matt, I'm glad I found you. We found something you might want to see. We have to take a skiff, but I think you'll be interested in seeing this."

It felt like Matt's throat sunk to his gut as the words struck a chord of fear. "Tell me what it is,"

Matt replied dryly. He could not quite prepare himself for the dreaded news he expected to hear next.

Chief Schlemer shook his head slightly, refusing to say. "Please, come with us. I think it's something you need to see for yourself. It has nothing to do with your son. I can tell you that."

Matt quietly sighed with a touch of relief. "What is a skiff?"

Chief Schlemer chuckled. "I forgot, you're not from a port town. It's a rowboat."

Curious yet suspicious, Matt stood to leave with the three officers. He had heard that there were corrupt police officers, and what Eric told him about a police officer being killed and thrown in the river in recent months, possibly by other officers, played through his mind. He wished William was with him, but William was out for the evening with Felix.

Matt had been outnumbered in the past and knew what he was capable of, but looking in the eyes of the chief and two officers, he didn't see the anxiousness of men who planned to ambush him. "Alright," he said, stepping out into the night with the three police officers.

Many police officers he had seen patrolling the streets were on horseback. However, they walked towards the river quietly and offered no information about where they were going. They descended some stairs to a floating dock and climbed into a large rowboat. The two officers took their seats and took hold of the oars to begin rowing.

Matt sat on a bench seat with his back towards the river, where he could keep an eye on the men. The boat swayed with their body movements as the sound of the water lapped against the side of the boat. The air was cooler on the river, and the slight touch of a breeze felt refreshing on his skin. Matt looked up at the stars in the clear night and noticed a shooting star flying through the night. It was a beautiful night that would have been wonderful if Christine was sitting beside him.

However, with his present company, uncomfortable silences during uncomfortable moments always made him cautious, and Matt could not trust any of the three men in the boat with him. He had already removed the leather thong that secured his Colt .45 in his holster, and it would only take a second or two to pull it and kill all three men before they could maneuver themselves to kill him.

The police officers rowed the boat just off the piers and rowed slowly past a moored three-mast vessel and then a two-mast ship. Floating past the large ships and gazing up at them from the water in such close proximity brought a whole new perspective of appreciation for the complexity and engineering of such magnificent means of world travel. The tall masts with broad furled sails and an unending maze of ropes and netting were fascinating.

The two officers rowed to an empty pier that looked deserted and in disrepair compared to the others. They rowed underneath the dock where the many pilings jutted out of the river to support the warehouse and pier above it. It was dark as the blackest night under the pier, with no light to reach under the empty warehouse above it.

Growing uneasy, Matt asked, "What are we doing here?" He was ready to draw his weapon and start firing if any of them made a suspicious move.

The boat drifted slowly as one of the officers reached out and used a piling to stop the boat. Chief Schlemer held a faintly lit lantern up to his face. "About two hours ago, while it was still light enough to see, two teenagers were fishing on a dock over there and saw someone hanging under here. They let us know, and then we made a discovery. I thought you might want to see this." He turned the lantern up fully and held it up as the officers rowed slowly forward.

The body of a young lady wearing what appeared to be a black dress slowly came into view. She was hanging by a rope around her neck that was tied to the handrail of a catwalk. Her feet were in black stockings with one boot missing as they dangled a foot above the water. Her face was contorted sickly downward and covered with dried blood from a severe beating that broke her facial bones. Her hands were untied, and a fingernail was pulled upwards from trying to pull at the rope. It was the most unexpected and haunting scene to be discovered between the pilings.

Matt gasped. His hand covered his mouth as he exhaled while a cold chill rode up his spine as he was filled with a horror that he had seldom experienced. The body was nearly unrecognizable from the vicious beating, but Matt recognized her immediately.

Chief Schlemer spoke as he held the light up to her body. "Her name is Rose Livingston, a local prostitute. But I think you know that because I heard you talked to her today. Would you like to tell me what that conversation was about?"

Matt closed his eyes as another blow to his mission to save his son had failed. To Matt's horror, Rose had been murdered and left hanging under a pier because she told someone she was going back to Branson with him. Matt rubbed his face and then ran a hand over his hair as the shock, disbelief, guilt, and fury all fought for a place to rule within his stirring soul. "She was, um…" He shook his head to get his thoughts straight. "I went to Lottie's Shore Leave Boarding House to talk to a young man trapped there named Henry, and she was there. She promised to pay Henry's bill as his stay accrued more debt. I called her out on it. It was all a scam."

"A scam for what?" Bruce Schlemer asked.

"To shanghai Henry. What do you think?" Matt asked irritably.

"I already told you, shanghaiing doesn't exist here. So how do you know this…Henry?"

Matt paused, dumbfounded. It dawned on him that he was being questioned about what he knew. "I didn't."

"Then how would you know of Henry or his debt to the boarding house?" the chief pressed.

Matt was in no mood for questions and answered sharply, "I was looking for my son. I asked if any teenagers were there, and the manager said no, but a sailor said there were. I went up to see if it was my son or Evan. Seeing her with him seemed suspicious to me, and I asked questions. I found out she was a prostitute hired by someone to keep him there. My guess was to be shanghaied on a ship. That's all I know."

"Did she tell you who she worked for?"

Matt shook his head slowly. "She refused to tell me. What brothel did she work at?"

Chief Schlemer answered, "None. She was a streetwalker."

"I don't believe that. Rose was too well dressed and clean not to have a madam or a clean home. Besides, she stated she was hired to persuade Henry to stay here."

Chief Schlemer shrugged questionably. "She was a very pretty girl, which usually makes for a very successful streetwalker. Clearly, she was hired, as you put it, for a good time that didn't go so well for her. It's the life of a prostitute, huh? Tragic. Well, boys, let's cut her down and return to shore. The marshal can help us."

Matt asked, "Do you know where she lived? We can probably find some answers there."

"*We*, meaning the Portland Police Department, will do just that. I think she just got caught up with a murderous customer, and it is nothing more than that." Chief Schlemer flashed a finger at Matt thoughtfully, "You know that Bender family from Kansas was never caught. Maybe John Bender Jr is in town and got mad at his wife, Kate. But since Kate's a murderous woman and a bit of a witch, too. Maybe he figured it would be safer for him to take his anger out on a pretty streetwalker. You never know."

Matt was quickly irritated by Chief Schlemer's ease of excusing the murder. "Yeah, you should tell the newspaper that," Matt replied sharply. "Somebody beat her senseless and killed her. And chances are it wasn't the headless horseman; we covered that ground earlier, right?"

"What are you getting at?" Chief Schlemer asked unamused.

"I bet a year from now, you still won't know who killed her, and her murder will never be solved."

Chief Schlemer grew frustrated. "Do you know how many thousands of people live here? Any one of the people you see on the street could have done this. Including the possibility of John Bender Jr. We don't know, and neither do you." He said with a shrug. "It's our case, not yours."

Matt spoke heatedly, "That's true. I'd find the person responsible, but you never will because I don't think you care. But here is your logic, we know it wasn't the headless horseman, but since the Bender family was never caught, maybe, just maybe, John Bender got mad at Kate and took it out on Rose. Case closed." Matt paused before saying pointedly, "You make me sick."

Chief Schlemer adjusted in his seat uncomfortably. "I'm beginning not to like you, Marshal Bannister."

Matt chuckled lightly. He wanted to hit the chief in the face. "If nothing else, Chief Schlemer, we do have that in common. I don't like you at all. I think there's more crap coming out of your mouth than floating in your stinking river."

Chapter 23

Rhoda told Matt that Officer Eric Stiles was in the saloon eating breakfast and wanted to speak with him. Matt approached the table where the Portland Police Officer was eating a bowl of oatmeal.

"Hungry? I'll buy," Eric offered as he waved a hand to invite Matt to sit across from him.

"No, thanks." Matt sat curiously. "Have you got any news about the boys?"

Eric gave a short shake of his head. "No. Did you not sleep well? You look tired."

"Not well enough," Matt answered. He was too shaken, heartbroken, and angry to sleep thinking about Rose Livingston being murdered. He could only assume she was murdered for wanting to leave with him, and it brought a heavy burden that weighed heavily on his heart. Between her being murdered and JoJo Perkins being beaten up for talking to him, it was clear that someone didn't want him around, and innocent people were paying the price for talking to him.

"I bet not. I heard Chief Schlemer paid you a visit last night. Rose Livingston's real name was Edna Ford. She was a twenty-three-year-old prostitute from parts unknown. I don't know anything about her life except she showed up here about two years ago, and Laura Eggers took Rose under her wing like a mother hen. Because of her youth, beauty, and stone-cold heart, Rose was perfect for making these young men fall for her. They fell hard like that boy you saved did—"

Matt raised a finger to stop him. "I spoke with her yesterday. She planned to return to Branson with me to change her life for the better and escape from all this. She wouldn't tell me who hired her, but she was going to tell them that she was leaving. I'm sure they killed Rose to keep her quiet. How do you know about Henry?"

Eric offered an empathetic smile. "Portland's a big city, but gossip spreads at the same speed as a small town. Nothing happens in the police station without it getting around. But please let me finish because it's important. Rose had a reputation for being the perfect bait. She was attractive and could act innocent and respectable. She claimed to be the daughter of a local businessman and worked at her father's office as a secretary; that was her story. She was rented out like a skiff down at Bert's dock by the crimps to meet certain young men hand-picked by the crimps.

"Someone marked Henry in a tavern by something so small as putting their hand on his left shoulder. Rose would then bump into him and fall in love at first sight. While she separated him from his friends and kept his attention on her, another professional would pickpocket him so he had no money. As we all know by experience, even the brightest young man still has a weak spot for a beautiful woman. Rose would get those boys all wound up, and instead of returning home, she'd convince them to stay, promising to pay for their room and board for a few days longer at Lottie's or elsewhere.

"If you know anything about young love, you know these young men didn't have a chance; they fall right into her trap. If I was twenty again, I might've fallen for her too." He paused to take a bite of his oatmeal.

"I was young once," Matt said, recalling his youth with Elizabeth. "I suppose the boarding house pays her?" Matt questioned.

Eric shook his head. "Not always. What I'm about to tell you is a secret, and there is no way to prove it now that the evidence disappeared when my friend was murdered. Ships arrive from and depart for ports all over the world every day. We have a busy harbor, and sailors jump ship to enter a crimp's boarding house daily.

"It's a big business here. The Ship Master or Captains are like anyone; some have much higher morals than others. Some are honest and want experienced seamen who sign on because they want to be at sea. Others don't care who is brought aboard as long as they are cheap labor. That is where the shanghaiing comes in, and it is usually done by the press gangs that prowl around the streets and taverns at night looking for victims or by other nefarious means, but as you know, people disappear. Those people are not kept in boarding houses. They are kept in secret places, out of sight, and well hidden.

"That kid, Henry, signed a legal contract stating the debt he accrued at Lottie's is to be paid in full when he leaves or by a certain date. If not, he will be charged with theft, burglary, and other miscellaneous jargon to make it sound criminal. If that man's debt isn't sold to a ship's captain by the date due, the crimp hands that debt over to the police, and the young man is arrested as a vagrant owing a substantial debt."

"I know all that," Matt said.

Eric hesitated to continue. "Here's the dirty secret. It's all off the record, meaning the court knows nothing about it. Lottie's and other boarding houses hand over young men like Henry to the police and take a loss on the debt, but in return, they are left alone by the police to do business free of suspicion and harassment. They can get away with murder like Rose's hanging last night. The police protect those places. That's where they benefit from the deal."

Matt gazed at Eric with a stone-cold expression. "How does that benefit the police department? It seems like it would just overcrowd the jail."

Eric lifted his glass of water to take a drink. "This is why my friend was killed, and I would be too if they knew I was telling you this. Chief Schlemer takes that debt and sentences the man to months of hard labor with the jail work crews digging ditches, building roads, or whatever is contracted with private owners, state or federal government.

"Fellas like Henry always work on a crew for financial gain, with laborers paid while living in a camp. The Henrys of the world get paid workers' wages, but since it's a jail sentence, his pay goes to the city. But remember, I said men like Henry are off the record? The city doesn't know about them, and their wages go right into Chief Schemer's pocket and those in on the scam.

"Now, one man sentenced to hard labor doesn't earn much, but multiply that by ten or twenty, thirty in a year, and it adds up over time. Technically, it's a shanghaiing business of its own. I don't know all the details, but I know that's basically how it works. It's all off the books and strictly between the crimp, the chief, and the work crew supervisor.

"As for men like Henry, they don't know the difference and think they are just paying their debt off. And after six months or so, they release the young man; his sentence is served, and no one knows the difference. Their debt to society is paid, and they go home wiser and happy." Eric laid his spoon in the empty bowl. "That's why Rose was used."

Matt narrowed his eyes as he stared at Eric. "So,

Chief Schlemer hired Rose, and that's why she was afraid to tell me?"

Eric wrinkled his nose. "Yes and no. He doesn't hire her, but he knows exactly who she is. The crimps around here try to bring in one Henry in a month to stay on the chief's good side. Laura Eggers, Big Richard, Potsy Jones, and all the others hire Rose and other young, attractive ladies to persuade young men to stay at their boarding house. Rose may have had four of five men she was swindling simultaneously; it's hard to say. She didn't have to sell her body anymore, just her charm, beauty, and acting abilities to entice them to stay. They can't leave, or they'll be arrested.

"Of course, not all those young men went to jail; some were seabound, but she was the bait used to supply a need without the press gangs grabbing men off the streets or drugging folks. It's just another means to an end. The crimps and madams work with the police and a few politicians to protect themselves and their businesses from being shut down. In other words, they feed the tiger to keep from becoming food themselves."

"Who killed Rose?" Matt asked pointedly.

Eric thought for a moment and shrugged lightly. "It could have been any of them afraid she told you too much or would tell you too much. Matt, our lower side is full of brutal thugs, and Rose had connections with all of them. It's impossible to say. But Henry was staying at Lottie's Shore Leave Boarding House, which none of them own.

"Lottie's was bought from Lottie Harmes three years ago by a man that lives in California named Colin Fairbanks. He's also a partner who owns half of the Maroon Squid Tavern. So, unless you can get something out of the old man Tom, who is as stubborn and sealed up as an iron-plated boiler, we may have no luck learning who killed her."

Matt frowned. He asked sarcastically, "So it wasn't John Bender mad at Kate after all, huh?"

"Huh?" Eric questioned with a strange expression.

"Nothing. So how do I stop your chief's enterprise?"

Eric shook his head. "The same way I could, you can't. Too many strands make up the cord, and they all protect each other to protect themselves. As I said before, I am barely hanging on to my job, and if I'm fired, I'll be run out of town because I know too much about all of them. They protect themselves, and I'm on the outside with few friends.

"And you can't go to the city council or the mayor because what Chief Schlemer has on them could cause quite a scandal. Some of the blackmail information he has was given to him by Laura Eggers and could hurt their families. So, the wheel rolls forward with the city denying the very things that fill their pockets. Men like me are given a choice: shut our mouths and learn to live with it or get run over."

Matt peered out the window at the city street. "I can't do that. I'll get the old man Tom to talk, and maybe I better visit Laura Eggers, too. I want to find the people that killed Rose."

"Matt, just be careful. You're making someone very nervous, and we don't know who that person is, but assume it's all of them because, as I said, it's a cord of many strands. If you get too close, they'll have no qualms about making you disappear too."

"I'm at the point that I hope they try, so I'll know who they are. I hope it's your chief."

Chapter 24

Matt walked into Lottie's in a bad mood and approached the old man, Tom, who was wiping a spilled drink from the bar top. "Who owns this place?" Matt demanded to know.

Tom's brow lifted. "Colin Fairbanks."

"Who is he?"

Tom shrugged uncaringly. "The owner."

"You've never met him?" Matt inquired.

"Nope."

"Who hired Rose to bring Henry here?"

Tom shrugged. "I don't know if anyone did. He showed up by himself."

Matt stepped closer as his eyes hardened. "I'm going to ask you again; who hired Rose?"

Tom grew uneasy. "I don't know. I just run this place."

"Yeah, I know. I don't care that you're an old man; I will hurt you if you lie to me again. Now, tell me what I want to know!" Matt shouted. There were three men in the small dining area, and all watched Matt with interest.

Tom's voice quivered, "I honestly don't know."

Matt grabbed Tom's palm and bent it backward in a wrist lock with enough force to drop Tom to his aging knees crying out in pain much quicker than Matt expected. Tom cried out, "My wrist! My arthritis...stop! Please stop!" he begged with a painful grimace.

Matt kept the pressure on the wrist as he knelt to look Tom in the eyes. "Who paid her?"

"I don't know! I just work here. Please..." he began to sob.

"Who pays you?" Matt's eyes burned into the old man's excruciating face heartlessly.

"The lawyer, Felix Rathkey!"

Matt let go of the wrist as a wave of rage swept through him. "Why does *he* pay you?"

"Huh?" Tom asked as he raised his head from the floor, where he wept while holding his throbbing wrist.

"Why does *he* pay you?" Matt demanded to know.

"He handles the owner's affairs. I just work here; that's all I know!"

Matt stood, turned around, and kicked a table over with a frustrated yell. He stared at Tom, his chest rising and falling heavily with the fury that consumed him. Felix Rathkey's name had been continuously coming up from the start, and Matt initially suspected him of having something to do with Gabriel's disappearance.

Tom remained on his knees, gripping his wrist and weeping in pain. Matt knelt again to speak to the old man, "Look at me." Tom raised his head from the floor; tears bubbled out of his eyes from his arthritic wrist being forced back beyond the limited rotation that the arthritis allowed. "If I discover you know more than you said, I will return and snap that wrist! Tell me what you know now."

Tom's voice was high-pitched as he cried in anguish, "I don't know anything! I sign people in, keep track of what they owe, and tend the bar. I give the contracts and money to Howard or Tony, and that's all I do. This is my home. The only one I have. That's all." His face fell back over his wrist as the throbbing continued.

Matt sighed and stood. He looked at a sailor staying at the boarding house who was watching nervously. Matt tossed him a coin. "Go get him a few pounds of ice. Make sure it's broken up enough that he can wrap it around his wrist."

***

Matt walked along Water Street to calm the fury that seized him. He was tempted to burst into Felix's office and shove a gun in his face, but for what purpose? There was no evidence that he knew where Gabriel was or had anything to do with Rose's death. The desperation to find his only son was a growing pressure in his chest that continued to expand with each dead end he came to. One lead pointed in this direction, another in that direction as he crossed the city repeatedly, making threats and talking to everyone he could talk to. Matt was beginning to feel like a caged monkey leaping at a banana on a string while being led around like a clown to entertain others. He was sick of dead ends and wanted to find out what had happened to his son.

Criminals have no laws to contain what they do, but law enforcement had a few that stopped them short of doing what they might want to do. Matt could not threaten to hang Felix, Big Richard, Potsy, or Laura Eggers from the underside of the dock to find his son and give them a push if he didn't like their answer. A criminal could hang a young lady for the same principle and get away with it.

More frustrating was learning that the man entrusted by the good citizens of Portland to hold the criminals accountable, Police Chief Bruce Schlemer, was just as dirty and crooked as the worst criminals. There was no way to win in a fixed game. Even if the police chief knew what happened to Gabriel and Rose, he would never admit it because, as Eric had said earlier, the cord of corruption had many strands. If Bruce Schlemer said a word, his life would end with the very twisted rope he helped create.

Calmly, Matt entered the Rathkey Attorneys at Law office and greeted the secretary. He was informed that Mister Rathkey was in a meeting and would be done shortly. She notified the attorney of Matt's presence, and before too long, he heard a door open and Felix's voice as he escorted his visitors out of his office.

Matt nodded at Morton Sperry and Tony Hurner as they left the office.

"Marshal," Tony said as he passed by.

Felix approached with an extended hand. "Matt, what a pleasure. Come in and tell me what I can do for you," Felix said pleasantly. "Do you know them?" he asked as Matt entered his office.

"Who? Those two? I met the one who said hello one day, but I don't know him. The other man with longer hair looks familiar, but I can't place him. What's his name?"

Felix sat behind his desk. "Um, Mitchell Grapes." It was the first name that came to his mind.

"Hmm. No, I don't know him." Matt adjusted himself in the chair comfortably. "Mister Rathkey, as you know, I have been searching for my son, and in the process, I stopped by a boarding house asking if they had a teenager staying there. The clerk denied it, but a sailor told me they did. I double-checked to make sure it wasn't my son, and the sailor explained to me that the pretty young lady with him was a decoy to make sure the boy stayed there to run up his tab so he could be shanghaied. I got the kid out of there. But the young lady was murdered last night; she was found hanging under a dock."

Felix narrowed his brow. "Why are you telling me this? Are they accusing you of her murder? I'll represent you."

Matt gave a soft chuckle. "No. I'm a lawman, so it is my nature to investigate, especially since I get the feeling she was murdered because she was planning to leave Portland with me to get out of prostitution. Unfortunately, someone murdered her last night. I'm looking for who did it."

Felix shrugged his shoulders, expecting Matt to continue. "I hope you're not looking at me."

"No. I went to Lottie's Shore Leave Boarding House to question Tom, and I may have been a little rougher than I intended with the old-timer. Tom mentioned you manage the owner's affairs here in town, including fifty percent of the Maroon Squid Tavern. It dawned on me that the Maroon Squid is where Bob worked, and he borrowed a lot of money from you to buy the other half of a company that you manage. Did you not want to work with Bob?"

A glimmer of hostility flashed through Felix's eyes. His mouth puckered thoughtfully. "My arrangement with Mister Fairbanks to watch over his investments is strictly confidential. Tom had no business mentioning my relationship with him."

Matt slowly wrinkled his nose. "Well, he didn't have much of a choice. Felix, I want to know who paid Rose Livingston to persuade Henry to stay at the boarding house you oversee."

Felix leaned back in his high-back leather chair. "Are you making an accusation that I would have anything to do with that?"

"I don't see how it could benefit anyone except the owner and perhaps you."

Felix removed his spectacles and spoke pointedly, "I don't know that lady. So, maybe they were lovers or something, I don't know. I am paid a flat fee for overseeing a few properties, but I do not manage them. Tom manages Lottie's, Hugh manages the Maroon Squid, and Bob would have managed it if he had not disappeared, but I think any accusations on my part are absurd. I'm an attorney, not a criminal."

"Some would say they are one of the same," Matt replied.

Felix was slightly amused. "I know. That's why I have security guards. I don't know who paid that woman or *if* she was paid, but I think any death is sad, especially a murder. If you meet her family, give them my condolences. Other than that, I don't know what I can do for you unless you have more on your mind."

"Quite frankly, I only have one thing on my mind: finding my son. I'm not having much luck with that."

"Well, that's why they're called *missing people*; they aren't found. But I do pray you find your son, Bob, and the other lad with them."

"Do you?" Matt asked abruptly. He was quickly irritated by Felix's blatant sarcasm.

"Do I what?"

"Pray I find them?"

"It's a manner of speech, Mister Bannister. But yes, I hope you do," Felix stated with frustration.

"As a Christian, prayer is more than a manner of speech. I believe God listens to our words and what's in our hearts. I won't say I'll pray for someone if I don't intend to. Prayer is sacred. Did you know the Bible says the angels are dumbfounded by how little people pray and call upon the Lord? They just can't believe how little we go to the throne of God in prayer. We know the Bible says the God of heaven and earth is our help, our shield, and our Father who loves us, and we have access to the very throne of God through Jesus, but we fail to pray as seriously and often as we should. Well, I believe God is just as active as ever, and I pray. I'm praying I find my son."

"Amen. I go to church, too," Felix said.

"Good," Matt said, looking at Felix evenly. "I won't judge your relationship with God; that's between you and him. But your name keeps coming up everywhere I look. I'm not accusing you, but I will warn you that if you have anything to do with my missing son, you might want to get right with God because you'll be meeting him soon."

Felix winced. "What? Are you threatening me? Don't answer that yet. Let me get this straight. You're threatening me because I gave Bob a loan that he paid back the same day, and I manage the affairs of a client that lives out of state. But I don't manage those properties; I merely oversee the financial aspects, and the managers manage them. I have no interest or idea what takes place inside those properties." He scowled as he leaned over his desk and glared at Matt. "I believe you owe me an apology."

"A warning isn't a threat; it is foreknowledge of a pending threat if corrective action isn't taken. I meant what I said, *if* you're involved in my son's disappearance, you can either return him to me or get right with God. If you're not, then you have nothing to worry about." Matt stood to leave.

"I have nothing to do with your son, but even if you found those who did take him, supposedly, they would have rights as American citizens. You can't just shoot them," Felix said.

Matt scowled. "Where are my boy's rights not to be kidnapped? What makes a criminal's rights any more valuable than my sons? I support the victims of crimes and not the predators that prey upon them. As far as I am concerned, whoever is responsible for my son's disappearance lost their rights when they took him."

"And what about the Bible saying to wait for God to take revenge? It says something about that too. Doesn't it?" Felix questioned.

Matt laughed lightly. "It does, indeed, Mister Rathkey. I happen to be a United States Marshal, a lawman. It is my job to bring criminals to justice." Matt said with a slight smile and a nod. "I have my rights, too."

***

Felix left his office at two o'clock with a long stem red rose that was delivered to his office shortly before. He saw William Fasana crossing the street with a wave and a shout to get Felix's attention. "William, what are you doing? How did you like the fights last night?"

"I thought it was great!" he exclaimed loudly. "I can't wait to move here and be a part of your fight

267

pit. I loved it! Hey, speaking of moving here, do you have time to look at some more properties? I heard a harlot was hanging from a vacant warehouse. I'm thinking she must've given something to someone, huh?" he chuckled with a soft tap to Felix's abdomen. He continued without waiting for a reply, "But I'm also thinking no one mentioned a warehouse to me. A warehouse on a pier would be exactly what I'm looking for, you know? Do you got time to show it to me?" he asked. He motioned towards the rose. "Or are you having lunch with Nora?"

Felix bit his bottom lip with a slight grin. "Yes, I am. We can look at that tomorrow if you like, or this evening. Now, if you'll excuse me."

"Sure. If you want to look at that warehouse today, you know where I'm staying."

"We'll do," Felix said and walked quickly away.

Matt Bannister had been told that Potsy Jones used an empty warehouse for his illegal deeds. Matt was curious to know who owned the warehouse Rose had been hung under and if the warehouse held any evidence of keeping prisoners inside. Matt had bet a dollar that William couldn't get Felix to tell him who owned the warehouse and get inside as a potential buyer. William was determined to win the bet and wouldn't take no for an answer. He'd get Felix Rathkey to get the keys from the owner and get inside the warehouse.

A single long-stem red rose seemed a nice choice for Nora, but her yard was filled with flowering rose bushes. A purple lily might add some variety to her vase, but another single rose seemed a little too dull when she had so many growing in her yard.

William wasn't the most romantic of men, but he knew a single rose symbolized romantic interest or love. Being a poker player for so many years, William could read facial expressions like a book and knew Felix was not just lying but anxious to get somewhere. Chances were the rose wasn't for Nora.

Having nothing else to do, William followed Felix five blocks into a residential area to a small house of lower social standing. Felix pulled a key out of his pocket as he approached the corner house with flaking white paint. He unlocked the door and went inside. William leaned against a neighboring house and watched. Fifteen minutes later, the beautiful blonde-haired lady that had spoken with Felix and Nora a few days before on the sidewalk slowly approached the home and went inside, closing the door behind her.

Chapter 25

Felix and Nora's seven-year-old daughter, Gretchen, had brown hair that was the perfect blend of her mother's darker and Felix's light brown hair. She was a sweet, affectionate little girl with a wild imagination and the prettiest smile. She enjoyed drawing pictures, and since Beth Hurner taught her how to draw flowers, Gretchen had drawn them by the dozens, and you couldn't wander too far into the Rathkey home without seeing her artwork lying on a table, the floor, or tacked to the wall. She enjoyed her dolls and playing with her cousins and friends at church. Gretchen loved Jesus and would pray with such sincerity that even the pastor of their church was impressed by her prayers. However, at home, she didn't have anyone to play with except her mother since her grandmother had gone to have lunch with her friend.

Nora Rathkey was busy cleaning the house and had just swept the family room when Gretchen came in from outside, tracking mud on the floor.

She had been making mudpies to have a tea party with her dolls outside.

"Gretchen!" Nora shouted irritably and then sighed to calm herself. "Your feet are muddy, and I just cleaned the floor. Please go wash your feet and hands off."

"Sorry, Mommy. Can I go play with my puppy?"

Nora never wanted pets in her house and despised Felix for getting Gretchen a puppy for her birthday two months before. It was a cute young white poodle that Felix couldn't resist getting for his daughter. Unlike her mother, Gretchen loved animals and affectionately named her new puppy Princess. Nora refused to let the animal enter the house, so Princess was kept in the kennel where Gretchen could let it run in the yard and play with her puppy.

"Sure, go play with Princess for a while," Nora answered.

Gretchen went outside to the kennel and stopped when she passed by Turk's pen. There was a bloody cut about an inch long that just narrowly missed the back edge of Turk's eye. Unaware of how it might have happened, Gretchen's concern and curiosity got the better of her, and she broke a promise to her mother never to enter the pit bull's pen.

"What happened to you, Turk?" She noticed another puncture wound on the dog's back that looked like a bite and touched them with her fingers as she petted Turk.

Turk gave a low, deep growl with a snarl twitching his short, powerful snout at the touch of her hand on the fresh wound. Gretchen had helped her father raise Turk since he was a puppy, and knowing he was hurt, Gretchen moved her face in front of Turk's to look into his eyes with a kind smile to show she loved him. "I'm just trying to help you, Turk. You shouldn't growl. It's not nice." She moved her arms to give him a loving hug.

A ferocious roar of a mixed growl and bark sounded as the powerful jaws of the fighting dog clamped down over her face, sliced through her flesh, and then viciously snapped onto her arm. Turk immediately began to shake her body from left to right like a ragdoll. The pit bull's teeth sunk into her flesh, tearing through the tissues as it continued to jerk, tear, shake, tighten the grasp, and tear into the girl. Gretchen screamed with terrifying volume and the sheer horror of what was happening to her. There was nothing she could do to stop the attack as her face, shoulder, and arm were all targeted in the fury that never seemed to end.

Nora Rathkey, who was outside hanging a rug to beat clean with a broom, darted with all the speed and endurance that panic can provide to the kennel and tried to pull the wrathful seventy-pound dog off her sixty-pound daughter. Knowing Turk intended to kill Gretchen like it did the dogs it fought in the pit, Nora swung the broom she carried with all her might to stop the dog from tearing into her daughter, but it had no effect. The powerful, deep, vicious snarling was nearly as loud as Gretchen's terrified screams. Nora swung the broom repeatedly while frantically praying the animal would release her daughter.

Another desperate swing of the broom and

Turk's attention turned towards Nora.

In an instant, the brutal beast ferociously leaped forward and grabbed her dress, knocking Nora to the ground as the animal clamped its bloody mouth onto Nora's arm with its powerful jaws. As if in a dream, all Nora could hear was Turk's enraged snarling, growling while his iron jawed grip and strong incisors tore through her flesh as the beast jerked her one way and then the other while he shook his head violently as if trying to pull the arm from her body. For a moment, Turk stopped shaking his head with Nora's arm firmly gripped in his mouth. Her body was vibrating with a deep growl.

For just a moment, Nora, in her nightmare-like shock, realized it wasn't Gretchen's screams she was hearing but her own. Turk's green eyes met with her own, and like a cannonball being fired, Turk released her arm and charged forward to attack her throat. Nora curled into a ball in the corner of the pen protectively while Turk's paws scratched at her face and body while his jaws clenched into her shoulder, sinking his teeth deep into her flesh. Nora screamed as Turk began shaking his head with the powerful neck and shoulders. The deep, enraged growls never stopped and vibrated through her body. He froze, holding her shoulder in his mouth with a deep growl, and then like a lion pouncing, he'd release his jaws to bite somewhere else, driving his teeth inside her, and began shaking his head wildly to tear her flesh away. The pain was as excruciating as the terror that filled her.

Laying on the ground screaming, Nora caught a glimpse of Gretchen lying still and unconscious, bleeding profusely from several areas of mangled flesh from the dog's wrath. They say a mother can do miraculous things when the child's life is in danger, but despite her daughter's life draining away six feet away, there was nothing Nora could do to escape the power, ferocity, and sheer madness of the pit bull, except scream.

Suddenly, a man ran into the kennel carrying a shovel. He turned the spade sideways and raised it above his head to bring the edge of the spade down across the dog's spine in an attempt to break Turk's back. Turk released Nora's bloody shoulder and spun toward the man with a snarl to attack the man with the shovel, but Turk's attention went to a second man who entered the cage to scoop up Gretchen's little body into his arms. Turk charged forward and snatched onto Gretchen's ankle to pull her back inside the kennel.

The man holding the shovel swung it downward with all his force, intending to slice the dog in half with the edge of the spade's blade. The spade was not sharp enough to puncture the animal's flesh, but the force of a second blow to the spine hurt the beast sufficiently enough to release Gretchen's ankle and turn on the man holding the shovel. Turk clamped his teeth into the man's leg before he could hit the beast with the shovel again.

Two more carpenters building the house across the street came running to help; one of the men carried an ax and, with three expert swings, guaranteed Turk would never hurt anyone again by nearly beheading the beast. Another man immediately used his suspenders and broke the broom handle to create a tourniquet around Gretchen's upper arm to stop the blood loss. The four men carried Gretchen and Nora to a carpenter's wagon and rushed them to the hospital as quickly as they could while trying to hold as much blood inside of the two ladies as possible.

***

With sutures in her bandaged arm and shoulder, deep red scratches on her face, and a blood-stained, ripped dress, Nora stormed angrily along the sidewalk from the hospital three blocks away to Felix's office, demanding to know where he was. His secretary, nor the other lawyers, could tell her as he left half an hour before with no information about where he was going. No one in the office knew where Howard Nicol was, but the secretary did tell her Tony Hurner and Morton Myers were across the river collecting payments. Felix had not gone with them. He wasn't in court, at the courthouse, or in his office.

***

Maggie Farrell watched her new friend, wearing a blood-covered and torn dress, clearly distressed, move along the street frantically glancing in the restaurants and stores to find her husband. Maggie left the butcher's shop to inquire what was wrong and immediately joined her friend in searching for Felix.

As they approached a corner, Maggie saw William slowly strolling towards them. He waved to her with a broad grin, but the grin faded when he saw the blood-covered dress and bandaged arm of a frantic Nora Rathkey.

"What's going on?" he asked with concern.

"Have you seen my husband? Our dog attacked our daughter, and she may not survive the surgery," Nora explained in a terrified panic. Her tears refreshed themselves continually as she feared the loss of their daughter. "Have you seen Felix?" she pleaded as if it was the last of her hope.

William moved his eyes from the terrified woman to Maggie and barely nodded. Reading his expression correctly, Maggie snapped, "Tell her if you know!"

William turned around and waved his arm, "Come with me." He didn't explain where they were going or why. He just quickly returned to the small white house a few blocks away. William stopped at the sidewalk leading to the front door and pointed. "You'll find your husband behind that door."

Nora stared at the place with a puzzled expression. "This is our first home. Why would he be here? I thought we sold it." She didn't wait for a reply before she walked hurriedly to the door and barged inside. The house had no furniture, just bare rooms with an empty kitchen towards the back next to the bedroom with the slight sound of a bed creaking behind a closed door.

Nora, far more concerned about their daughter, opened the bedroom door and stared at her husband, nude as the day he was born, with Beth Hurner. Nora's voice was cold, "When you're done, Gretchen is in the hospital fighting for her life! Maybe you could join us there."

"Nora!" Felix exclaimed and quickly sat up while covering his nether region. Beth also sat up alarmed and wrapped herself in shame with her dress. She began to cry.

"Um...a..." Felix was caught with his pants off and couldn't explain himself.

Nora's glaring eyes narrowed in wrath. She shouted, "Did you hear me? Gretchen is in the hospital and may not survive surgery! I came to tell you, and I've been looking everywhere. I don't know if our daughter is still alive or has bled to death already. And...I find you here? With Beth?" Nora's jaw clenched tightly with more mixed emotions than a lady should ever feel at once.

"Nora, what...what...what happened to Gretchen?" Felix stuttered as he reached for his clothes.

"Your damn dog tore her up, Felix! They have to amputate her arm." The words being spoken brought the reality of it to life, and Nora burst into uncontrollable sobs. She turned away from the door, and Maggie quickly went to her with a supportive hug.

"Nora," Felix said, coming out of the room half dressed.

Nora forced herself to stand straight and turn to look her husband in the eye. She shouted, "If Gretchen dies, I'll never forgive you! This is all your fault! I told you to keep that dog away from my house. I told you!" she screamed before breaking into horrified tears.

Beth came out of the room with her dress pulled on loosely. Her expression was both shame and sincere concern for Gretchen. Her tearful voice trembled, "Nora, I'm sorry."

Nora snapped, "Tell it to Tony, not me!" Nora quickly walked past William to return to the hospital. Maggie hurried out the door to support her friend.

Felix stared at William standing in the family room, watching him get dressed. Beth went back into the room to finish dressing. Felix asked William with annoyance, "Did you follow me here?"

William nodded slowly, "Yep. And you should be darn glad I did, or you wouldn't know about your little girl. It sounds like you better get your ass to the hospital."

Felix knew William was right. Hopping on one foot and then the other, he pulled his boots on as fast as possible.

Beth came out of the bedroom shaking and visibly upset. "Damn you, Felix! This is your fault. I'm telling Tony the truth tonight!" She began to weep. "This is your fault. If I lose Tony because of you..." She wept.

Felix pointed a finger at her and snapped, "No, you won't! You just shut up and leave Nora to me! Nothing changes. Got it? I haven't got time to worry about that right now. Gretchen's hurt; didn't you hear anything!" He quickly departed the house.

William stood awkwardly in the family room,

watching Beth lean against the wall and slowly slide down to the floor, sobbing with her head buried in her clenched fists. "It's not my fault," she said through her tears. She hit the wall in her agony. "It's not my fault," she sobbed.

"Miss, are you okay?" William asked softly.

She looked over and, seeing him, turned her face back into her hands. "Oh, Jesus, it's not my fault," she repeated through her sobs.

Chapter 26

Matt Bannister sat at an empty table in the Silver Casterlin Saloon after receiving a wire from his deputy, Truet Davis, back in Branson.

It read:

D.A. Jackson Weathers acquits Jesse Helms— Crowe Brothers in town.

"Unbelievable," Matt said to himself as he rubbed his beard. He had left Truet Davis in Branson to look after Jesse Helms, who was in their jail for the rape of a young girl named Laura Whitehead in Hollister. The Crowe Brothers from Prairieville had come over the mountain and intimidated the District Attorney, Jackson Weathers, to let their cousin Jesse walk away a free man.

There were times when being a lawman could be one of the most frustrating careers a man could get into. All the effort to make the arrest of Jesse

Helms and bring him back to Branson to stand trial for what he did to that young girl was now null and void.

More discouraging was learning of the corruption within the Portland Police Department. The city's only real power and authority belonged to the criminals controlling the wharf and sailors' houses. However, that's what corruption does to law enforcement; it gives the balance of power to the criminal element and puts innocent citizens at risk. Portland's corruption went too deep for Matt to do anything about, but he wasn't there to fret over that.

Matt reread the wire and sighed as his discouragement lowered another level to the origins of defeat. He was beginning to accept that too many days had passed and Gabriel was no longer in Portland. He had not gotten to Portland in time to save his son, and he could do nothing about that. Even the trail of suspects had so far led to nothing more than speculation with no evidence to tie any one person to the vanishing of the three young men. It seemed he would go home a beaten man and admit to Elizabeth that he had failed to bring Gabriel and Evan home. Worse than that, he had no answers to any questions she might ask.

Rhoda Bannister, Matt's stepmother, sat down across from him uninvited. Her usual no-nonsense eyes were brimming with tears. Her voice cracked as she asked, "Don't lie to me, Matt. Where is my son?"

Matt shook his head quietly. "I don't know, just

like I don't know where my son is. And before you ask, I don't know who took them either."

Rhoda snapped, "Well, are you going to find out or just sit here? Every day I expect Bob to come home, and he's not here. Something is wrong, and I want to know where my son is!" Her bottom lip repeatedly quivered as she fought to hold herself together.

"I'm trying," Matt said softly. "I have spoken with the police, hospital, city hall, dock workers, every boarding house, sailor house and crimp, pimp, and others and have come up with nothing. Back at home, our cowardly District Attorney released an outlaw we arrested for a terrible crime. I just found that out." He held up the wire. "I'm not in a very good mood right now either. My son is missing too. So, if you think I'm not trying to find them, you're wrong. I don't know where else to look!"

"So, what are you going to do, give up?" Her eyes bore into his with a hardened glare.

"No. I'm not giving up." He added softly with a defeated tone, "Sometimes in life, situations are simply out of our hands, and all we can do is trust God and give him room to work without us getting in the way."

Rhoda scoffed as she twisted in her chair and hit the table with the bottom of her fist with a loud bang. "That's a nice little cliché to hear, and I'm sure it's supposed to make me feel better. But damn it, Matt, I don't want to feel better; I want my son back home! You can trust God all you want, but if the Bible is true, God quit doing miracles long ago.

I believe in God and pray too, but miracles don't happen! Getting off your butt and doing something is what is going to bring the boys home."

Her voice struck him like falling into a patch of briars, aggravating wounds already festering. He took a deep breath to help control his growing frustration. His eyes hardened as he said, "I didn't say I was waiting for a miracle, did I? Saying you're going to trust the Lord isn't a cliché; it is a decision to put your trust in the Lord. Saying something like, 'God will never give you more than you can handle' is a cliché and does more harm than good because it isn't true. Life does give us more than we can handle. That is exactly why people like me put our trust in Jesus to get us through the tough times that appear hopeless—like right now.

"I don't know where those boys are or what happened to them. I haven't learned anything. I haven't been sitting on my butt and am in no mood to be accused of it. So, let me repeat; I am putting my hope in the Lord. I am trusting Jesus to reveal something to help us find the boys or answer what happened to them and who is responsible. If you don't like that answer, I suggest you pick up your little golden calf sculpture or whatever it is that you pray to and try to do better."

"Don't be ridiculous!" she snapped. "I pray to God."

"Which one?" Matt asked sharply. "If you can't believe the Bible, what god do you believe in? All we know about God is from the Bible. The Bible says *all scripture is breathed out of God.* If you can't believe that, then you start to pick and choose what you think is okay and discount what you disagree with, like shopping for apples at the mercantile. And that is very foolish to pick and choose what you think is good and right when God is the creator of life, and he makes the rules, not you or me. We'll be accountable to him, not him to us. So whether you believe it or not, it is still true."

"Matt," Rhoda said with her eyes glowering at him. "I didn't come down here to hear a sermon. I want my son back. He's missing, and here you are sitting in the sun having a drink! Now, are you going to get out there and find him or not?" She nodded towards the window he was sitting beside.

Matt lifted the glass and shook it slightly. "It's water. I want to find my son as much as you do. I offered a five-thousand-dollar reward, and not one person has offered a single bit of information. I'm not giving up, but so far, we haven't discovered anything. There is no trace of them. I wandered in the underground tunnels, and there was nothing there. The only thing I've done so far is getting a man beat up and a young lady murdered for speaking with me." Moisture clouded his eyes. "So, to say I'm doing nothing is a bit of an insult. I'm making someone nervous."

"Well, you need to find out who because Bobby has never gone this long without coming to see me." She covered her mouth to fight the tears that refused to remain in her eyes. "I'm terrified that I'll never see my son again."

Matt reached over and took hold of her hand on

the table. "I know. I feel the same way. There is a vast canyon between saying I believe in God and knowing who God is and having a relationship with him. The difference between you and me is I put my trust in the Lord, and you don't."

"I do, too," she said, wiping her tears away.

"Rhoda, there are some dangerous people in this city that don't like me, and if one of the people I irritated sent men in here with shotguns to kill me but killed you too—would you go to heaven?"

Rhoda's brow lowered in consideration. Her shoulders slumped as her bottom lip quivered and her eyes filled with tears. Her head shook. "No."

Matt watched a tear slowly stroll down her cheek. "Then pray with me, Jesus—"

"Matt!" Eric loudly called as he crossed the saloon. "I'm sorry to interrupt your conversation, but I need to speak with you." He was in his royal blue police uniform with a large badge.

"I'll meet you outside in a minute," Matt said irritably. He waited for Eric to walk away. "Let's pray—"

"No," Rhoda said, standing. "He might have news about Bobby. We'll talk later, Matt," Rhoda said as she left the table and walked away.

Matt was annoyed by the interruption, but he wasn't too surprised. It wasn't uncommon to be interrupted when talking to an unbeliever about Jesus.

"Have you found anything new?" Matt asked as he stepped outside the Silver Casterlin.

Eric said, "The warehouse Rose was hung from

was owned by a man named Alex Webber, who had a small company called Webber's River Distribution Company, but it closed down after he died six years ago. It's been vacant ever since. As for the current owner, it's still in his name, and he had no family. But I did learn from a bartender, whose name I promised not to share, that Potsy Jones has a key to the place. Shall we go talk to Potsy?"

Chapter 27

Potsy Jones grimaced with annoyance. "What do you men want from me? You've been nagging me about these missing men I know nothing about, and it's getting monotonous. I told you I don't know anything about your son. I liked Bob, and I hope you find him, but I don't know anything. How many times do I have to say that?"

Eric said, "We're not here for that. Rumor has it you have the key to the old Webber distribution warehouse?"

"Yes. So?"

"Where did you get the key? Alex Webber died before you came to town."

"I bought it from his old supervisor, who didn't know what to do with the key. No one owns the warehouse now, and the last I heard, it was tied up in probate. It's not illegal to have a key to a vacant property, so what's all this about?"

"Well, you know Rose Livingston was hung un-

KEN PRATT

derneath it, right?" Eric asked.

Potsy quickly said, "Anyone could have taken a skiff under there and done that. I hope you aren't trying to pin that on me because I have a key to the place."

"No, we're not accusing you," Eric admitted. "Whoever did it used the catwalk, not a boat. I was just wondering how you got a key. Could I borrow that key so Matt and I could look around the warehouse?"

Potsy grimaced with a perplexed shrug. "Why is everyone interested in that building today? Felix Rathkey came by here twenty minutes ago with some fella from Seattle to look at the place. I told him I didn't own it, but the hustler wanted to look at it anyway."

Matt chuckled. "That would be my stepsister's beau. He's a jackass," he explained to Eric.

"Oh. Well, let's find them before they close the door."

***

William Fasana slowly grinned when Matt entered the warehouse with a uniformed Portland Police Officer. He tapped Felix's belly a few times and pointed towards the door. "Are you sure your wife didn't call the police for trespassing on your marital oaths?"

"Shut up!" Felix snapped quietly. "I'm already irritated at you as it is."

"Felix, you should thank me for telling your wife

288

where you were. Otherwise, you wouldn't know about your daughter, and that's where you should be anyway, not here with me."

Felix shook his head slowly as he watched Matt and Eric walking towards them. "I couldn't stand being at the hospital any longer. My daughter is in surgery, and Nora hates me right now. I couldn't take it."

"I bet not," William said quietly. He motioned to the two lawmen. "Well, would you look at that, Felix? You're in so much trouble they didn't know if they should send the city police or a federal marshal for broken marital oaths, so they sent them both!" He snickered. "Where are the cavalry, boys? It's the only thing you're missing."

Felix turned his head quickly to glare at William irritably. "Officer Eric Stiles, Marshal," he greeted the two men. "What can I do for you?" Felix asked.

"We're just here to look around," Eric answered. "We stopped by Potsy's to ask for the key, and he said you were here. May I ask why?"

Felix motioned to William. "I'm showing him the property. He has some interest in purchasing it possibly."

"I didn't know you were in real estate, Felix," Eric said bluntly as it sparked his interest.

"I'm not. William asked me to look over any offers he may make. I just got the key for him."

"How did you know Potsy had the key?" Eric asked.

"Everyone knows Potsy has the key. He has his New Year's Eve party here. Certainly, you knew that."

"I knew he had big parties but thought it was in his tavern. I work security at the Mayor's Ball every New Year's Eve."

William chuckled as he gazed at Eric's thick mustache. "The mayor must be a man of great foresight to keep you away from fireworks. If a random spark ignited that bushy lip, you'd set the whole city ablaze."

Eric cast an annoyed glance towards William but ignored the comment and continued speaking with Felix, "I'm investigating the death of Rose Livingston and the disappearance of Bob Mears along with Matt's son. I thought we'd look here and see if we could find anything."

Felix waved a hand around the warehouse invitingly. "Have at it. If there is anything here, I hope you find it."

William tapped Felix's belly again and waved towards Eric, "Do you know what we do for entertainment in Seattle when we see a policeman? Watch this..." He reached for his billfold, pulled out a dollar bill, and dangled it above Eric's head. "Jump for the dollar, Maurice. Be a good monkey and jump for me."

Eric stepped forward and drove a right fist toward William's mouth. William jerked his head back just enough for the hardened fist to breeze past his mouth. The straight right fist thrown with the power of the policeman's body weight behind it was too close for William's comfort. It was quickly evident that Eric knew how to hit and how to hit hard. The blow would have knocked out several of William's teeth if it had connected.

Caught off guard, William stumbled backward as the offended officer kept moving forward like an angry bear ready to rip him apart. William extended his hands out in surrender while glancing at Matt for help. He hollered, "Whoa, horsey!"

Unmoved by the cowering loudmouth, Eric dipped his body to the left and drove a hard left fist upwards into William's exposed liver. William gasped as the wind was knocked out of him while his body stiffened with the painful blow. An overhand right fist connected with William's left eye with explosive power; all William could see was the wooden timbers of the warehouse floor coming towards him as he fell. William hit the floor, suffering from the pain of the two quick blows. He could feel the swelling around his left eye start immediately.

Eric stood above William with a harsh scowl and wild-eyed. "Say another word. I dare you to make one more joke at my expense."

Matt had never seen his cousin lose a fight so quickly. The swelling of his eye and grimacing face showed William was finished. Matt stepped close to ensure Eric wouldn't strike William again. "Eric, I think he's had enough. I don't like the jackass either, but he is my stepsister's friend. Hopefully, she'll wise up and have nothing to do with him. Let's go see what we can find here."

William, still on the floor, pointed a finger at Felix. "He said you were bought and paid for."

Felix's eyes widened as he shook his head innocently. "I never said that, Eric!"

As Matt and Eric walked into another area of the warehouse, William got back on his feet. "Well, let it be known; it's not a good idea to joke around with a Portland Police Officer." He chuckled as he touched the swelling of his eye. "They don't have much of a sense of humor."

"You're nuts," Felix said, staring at his friend. "You're crazy."

William chuckled. "No. Crazy is having a fling with your friend and right-hand-man's wife. That's crazy. I'm just adventurous."

***

"What were you thinking?" Matt asked, looking at William's swollen and blackened eye. His eyeball was bloodshot from the broken vessels. They were on top of the Silver Casterlin building for their nightly meeting at midnight.

"I was just playing around," William said with a chuckle. "You could've stopped him, you know."

"It was two hits, William. There was no time to. Besides, I told him I didn't like you. Why would I stop him? You're the one that decided to try to humiliate him. It didn't quite work out too well, did it?"

William shook his head slowly. "No," he admitted. "Felix had a bad day today. It started good, though. He met Morton's big friend Tony's wife for a private meeting..." He told Matt what had happened throughout the day with Beth Hurner and the dog attack. "So," William finished, "I decided to have some fun with your policeman friend. I don't think he liked me. Anyway, Felix said I was crazy. But I told him he was crazy for...well, for your benefit, I'll use the Biblical terminology that you might understand, Felix *knowing* his strongarm man's wife."

Matt gazed at William for a moment as all the information was digested. "I know you're not crazy, but I'm beginning to think you're not too bright. Eric told me he was quite a successful pugilist before joining the police department. And he sure looked like one, didn't he? Two hits put you out." Matt chuckled.

"I wasn't out! Down, but not out," William argued. "Where is Morton? He's late."

"I don't know." Matt opened his pocket watch and tried to see the time in the lack of light. "How is Felix's daughter?"

William shrugged empathetically. "I don't know. I feel bad for her and their family. I offered to kill the dog, but it was already dead. Maggie and I went to their house that one night for dinner and met the little girl before she went to bed. She is a cute kid."

Matt thought about telling William about Rose, but since he had no direct knowledge of her or Henry, he decided to keep it to himself. "I plan to go to the hospital to visit JoJo Perkins for a bit. Maybe I'll stop by the little girl's hospital room and bring her some flowers. Perhaps Felix's wife will share some information now that she's mad at him. If not, we might be wasting our time, William. We can't find any evidence on him."

William twisted his head slowly. "It only feels like we're an apple bobbing on a stagnant pond. I believe with all my heart that we're not here for nothing. Gabriel is a smart boy and he has Fasana blood in him, just like you and me; he'll survive whatever he faces. If he's out to sea, he'll come home. Evan, too; Gabriel will see to that. I don't think we're wasting our time. I believe this is where we are because, as the book of Proverbs says, *A man's heart plans his way, but the Lord directs his steps*. Let's stay the course and not get too discouraged. As you've told me a thousand times, God is in control."

Matt looked at his cousin and smiled slightly with appreciation. "Thank you."

"For?"

"A bit of encouragement. I haven't had much of that lately."

"Matt, I want to get Gabriel back as much as you do. So, I suggest we do it."

The door squeaked open, and Morton stepped slowly onto the rooftop with an uncomfortable scowl.

"Wow, you look more miserable than your sister Jannie on a sober night. What happened to you?" William asked.

Morton gave him an irritated glare as he sat on the roof's brick rail and began pulling his new shiny black boots off. "I have never walked so much in my life. My feet are blistered from these boots, and my feet hurt." He pulled a jackknife from his pocket and opened the narrowest blade to poke a small hole at the base of the blisters to drain the fluid.

"Where did you go?" Matt asked.

Morton waved towards the river. "Everywhere across the river. From the west side clear to the east, north, south, and just about everywhere in between, collecting payments for attorney fees and other fees which I don't know about. We must have walked five miles, if not more." He squeezed the liquid from a blister on the side of his foot. "I miss my horse."

William asked, "What did you think about the dog fights last night?"

"I thought it was brutal and sad. I wanted to keep that little dog that got hurt. I hated seeing it torn apart by that beast of Felix's. I didn't like it," Morton said tiredly.

"Yeah, but you won money, right?" William asked. He continued more sincerely and empathetically, "That beast of a dog tore into Felix's little girl today, and the doctor had to amputate her arm."

Morton's head dropped in silent prayer. He looked back up at Matt. "With all the sadness you see doing this job, how do you do it? I watched that dog, and the ferociousness was incredible. I cannot imagine what it did to that child. I feel bad enough about what I did to that man, JoJo, but now I have a vision of that dog doing what I witnessed to a child. I keep thinking about that girl in Hollister and how much my cousin and friend hurt her." He shook his head. "I don't know if I can keep doing this if we can't bring Gabriel and Evan back alive. I mean, how much can you take?"

Matt answered the question thoughtfully, "Where there is crime, there are victims. The only justice those victims have, depends on us catching the criminals and bringing them to trial. I never said this was an easy job or that your heart wouldn't get broken from time to time. This is not a job for a weak-willed man. I don't know how a human being can do what we do without the Lord being there to make some kind of sense out of the pure evil and wicked things we see. Morton, I've seen crimes so heinous that it's unbelievable that a man or woman could do them to another human being. It is our job to take that heartbreak and empathy we may feel and apply it to getting justice for that victim and their families.

"I remember the Dobson Gang terrorizing Elizabeth, Joseph, Tom, and me down at the swimming hole on Pearl Creek, and I get angry to this day. What they did to Joseph..." he hesitated. "That's why I choose to wear this badge and why it means as much to me as it does. I have the right and obligation to stop men like them from ever harming another group of friends again. Turn all those emotions for the victims around and focus them on finding the criminals responsible. That is what I do."

Morton sighed heavily. "I still can't believe Jesse did that to her."

"I got a wire from Truet today stating that your cousins, the Crowe brothers, showed up in town, and Jesse is now a free man. The charges were dropped. Focus on that."

Morton shook his head silently.

William knelt to speak at the same level as Morton, "And I caught Felix and Tony's wife in bed together; well, Felix's wife caught them. So that will add some excitement to your day tomorrow."

Morton raised his head and squinted his eyes. "You're kidding me. Beth? I have a hard time believing that. I thought she loved her husband too much to do that. Well, that's going to kill him. If there is anything I have learned, it is that Tony loves his wife. I've learned that much. That's not going to be good when he finds out. Did Felix give you the black eye?"

"No!" William chuckled. "Matt failed to act like family and let his police officer friend hit me for no reason."

Morton smiled slowly. "I'm sure there was a reason, William. If my feet didn't ache, I would blacken your other eye for what you said about my sister." Morton pulled his stocking and boots back on and stood. "I'm heading back to my hotel room. I'm exhausted. If Tony finds out about his wife and Felix…things could get bad, but he might kill himself. I don't know. She is his world."

Matt spoke to Morton, "As William said earlier, the Lord directed our paths right into the center of this, whatever this is, for whatever purpose he has in mind. Whether it has anything to do with Gabriel or not, if the Lord opens the door to spread the Gospel and save a man's soul, marriage, or a man's life, let's all be there to answer the Lord's call."

William snickered. "I may not be the best fella for that."

Morton waved a hand towards William, "Maybe Felix will start praying for the Lord to accept him into heaven, just so that he doesn't have to listen to you for eternity."

William's brow lowered thoughtfully. "Do you think that would count as me saving someone? If so, I'll have more treasures in heaven than I think because I've been told to go to hell a thousand times at least." He laughed.

Chapter 28

Since they had been taken to the cabin, Gabriel Smith had heard steam-powered paddlewheel boats passing by the cabin. But this steam engine was different; the sputtering thud drew closer and seemed to echo in the forest around the cabin as it pulled him from his dreary dream that was quickly forgotten as his eyes opened. The surreal realization that the boat came to rest near the riverbank sent a chill down his spine.

He shook Evan awake while he listened to the curly black-haired man that watched over them speak to someone outside the cabin. Gabriel spoke urgently as he leaned over his adopted brother, "Evan, wake up. I think we're being moved," Gabriel said anxiously.

"Hmm? To where?" Evan asked, sitting up on the bed.

"I don't know."

Howard Nicol opened the door and glanced

back at someone outside talking to him while holding a clear bottle in his hand. Gabriel could see it was dark out except for the lantern Howard had placed outside the cabin to mark its location in the darkness. Howard was followed inside by the big man with short brown hair wearing a blue suit and a derby hat. Pan, the little Chinese man, entered the cabin as well.

Howard pulled the cork from a clear bottle filled with what appeared to be water. "Drink half of that and then give the other half to him."

Gabriel's heart beat rapidly as an overwhelming sense of dread filled him. He shook his head. "No," he sputtered. "I...I won't do it."

Tony Hurner took the bottle from Howard. "Get the funnel." He turned his attention to Gabriel while Howard left the cabin. "Listen, little Bannister, I don't care if you want to drink it or not; you will. I'll see to that."

"What are you going to do to us?" Gabriel's dry throat squeaked out with a frightened tremble.

"You're going on a trip. You'll enjoy it, and someday, you'll thank me for it."

"No, I won't! I have a little brother and sisters. Please, let us go. It's not too late to let us go," Gabriel pleaded, barely able to keep his heavy breathing and racing heart from breaking down and bawling from the panic that seized him.

Tony gave a slight wave. "Pan."

Pan lunged at Gabriel and expertly slithered his arms and legs around Gabriel's with the efficiency of a constricting snake. He pulled Gabriel's arms and legs back as far as the chains allowed while bowing his body outwards to limit Gabriel's mobility significantly. Gabriel tried to slam his head backward to headbutt Pan but found no target to connect with.

Howard returned to the cabin with an eight-inch metal funnel. He grinned with a slight chuckle to see Gabriel stretched out and helpless; the anguish on the young man's expression as he wept, trying to fight to break free, was a pleasing sight for Howard. "Mind if I pour it? I owe him one."

Tony handed the bottle to Howard and took the funnel. Tony quickly grabbed Gabriel's hair and jerked his head back, forcing his mouth open, saying, "If you don't want to drink it willingly, we'll pour it down your throat!"

Tony shoved the funnel into Gabriel's mouth, causing him to gag until the funnel was pushed further down his throat. Howard poured half of the bottle of laced water down Gabriel's throat before the funnel was pulled out.

Gabriel wanted to roll to his side and stick his finger down his throat, but Pan held him securely as the other two men unshackled his wrists and resecured them behind Gabriel's back before Pan let him go. Once free, Gabriel rolled to his side and wept.

Howard held the bottle out towards Evan, who had sat silently watching with a trembling lip and watery eyes. "Drink the rest, or we'll do the same to you." Evan's hands shook noticeably as he took the bottle and drank the remainder of the water obediently through intermittent gasps of air and submissive guttural sobs.

Tony explained, "There's enough morphine in that bottle to knock both of you out for several hours. When you wake up, you'll be in your new home, the *Everson Solstice,* out on the open Pacific Ocean. If you don't wake up because we gave you too much, well, then you'll be crab food. We're already paid, so we don't care either way. One thing is for sure, though, if you do wake up, you'll be true sailors by the time you reach Africa, and you may learn to love it." Tony smiled. "You two won't be back home for at least two years, if at all."

"I can't swim," Evan blubbered.

Gabriel sat up quickly and shouted, "I'm only seventeen. You can't do this to me. Please, let us go," he pleaded through his frightened tears.

Howard snickered and knelt. He lifted Gabriel's chin to look into his tear-stricken, frightened eyes. "You're not so tough now, are you? Listen, I could let you go if I wanted to, but I don't care about your family or you. I'll say hello to your father tomorrow night when we take him out for dinner to celebrate you going to sea. He won't know it, but the money buying his meal will be from my share of selling you." Howard smiled as he watched the torment on Gabriel's expression.

Gabriel could feel himself beginning to drift toward sleep. "You won't...get..." He fell back unconscious.

In the darkness of the earliest morning, the two boys were hoisted aboard the *Everson Solstice,* carried into the loaded hull, and set on hundred-pound burlap bags filled with wheat bound for Port Lagos in West Africa. Once aboard the three-mast, one hundred-and-eighty-foot, iron-hulled schooner, the tugboat tied onto the vessel and towed the *Everson Solstice* down the Willamette and into the Columbia River for its hundred-and-thirteen-mile journey to the Pacific Ocean.

***

Gabriel woke up feeling sick to his stomach, confused, and quickly afraid, as he was surrounded by pitch-black without a glimmer of light. He could feel the burlap with his fingers and the scent of the wheat that filled the bags that were as solid as bricks. The shackles on his wrists and ankles were gone, leaving him free to move around, but there was nowhere to go without some light to guide him through the darkness. His dry and sore throat were reminders of being forced to drink the tainted water laced with morphine.

With a gasp of breath, he realized he was no longer in the cabin or the brick cell but in the hull of a ship that lightly swayed with the water. The momentary confusion about where he was became apparent as he realized he was a prisoner on a ship.

Gabriel cried out, "No! No! No! Lord Jesus, please, no!" He tried to swallow, but his throat hurt from being scratched by the funnel. "Jesus, Lord, my Lord, no. Evan!" He pushed his body across the tightly stacked bags surrounding him, shouting,

"Evan! Evan, are you here?" He was quickly alarmed that they had been separated. "Evan!"

"Gabe?" Evan's shaken voice came from the darkness. "Gabriel, where are you?"

"I'm here," Gabriel said with relief. At least he wasn't alone in the deep darkness.

"Where are we?" Evan shouted and then added with a subdued voice, "I'm not feeling good."

"I...I don't know."

"We're moving!" Evan exclaimed loudly. "Are we on a boat? We *are* on a boat!" Evan began to blubber, "We're never going home! He said we're never going home. Gabriel, you promised God would help us! You promised!"

A cold hollowness swept through Gabriel. The hope of being rescued by Matt Bannister, like his mother was from the grip of Donovan Moskin and John Birch two years before, constantly renewed itself in Gabriel's mind. He had faith that his father would rescue him. Granted, there was no snow to follow the tracks or landmarks to mark the cabin by the lake, but Gabriel had prayed continuously that the Lord would guide Matt to them. He believed the Lord would. Now in the cargo hull of a ship on the Pacific Ocean where no help could be found, Gabriel realized his prayers had not penetrated the brick walls of his underground cell or the log walls of the cabin. He knew God heard every prayer, but not every prayer was answered the way that was wanted. His Grandfather, the Reverend Abraham Ash, used to say, "Every prayer is answered in one of three ways—yes, no, or wait."

It was a bitter taste to swallow, more bitter than morphine-laced water, to realize God's answer was *no*. Gabriel wasn't going back home to Willow Falls.

The horror of realizing that he was leaving the country and would be at sea for months to years if he survived at all, brought a wave of anxiety heightened by the frightening darkness surrounding him like a buried casket. He would not go home to see his loving parents or younger siblings. He would not be going back to see Tiffany Foster, nor would she ever know how important she was to him. Tiffany would never know; she would always be his first love.

Now in the darkness, with his future as dark and unknown as the room he was in, it was becoming a nightmarish reality that he may never see any of them again. His family would never know if he was alive or dead. Gabriel's chest heaved with a swell of emotion. He couldn't speak as an invisible bulge about the size of an egg felt caught in his throat, choking any attempt to speak.

"Gabriel?" Evan questioned as he shuffled over the wheat and suddenly dropped to the wood-beamed floor. "Ouch! You can't see anything!" he yelled angrily. "I just fell!"

"Are you okay?" Gabriel choked out.

"I landed on my elbow on the floor," he said painfully while rubbing his elbow. "Gabriel, we're on a boat."

"I know."

"What are we going to do?" Evan began to weep.

"I don't know," Gabriel's voice quivered as much

as Evan's.

Evan's voice rose, "I can't stand the darkness! I can't see anything. What's going to happen to us, Gabriel? Where are we going?"

"Evan—"

"What's going to happen to us, Gabriel? When can we go home? I want to go home!" he yelled, breaking emotionally into loud sobbing.

"I want to go home too," Gabriel choked out.

A door squeaked open, and a light shined into the crowded hull from the top of a steep stairway where a man holding a lantern stepped down the stairs and took a few steps towards them. The man was in his fifties with a gray beard and shoulder-length yellow hair that appeared windblown, tangled, and not brushed in months. He looked mean, intimidating, and heartless as he shined the light on the two boys. He spoke in a deep and commanding voice, "You two men signed on with the *Everson Solstice*. This is my ship, and you'll do as I say. My name is Captain Horace Smithrud. I'm the Master of this ship, and you will call me *captain* at all times. Which one of you is Evan Gray?"

"Me," Evan said through a squeak of a voice.

The captain shifted his eyes to Gabriel. "You're Smith?"

Gabriel nodded.

The man shouted abruptly, "Say, 'Yes, Captain!'"

Gabriel, frightened and breathing hard, complied, "Yes, Captain."

Captain Smithrud continued, "As greenhorns, you signed on to do the grub work. That starts now.

Let's get you topside and shown your quarters. I'll show you the galley, where you two will begin peeling potatoes for supper. Afterward, you'll clean the galley and start learning the nautical terms and locations of the ship. This is your home, and you will do as you are ordered. Any questions?"

"Where are we?" Evan asked skittishly. He wiped his tears away.

The captain glared at him with a perplexed expression. His tone was sharp, "Are you stupid? I just told you. You signed on with the *Everson Solstice*."

"We didn't sign on to anything. We were kidnapped," Gabriel explained. "You have to let us off the boat."

Captain Smithrud stepped forward and shined the lantern's light in Gabriel's face. "I have Articles of Agreement signed by both of you stating you willingly and knowingly signed on with this passage to Port Lagos, Africa. Once we reach port, you can collect your pay and disembark if you choose, or I can terminate any agreement and leave you there if you don't carry your weight. You signed your names to a legal document, and now you both belong to me. You can work or jump ship. Those are the only options you have."

"Jump where?" Evan asked without thinking about it.

"Overboard!" Captain Smithrud shouted impatiently. "For crying out loud, boy, you are as dense as artic ice, aren't you? Well, I'll tell you what, this might be a long journey for you because if you refuse to hold up your part of the deal, you will be beaten black and blue, flogged with the cat-o'-nine-tails or keel hauled. I promise you one thing: you will work, or your life will become so hellish you'll choose to jump ship. And if you can't do the work, I'll toss you overboard myself. I won't waste food and water on dead weight. Is that clear?"

"Yes, sir."

Captain Smithrud leaned over Evan and shouted, "Yes, Captain!"

"Yes, Captain," both boys repeated.

He spoke in a calmer tone, "Good. We'll be crossing the Columbia Bar before long. Come topside for the last look of land you'll see for quite a long time."

They ascended a steep staircase to the lower deck, then another set to the upper deck, and finally a third set to the top deck. The late afternoon sunshine stung their eyes as they walked out onto the open top deck of the *Everson Solstice*. The Willamette Valley had been in the nineties, but the Oregon Coast temperatures hovered in the mid to high sixties despite the same blue skies that heated the rest of Oregon.

Gabriel shivered in the cold breeze as he looked out over the blue water of the Columbia River at the green forested mountains that hugged the river's bank. He was amazed to see how wide the Columbia River had become. It was broader than he imagined a river could ever be. The train coming west had paralleled the Columbia River from Walla Walla to Portland, and it was the widest river Gabriel had ever seen, but the mouth of the Columbia

River had become so vast he would have thought it was part of the ocean.

Captain Smithrud pointed at a small city built on piers stretching out over the mudflats of the river's outgoing tide. There were tall ships anchored around a port much smaller than Portland's. "That is Astoria. The last civilized place you boys will see before landing in Argentina to refill our water and food supply for the journey around the cape and across the Atlantic."

Gabriel's head turned to gaze at the captain and then back at the city of Astoria. Help was only that far away, but the distance between the ship and shore was still quite vast.

Captain Smithrud's deep voice discouraged any foolish notions, "You might think about diving in to escape, but the current is treacherous, and the undertow will grab you before our ropes will. The river is four miles wide here, and I doubt either of you pups could swim two miles to shore in either direction. Sea Lions and seals follow the salmon up this river, bringing in the sharks. If the current doesn't kill you, the sharks will, and if the sharks don't, the water's temperature surely will. The current will take you out to sea, sure as hell. So now is your chance to jump in if you want to." He chuckled as the two boys helplessly stared at the city of Astoria as they passed by with the fast-moving tide.

The current was swift as it rolled straight toward the open sea a few miles away. Gabriel could swim, but he wasn't that good of a swimmer. The only places he'd ever swam were the small swimming hole along Pearl Creek and rarely the Modoc River. The Columbia River was the largest body of water he had ever seen, but it was swift, powerful, and wild. To consider jumping into the river would be suicide.

Evan answered Captain Smithrud, "I can't swim."

"Then you better work your ass off and make me happy," the captain replied.

Peter Swan took notice of the two boys and approached to introduce himself. "Captain, are we going to weigh anchor and wait for a river pilot to cross the bar?" The Columbia River Bar was one of America's most hazardous and deadly bar crossings. As such, Astoria had river pilots who navigated every ship in and out of the Columbia River.

Captain Smithrud wrinkled his nose distastefully. "No. I watched a pilot board the English schooner. Dirk is on the helm and trailing his tail. I don't need to pay for a pilot; we'll follow him out. We'll be fine."

Peter nodded to the two young men. "I thought I met all the crew."

"Oh, we found a couple of stowaways that joined us. Gabriel, Evan, this is Peter."

Peter recognized the frightened expressions on the two boys' faces immediately. He had seen it before on other ships fresh from leaving ports where men had been shanghaied. He knew exactly who the two teens were and which one was Matt Bannister's son. "Boys," he said as he shook their hands. "Captain, I could show them around if you'd like?"

The captain knew following a ship across the bar navigated by a river pilot wasn't the safest gamble, but it was one he was willing to take to save a few dollars. He was needed at the helm to protect his cargo and ship through the most dangerous part of the river. Captain Smithrud quickly obliged Peter's offer to show the greenhorns around the ship.

Peter gathered the two teens at the rail and spoke softly, "You're Matt Bannister's son, right?"

Gabriel nodded with surprise. "Yes."

"He's been looking for you. I was just on the bow and saw a sternwheeler coming in against the tide; that will slow it down quite a bit. The passengers are out on the deck, which is perfect. Listen to me. The river is too wide, cold, and fast to swim across, but if you dive in and start swimming when I say, those passengers will see you and throw you a lifeline. It's a risky and dangerous gamble, but you won't see your Pa and family again for years if you don't take it. You don't have much time to choose." He peered forward over the rail to gauge the incoming steam-powered sternwheeler's distance and speed.

"I can't swim," Evan said with a quivering lip as his fate was sealed upon the *Everson Solstice.*

"Can you?" Peter asked Gabriel anxiously.

Gabriel nodded with a tormented expression as he looked at Evan. "But I can't leave Evan."

Peter sputtered, "Your father has been looking for you two. If you don't go, your family will never know what happened to you. And this is your only chance; you're doomed once that boat passes us."

Evan grabbed Gabriel's bicep. "Gabe, you have to go. Mom and Dad, the kids, they need you. They don't need me, but they do you. Go. I'll be okay."

Peter put a protective hand on Evan's shoulder and said, "I'll watch over him, I promise. I'll treat him like a little brother and get him back to you someday. You have my word; I won't leave him. If you're going to go, you need to go *now*."

Gabriel was terrified as he stared at the raging waters that carried the ship toward the western horizon. The only places he had ever swam, didn't have a current and were not much wider than the ship he was on. The four-mile width of the Columbia River was overwhelmingly terrifying to a boy who swam in a creek.

Peter spoke pointedly, "Run and dive overboard and keep swimming as hard as you can towards the shore. Someone on that sternwheeler will see you. Now, Go!"

Gabriel was torn. Evan was not just an adopted part of his family; he was also Gabriel's best friend. He didn't want to leave Evan behind or drown in the turbulent water below them. He was too scared to make the dive overboard and felt the pressure building as time passed, allowing the two vessels to draw closer together. He looked at Evan with frightened tears filling his eyes. "I don't want to leave you here."

"Quit being stupid! Tell Mom and everyone I love them. Now go, Gabriel. Now!" Evan shouted.

Gabriel gasped. "I love you, brother."

"I'll be back," Evan said with a forced smile,

quivering lips, and a sniffle.

Gabriel knew there would be no turning back once he made the dive off the ship into the river. There would be no mercy between the chance of rescue and certain death. His hands shook, and his heart pounded so hard that the pounding in his ears began to block out the sound of Peter ordering him to jump. "Evan, I don't feel right leaving you."

"Go!" Evan yelled angrily.

With a deep groan, Gabriel ran forward and dove over the rail. Not knowing how to dive from a higher elevation than a three-foot bank back at home, Gabriel's lower body came over his head, doing a flip in the air, and fell ten feet to the water below, landing abruptly on his back. The jarring of the landing was hard enough, but the water's cold temperature took his breath away while the swift current grabbed him with the force of a galloping horse running into him, pushing Gabriel towards the sea at an alarming rate.

"Swim!" he heard Evan yell.

Gabriel began to swim away from the *Everson Solstice* towards the approaching passenger ship's pathway. He glanced back briefly to see Evan at the rail, watching him as the vessel moved further away. Twisting his head from left to right as he swam, Gabriel could taste a hint of salt in the water as he pulled his face out of the water to take a breath. He had no time to wonder how far he had gotten, but it felt like he wasn't getting anywhere being surrounded by miles of water. He swam across an outgoing tide and knew he was going further down the river than he was across it.

He could hear the large steam-powered stern-wheeler drawing closer. The fear of missing it and being stuck in the middle of the river kept him swimming harder, even though he was quickly tiring and running out of energy. Rhythmically, his arms rowed, one after the other, while his feet kicked in the water while twisting his neck back and forth to inhale and exhale in a race to get near enough to be rescued.

The water was as cold as an early spring dive into Pearl Creek after a harsh winter. His skin was turning red with the cold, and his chest was burning from the exertion he was putting forth, as his body required more oxygen to keep up with the energy he was using. He could dig fence post holes all day, but swimming was wearing him out fast.

"Man overboard!" Peter yelled as loud as he could towards the steam-powered passenger paddle-wheeler nearing Astoria. He pointed where Gabriel fought to keep swimming. Several passengers on the ocean-going sternwheeler began to point and holler at the crew members on the ship. Peter's cry had caught the attention of all hands on the *Everson Solstice* too.

The distance between the sternwheeler and the *Everson Solstice* was greater than it appeared, and Gabriel prayed desperately to the Lord to give him the strength to keep swimming fast enough to meet the approaching boat in time to be saved.

He could hear the cries of the passengers alertly wanting to reach him and the faint yells of Evan and Peter to keep swimming.

The sternwheeler slowed and steered towards Gabriel to draw nearer to him. A crewman threw a life buoy connected to a rope for Gabriel to grab. The life ring didn't reach him, and the current swept it away before Gabriel could get it. Gabriel stopped swimming and bobbed in the water as the large sternwheeler with a deck of people slowly passed him. The people called to him and others for a life preserver to be thrown and lower a life-boat. Their concern for him was clearly evident, but Gabriel was exhausted. If the ship passed by, he would surely drown as his strength was failing fast.

The crewman who had thrown the life ring yanked on the rope to pull it back to him as fast as he could. Another crewman forced himself in front of the curious passengers at the stern, tossed a life ring upriver from Gabriel, and yelled for him to swim to it as it approached him. With an urgent prayer, Gabriel swam towards the life ring and reached an arm through the ring just as it passed by him. He clung to the life ring like a frightened child while the crowd on board erupted in applause. Gabriel held on while the crew members pulled the rope drawing closer to the ship, and pulled him out of the cold water.

Gabriel was too exhausted to speak as the men pulled him to safety on the steel deck. He ignored their questions and wept as he watched the *Everson Solstice* drift with the tide toward the sea.

"Goodbye, Evan," he said quietly through his tears.

He was taken to the warmth of a room and wrapped with a wool blanket to warm his chilled body. He was given a cup of coffee, and shortly, the captain of the passenger liner entered the quiet room away from the curious passengers.

The captain sat across a table from Gabriel and looked at the young man curiously as if studying him. "Hello, Gabriel. You're a very blessed young man or the luckiest fool I've ever seen. First Mate Jackson tells me that you dove off that schooner intentionally. Is that true?"

Gabriel nodded. "Yes, sir."

"Why? I suppose it wasn't a suicide attempt."

"No, sir. My brother and I were kidnapped. He can't swim; he's still on the boat," he said emotionally.

"Shanghaied?" the captain questioned.

Gabriel nodded.

"Oh boy," the captain sighed. "I'm Captain Luke Hawman, and this is my vessel, *The Reverence Nine*. We're not scheduled to dock in Astoria until our return trip to San Francisco, but we are anchoring for a little while to take the river pilot back to shore. If you need to go ashore to notify the Astoria Police, I can arrange for him to take you."

Gabriel shook his head. "No. My father is in Portland."

Captain Hawman narrowed his brow. "We'll be in Portland late tonight."

Gabriel's eyes widened. "Can I go to Portland with you?"

Captain Hawman smiled empathetically. "I

think we can handle one more passenger. I'll tell you what, how about we get you into some dry clothes, something to eat, and then you can meet me in the wheelhouse to tell me what happened."

"When will we be in Portland?"

"Tonight, between ten and eleven. Thereabouts."

Gabriel was worried. "When we get to Portland, can you accompany me to my grandfather's house? I don't want the men that took me to see me walking alone."

"Don't you think you should go to the police?"

"My father is Matt Bannister, a U.S. Marshal, and he's been looking for me."

The captain's brow raised. "Yeah, I'll take you. I like to meet him myself."

Chapter 29

Felix Rathkey sat in his daughter Gretchen's hospital room, heartbroken to see his baby girl whimpering in pain. Her arm had been so severely damaged that the artery had been severed in several places. Gretchen would have bled to death if it weren't for the wisdom of the carpenters that came to her rescue and tied a tourniquet around her bicep. Her arm was amputated at the shoulder, and even with the help of morphine, she was still in great pain. Her other shoulder, arm, and leg had been bitten and needed a few sutures, but a wide gash that took forty-nine stitches to close promised to deform her angelic face with a large scar from her eye to her chin. Gretchen slept with the help of the painkiller, but the doctor was concerned about the risk of rabies and infection. Felix's only daughter was not out of danger, and it weighed heavily upon his heart.

His bottom lip was stuck outward, and his eyes were moist. The fun, excitement, and gambling of dog fights were a thrill that Felix enjoyed. He had paid a lot of money to purchase a breed of fighting dog with a fierce reputation and a nature for being aggressive, fearless, yet loyal to the owner. His pit bull had been sired by a well-known champion in the dog fighting circles back east. Felix took a train to Philadelphia and brought the pup home to raise with the intent of becoming a champion he could fight up and down the west coast. Turk had the right temperament, endurance, ferocity, strength, and power in one impressive body that made him the undefeated local champion and earned Felix some good money. Turk was naturally aggressive and would attack another dog with murderous ferocity, but he was never aggressive toward Felix or any family member, including Gretchen.

Nora was not an animal lover and didn't want any pets, and she certainly never wanted the fighting dogs near her home because she feared someone would get bit eventually. Now Gretchen wasn't bit; she was mauled and fighting for her life.

Felix couldn't understand why Turk would attack Gretchen with the intent to kill her like one of the dogs he was pitted against. The doctor feared Turk may have gone mad from contracting rabies from an undiagnosed rabid dog it fought. To add more horror upon a horrific situation, Felix could not answer the doctor's question with any surety. The threat of rabies raised Felix and Nora's anxiety level dramatically in fear for their daughter's life. The high likeliness of just one of Gretchen's many bite wounds becoming infected and turning gangrene was a fearful thing. Now the doctor brought up the possibility that Gretchen and Nora's lives could be lost to the wretched disease of rabies. Felix had never considered the risk of fighting a rabid dog, but if Turk did go mad from it, the lives of his wife and daughter were solely in the Lord's hands because there was no cure for rabies.

Nora Rathkey was facing the most challenging moment of her life, yet she had no desire to sit beside her husband. She sat in a chair next to the bed holding Gretchen's hand. Her little hand was scratched and had puncture wounds from a bite, but she didn't need stitches. Nora had her own injuries, which were relatively minor compared to her daughter's. Nora had not left Gretchen's side or stopped praying for her little girl.

Nora smiled like only a broken mother could as she stroked her little girl's soft brown hair affectionately. "She'll have to learn to brush her teeth, brush her hair, and write with her left hand now," Nora mused to herself with a soft voice.

Felix answered gently, "She's smart. She'll accomplish that quickly."

Nora's eyes hardened at the sound of his voice; she glared at her husband. "This is your fault! I told you I didn't want those dogs kept at the house," she kept her voice low so her resentment wouldn't travel through the hospital, but the hostility was as thick as cold honey.

Felix closed his eyes with a heavy sigh. "So, you've said many times now. I'll take the blame. You're right…" He didn't know what else to say that he hadn't already said. She was right, but how many times could a man say he never thought it would happen? It was a tragedy that he never expected.

"You and your stupid dog fights! If you had listened to me, this never would have happened. I told you!" Her watery eyes glared at him accusingly. "You make enough money; I don't understand why you insist on fighting dogs. Never again, Felix! And if all those dogs aren't moved away from my house, I'll hire those good men who saved your daughter to kill all your dogs. I'm not making empty threats. Do you hear me?"

Felix was quickly aggravated. "You just mind your house. Turk is gone; the others are fine."

She spoke plainly, "Don't be surprised if they're all dead tomorrow. I'll put poison in their food myself if need be."

"Oh, yeah?" Felix asked irritably. "If one of those pups is hurt, I'll cut down all of your prized rose bushes and every other bush around the house," he countered.

Her eyes widened in a fury. She shouted, "I don't care about rose bushes. I care about my child!"

Felix stood to shout back at Nora, but his attention went to an unexpected knock on the already-opened door. His contorted, angry expression faded as he watched Matt Bannister enter the room quietly, carrying a ceramic pot with a lily plant with pink flowers in full bloom and a soft fabric doll with yellow yarn hair in a blue dress.

"Matt...what...what are you doing here?" Felix stuttered with surprise.

Matt spoke, "I heard about your daughter and wanted to offer my best wishes for her recovery and give her this pretty plant and a doll to snuggle

with. I am so sorry to hear what happened to her."
His eyes went to Gretchen sleeping on the bed, and
his heart immediately broke to see her bandaged
face and a missing arm.

"Thank you," Felix said, taking the potted plant
and doll.

Nora noticing the silver badge on his left lapel,
asked, "Who are you?" Her sharp and rude tone
revealed her hostility towards her husband.

Matt pulled his eyes from Gretchen to speak to
Nora, "I'm Matt Bannister, Ma'am. I just wanted to
stop by and offer my best wishes and prayers for
her recovery. I heard the dog attack was bad; I just
didn't realize it was *that* bad." His sincerity was
genuine as his eyes went back to Gretchen.

Nora took a deep breath. "For her, it is going
to be an entire life transformation. She liked to
draw pictures and paint them. Now, she'll have to
learn how to do that with her left hand. But I think
looking at herself in the mirror every day will be
the hardest part of her transformation." Nora's lip
quivered as her eyes filled with deep wells of fresh
tears. She wiped the tears away and asked pointedly, "Are you on my..." She paused as a quick twitch
of a snarl flexed her lip, repulsed to call him her
husband. "Felix's payroll too?"

Felix spoke firmly, "That's enough, Nora."

"No, Ma'am, I am not. It's just the opposite. My
son went missing, along with his stepbrother Evan
and my stepbrother Bob Mears. Felix is one of the
last people to have seen Bob, and I had some questions for him; that's how we met."

Nora's hardened expression softened. "Did you

find your son?"

Matt shook his head as his lips tightened. "Not yet."

"I'll pray that you do and that they are okay. I couldn't imagine if my daughter went missing." She turned her head toward Gretchen and sniffled as her lip twitched. "This is far too heartbreaking enough."

"I can imagine so," Matt said. "Well, I just wanted to stop by and let you know I'll be praying for her and say I'm sorry to hear about such a tragedy."

"Thank you. And I apologize for being rude, Mister Bannister. I'm normally not," Nora explained.

Matt pointed at Gretchen. "You have a lot to deal with. I understand."

"If you'd like, you could go to my house and use that gun to kill all my husband's dogs. I would appreciate it," Nora said plainly with a finger directing his attention to his sidearm.

"Nora, stop it," Felix argued. "Thanks for coming by, Marshal, but now isn't a good time."

Matt ignored Felix. He nodded towards Gretchen. "I would have loved to kill the dog that did that to her. But I can't go do that for you."

***

Tony Hurner was tired after a short night of sleep. He yawned as he, Howard Nicol, and Morton sat at a table in a restaurant, eating a piece of pie with a needed cup of coffee. "I just didn't sleep well last night," he explained.

"I slept like a baby. I'm getting used to that hotel's bed," Morton offered.

"I'm glad to hear it," Tony said, followed by another yawn. "Oh, my word. I need a nap."

"Me too," Howard yawned. "You gotta stop yawning, Tony."

"I'm trying," Tony agreed. "Let's go to the hospital and give little Gretchen our love. We should stop by a tavern and bring a bottle with us. I'm sure Felix and maybe even Nora could use a drink. That dog was always mean. I wish I could say I was surprised to hear it bit someone, but I'm not. Once a dog gets a taste of blood and likes it, I don't think it stops; it just kills."

Howard finished his coffee. "Good old Turk; I won a good amount of money on him. It's sad about Gretchen, though. I agree; let's get a bottle and maybe some flowers for Nora. I'm sure she's devastated."

They left the table and approached the counter to pay. In front of them, a lady with light brown hair had her back turned to them while ordering a single piece of frosted cake with a candle on it. She paid the cashier and turned around, carrying the cake with a lit candle on a saucer. She smiled at Tony, "Excuse me." The excitement on her face transformed into horror when she made eye contact with Morton. The saucer fell from her fingers and shattered on the floor as she stepped back against the counter in terror, beginning to shake while tears welled in her eyes. "Morton," she gasped.

Surprised, Morton quipped, "Rachel?" It was

Rachel Sperry, his brother Alan's ex-wife, who had disappeared with their daughters after Alan went to prison.

She was frozen in place, staring at him, willing herself to run, but was too afraid to move. The life she had built with her daughters was over now that Morton had found her, and there was nothing she could do about it except shake and suffocate with her tightening throat.

"Excuse me," Morton said abruptly to his friends and roughly grabbed Rachel by the arm. She screamed and began sobbing as he quickly pulled her out of the restaurant and dragged her down the sidewalk to speak privately. Rachel wept and went along with him in total surrender, terrified to make a stand or fight against him. She wailed bitterly.

Morton reached the restaurant's corner, shoved her back against the wall, and glared into her downcast eyes. He put his face close to hers and sneered, "Look at me! I'm not here for you, Rachel. Look at me!" He demanded with a slight slap to her face. She cried out, terrified, and began to lose control of her bladder, urinating on herself as her body trembled. Morton's cold green eyes were murderous as he warned with a cold sneer, "Don't tell anyone that you saw me or say my name. If anyone asks you, I'm Morton *Myers*. If anyone hears differently, I *will* come after you. Understood?"

Tears streamed down her cheeks, and her frozen body was as stiff as a board, with her elbows tight against her sides and arms across her breast. She nodded quickly and squeaked out, "Yes."

"What is my last name?"

"M...Myers."

He exhaled with a nod. "You didn't see me, Rachel, and I didn't see you. Agreed?"

She nodded as her neck slunk into her shoulders like a frightened child about to be whipped.

"Goodbye," he said and left her at the corner as she slid down the wall to a sitting position, bawling.

Howard and Tony were waiting on the sidewalk watching. Howard motioned towards Rachel. "Who's that? I thought you didn't know anyone around here?"

Morton cast a deadly scowl toward Rachel. "She's my former sister-in-law. I had to ensure she didn't tell anyone who I am." He explained, "I told you I had an outlaw gang, and Matt Bannister is in town. If he finds out who I am, someone will die; him or me."

Tony grinned. "I love it. She pissed herself." He chuckled as Rachel slumped against the wall, still sobbing in a wet puddle on the sidewalk.

Howard asked, "What happened to her husband? She's not bad looking, you know?" Howard was a bachelor.

Morton was troubled by seeing her but answered honestly, "I killed him."

"Your brother?" Tony asked, astounded.

"Yes."

"Do I dare ask why?" Howard questioned.

"We didn't get along," Morton answered.

"You *are* a dangerous man." Tony chuckled. "I'm glad you're on our side."

Morton exhaled to relieve the anxiety he was hiding as they walked around a corner and put her behind them. "She knows what I'm capable of."

"What about her girls? Aren't they your nieces?" Howard asked.

"What girls?"

Tony laughed. "Morton, she was getting a birthday cake for one of her girls. Didn't you see them at their table? I suppose you wouldn't; they were sitting behind you about three tables back. Cute kids. They were about as shocked as we were when you rushed their mother outside."

"I didn't see them," Morton answered softly.

They stopped by a tavern, got a bottle of whiskey and some flowers from a store, and rode a street trolley to the hospital. Tony entered the hospital room with the bottle held up in the air. "We're here to offer our condolences and bring gifts. Flowers for the pretty mama and a stiff drink for the father."

"She's not dead," Nora answered spitefully. "Who are you?" she asked Morton. She was exhausted, worried, and in no mood for her husband and his friends.

"Morton Myers, Miss. I'm sorry about what happened to your daughter."

Nora nodded her thanks with tight uninterested lips. "Where is Beth, Tony?"

Tony opened the bottle and handed it to Felix. "Planning what to make for dinner, I imagine," he answered before speaking to Felix, "Drink up. It will make you feel better."

Felix stared at Nora with a combination of a

warning, weakened significantly by a pleading in his eyes for her not to mention catching him in bed with Beth the day before.

"Drink!" Tony urged.

Felix offered a troubled attempt at a smile and took a long drink. "Thanks."

Nora's expression was as cold as a winter's night as she stared at Felix bitterly. "You better drink some more, Felix. I'm sure you'll need it when you tell Tony what you must tell him."

Felix nearly choked on the liquor he was swallowing. "Not now," he said with a forced smile to Tony. "This just isn't the right time or place, Nora."

Nora looked around the hospital room and said with a slight smirk lifting the corner of her lips, "Oh, I think the hospital is the perfect place for you to tell him. I won't keep it a secret. You can tell him, or I will."

Felix took another long drink while beads of sweat began forming on his forehead.

"What is it?" Tony asked. "Am I getting a raise?"

"Maybe, if you play it right," Nora quipped. "Howard, why don't you take your friend and leave? We don't want company today, but Felix does have something to tell Tony."

"Nora…" Felix said with a pleading in his tone.

"Now, gentlemen," Nora said firmly, waving towards the door.

When the two men left, closing the door behind them, Nora said, "Tony, you better sit down."

Tony watched Felix take another long drink and realized it probably wasn't good news by the expression on Nora's face and Felix's anxiousness to drink from the bottle. "Better slow down there, boss. By the way you two look, I might want some of that when we're done."

Felix handed him the bottle with a nod. "You might."

"What is this all about? Did I do something wrong?"

"No," Felix answered and paused.

"Tell him, or I will," Nora said pointedly.

Tony was suddenly alarmed and asked frantically, "Don't tell me I left the dog gate open? Is Gretchen being mauled my fault?" he asked with a frantic wave towards Gretchen.

Felix shook his head. "No."

"Thank goodness. That scared me for a minute." He relaxed.

Nora asked mockingly, "Felix, my dear husband, do you not have the spine to tell him?"

Felix cast a resentful glance toward Nora, "Can you leave the room so I can talk to Tony alone?"

"No."

"Nora, it's the least you could do to make this easier."

Nora kissed her girl on the forehead. "Alright. But you better tell him because I'll ensure he knows when I return."

"I'll tell him, just go!" Felix exclaimed with a glare.

Tony smiled uneasily. "What's this about, Felix?"

Felix paced back and forth across the room. "Tony, you know I would never do anything to harm you, and I hope you feel the same for me. I know you are a faithful man to me and everyone else. You're a loyal friend that would do anything for me, and I love you like a brother."

"Are you firing me?" Tony questioned.

Felix shook his head. "No. But you might want to quit when you hear what I have to say."

His brow narrowed with concern. "What is it?"

Felix took a deep breath and sighed. "Tony, Beth has been..." He paused and leaned against the wall. He looked his friend in the eyes and said, "I ran into Beth yesterday when I was going to lunch, and we started talking a little bit, so I asked her to join me. She confided in me that she's been having an affair—"

"Bullcrap," Tony chuckled. "Quit joking around and tell me what you need to say."

"Tony," he paused to take a deep nervous breath. "You told her about my hideaway, didn't you? You must have told her, or maybe Howard did. Tony, she asked me for a key to it so she could meet her lover there in secret, but I said no."

"You're not serious," Tony said in a low, stone-cold voice.

Felix grimaced. "That's not all, Tony. When I said no, Beth propositioned me for a key. If it's not obvious, Nora and I haven't been getting along lately. Beth is just so beautiful that I wasn't strong enough to tell her no. I succumbed to her temptation and committed the sin of adultery with my best friend's wife. I felt bad enough, but then Gretchen was attacked, and William brought Nora to the hideaway, and she caught us. I'm sorry, Tony."

"Bullcrap. Tell me your joking," Tony said warningly.

Felix raised his hands innocently. "In my defense, I don't think any man could resist Beth when she tempts you as she did. Honestly, Tony, Beth wanted a key to the hideaway, and when I refused to give her one, she turned on that seductive charm that I never imagined she had. I couldn't resist her, and I am so sorry."

Tony stared at the floor with his eyes misting just a touch. His chest heaved up and down with his deep breathing as he brewed in the shock that his bride had allowed another man to touch her. Fury rose like a lit fuse towards a stick of dynamite, drawing ever closer to exploding.

"Tony," Felix said softly as he pulled a chair a few feet in front of Tony and sat facing him. "I'm sorry for crossing a line that should never be crossed. I can't believe it happened myself. I mean, you know me better than that. I would never try anything on Beth, not ever. I was shocked that she'd do that. I was absolutely stunned when she said she was having an affair with…well, and then she wanted a key bad enough to proposition me for one. I'm not the most handsome man in town, you know."

Tony's eyes narrowed as he lifted his head to ask, "You took my wife to your hideaway?"

"Not intentionally! No, I told her no at first. I wasn't going to ruin our friendship by giving her a key to continue her affair. But then she started coming onto me with this trade, and it just kind of happened."

"It didn't just happen!" Tony snapped abruptly. "You had a choice!"

"I did. And as I said, I made a terrible mistake. I feel guilty about it like you wouldn't believe." He closed his eyes and sighed. "I won't lie to you, Tony. Beth wanted a key because she was too afraid to meet this fellow at your place because neighbors talk or you might come home. He lives in an apartment, and they can't go there for the same reasons, so they've met in a hotel or a cabin somewhere. Tony, she tempted me, and I gave in. But she was cheating on you before that. And if you don't believe me, you can look for my key; it's a brass key with the letter H stamped on it. Beth seduced me to get my key, and now she has it. She wouldn't have taken it if she wasn't planning to meet her lover. I hate to tell you this stuff, but I can't keep it from you because you're like my brother. We're partners, and I betrayed you." He lowered his head shamefully. "I hope you will forgive me because I know I've done you wrong."

"Who is he?" Tony questioned harshly.

Felix spoke emphatically, "I can't tell you that. All I can tell you is we both know him."

Tony stood slowly. "Howard?"

Felix stood weary of what Tony might do. "Tony, I can't say."

Tony gasped and bit his lower lip in a sneer. "I'm lost for words. Part of me wants to beat your face in, but I really want you to tell me this is all a lie. I'll even say please," he said with a heartbroken smile.

Felix looked his friend in the eyes. "It's all true. Nora caught us. Tony, find that key, and you'll know I'm telling you the truth. She's cheating on you, Tony."

Tony gasped as his knees weakened at the words. He blinked repeatedly to push the moisture from his eyes. "I never imagined she'd do this to me. I just never imagined."

"Me neither. I was shocked to learn Beth is unfaithful, Tony. Now she might deny it or devise an excuse, but the proof is in the key. She wouldn't have it if she didn't want it. Right?"

Tony took a deep breath and squeezed his lips tightly together. "I'm going to go." He paused. "I love your family, Felix. I never expected her to do this to me, especially with you. You're supposed to be my friend, not just a boss. I would love to beat you senseless right now. I really would."

"And deservedly so. There is no excuse for what I did, period."

"There's not," Tony agreed. "But you know, Felix, maybe what Turk did to Gretchen is punishment enough for you. Because for the rest of your life, when you look at your daughter, I hope you remember where you were when your dog attacked her. That's what it costs you."

"Tony, you have no idea how sorry I am."

"Sorry, doesn't fix it!" Tony snapped. "She's my life, Felix! And now it's over."

"As hard as it is to believe, maybe I did you a favor," Felix replied. "Maybe it's better to know now before you raise Howard's, I mean, someone else's child."

"I can't work for you anymore. I quit, Felix."

"You can't quit on me. We're partners. You're my best friend. Tony, take a day or two and think that over. You and me, we could run everything together."

Tony's fist folded and swung around to connect with Felix's jaw sending him to the floor. With a growl in his voice from deep within, Tony hissed, "You're damn lucky I don't shoot you! We're not friends, Felix. Hell no, I won't forgive you! You destroyed my life; now I'll destroy yours." He looked at Gretchen, struggling to open her eyes from being woken up by the shouting. He gasped emotionally. "Or maybe you already did destroy yourself. I love your daughter, Felix; I hope she feels better. But you and I—watch your back!"

Nora heard the commotion and came into the room to see Felix lying on the floor with a bloody lip. She said to Tony, "I see he told you."

Tony pointed at Felix. "Don't forgive him, Nora. My wife isn't the first woman he's taken to your old house. There's been several." Tony left the room quickly.

Nora looked at Felix and smiled slightly. "And all the little piggies went wee, wee, wee, all the way home. So, the truth comes out."

"Hardly," Felix said as he returned to his feet. He pulled a handkerchief from his vest pocket and dabbed his bloody lip as he sat in the chair. He smiled slightly. Confidentiality was everything to Felix. Howard had let it slip out that Bob

Mears wasn't ever returning home to one of Laura Eggers's ladies. That information could ruin them all. Tony would get rid of Howard and forgive his wife. He loved Beth too much not to, and then he would come back to work.

"I was listening through the door," Nora continued bitterly, "I know about your *hideaway.*"

"Mom," the whimpering voice of Gretchen took Nora's attention from her husband. "It hurts, Mama."

Nora's heart melted like wax and filled her eyes with warm tears. "I know, baby. I know. Mommy's here."

***

Tony Hurner was devastated. He sat down in the hallway to weep before going outside, where his friends waited. It broke his spirit to learn that his beloved Beth had been unfaithful. It was hard to believe that a woman loved like a princess and lavished with affection would seek the attention of another man while knowing it would destroy the heart of the only man on earth who loved her in such a profound way. Tony could not believe the people he trusted the most would betray him in such a way; the thought of another man with her infuriated him. He pulled himself together and wiped the moisture from his eyes. He walked out of the hospital into the sunshine, where his two friends were waiting for him.

"What did Felix want?" Howard asked with interest. Perhaps slightly envious if Tony got a raise.

Tony glanced at Howard accusingly. He took a moment to collect his thoughts before answering. "He said you boys could go home and get some rest. We're going fishing tonight. Morton, it's time you get your feet wet. I'll meet you at the hotel around midnight."

"Catfishing?" Morton questioned. "I never liked the taste of catfish myself. I prefer trout or salmon, not bottom fish."

Howard chuckled, but Tony looked annoyed. "Just be ready to go. I'll see you tonight."

Chapter 30

Beth Hurner was devastated to learn the extent of damage the dog mauling had done to sweet little Gretchen. However, shame, guilt, and a heavy dose of fearful anxiety created a wall that forbade her from visiting the hospital. Beth had left Felix's hideaway frantically, afraid that Nora would reveal her act of treason to Tony. Beth had discovered what real panic felt like when Tony came home that evening, but true to Felix's word, Tony knew nothing about what had happened. He was as affectionate, kind, and loving as always.

Beth woke up every morning and could almost count down on her fingers when Tony would swoop her into his arms in a tight embrace. He'd tell her how beautiful she was and reassure her that he loved her as far as the left was from the right. Every morning, he did his best to treat her like a princess waking to a brand-new day. He was attentive, caring, and as loyal as a faithful dog. Many women dreamed their husbands doted over them as Tony did with her. Sometimes, Beth found Tony's constant affection a bit stifling and even annoying, but she wouldn't change it for the world. He was her husband, and she loved him.

Tony was employed by Felix long before Beth married him. Once they married, Felix and Nora began to invite Tony and Beth over for dinner and attend plays at the theater with them, among other social events. They were all friends and had been for a few years now.

That changed about three months before when the body of a Portland Police Officer was found floating under one of the piers. The officer had been murdered with a bullet placed in the back of his head. The murder had outraged the city, and a large reward was offered for any news leading to an arrest.

Felix Rathkey approached Beth with the officer's journal that was found in the river and given to him. It was a leather-bound journal that was of interest to Felix, especially the two or three pages leading up to a late-night meeting at the pier with Tony Hurner the night that the officer was killed. Beth had read the few watermarked pages in the journal, and the words the victim wrote undoubtedly painted a picture that would give Tony a motive and opportunity to murder the policeman. There was no doubt that the officer's journal entry written hours before his death would condemn Tony.

Then, like reaching for a cookie and pulling a snake out of the cookie jar, Felix threatened to turn the journal over to the police and agree to testify against Tony if Beth did not do what he asked. Beth was given a choice between a nauseating proposition that turned her stomach or watching her husband be sentenced to death and hung.

It always made her sick to her stomach, but she preferred to pay the ransom for her husband's freedom than go through life without him. She was often tempted to tell Tony that Felix was blackmailing her, but she could never find the right time to admit that she was unfaithful, even if it was being done for him. Beth always came home and vomited. Felix made her feel dirty, unclean, and filthy. She was ashamed to look in the mirror, and the center of her sunflower paintings took on a darker core while the petals shined bright. Her paintings were very much an image of her—bright and happy for Tony and the world to see, but her core was blackened with shame.

Now that Nora had caught them together, anxiety fluttered like moths, causing her to jump at every sound with the expectation of Tony coming home in a rage. Beth knew Tony's job consisted of collecting money and protecting the attorneys, but she also suspected he hurt people judging by the occasional blood spots on his suits. Beth was no fool; she had come to realize that Tony wasn't just a bodyguard, as she initially believed. After reading the policeman's journal, she knew he was involved in illegal activities and had murdered the police officer and doubted it was his first murder. If Tony had a dangerous side to him, he had never shown a hint of it to her. He was always the most loving and kind man she had ever known. What he did at work, to her knowledge, was collect money and guard the attorney's office. He never spoke to her about anything more.

A cold chill crept up her spine when she heard the front door open as Tony came home earlier than usual. She was slicing apples for a snack and left the kitchen to greet Tony at the door.

"You're home early. Did you miss me that much?" Beth teased while wrapping her arms around him with a kiss. His arms circled her like usual, but he cut the kiss short. She pulled away to notice he gazed into her with a touch of moisture in his eyes. "What's wrong?" she questioned with a nervous swallow that nearly choked her voice away.

Tony's lip twitched emotionally. "I went and saw Gretchen…"

"Oh," she said as a wave of fear larger than the tallest tree in Fairview Park swept over her. "And?"

Tony shook his head slowly as he lowered his arms. "They amputated her arm. She's in bad shape and may not make it. You didn't go see her and Nora?"

"No," she said as her bowels dropped at the news of Gretchen. Tears filled her eyes as guilt heaved a ton of debris onto her spine to carry. "My heart is broken enough without seeing her like that. Maybe I'll go tomorrow." She covered her face emotionally.

"I bet," he said with a stone-cold expression. "Listen, I'm exhausted. I'm going to lie down for a while. Maybe you could wake me in a few hours?"

"Tony? Is everything okay?" A part of her wished he'd yell at her for what she'd done and get the burden of a wall out of the way.

He forced a sad smile. "I'm just tired, and Gretchen...broke my heart."

"Do you want to talk about it?" Beth asked.

He avoided looking at her. "No. I just want to sleep for a while."

"Okay. I love you."

His eyes grew glossy and warm as he watched his precious wife. "I love you more." His lips began to quiver emotionally.

Beth's expression tensed. "Do you want to talk?" Deep down, she knew by his hurt expression that he knew about Felix and her.

He shook his head slowly. "Not right now. I'm going to lie down." He went upstairs to his bedroom and closed the door.

Tony sat on her side of the bed and pulled open the small drawer of her bedstand. He shuffled through her things. Finding nothing out of the ordinary in the drawer, he went to her dresser and searched two drawers before opening the third; under some night dresses, he spotted a brass skeleton key. Tony picked it up, stepped backward, and sat heavily on the bed. He swallowed hard, almost choking on a suddenly dry throat as he turned the key over to see an H stamped into the brass.

Tony covered his mouth to silence his muffled sob. He loved Beth more than he had ever loved anyone and gave his life to her in every way; now, his life was crumbling before his eyes like a nightmare he couldn't wake up from. He had hoped Felix was lying, but everything Felix had told him was true. Beth was having an affair and allowed Felix to touch her for the price of a key to the hideaway.

Fury filled him like fire spreading over pitch-coated kindling, but alongside the rage, fighting for a more significant percentage of him, the brokenness of her betrayal swept his strength away. He rolled to his side on the bed and wept.

A half-hour later, Tony descended the stairs and paused at the front door. "I have to leave. I forgot all about an errand I was supposed to do. How about we go out for dinner tonight? We haven't gone out for dinner in a while."

"I'd like that," she said.

He smiled and gave her a quick kiss. "Dress nice. I love you, Beth. I'll be back soon."

***

Beth had changed her old blue and white house dress into a prettier red dress with a yellow floral design. She put her blonde hair in a lovely bun and wore a wide-brim white hat with a black band. She appeared as beautiful as ever while Tony escorted her from their home towards a trolley to Chinatown.

They entered a single-level building marked by Chinese writing. A large and powerful Chinese man escorted them to a private table behind a series of red curtains with various patterns of lions and mystical creatures on them. Being isolated from the other guests made Beth uneasy, and she asked, "Do they not like Americans? It seems weird our table is separated and hidden from everyone else, don't you think?"

Tony wrinkled his nose with a slight shake of his head. "The Chinese think giving a man and woman some privacy is respectful. If it were me and Howard eating, we'd be out there too, but since you're a lady, we have some privacy so we can eat without all those single Chinese men drooling over you." He forced a smile.

"Oh," Beth said, satisfied with his answer. "Well, the perfume they use is very intense. It smells good but very strong."

He nodded in agreement without saying a word.

Beth could tell Tony was brooding over something, and it scared her. "I got a fantastic bread pudding recipe from Polly's Bakery. I can't wait for you to try it," Beth said with mock excitement. "I'll make it tomorrow with some pork chops and beets. Does that sound good?" she asked to make the quiet dinner more comfortable with some conversation. His silence and lack of enthusiasm were growing uncomfortable.

Tony nodded slowly. "Very good."

"Tony, are you okay? You seem troubled. Is something wrong?" she asked. She tried to remain calm, but her hands shook anyway when she saw the moisture in his troubled eyes.

He sighed. "I didn't lock the kennel door, Beth. Gretchen being mauled is my fault," he lied, explaining his troubled countenance.

"Oh…baby. It's not your fault," she said compassionately, leaving her seat to walk around the small table to hold him in a supportive embrace. A part of her was relieved to hear he was troubled by that and not her betrayal. She kissed the top of his head and pressed him against her lovingly. "Don't blame yourself, sweetheart. It was an accident. Everyone knows you would never do anything to harm that sweet girl."

Tony sniffled as he wrapped his arms around her and began to weep, pulling Beth's body against him.

"It's okay," she soothed. "I'm sure Nora and Felix don't blame you."

He lifted his head at the sound of her voice and gazed into her eyes. He grimaced and clenched his jaw at the sound of her saying Felix's name. "I'm sure you're right. They know I would never do anything to hurt Gretchen."

"Hello, My name is Pan. I brought you soup to start and a glass of wine. Please enjoy your soup while we prepare your meal," Pan Ching said as he delivered two bowls of soup and two glasses of wine on a tray. He was friendly and spoke English well enough to explain to Beth what was available for dinner and take their order. He was pleasant, friendly, and a joyful host to have them in the restaurant. Pan nudged Beth's arm as he laughed with her about her hesitation to try the fish soup, "You're silly. Finish your soup, and I'll refill your wine glass."

Thirty minutes and two glasses of wine later,

Beth leaned her head over the table to gaze at Tony. "I'm...not feeling well," she said softly.

Tony checked his pocket watch. "I'm not feeling too good either."

"You're not? Maybe it was the soup," she suggested as she blinked her eyes to focus on Tony.

"Or the wine." He reached into his pocket and held the key for Beth to see. His expression turned to stone. "I found the key. You shouldn't have cheated on me, Beth. I won't raise my voice right now, but when you wake up, we'll chat."

"I didn't...I'm...I..." Beth's eyes closed as her body collapsed onto the table's edge and slumped down to the floor with a muffled thud.

Tony rubbed his face with a troubled expression. "I never thought it would come to this, Beth," Tony said with more heartache torturing his soul than he had ever known. He had Pan give her enough morphine, according to her weight, to put her out for about six hours. It was just after seven in the evening, and he had several hours to wait before sunset and the darkest hours of the night.

Pan Ching and the big man, Bolin Zhao, came through the heavy curtain, grabbed Beth, and carried her into the back of the restaurant, where they tied her feet and hands together before placing her in a simple pine coffin. The coffin had papers tacked onto it written in Chinese and painted on the sides in English were the words: *Human Remains...ship to Shanghai, China.* Tony had no idea what the Chinese writing said; he just instructed Pan to make it look official so that no police officers would question what the coffin contained. No police officer would spend a moment's thought on two non-English-speaking Chinese men hauling a deceased Chinaman across town to be sent home for burial.

Finding the key proved that Beth pushed herself onto Felix like a starving prostitute without the decency to even ask for money for her efforts, just a key for more privacy to sneak around. It made Tony wonder how many men in Portland who smiled at him on the street did so because they had relations with Beth, too. The idea of it drove him crazy. In one day, Tony's wonderful life had been changed; it was collapsing before his eyes.

Chapter 31

Darkness had fallen over the west coast when the sea-going sternwheeler The *Reverence Nine* berthed alongside the well-lit pier of the R.L. Lattimore Sternwheeler Terminal. Captain Luke Hawman was never comfortable allowing the passengers to go ashore when arriving late at night in Portland, Astoria, and San Francisco; the three cities that the *Reverence Nine* routinely traveled to and from. The wharves of all three towns were known for their dangers, and Captain Hawman strongly encouraged the passengers to wait until the morning to go ashore. However, there were always the anxious ones who couldn't wait and took fate into their own hands as they left the ship.

Gabriel was nervous, perhaps a little paranoid, about being spotted by the men that had taken him. He feared they would take him again or kill him on the spot to protect themselves. He stared out over the pier looking for any of the men that had held him captive but didn't see anyone that looked familiar in the available light. Even with the reassurance of being in the presence of Captain Hawman and several of his crewmen, Gabriel was afraid to walk from the R.L. Lattimore Sternwheeler Terminal across town to the Silver Casterlin building. He worried his father may have given up looking for him and returned to Branson, leaving him at the mercy of Bob Mears again.

When Captain Hawman's official duties were completed, he asked Gabriel, "Are you ready to go find your father?"

"Yes, sir," Gabriel said uneasily. "I'm afraid we might run into the men that took me. It was my grandfather's stepson that introduced Evan and me to them. What if my father is gone and Bob is there?"

Captain Hawman spoke reassuringly, "You let me worry about that. We'll be armed, and I won't leave you until I know you're safe and that justice will come to Bob. We didn't pluck you from the water to throw you back in. You're going home, young man, even if I must put you on the train myself."

The captain and four crewmen escorted Gabriel across town to the Silver Casterlin. Afraid of Bob Mears being at his grandfather's apartment, Gabriel asked one of the barmaids to knock on his grandfather's door and ask him to come downstairs for an immediate situation.

Floyd came rushing downstairs, expecting to find a burst pipe spraying water in the kitchen but stopped when he saw Gabriel. Floyd's eyes widened and filled with moisture while an emotional grin revealed the relief and gratitude that filled him like a refreshing breeze on a sweltering day. He immediately wrapped his arms around Gabriel in a tight embrace.

"We have been looking everywhere for you! Thank God you're okay. Where have you been, Gabriel? We were so scared." He grabbed Gabriel's shoulders and pushed him back to look at him fondly. His eyes maneuvered to Captain Hawman. "Who are these men?" he questioned.

After a short explanation, Floyd led Captain Hawman and Gabriel to the roof where Matt, William, and Morton were having their nightly meeting. Floyd opened the bulkhead door with its annoying creak. "Boys, look who came home!"

"Gabriel!" Matt exclaimed and moved quickly to hold his son and pull him close. "Thank you, Jesus, thank you," Matt said lightly through tightly closed eyes that burned with grateful tears.

In his father's embrace, Gabriel was overwhelmed by the knowledge that he was finally safe and no one would harm him again. Gabriel's strength evaporated, and he wept as he clung to his father tightly. "They took Evan," Gabriel mumbled through his tears. "I left Evan," he said with the weight of his guilt and then began to sob as he clung to Matt.

Matt remained quiet to let Gabriel cry with the mixed emotions he knew Gabriel had to be going through. Matt sniffled and opened his moist eyes to see a sea captain dressed in a black uniform standing by the door, who gave Matt an approving em-pathetic nod. Matt closed his eyes in a silent prayer of heart-felt thankfulness while he held his son in his arms. He could feel Gabriel's body jerking with his sobs, and it tore at Matt's heart, knowing the boy was agonizing over Evan and the experience he had gone through. After a few moments, Gabriel began to get himself under control.

Feeling the time was about right, Floyd quietly explained, "Matt, this is Captain Luke Hawman. We have him to thank for bringing Gabriel home."

Matt wiped his eyes and then shook the man's hand firmly. "Thank you. I'm Matt Bannister. This is my father, Floyd, and my deputies, William and Morton. I don't know how to thank you. Where did you find him?" He continued to hold Gabriel with one arm while the boy wept softly.

Captain Hawman answered, "Your son is very fortunate. Blessed by the Lord Almighty is more like it. We saw him jump ship into the mouth of the Columbia, and fortunately, we were able to snatch him from the current, which, again, is *very* fortunate," he emphasized. "Unfortunately, his brother didn't know how to swim and was left aboard a merchant ship named the *Everson Solstice* and was taken to sea. They were shanghaied here in Port-land. I felt it was our responsibility to get him here safely. My crewmen are downstairs having drinks."

Floyd placed his palm on the captain's shoulder. "Well, let your crew know it's on the house! Whatever they want tonight is on the house as a token of our appreciation. If they want to drink until they puke and then drink some more, they're welcome to do so." He laughed joyfully.

Matt shook the captain's hand again. "My deputies and I will come down a bit later and visit with you and your crew, but I'd like to talk to my son if you don't mind."

William pried Gabriel's face from Matt's chest to look into the boy's tear-filled eyes with a mock scowl. "If I were your father, I'd grab a strap and tan your hide for giving us such a scare," he said with a wink and quick smile.

Matt stepped back to look at his son and asked gently, "What happened?"

Gabriel explained through nervous and labored breaths what Bob had told Evan and him to convince them to break their promise to Floyd never to leave the Silver Casterlin building and everything that had happened since, to the best of his foggy memory.

Floyd was horrified. "Bob did this to you?"

"Yes, sir. If he says he didn't, then he's lying!" Gabriel answered quickly. The anxiety of seeing Bob again showed in his worried expression.

"Bob hasn't been seen since that night either," Matt said. The words Eric told Matt about the possibility of Bob being killed to protect the kidnappers returned to him. "Do you know who those men were that Bob met?"

"No. It was the same two men that came to where we were being kept sometimes and a Chinese man. Most of the time, it was a Chinese man that watched us. They were the only people we saw until Evan, and I woke up on the boat. A man named Peter told me to jump overboard and swim toward Captain Hawman's ship. Peter said he knew you were here looking for me," Gabriel said to his father with affectionate eyes.

"You better believe I was," Matt said, reassuring the boy. "I want you to know that Tom wanted to come too, but I wouldn't let him. He needed to stay with your mother in case bad news was all I could send back. But he wanted to be here."

"Peter?" Morton questioned. "I know him. I told him I was looking for you and Evan. Do the names Tony, Howard, or Felix sound familiar?"

Gabriel shook his head. "I never heard their names. Except for the Chinese man's name, it was Pan. Like a frying pan."

William quipped, "Well, with ten thousand Chinese in town, we should easily be able to find two or three hundred named Pan. A few more hundred named Tran, Xan, San, and even a few named Han and every other *An*, but I'll bet you we won't find a single one named Dan. I don't know why they don't use American names."

"Can you describe the men?" Matt asked, slightly annoyed by William's flippant words.

"The one with us most often had short black curly hair and a mustache; the other was clean-shaven and had short brown hair, but he was only there a few times. That man wore a derby hat all the time. The other man didn't wear a hat at all. They were both big and wore suits."

"That sounds like Tony and Howard," Morton

said to Matt. "As I said earlier, Tony's coming by my hotel at midnight to go fishing," Morton said with an added questionable shrug. "I don't even like catfish."

"Tomorrow, we'll have Gabriel identify them to be sure," Matt said.

Morton spoke, "I can suggest having lunch here tomorrow so Gabriel's not seen. I'll suggest that tonight."

"Sounds good."

William pointed at Gabriel. "Now that he's safe, I'd like to take Maggie to visit Aunt Eleanor in Astoria for a few days before I return home."

Matt was quickly incensed. "We're not done!" he exclaimed in a raised voice. "We still have to find Bob and those responsible, whether it's Morton's friends or not. We'll find that out tomorrow. But don't think you're wandering off to have fun just yet, William!" Matt's eyes glared into his cousin harshly.

"I didn't mean now!" William replied coarsely. "I'm looking forward to kicking the snot out of the men responsible. Even if it is my buddy, Felix, I'll still bust his head open."

Morton nudged William's arm, "You might be in trouble with your buddy anyway. I'll let you know if I hear anything."

"Huh?" William chuckled. "Trouble for what? Not flushing that nifty water pot thing downstairs? I figured the next person might want to pull that chain."

Morton's brow lowered slightly, perplexed. "No.

Felix can't be happy with you for bringing his wife to his little love nest. As I mentioned earlier, Tony was upset when he left the hospital today. Felix's wife must have told him about finding Felix with Beth. If things go bad for Felix, he may blame you."

Matt suggested to Morton, "You should go by and check on Tony's wife just to make sure she's okay. A man like that might get violent with her."

Morton nodded in agreement. "I'll do that in the morning."

William added, "Well, Mort, I'm not too concerned about Felix being mad at me. What's he going to do, write me a nasty note?" he chuckled. "And if he sends his big dogs on me, you'll be one of them. So, I should be okay."

Morton chuckled. "William, I'd be the first to hit you."

William laughed and padded Morton's back. "I know. Well, fellas, we got Gabriel back, so it's a good night. Now, if you'll excuse me, I'm going to join the captain and crew that saved Gabriel and see if I can't swindle a free passage to Astoria for Maggie and me."

***

Morton had nearly fallen asleep by the time Tony knocked on his hotel door well after midnight. Tony was quiet, in a foul mood, and smelled of liquor as he led the way to the waterfront. Morton had no idea where they were going or why, but he followed along and asked a few questions, which were either ignored or answered abruptly by the words, "You'll see."

The two men walked a long way to a warehouse with Chinese writing on the front. A tall fence lined the entire front of the property, including the locked double gate that opened to the dock. At the outside edge of the warehouse, Tony stopped towards the end of the fence, reached a finger in a slot, and opened a concealed walkthrough gate, which appeared to be a solid part of the fence. Opening the small gate revealed a walkway that snaked its way to the catwalks under the pier that hovered above the river. The tugboat was tethered to a platform connected to the catwalk.

The tugboat's engine idled while Howard, Bolin, and Pan waited for the two men to come aboard. "Watch your step," Tony said as he leaped aboard the tugboat. Morton did the same. He was curious why they were boarding a tugboat in the middle of the night and why the two Chinese men were there. He had a bad feeling stirring in his stomach and wished he had brought his gun belt to have his trusty .44 on his hip instead of the clumsy shoulder holster with a brand-new Colt .38 double action which he had never fired once. As the stirring in his stomach grew, he began to wonder if Tony had discovered he was U.S. Deputy Marshal. His suspicions grew as the other three men all seemed uneasy, with Tony being the most quiet and brooding. The thought heightened Morton's senses, and he readied himself to fight for his life at the earliest sign of trouble.

Morton wasn't at all reassured when Howard asked, "What's going on, Tony? Who is in the wheelhouse? Hector won't open the door, and these two aren't saying a word either." He motioned at Bolin and Pan.

"Good," Tony said and knocked on the wheelhouse door and waved the captain on. The steam engine picked up speed, and the two paddlewheels began to churn in the water, moving the tugboat out into the center of the Willamette River to go upriver. The tugboat had no lights burning in the wheelhouse or on the deck as it passed the other ships anchored to wait for their dock to open.

Howard was concerned. "Tony, what are we doing? Who do you have in there?"

"Howard, it's none of your concern. Just leave me alone!" Tony snapped sharply. He pulled a flask from his coat pocket and took a long drink of whiskey. Tony's eyes burned with anger as he watched the city lights fade behind them as they entered the darkness of the forests that lined the river.

Tony was filled with mixed emotions between fury and what the priests of his youth called grace. Grace meant unwarranted favor, which part of him wanted to offer. There was the temptation to hold Beth in his arms, feel her soft embrace, and tell her he loved her enough to forgive her if she would only love him. But the fury within him reasoned that the truth remained, if Beth loved him, she never would have cheated on him. Since she took the key to the hideaway and planned for future infidelities, there was no grace left to offer, just condemnation for her.

A man could love a woman to his dying day, but she would never be loyal to him if she didn't love him. He could set Beth free and get divorced, but if he couldn't have Beth, then no one would. No one could love her more or better than he did, and he would not allow her to find happiness without him. He couldn't live with that.

Howard Nicol watched the last of the city's lights disappear behind the trees that left a wall of darkness along the river's edge, leaving the moon's faint light illuminating the boat. He asked Morton, "Do you know who is in the wheelhouse?"

Morton shook his head. "The captain?"

Howard scoffed irritably, stepped across the deck, and physically spun Tony around to face him. "Tell me what is going on! Who is locked in the wheelhouse? What's with all the secrecy?"

Tony jerked his revolver from his shoulder holster and shoved it in Howard's face, his enraged eyes bulging as he stepped forward, forcing Howard to step back towards the short deck rail.

"Whoa, Tony!" Howard exclaimed, surprised. "Hey, Pal, what is wrong with you?"

Tony's lips twisted into a wicked snarl as he sneered, "You knew she was my wife! You knew it." he yelled.

Howard was startled by the venom in Tony's eyes and the words that he was yelling. "What? What are you talking about?"

"You know exactly what I'm talking about! You were supposed to be my friend. You and Felix both were. You betrayed me!"

"I didn't betray you. Are you talking about Felix and Beth? I didn't tell you because I knew you'd find out eventually."

"Was it your idea for her to get the key?" Tony was sickened. "She's my wife, and you didn't betray me?" Tony yelled.

Tony stuttered anxiously, "Tony, I couldn't tell you, or I'd lose my job. I knew you'd find out—"

Tony accused bitterly, "So you had Beth get it!"

"Huh? What are you talking about? I—"

The percussion of the .38 revolver echoed across the river as Howard fell against the short rail of the tug clutching his chest. Howard was wide-eyed and gasping for breath, in shock that he had been shot.

Tony's snarl tightened. "You'll never know how bad I want to empty the cylinder into you, but you don't deserve it. You're going to drown." He ordered Bolin and Pan. "Throw him overboard."

Howard tried to speak, but his attempts were a mumbled stutter. The terror showed in his eyes as the two Chinese men grabbed Howard obediently and threw him over the side of the tugboat into the Willamette River's current. Howard tried to stay afloat, but he went under before he went out of sight in the darkness.

Morton stood, shocked to have witnessed not just what had happened, but the quickness of it. He had been in gunfights before and knew the most unexpected things could happen, but he wasn't expecting Tony to turn on his friend. Tony turned to Morton and raised one finger. "I won't allow anyone to betray me. Not a friend, not anyone. Did you know Howard and Felix were bedding my wife?"

William told Morton what had happened, but now it all made sense. Morton had just watched Howard being killed for admitting he knew about Felix and Beth. Morton shook his head. "How could I? I've been with you this whole time."

Tony accepted the answer. "Howard was as slimy as a slug. I just never expected him or Felix to betray me. I know Felix is as crooked as a snake, but I never expected him and Howard to do this to me. My wife's a whore, Morton." He gave a pain-filled grimace. "How's that for gratitude? While I'm out making money to give her a nice home, she's pleasuring herself with him!" He shouted as he pointed at the water behind the boat. Tony bit his lip emotionally as his breathing became strained. "Felix, too, now. I can't allow that." He took another drink from his flask.

Morton suggested, "You could go find the marshal, Matt Bannister and tell him everything you know about Felix."

Tony nearly spat out his whiskey. "I'm not telling anyone anything! I may not be a lawyer, but I know my business. I'll get my revenge." He took another drink from the flask and then looked around. "Hell with it." He banged on the wheelhouse door and shouted. "This is good. Stop here."

There were two curves in the river to reach the cabin, which was four miles outside of Portland. Where they liked to go fishing, as they'd say, was six miles upriver in the wilderness where the river cut through the thickest forests without a town or cabin anywhere near the Willamette. The Willamette River was a fast-moving river with gravel bars that shifted with every winter and spring flood. Some areas were shallower than others, but where they usually went was a deep hole, over twenty feet, even in late August when the water levels dropped to their lowest. The bodies would never be discovered in the hidden depths, and where there was no body—there was no murder.

"Morton, have you ever killed a woman before?" Tony asked, turning from the wheelhouse.

Morton nodded in the darkness. "Regrettably, I have."

"It's no different than killing a man," Tony said coldly.

The wheelhouse door opened, and an older man with a stern expression on his unkempt, gray-bearded face said irritably, "It's only ten to twelve feet here? Are you sure?"

"I'm too tired and drunk to travel six miles and back, Hector. We'll just shorten the chain. It'll be fine." Tony took a deep breath and exhaled before taking another drink from the flask.

"She's awake," Hector said.

Tony stepped into the wheelhouse, grabbed the chain around Beth's ankles, and dragged her out onto the deck. Her ankles were chained with a padlock connecting a six-foot chain to the fifty-pound anchor. Her wrists were bound with rope while another cord tied her arms to her waist, making it impossible to pull the gag out of her mouth. The gag was held in place with a sash around her head.

Beth was petrified. Her widened eyes pleaded desperately with her husband while she tried to scream through the gag.

The tug pilot carried the anchor out of the wheelhouse and dropped it beside Beth with a heavy bang. "My hands are clean of this. They're starting to ask questions about me buying anchors."

Tony didn't want to hear it. "You're paid well, Hector! Just do what you're paid to do and keep your mouth shut!" He gazed down at his wife, lying on the deck helplessly, scared, weeping, and trying to plead through her gag.

Morton stepped forward, outraged, "What are you doing? Cut her loose. She's your wife, Tony!"

Tony pointed a finger in Morton's face. "Stand back, or I'll kill you too!" He shouted. "This is my business, not yours! Bolin, put your gun on him, and if he moves, shoot him."

The big Chinese man pulled one of his revolvers from his shoulder holster and aimed it at Morton. "Don't move, or you die." He said coldly.

Morton glanced back at Bolin and shook his head, astounded. "Tony, Beth is your wife."

Tony stepped forward with a hard swing of his right fist and knocked Morton to the tug's deck. He shouted while Morton rubbed his jaw, "One more word, and I'll tie that anchor to your ankles too! Pan, take his gun away from him. He might try to use it."

Pan obediently reached for the shoulder holster, but Morton grabbed his wrist to resist. Pan curled the knuckles of his left hand and shot them downward into Morton's throat with just enough force to interfere with Morton's breathing to make him choke. Morton immediately released Pan's wrist and held his throat while coughing to get his breath. Pan removed Morton's only weapon.

Tony knelt beside Beth and took another drink from his flask. "I gave you my life. I would never betray or hurt you if you were true to me. I'm not a god-fearing man, but I meant my vows before God when I said them. I loved you, Beth. I didn't treat you wrong, and I gave you everything I could give you. I suppose it wasn't enough because you sure gave yourself to Felix for something so little as a key!" He pulled the key to the hideaway out of his pocket and held it in front of her. "This key must be awfully important to let that fat, sweaty side of pork touch you. I didn't realize Howard was that important to you, Beth. Well, sweetheart, your lover is dead, and he's waiting down there somewhere for you. I should have chained him to you, so you two lovers could be together forever at the bottom of the river!" He stood and pulled her feet towards the boat rail.

She shook her head frantically with tears streaming down her cheeks. She gagged as she tried to swallow.

Morton shouted. "Let her have her say, at least! You're making a big mistake, Tony. You said you love her!"

Bolin kicked Morton in the face. "Shut up!"

Tony paused and nodded agreeably. "Alright,

let's see what the whore says." He took a knife from his pocket and cut the rope tied around her waist that held her arms.

Beth immediately pulled the sash away and the wad of cloth out of her mouth. She took a deep breath and began sobbing. "I love you! I have always loved you! I didn't have a choice! Tony, listen to me! If I didn't do what Felix wanted, he would turn that police officer's journal over to the police. He threatened to have you arrested. You would have been hung; Felix said he'd make sure you were. I read the journal! What choice did I have, Tony? I did it for you! I did it for us; so we could be together," she sobbed. Her words and wails echoed through the silent forests like a lamenting ghost seeking a lost lover in the river.

He ignored her words. "How long has it been going on with Howard?" he asked boldly, unphased by her pleading.

"What?" she wailed loudly. "Nothing is going on with Howard!"

Tony kicked her in the side viscously. "You know exactly what I'm talking about! Felix said you seduced him for this key!" He held it in front of her face. "So you could meet Howard in the hideaway instead of hotels. I found the key in your drawer, Beth. Don't lie to me!" he screamed in her face. "You seduced Felix to get this key so you could meet Howard whenever you two wanted. Well, like I said, he's dead now. Take this key here and use it when you two meet up." He grabbed her red dress with yellow flowers and ripped the front open to shove the key between her breasts.

"Tony, stop it!" she screamed as she fought him.

He slapped her face with a solid blow that stung her cheek. His handprint reddened her face. She began to sob, shocked by the blow, but choked it down as he left the key over her heart. "You think I slept with Howard?" she asked angrily. "How stupid can you be? Felix is the one lying to you. He blackmailed me to be with him or you'd be hanged. Don't you understand? He would give the police that man's journal with your name in it! I read it, Tony! I love you enough to let that disgusting pig touch me, but it was only so we could be together. I couldn't lose you. I swear I never wanted to, Tony, but I didn't have a choice, or I'd lose you. I love you!" She began to sob. "I wanted to tell you. Oh, Lord, Jesus, help him to see. Tony, I did it to save your life."

Morton knew if he had his sidearm, he could draw it faster and perhaps kill them all, but on his hands and knees on the deck without a gun, there was very little he could do against three men with guns. He stood slowly. "She sounds sincere, Tony."

"Mind your business, Morton!" Tony snapped with a harsh scowl. Bolin slammed his revolver across the back of Morton's head with a ferocious hit. Morton fell back to the deck, wincing in pain while blood seeped between his fingers while holding his head.

Tony glared at Beth with hatred burning in his eyes. "I don't know what you're talking about; I didn't kill any policeman. I don't know about a journal or what you're talking about. All I know is you coerced Felix to take you to his little house, so you get that key to meet Howard there whenever you want to."

"You didn't kill the policeman?" Beth gazed at Tony with her mouth open as her head shook slightly.

Tony knelt and squeezed her cheeks forcefully, staring into her eyes bitterly. He shouted every word slowly so she would understand him, "I HAVE NEVER KILLED A POLICEMAN! All I know is you're a whore! The key proves that." He forcefully tossed her head down against the deck as he moved around to her feet to open the padlock and shorten the chain length to the anchor.

Beth winced at the bump forming on the back of her head as she held her head with her two hands from the tied wrists. "Felix lied to you, Tony. He was lying to me, too," she said, realizing she had been deceived. The whole thing was based on a lie. "Why don't you believe me? I have never lied to you, Tony. Why won't you believe me!"

Tony yanked her up onto her feet next to the short rail and glared into her eyes.

Beth shook her head, terrified of the water. "Why don't you believe me? I have never lied to you, Tony. Felix lied! Why won't you believe me?" she sobbed.

His voice was cold, "A woman that cheats on you will lie too, Beth. I love you, but I can't trust a word you say!" Tony hit her forehead with his palm, abruptly forcing her over the rail into the water.

"I can't...swim!" she exclaimed as she splashed

frantically to keep her head above the frigid water, but her ankles were chained to the anchor on the tug's deck, holding her legs upward.

Morton, still lying on the deck, suddenly got to his hands and knees and then sprinted forward and dove overboard to save her. He hit the cold water and felt the current trying to gently pull him away from her. He lifted her shoulders to hold her face out of the water while he tread water to keep himself at the water's surface. Beth frantically reached her tied hands over his head, forcing him underwater in her panic. He kicked his feet frantically to keep himself and Beth above water.

Tony stood next to the rail holding the anchor. He'd lift it to pull her feet upwards, which forced her upper body to go underwater, and with it, Morton too. It humored him. "What do you think you're doing, Morton?" Tony asked with a slight smile. "Get away from her and back on board."

Morton, struggling to keep Beth's head above water, said, "I can't let you kill her!"

Tony paused. He stared at Beth, clinging to Morton's neck tighter than she ever clung to him. It angered him as he pictured Howard's face on Morton's and how his wife must've held onto him. "That's too bad. If you want to betray me like that, you can die with her. Bolin, shoot him. Bye, Beth." He tossed the anchor into the deep water. "Goodbye, Morton."

With a sudden jerk, Morton was pulled underwater like a bull taking off on a dead run with a lasso tied around his neck. Morton was choked by the short length of rope between Beth's wrists as they clamped around his throat with the force of the falling anchor deeper into the blackness of the cold water. He could feel his body being pulled down as his feet separated from her and began to rise, lifting his body while his head was still being pulled down.

Frantically, Morton pushed Beth's arms off his head to free his neck, but she clenched onto his hair to keep him from leaving her. Her grip on his hair was unrelenting as he tried to break free. Desperate to open her clenched fist full of his hair, he felt for her face and poked a finger in her eye. It wasn't meant to hurt her, just enough to release his hair. When she let go, Morton hooked the binding of her wrists with the crook of his elbow and tried to pull Beth up to the surface, but it was hopeless. The chain around her ankles and the anchor's weight were unforgiving.

The anchor hit the bottom of the river, and the blackness was terrifying, not knowing how deep they were nor able to see any light above. Bolin's gun was heard as a faint thudding, but no bullets could be seen. Glancing down, he could barely distinguish the blonde hair floating upwards and the bright yellow flowers on her dress. She was panicking, and her fingernails scratched and tore at his arms and body.

Silently pleading with the Lord to give him the strength to save her, Morton knew there was only one way to help her, and it would likely end up killing him as time was short. Unable to hold his breath for too long, Morton knew he would be shot if he returned to the surface to get a breath. Even if not, he could not swim back down to reach Beth in time to save her. He swam downward, allowing Beth to scratch him with her nails, and reached blindly for the chain on her ankles and followed the chain to the anchor. He tried to lift the anchor and carry it. But his feet slipped on the loose gravel bottom, and the anchor fell. Beth clenched onto him desperately.

If he had a gun, maybe he could shoot the padlock and hope it would open, but it was useless. He could not save Beth, but she would drown him if he didn't break free from her grip and save himself. Her fists had clenched onto his suit coat, and she refused to let him leave her. Desperate for oxygen, Morton kicked her abdomen and pushed himself out of her clenched hands and away from her. The kick forced what oxygen she had left out of her lungs as he swam upwards.

Morton felt like he was dying inside as he knew Beth was drowning at that very moment, and there was nothing he could do about it. He was only moments away from drowning himself. His lungs ached to breathe in fresh air, but he had no idea how deep he was or how far he had to swim upwards to reach the surface. His legs kicked, and his arms reached out in the blackness for the surface while every physical movement cried out for another breath. Every second grew more desperate with every kick of his feet and reach of his hands as he hoped every stretch of his arms would break through the surface.

Empty lungs demanded his body to inhale, and Morton could only fight it for so long before his chest would exhale involuntarily and inhale nothing except water if he didn't reach the surface in time. Desperately he strived harder, not caring if he'd be shot at the surface; he was desperate to breathe in fresh air. Unable to hold his breath any longer, he exhaled his lungs as the bubbles rolled over his face toward the surface. Faintly, he could see a glimpse of moonlight through the blurry lens of several feet of water and then burst through the surface with a desperate inhaling of cool fresh air.

He tread water as his chest heaved with several heavy breaths. His eyes narrowed on the departing tugboat nearly thirty yards away, going full speed down the river towards Portland. He sucked in a deep breath, followed by another, to get some oxygen moving in his blood. With the noise of the steam engine and paddlewheels churning the water, he doubted Tony would hear him if he yelled with the fury that filled him, but Morton wasn't about to take a chance.

Morton swam slowly towards the shore, knowing it was a long way away for a tired man to swim. He wasn't the best swimmer, but if he continued to swim and did not think about the distance, he might be able to make it.

He was still too far from shore to feel confident about his swimming when he paused to rest again, and to his surprise, his feet touched gravel. Morton stood on his feet and walked through the chest-deep water across the river on a gravel bar. Just as

KEN PRATT

surprising, the last ten feet of water, which should have been knee-deep, dropped off into a deep hole just wide enough for him to swim across before reaching the bank. Morton collapsed on the bank, exhausted.

Silence had overcome the river as it gently flowed by. A few frogs croaked, and crickets chirped. The sound of a distant owl hooted, and all was as it should be in nature. Except out in the river, a young lady was dead that should never have been. Morton buried his head in his hands. He had done all he could to save Beth, but it was useless. Morton could see the deep scratches that burned on his hands from Beth's fingernails in her desperation to hold on to what little hope he offered. He could feel other scratches on his neck and face as well.

Morton Sperry, the man that once terrified a county, had never felt more broken. He peered at the slight bleeding of a deep scratch on top of his hand and knew right then that Beth would leave a scar on him that ran far more profound than the scratch.

Chapter 32

Tony Hurner opened his eyes to Beth's empty pillow. For a moment, he wondered if she was boiling a pot of coffee in the kitchen, but then the pleasant thought was washed away by the memory of the night before. Beth's pillow was inside a white pillowcase with embroidered sunflowers of various sizes that she had embroidered herself.

Tony pulled the pillow close to smell the fragrance of Beth's hair and closed his eyes as he breathed in the unique scent that belonged to his sweet bride. All the fury he had felt towards her the night before was replaced by the hollow yearning to have her beside him and hear her soft voice telling him about her night's dream. It was the first morning he had woken up alone since the day they married, and suddenly, the house, his life, and his soul felt empty and bitterly cold, like an empty tomb with no way to exit and no avenues of escape except to join her in death himself.

The scent of his beloved lady penetrated his soul, and he would never forgive himself for what he had done to Beth. The weight of regret that filled him was more than any alcohol or Chinese opium could cover. Felix Rathkey was once a name he admired, but now Felix would pay with the savagery of a broken man with nothing to lose. Afterward, Tony could join Beth in the afterlife, and maybe she would forgive him for not hearing her final words. Like kindling on an ember, the whiskey fueled his fury and numbed his ears to anything she had to say. The words Beth tried to tell him deflected off him like a mirror deflects light. His rage blinded him from seeing that she was telling the truth, at least as she knew it. The memory of her voice begging him to believe her repeatedly echoed in his head. He would never be able to forget them.

He was a fool. In his immediate wrath, he succumbed to drinking and focused on the accusations by Felix without having the decency to ask his bride for the truth. He assumed the worst and cruelly murdered her.

Regarding a journal that supposedly condemned him, Tony had no idea what Beth was talking about unless Felix manufactured one to deceive her. Knowing his former boss, it was not out of the possibility of a Felix scam. They had done similar things in the court of law for paying clients.

The longer he held her pillow to his nose to smell her sweet fragrance, the more clearly he finally heard what Beth was saying and understood that the truth was written on her face; he was just too enraged to see it. Her meeting with Felix was wrong, but she thought she was protecting him. The thought left a dull throbbing in his chest. He pressed his face deeper into her pillow and began to weep. Despite his horrific actions, Beth was the only woman he truly loved. He doubted he could have ever dropped the anchor into the river without the mind-numbing effects of the whiskey dulling his decision-making. It was too late now, though. She was gone, and so were his friends, Howard and Morton. He would never touch alcohol again; he swore it. The guilt and memories that would forever haunt him could confirm it.

He wiped his tearful eyes and sat up on the bed, still wearing the clothes from the night before. He stood and walked out of the bedroom and downstairs. He turned to enter the silent family room when the steel of a Colt.44 slammed down on the back side of Tony's head. He collapsed to his knees when he was struck again.

***

Tony woke with a pain that throbbed his head. He opened his eyes and squinted as the bright mid-morning sun shone through the window into his eyes. Sitting upright on a small davenport in the family room, Tony lifted his hand to cover his eyes from the sun and realized his wrists were shackled together. He had blood on his shirt, and after wiping a sore on his head, he glanced at the blood smeared on his fingers.

"You should have made sure I was dead," Morton Sperry said plainly. He was sitting in a padded chair in a corner facing the davenport. He had changed into his regular clothes and wore his gun belt with his Colt .44 Caliber revolver. On the left lapel of his shirt was a silver badge that occasionally flickered in the sun. Morton's voice was cold, "Now it's my turn."

Tony smiled slightly to see his new friend. "Then kill me."

"My name is Morton Sperry. I led the Sperry-Helms Gang for many years. Do you see this badge?" He pointed at the silver star on his lapel. "I'm a U.S. Deputy Marshal in Matt Bannister's office. Matt's son went missing, and we came looking for him: Matt, William Fasana, and myself. We fell short of finding him, but I found you and witnessed you murdering Howard and Beth. That is enough for you to be hung."

Tony sat calmly with his fingers interlaced; he lifted his thumbs uncaringly as he shrugged. "It doesn't matter to me anymore. If you want to arrest me, do so. I'll plead guilty. The sooner I hang, the better. Or you could take these shackles off and shoot me. Put my gun in my hand and say you had to. You're a killer, Morton, just like me."

"I'm not just like you; I never harmed a woman I loved."

"Bull. What about that woman at the restaurant yesterday? You had her pissing herself. Don't tell me you wouldn't hurt a woman. She was terrified! You're more like me than you know," Tony accused.

Morton frowned. "My former sister-in-law knew me at a different time. I said a woman that I loved."

"You killed your own brother. How's that for love? Or was that a lie too?"

"I didn't have much of a choice with him. But with you, I do. Put this over your head. We're going to meet Matt." He tossed a pillow slip to Tony.

"I've met him. I even offered to help find his son." He chuckled lightly. He pulled the pillow slip over his head. The sunlight shined through the white cotton of the pillow slip but blocked him from seeing anything else. "Now that you got a hood over my head, you could execute me, and I won't see it coming if that helps."

"If it makes you feel better, I'd like to kill you right now. I absolutely would. But I'm not like you, and I hope you get to live with what you did to Beth for a long time before they hang you. Stand up; let's go."

***

Matt Bannister pulled the pillow slip off Tony's head, and Tony gazed around at the roof of the Silver Casterlin curiously. "Why are we here?" he asked, blocking the sun's bright rays from his eyes. Morton stood at his side with a loose grip on his arm. He squinted as he recognized Matt and, with a bit of surprise, Felix's new friend, William Craig, Floyd Bannister, and to his astonishment, Matt's son, Gabriel.

Tony grinned incredulously. "You found your boy?"

"Where is Bob Mears?" Matt asked plainly.

Tony stared at him, unconcerned. "How did you find your boy?"

"Gabriel jumped off the ship yesterday and made it back here," Matt explained quickly. "We know you took him and Evan. Now, where is Bob? His mother is dying inside with worry. Is he hiding or dead?"

Tony remained silent.

Matt took a drink of water from a glass. "Your freedom is gone. So, who are you protecting? Morton told me that your boss was blackmailing your wife into pleasing him. Why would you protect Felix?"

"Oh, I have no intention of protecting him!" Tony exclaimed bitterly.

"Good," Matt said. "Was it—"

Tony interrupted sharply, "You have no jurisdiction here to arrest me, so you better let me go. I won't answer any more questions."

Matt chuckled lightly. "Yeah, that's true, but you don't see a Portland Police Officer up here, do you? No, you don't. It's just my family and me. You asked, so I'll tell you, you're up on the roof because no one can see or hear you. I'd answer my questions because if you don't, we'll strip you down naked and leave you tied to a chair up here all day in the hot sun with a glass of water three feet away, day and night, for as long as it takes for the thirst and burning of a blistering sunburn to convince you to speak. Generally speaking, I'm a fair man, but you bastards stole my son, and now I don't give a rat's ass about you. There is no more niceness in me. If you don't believe me, I'll send William down for a chair, strip you down, and leave you here for four or five hours starting now."

Tony lowered his head quietly for a moment. "I'll tell you everything you want to know if I can have ten minutes alone on this rooftop with Felix first." Tony's lips snarled as he spoke.

"I don't have a problem with that, but the District Attorney might," Matt answered. "Right now, you can start by answering my first question, where is Bob hiding?"

Tony lowered his head. "Bob is hiding upriver from my wife in twenty to thirty feet of water." He sighed heavily. "I suppose I have nothing to lose by telling you that. He's dead; we drowned him the night we took your son. Felix ordered it to be done. And no, by the way, it wasn't Bob's idea to take your boy. It was Felix's. Felix blackmailed Bob into it. He bought all the debt Bob owed from others and called it in. Bob had no choice, or he'd be killed, which he was anyway."

"Oh, my Lord," Floyd said as the words cut into his heart. "Oh…I better break that news to Rhoda. Oh, Lord, give her the strength to get through this." Floyd left the roof to go downstairs.

Matt asked William. "I told Eric to meet me here around eleven. Can you go downstairs and wait for him?"

"Sure, send me, right? Maybe he'll blacken my other eye so they match," William complained as he left.

377

Matt explained to Tony, "You're right, I don't have jurisdiction here, but Eric does. Since I don't have jurisdiction, I don't have to play by the rules. Don't feel too protected by Eric coming up here, though; he'll let me do whatever I want to get information from you and say he wasn't here. You understand, right?"

Tony peered out over the view of Portland. "In some ways, we owned this city. If I can't kill Felix myself, I'll just have to tell you everything I know to hurt him. It's pretty simple; Felix is a record keeper and writes everything down. If you want to know everything, I suggest you search the safe in Felix's office. It's behind the painting of the ocean. Push the paneling, and it will open the panel door to expose the safe. The safe can only be opened with a key, which is kept in a hidden compartment under his desktop.

There is another safe at his house behind an ugly drawing of his wife in his home office. It's the same thing, push the paneling, and it will open the panel door. You'll find that key in the same place inside his home desk; they're matching desks. Both safes will be a goldmine for you, I promise. You won't need me to testify because everything is right there." He spoke to Gabriel, "Howard is dead if that is any consolation."

Gabriel didn't answer.

Tony's eyes watered, and his lips tightened. "I killed my wife, and I don't want to live with that. I can't live with that." His lips twisted emotionally. "You'll hang Felix once you know what he's done." He took a deep breath and then rammed his shoulder into Morton, knocking him off balance and falling to the tar roof. Tony took advantage of his momentary freedom and sprinted toward the roof's edge.

Matt scrambled after him to try to reach him before Tony jumped off the roof; Matt gripped the back of Tony's collar just as Tony lowered his center of gravity and tried to dive off the building, but Matt wrapped his arms around Tony's waist and pulled him to the roof short of the brick rail. They rolled on the ground to a stop. Tony could not fight due to his shackled wrists, but he cursed Matt with an alphabet of foul words.

Matt slammed his forearm down on the back of Tony's head, driving his face into the roof. Matt snarled, "I have news for you; you're going to live with your wife's murder until your execution anyway."

"I told you everything you need to know. Let me jump. Please," Tony begged.

"I'm afraid not. I think I'll let you lay here until Eric comes up."

***

Within twenty minutes, William and Officer Eric Stiles came onto the roof with two other police officers that Eric trusted. Eric said, "Matt, you didn't tell me William was one of your deputies. I wouldn't have hit him if I had known that."

William agreed, "Yeah, Matt failed to be much help there."

"William, you deserved it," Matt said. "Eric, we're

going to need some search warrants. Tony, tell him what you told us about the safes." Tony told him the same details about the safes and their contents.

Eric told the other two officers to take Tony to the city jail. "Matt, let's you and I approach the District Attorney and ask a judge for search warrants." He turned his attention to Tony. "It's a pleasure to arrest you. We'll put warrants out for Bolin and Pan too."

They let the two officers lead Tony down the stairs first to the fourth floor, where Rhoda and Floyd waited outside their apartment near the stairs. Rhoda was visibly upset and had been sobbing. Her eyes glared at Tony as he was escorted down the stairs from the roof. "You drowned my son?"

"Hold up, fellas," Tony said.

"We can't do that," one of the officers said.

Eric stepped around them to Floyd and Rhoda. "Give Tony a moment or two to answer her. It's the least he could do. Matt, we must hurry."

"Excuse me," Matt said as he passed by them to continue downstairs.

Rhoda repeated, "You drowned my son?" Her jaw clenched tightly.

Tony's lips lifted slightly. "I did."

"Why?"

"It was my job. It's no different than you evicting people that don't pay their dues here. It wasn't personal."

"He was my son!" she shouted with a trembling lip. "You had no right to do that!" she sobbed.

"Ma'am. As I said, it wasn't personal. That's all I

have to say. Oh, except that Bob cried like a baby." He laughed.

Outraged by the blatant disrespect, William Fasana hit Tony with his fist on the back of the head. "Shut your mouth, you piece of—"

Tony tried to attack William but found it difficult with secured wrists. The two police officers were trying to hold Tony back and get control of him. William hit Tony with a quick left jab and an overhand right to the face. The right fist broke Tony's nose. He cried out in pain as the blood flowed heavily from his bent nose.

The two officers turned their attention to pushing William backward while Morton and Floyd tried to hold onto him to stop him from hitting Tony again. William was incensed and yelled, "You murdered her son and laughed about it. I'll break your head open. You son of a—"

Tony looked at the blood on his hands and saw a flash of silver through his water-filled eyes that caught his attention. In the commotion of separating the two men, Rhoda had pulled a small .32 silver-plated derringer out of her pocket and aimed at Tony's face. His eyes widened just as the hammer fell, igniting a flash.

Tony's collapsed at the top of the stairs like a grain bag being dropped off the pier. His upper body slid down three stairs ending with the iron shackles cracking against the stairs above his head. Blood flowed from an entry wound in the center of his forehead.

The unexpected percussion of the gun left them all speechless for a moment until Tony's fall ended abruptly.

Rhoda stood with the gun still pointing where Tony had stood. Her breathing was heavy. "It's personal to me!" she shouted. The derringer dropped to the floor as she bent over and began sobbing. Floyd, in shock, moved to put an arm around her. She held onto him and loudly wailed.

William picked the small weapon off the floor, still slack-jawed. He was speechless; it was his derringer that he had left in his belongings inside the apartment.

One of the officers checked Tony's pulse and shook his head. "He's dead."

The other officer told Rhoda, "Miss, I must arrest you for his murder. And I have to take that weapon for evidence."

Floyd stammered, "What did you do? Rhoda, why? How? Where did you get the gun? What did you do?" He hugged her while he wept.

Rhoda kissed her husband and allowed the policeman to secure her wrists. She sniffled as she gazed lovingly at Floyd. "I'm sorry, Floyd. You're a good husband. I want you to know that. William, take care of Maggie. I'm sorry, Floyd, but he murdered my baby. I had to," she said before she was escorted past the dead man lying on the stairs.

William and Morton looked at each other; neither could find any words to say. Floyd pressed an arm against the wall and wept.

Chapter 33

The news of Bob's death had left Maggie Farrell devastated, but adding her mother's arrest for the murder of Tony Hurner doubled the blow. William stayed in the apartment with Floyd and Maggie. In a moment, everything had changed; Rhoda was in jail, being charged with the most severe crime known to man—taking another human being's life with the intent of doing so. The truth of what happened to Bob was traumatizing for Rhoda. Worse, not having a body to bury outraged her to the point where any true justice could only come from her hand. Maybe she could plead momentary insanity, maybe not. All Floyd knew was that in a moment, Rhoda's decision had destroyed their home, and his and Maggie's lives would never be the same without her.

Across town, Eric introduced Matt to the District Attorney, David Fisher, who immediately approached a Superior Court Judge, John Groom, with Tony Hurner's information. Judge Groom signed search warrants for Felix's home, attorney's office, and one for Lottie's Shore Leave Boarding House. Three teams searched the three warrants with District Attorney David Fisher, two of his assistants, Officer Eric Stiles, and four police officers he trusted. Matt Bannister and Morton Sperry were invited to help.

Opening the safes that Tony Hurner mentioned revealed a treasure trove of well-kept records containing names, dates, financial payments, and precisely how corrupted Felix was. After just a half hour of reading files, receipts, and contracts, the evidence revealed that Felix was involved in witness tampering, extortion, shanghaiing, and ordering the murder of several individuals like Bob Mears through his hired help.

Felix kept meticulous records, and the first entry on the earliest date of his journals explained why: When he retired from practicing law, he wanted to write a biography telling his story about having the reputation of being the finest defense attorney in Oregon with an upright and honorable reputation, while being one of the most notorious criminals that no one knew about. He believed it would prove his brilliance and bring him the fame that being an attorney never would. He wrote, "I am too intelligent to fall and too slick to be caught." His records revealed in detail, enough incriminating material to convict Felix to an extended sentence, if not a lifetime, in the Oregon State Prison.

The journals and collaborating records would

bring several other search warrants and possible jail sentences for Police Chief Bruce Schlemer, several officers on the police force, business owners, and a particular judge in the judicial system. Corruption, like mildew, has a way of spreading to the weaker souls that lack integrity. But discovering a written record of corruption in the city officials and business owners promised to shake the city to the core when it was revealed through the press.

***

Felix had wondered how Tony would react to learning that his wife was unfaithful. He liked Tony quite a lot, but Beth was too beautiful not to be attracted to. Felix was a man that usually got what he wanted, and if not, he'd find a way to retrieve what he was after. He discovered right away that Beth would never be unfaithful to Tony. It took some thinking and a week's worth of fictional writing in a leather-bound journal and dipping it in water to make the journal of a deceased police officer found in the river look authentic. It was all a deceptive con, but Beth fell for it like a timid mouse taking a piece of cheese.

It was terrible luck that Nora caught him in the hideaway with Beth. It ruined a good thing he had going and would have continued for years. He hoped to hide it from Tony, but when Nora insisted on telling Tony, Felix had to think quickly. He could not tell the truth, or he would suffer Tony's wrath. Felix had given Beth a key to the hideaway months before so she could go in if he was late. Knowing she had a key hidden somewhere in her home, Felix made a brilliant move. Sometimes a man could impress himself with his own brilliance, and Felix had done just that by casually shifting the narrative and the bulk of Tony's wrath towards Howard Nicol. In doing so, he had settled an issue that had recently come up while having lunch with Big Richard; Howard's mentioning of Bob Mears never coming back home. That short statement could end everything for Felix if the wrong set of ears caught hold of it.

Felix wasn't too surprised when Howard hadn't shown up at work that morning. He doubted Howard would ever show up anywhere again. Beth would be thrown out of her home and have nowhere to go except to Felix, and Tony would have no one left in his life either until he returned to Felix as well. It was a messy and heartbreaking deal for Tony and Beth, but like kicking a dust pile, it would settle down, and Felix would still have his beautiful lady on the side and Tony working for him.

Seeing District Attorney David Fisher enter the law office with Matt Bannister holding a search warrant was a surprise that Felix had never expected. He was informed that his home was being searched too. Felix was aggravated, but he wasn't too concerned. Nothing in his desks or filing cabinets was out of the ordinary for an attorney, including his case files. He covered his tracks thoroughly. To calm his nerves, he assured himself that they had no reason to want to look behind the paintings on the walls, but even if they did, all they would find was a paneled wall like the rest of his office. The wall had to be pressed inward to open the paneling door to reveal the safes in his office and home. He could reassure himself that everything was secure.

***

Knowing he had to leave the office and couldn't go home, Felix visited his daughter at the hospital. Gretchen still had a long fight ahead of her, but she was doing as well as the doctor could hope. It was a heartbreaking situation that no parent ever wants to be in, but they still had Gretchen, and Felix and Nora were thankful for that. Nora had stayed overnight at the hospital to be with Gretchen and had not spoken more than four words to him since his arrival. Those four words were, "Don't speak to me."

Three hours of silence later, a knock on the hospital room door drew his attention. Matt Bannister entered the room.

Self-confident, irritable, and perhaps with a sense of superiority, Felix asked, "Well, Marshal, did you find anything?"

Matt raised a single finger indicating for Felix to wait. Matt knelt in front of Nora beside the bed. "Missus Rathkey, I am sorry for what happened to your daughter."

"Thank you," she said with moist eyes.

Matt grimaced as he hesitated to speak. "I am

also sorry because I am about to make your life much harder. I'm sorry for you and her, not him." He stood.

"What do you mean?" she asked with concern.

Matt ignored her and spoke to Felix, "Did I find anything? You asked. Yes, I found my son. I figured you wouldn't believe me, so I brought him with me. Gabriel," Matt called.

Felix's spine stiffened as his mouth dropped open, stunned to see the young man walk timidly into the hospital room.

Matt motioned towards Felix. "Gabriel, this is Felix Rathkey, the man who had you and Evan kidnapped and sold to Captain Horace Smithrud for two hundred and fifty dollars."

"What?" Nora Rathkey questioned in horror. "What's this all about?"

"Uh…" Felix was too stunned to speak. His eyes widened while his breathing became heavier. Sweat began to bead on his forehead. He knew the only way Matt would know that information was if Tony told him so. He took a deep breath to regain his composure and think.

Felix forced a smile. "First, let me just say, praise the lord, you found your son. I know how difficult that was for you and him, I'm sure. But you're mistaken. I never met the individual you mentioned, nor did I have anything to do with your boy's disappearance. I can only assume someone told you this ridiculous accusation unless you have some kind of proof?" he asked skeptically. "I will confess that I was caught yesterday with my right-hand man's wife. I'm ashamed to say I gave in to her temptations and told him so. If Tony is your source of information, I can surmise that he is justifiably angry and is trying to use you to get revenge for what I did. You can ask my wife; she's the one that caught me," he suggested shamefully. "I had nothing to do with this young man's disappearance, wherever he was."

Nora stood from her chair to speak with Matt. "That is true. I found him and Beth Hurner..." She paused with disgust as she chose her words carefully. Her voice faded to a whisper with each word, "in our old house committing adultery."

"I'm very sorry to hear that too, Missus Rathkey. That must have been hurtful, especially when your little girl needed you both with her. Your husband had my son and his adopted brother shanghaied and sold them to a ship's captain. My son jumped overboard and got away. His adopted brother is on his way to Africa aboard the *Everson Solstice*."

"You must be mistaken," she said defensively. "Tony is lying to hurt Felix."

Matt wrinkled his nose and shook his head. "Would you like to know why he did it? Would you like to tell her why, Felix?" Matt asked with an embittered tone to his voice.

Felix chuckled. "I don't know what reason Tony would come up with. Did he see your son with you and come up with a great story? What did he say?" Felix asked with an expectant grin.

Matt's expression slowly hardened. "To create a mystery I could never solve. To gain a sense of power, simply because you could."

Felix laughed lightly. "That's the most ridiculous excuse I've ever heard."

Matt turned to Nora. "Your husband wanted what little notoriety it might bring him to be the cause of the one thing that would haunt me forever, my missing son. He almost got away with it, but I'm about to show him what a powerless little worm he truly is."

"That can't be true," Nora stated. "You don't believe that? You must know that Tony is just trying to hurt my husband for what he did."

Matt turned his eyes back to Felix. "I would agree, but Tony didn't tell me anything except where to find your two safes and the keys."

"What?" Felix gasped and began to step backward towards a corner. His face lost its color with the shock of being betrayed.

Matt's eyes narrowed as he said, "When I first came to Portland, I swore I would kill the men responsible for my son disappearing, and I meant every word of it. But now, I think forcing you to leave your family when they need you the most is even more punishing for you. Because that little girl is going to wake up, and her life is going to be completely different. She'll need you to help her learn how to use her other arm and reassure her that she will be okay. You should be there to help her work through all the emotions she'll have. She'll need her daddy to tell her how beautiful she is, even with a scar. She needs her daddy to make her feel safe at home.

"A girl needs her father to be home. She needs her

father to be a good husband. She needs her father to be everything you're not going to be. It breaks my heart, and it honestly does break my heart to know that you won't be there for her or your wife. When your little girl cries for her daddy because she's sad, you'll be behind jail and prison bars for a few years at least. By then, your attractive wife will probably want a divorce and be married to someone else to raise your daughter." Matt paused. "But don't get me wrong; I have absolutely no pity for you. I suggest you say goodbye to your wife and daughter while you can. Fellas, come on in."

Portland Police Officers Eric Stiles, David Fisher, Morton Sperry, and William Fasana entered the room with two other police officers.

Felix backed into a corner with a terrified expression on his face. Panicking, he said, "Stand back!" he pulled a small .32 caliber revolver from behind his back, where he kept a holster on his belt.

Alertly, Matt drew his revolver with blinding speed, pulled the hammer back, and aimed it at Felix before Felix could raise his hand holding the weapon. "I don't think you're going to win! Might as well drop it or continue," Matt said with a hardened voice. His penetrating eyes showed no doubt that he would pull the trigger if disobeyed.

Felix had frozen with his gun, barely clearing his waist. He stared at Matt as his bottom lip trembled. The ivory-handled silver-plated .32 dropped to the floor as a guttural sob broke loose from his lips. His body jerked as he fought from wailing. He blinked rapidly as wells of tears filled his eyes.

Nora's voice cracked with emotion, "Felix, what have you done?"

David Fisher spoke frankly, "Felix Rathkey, you have been a thorn in my side for far too long. I have been waiting a long time to say this; you are under arrest for soliciting the murders of Bob Mears and Rose Livingston. Officer Eric Stiles, please take Mister Rathkey into custody."

"My pleasure," Eric said and pulled out his wrist shackles.

Felix could not fight the fear of being arrested any longer and sobbed as the three officers shackled his hands in front of him. He barked out an emotional sob. "I'm sorry, Nora." His body involuntarily jerked with his deep erratic breaths.

David Fisher said, "It's good to know your alias is Colin Fairbanks, Felix. You're the mysterious owner of Lottie's Shore Leave Boarding House and The Maroon Squid Tavern. Needless to say, your list of crimes will be substantial."

Eric explained to Matt, "We discovered Felix had Howard Nicol and one of his other thugs from Chinatown beat Rose and then hang her as a warning to others. You were right; Felix feared she'd tell you about him."

Matt shook his head with a heavy sigh. What had happened to Rose broke his heart. "Felix," Matt said sternly to get his attention. "It is a pleasure to see you whimper like a scared child because your days of crying are just beginning. Say goodbye to your family. We're taking a walk." The anger in Matt's eyes sent a chill down his spine.

Felix hadn't noticed Morton and William standing back near the door. He stared at the silver star badges on their lapels with bewilderment. "You two are Matt's deputies?"

William Fasana put a friendly hand on Felix's shoulder with a heavy sigh. "Yeah. I knew I was forgetting to tell you something; I just couldn't remember what. Well, that was it!" he exclaimed with excitement. "I'm a Deputy U.S. Marshal. I'm also Matt's cousin, William Fasana. Morton works with us too. And you thought you were smart?" He shook his head doubtfully. "But hey, when you get out of prison, we'll do it again. I've had fun."

Felix gazed at Matt bewildered. "We covered everything. How did you know it was me?"

Matt shook his head. "I didn't. I trusted the Lord would lead everyone where they needed to be. And thankfully, he did. But it was your own lust and lies that caught you. We may never have known if you were not caught with Beth. Tony pointed us towards your safes; your meticulous record-keeping told us the rest. You can't lie; everything is written in your own words."

After hearing Matt's words, Nora burst into tears and buried her face in her hands. "Get him away from me!" she shouted. "Just go! I won't be married to a criminal."

Felix's brow twisted with emotion. "Nora...I'm sorry," he bellowed. "Nora...I need you more than ever now. You're my wife."

"Get him away from me!" Nora screamed. The loud volume seemed to startle Gretchen, and her eyes fluttered open and closed, tiredly.

Matt grabbed Felix's arm to lead him out of the room. "Let's go."

"No! No! My daughter…Matt, my daughter, is waking up. I want to say goodbye to my daughter. Nora…Please, Lord, please," he pleaded as Matt pulled him out of the room.

Matt said as Felix wept, "Speaking of the Lord, maybe while you're in prison, you should spend more time reading your Bible. Being a Christian isn't about saying so; it's about trusting Jesus to be the Lord of our lives in every way. Now that you're going behind bars, trust the Lord because sometimes paths that look like dead ends lead to the greatest blessings. Spend some time with the Lord, Felix. He'll make you a better man."

William put an arm around Felix's shoulders and jerked him close as they walked down the hospital hallway. "Oh, don't talk like that, Matt. Felix is a great guy. How would he know his actions would get Beth, Howard, and Tony murdered on the same day? Getting three people murdered at three different places and times on the same day? Now that takes talent!" William said. "Felix, I think you're brilliant. Never mind breaking your wife and daughter's hearts and losing your career. I believe you are brilliant, and like I said, when you get out and have nothing left except crime, I'll come back, and we'll do this again.

Felix asked, "They're all dead?"

William shrugged, "Your dog Turk isn't the only big dog that went a little crazy. So did Tony, but he was put down too. I told you, you were the crazy one for messing with Tony's wife, not me," he said pointedly.

Matt stopped suddenly when he walked past JoJo Perkin's room. "William, I'm stopping here to visit a friend of mine. Goodbye, Felix. You might think I'm the man that ruined your life, but when you start to think so, be sure to look in the mirror. You made your choices, I just helped bring them to light. You can blame me for that if you want."

Felix glanced at Matt with hatred burning in his eyes, but didn't say a word as he was led away.

***

JoJo was feeling better, though his ribs were still quite tender. Being technically homeless, the hospital kept him a few days longer than usual. Matt had visited him twice and given him the knife Dillon had bought him. To his surprise, even Dillon and his friends came by to say hello. His best surprise was his older sister stopping by to make amends.

A quick knock on the door and Matt Bannister stepped into the room. "Hello, JoJo. How are you today?"

"Good." His happy grin was broad. He enjoyed having visitors. "Did you hear the yelling a little bit ago? It was scary."

Matt smiled sadly. "It was. I wanted to come by and say goodbye. I'm going back home tomorrow."

"You don't have to. I could make a bed in my place for you if you wanted to stay. I wouldn't make you pay." The sadness of losing a new friend showed in his eyes. He didn't have many friends.

"In the rat barn?" Matt asked.

JoJo grabbed his ribs as he laughed lightly. "Yes. You don't have to leave. You could stay."

Matt shook his head slowly. "JoJo, I'm getting married. My fiancée would be pretty upset if I didn't go back. I haven't seen her in nearly two weeks or longer, it seems like. Too long, anyway."

"Is she pretty?"

"Yeah, she is. And I can't wait to see her. Besides, I heard your sister is going to be helping you. Does it feel good to know she loves you after all?"

JoJo smiled. "I love her. Look, she gave me my papa's wedding ring." He held up his left hand to show a silver ring on his finger. "It fits too!"

Matt smiled. "I think I'll take that for my wedding," Matt teased.

"Do you want to?" He began taking the ring off.

"No! I was teasing. That's for you."

"I'd let you use it. You're the best friend I have."

Matt could not explain why, but his eyes watered just enough to become blurry. "I'm honored to be your friend, JoJo. Listen, if you ever need anything, my father manages the Silver Casterlin Saloon. Go there and talk to Floyd Bannister. He knows how to reach me, Okay? It's been a pleasure to get to know you, JoJo. I need to go."

"Are you coming back? When will I see you again?" JoJo asked sadly.

"Someday. Take care, my friend."

Chapter 34

Rachel Sperry had changed her name to Shirley Hotchkiss to evade the Sperry family from finding her and forcing her back into the hell of the Sperry home in Natoma. Her eternal appreciation went to several friends who helped her to escape Natoma and start a new life in Portland. She and her daughters lived in a small peaceful home and owned a shop called Hotchkiss Fabric, Sewing, and Mending.

Known as Shirley to everyone in Portland, she was alarmed to hear a man's voice say, "Rachel, you are as pretty as ever," William Fasana said with a grin. He had come into the store with Matt. "But I'm no longer single, so don't be kissing on me if you can help it."

Her mouth dropped open before a wide grin formed. She didn't say a word; she just quickly walked around the counter and tightly wrapped her arms around him. He chuckled as he held her.

She pulled back to look at him with an emotional grin. "William..." She stared at him appreciatively as her eyes filled with tears. William was one of the friends that helped her escape Natoma and the Sperry family.

"Well, don't start crying," he said. "I know it breaks your heart that I found someone else, but you know those things happen when you take too long."

"They do, indeed. How are you, my old friend?"

"I'm good. You?"

She shrugged. "I'm okay. I miss you all, though. Remember when we were young and all the crazy things we'd do? I was just thinking about you recently. You still need to get your haircut," she laughed with a wipe of a single tear that escaped her eye. She glanced at Matt, and her brow narrowed questionably. "Who is this?"

Matt spoke, "I was younger. You might remember telling me to get lost once or twice," he offered as a hint.

Her grin widened. "Matthew Bannister! I should have known. You look like Lee but with a beard." She let go of William to give Matt a quick hug. "You've become famous since then, and you came home! The last I remember of you is you ran away. Lee was devastated. I remember that. The Ash girl married your friend, and you left. And then she had your baby, or at least that's what everyone thought." She paused with a cautious glance at William. "Maybe I shouldn't have said that."

Matt chuckled. "My son, Gabriel. You're right.

That's why we came to Portland. Gabriel was visiting his grandfather, *my* father, and was shanghaied..."

"Good Lord!" she gasped.

"Gabriel got away. We are heading home tomorrow morning on the train. We wanted to stop by and say hello. But most of all, there is someone that needs to talk to you." Matt turned and waved for someone to enter the shop.

Morton Sperry stepping inside her shop sent a wave of involuntary terror through Rachel, and she scooted back against the counter and began to shake.

"Rachel," William said comfortingly, "You're okay."

Morton raised his hands innocently and pointed at the badge on his lapel. "Rachel, first and foremost, I must apologize for scaring you the other day. I was pretending to be someone else to find Gabriel and couldn't have you ruining it. So, I am sorry for scaring you."

Rachel's voice trembled, "What...what is this? What's going on? You can't take me back! I won't go back," she fiercely shook her head, refusing to go.

"I'm here right with you, Rachel. You're safe," William said to comfort her.

"Rachel, please listen to him," Matt said softly.

Morton continued, "I'm not here to take you back or anything like that. I'm not the same man I used to be. I was a monster when you knew me, and I ask you to forgive me. I apologize for everything I did and what happened to you in Natoma. I wanted to let you know that you are free. You don't have to worry about Alan anymore because he is dead. No one will be looking for you or coming after the girls. The Sperry-Helms Gang no longer exists, and I'm sorry for any fear, pain, or anxiety I caused you. I'm a Christian now and marrying a Christian lady when I get back to Branson."

"Alan's dead?" she questioned.

Morton was hesitant to answer as his eyes watered. "I had to shoot him. Daisy is dead too. He shot her by accident while shooting at me. Rachel, I wanted to let you know that if you want to go home to your family in Willow Falls, it's safe to do so. I changed my life, and I'm not the same man I was. I don't expect you to forgive me for the past, but the least I could do is apologize and let you know you have no reason to hide."

"Daisy's dead? She was so sweet," she said softly. "You're a Christian?" she asked doubtfully.

He nodded.

"I can vouch for that," Matt said. "Morton is a changed man and my deputy now. And he is marrying a fine Christian lady."

William added, "You know me well enough to know I wouldn't be with him if he was lying about that or a threat to you. I have an idea, how about you close the shop and join us for dinner. We're leaving tomorrow if you want to come back home."

"My life is here now," she said with a wave around her store.

"You don't have to pack up and move to join us for dinner." William chuckled.

"I don't know..." Her eyes went to Morton suspiciously.

Morton volunteered, "How about you three go out for dinner and I'll stay with Floyd."

Rachel had never liked Morton, but she could see a change in his green eyes, and his voice had lost the fierceness she had known. It was nearly impossible to believe that Morton had become a Christian man, yet, she knew the Lord could do amazing things, even change someone like Morton Sperry. She took hold of William's hand and squeezed it. "Morton, why should I forgive you?"

He shook his head slowly. "Rachel, I have learned that forgiving somebody isn't for them as much as it is for me. I have lived my whole life being a criminal; you know that probably better than anyone. I'm not proud of it, not at all. I'm trying to forgive myself for all the wrongs I have done. I know I've done you wrong; my whole family did. I regret my part in making your life hell. I hope that you might forgive me because I am sorry.

"I'd like someday to see you on the street and say hello without the weight of the past bearing down upon me or you being afraid of me. For that to happen, I have to ask for your forgiveness. Whether you do or not is your decision, and I'll respect it either way. You have cause to hate me, and I know that. I just want you to know that I'm aware of how wrong I was and how much I regret the things I did. You deserved far more than my brother ever gave you and how we treated you, especially me."

Rachel wiped her eyes. "Morton, this is very

scary for me. But would you like to meet your nieces at dinner tonight?"

"I'd love to," he said.

"I never thought I'd say it, but I'll try to forgive you, Morton. It will take some time, but I will forgive you."

He smiled tightly. "Thank you."

"Well," Matt said, "Let's go have something good to eat. And then, let's get ready to go home. I can't wait to leave this city and return home to Branson. I miss Christine."

William added, "Matt's getting married at the end of this month. Maybe you and the girls would like to come to Branson and join in the family reunion. It's going to be quite a party and might be a nice visit for you."

A Look At:

When The Wolf Comes Knocking

Some wolves attack when their prey is at its weakest. Some charge fiercely. Others...knock softly.

When Greg Slater returned home from college for winter break, his whole world changed. After rescuing his high-school sweetheart, Tina Dibari, and helping sentence his best friend, Rene Dibari, to life in prison, Greg fell in love for the first time.

Fifteen years later, life isn't easy, but Greg and Tina are working on their marriage. But an old fear has come back to haunt them...

Rene has escaped prison, and he's thirsty for revenge.

As shocking truths unfold, Greg and Tina face a ripple in their faith and in their home. Tina starts doubting her faith and seeks comfort in a friend with lustful intentions. Meanwhile, Greg struggles to navigate this new unrest in their relationship.

Unfortunately, evil stops for no one, and three very different wolves are after the Slater family.

Will Greg and Tina's love be enough to keep them together, and—more importantly—will their faith hold true when the wolves come knocking?

AVAILABLE NOW ON AMAZON

About the Author

Ken Pratt and his wife, Cathy, have been married for 22 years and are blessed with five children and six grandchildren. They live on the Oregon Coast where they are currently raising the youngest of their children.

Ken grew up in the small farming community of Dayton, Oregon, where he worked to make a living. But his true passion always lay with writing.

Having a busy family, the only "free" time Ken has to write is late at night—getting no more than five hours of sleep every day. He has penned several novels that are being published, along with several children's stories.

Printed in the USA
CPSIA information can be obtained
at www.ICGtesting.com
LVHW032346220923
757294LV00031B/205